DREAMWORLD

Jane Goldman has written extensively for national newspapers and magazines, and was the recipient of *Cosmopolitan*'s 'Women of Tomorrow' award for achievement in journalism. She is the author of several books, including a series of highly acclaimed works of teenage non-fiction, number one best-seller *The X-Files Book of the Unexplained, Volume One* and its sequel, which were nominated for non-fiction awards by the British Publishing Association and the Writers' Guild, respectively.

She and her husband are based in North London, but spend as much of the year as possible at their home on Florida's Space Coast. Their three children provide an excellent excuse for spending a ludicrous amount of time at theme parks.

DREAM WORLD

Jane Goldman

HarperCollins*Publishers*

'I've Got a Match'
Words and Music by John Flansburgh and John Linnell
© They Might Be Giants Music and W. B. Music Corp
Warner/Chappell Music Ltd, London W6 8BS
Reproduced by permission of International Music Publications Ltd.

HarperCollins*Publishers*
77–85 Fulham Palace Road,
Hammersmith, London W6 8JB

The HarperCollins website address is
www.**fire**and**water**.com

This paperback edition 2000

1 3 5 7 9 8 6 4 2

First published in Great Britain by
HarperCollins*Publishers* 2000

Copyright © Jane Goldman 2000

The Author asserts the moral right to
be identified as the author of this work

ISBN 0 00 651334 4

Set in Meridien by
Rowland Phototypesetting Ltd,
Bury St Edmunds, Suffolk

Printed and bound in Great Britain by
Clays Ltd, St Ives plc

For Amanda Goldman
and Stuart Goldman,
with love

Acknowledgements

I'm forever indebted to Mary Pachnos, my wonderful agent and great buddy, without whom this book would not exist. Profuse thanks too, to Gillon Aitken, and the folks at HarperCollins: Susan Opie, Lucy Ferguson and Nick Sayers.

Likewise my husband, Jonathan. In the eleven years since he vowed to stick with me for better or for worse, he has inspired me and believed in me, tolerated all kinds of crap, been my greatest friend, given me both roots and wings, and made me happy beyond belief. Jonathan, thank you. I love you.

My gratitude also goes out to . . .
. . . My wonderful family, including Ursula Landsberg (a.k.a. Kinny) and Toula Mavridou, the sister I always dreamed of having, only better. Big, big love and thanks to you, Tulip.
. . . Emily Dean – for support with this book, for all our amazing adventures, for matching me in compulsive behaviour and puerile sense of humour and being the best damn best friend anyone could wish for. Hey, Em, my points are your points, always.

. . . Kate Anderson – for her wisdom, tolerance and friendship, for scaring off the burglar and for the remarkable feat of helping to make our family more Waltons than Simpsons.

. . . Jack Barth – for his professional assistance and being a pal in a million.

. . . Lynda Spiro – for always being there for me.

. . . Adam Buxton, Joe Cornish, Sarah Evans and Annabel Hutton – for never failing to cheer me up, which during this last year was often quite a feat. I count myself wildly lucky to have friends like you.

. . . Cleo Paskal, Michelle Alexander, David Baddiel, Frank Skinner, Tracy Towner, Debbie Marrow and Max Ellis – for their friendship and support.

. . . Ed Robertson – thanks.

. . . Neil Gaiman – for encouraging me to write a novel in the first place.

. . . Lee Brown and Miles Cruickshank – for their expertise re: dangerous construction equipment.

My home is your home
We may live far apart
but never forget it
You're my neighbour at heart

'My Home is Your Home'
Theme from the Global Village Cruise
at the ImagiNation theme park,
Dreamworld, Florida

One

Of all the songs that accompany theme park attractions, which is the most insidiously catchy, the most precious, can't-get-it-out-of-your-head annoying? 'It's a Small World' from the ride of the same name at Walt Disney World, perhaps? Or, 'My Home is Your Home' from the not dissimilar Global Village Cruise at Dreamworld?

Up until about three seconds ago, before she heard the thunder of footsteps on the concrete staircase behind her drowning out the distant festival of theme park noise from above, before she felt hands on the back of her furry costume pushing her through a doorway, before she heard the door slam and struggled to see who was behind her and felt an arm snake around her and plunge something sharp into her thorax, Lisa Schaeffer would have loved to have debated the matter at length.

Lisa Schaeffer liked that kind of thing very much. There were few things she enjoyed more than getting some friends round, cracking open a nice cold microbrew, firing up a Camel Light and talking about theme parks or seventies' Saturday morning cartoons, or seeing who could come up with the most outlandish idea for a new Fox 'real TV' special. 'When Buildings Collapse' was her best effort, she felt, and although she'd always had a sneaking

1

concern that it may originally have been a gag she'd heard on *The Simpsons*, no one had picked up on it to date. In fact, since her recent relocation to Orlando, no one had hauled her up on anything at all. When it came to gloriously pointless riffs on pop culture, she was way ahead of everyone else and she loved it.

In Los Angeles, for instance, everyone she knew had already worked out their porn name (name of your first pet plus the street where you grew up – Lisa's was Fluffy Mulholland) and had spent many a jocular soirée trying to remember the difference between the theme tunes to *Superman, Star Wars* and *ET*. Here in central Florida, however, Lisa's new friends had received these games with glee and delight and Lisa had felt sure that once she headed back to the West Coast, she'd eternally be remembered as just about the most riveting raconteur ever to grace the Orlando social scene. But it had taken only seconds for everything in Lisa's world to change.

'It's a Small World' versus 'My Home is Your Home'. Which sugary paean to the spirit of global community *is* the most contagious? The salient answer, at this moment, was that for the first time in her life, Lisa Schaeffer didn't give a damn. Because right now, as it piped on distantly through the speakers somewhere overhead, she had to contend with the possibility that 'My Home is Your Home' might be the last piece of music – and, for that matter, the last earthly sound – that she would ever hear.

Even for a worshipper of kitsch, it was not an entertaining notion. No no no. Surely life – *her* life – was more sacrosanct?

Besides this thought and the other, more obvious ones – the fascination with the things that looked like free-floating balls of mercury that danced before her eyes as unconsciousness encroached, the nasty awareness of the warm wetness of blood as it pulsed out of her and soaked into her costume, the horror at the hideous, rasping, rhythmic noise of air passing in and out of her punctured lung and pleural cavity – the only other notion that stood out from the crowded clamour of confusion in Lisa Schaeffer's mind was mild surprise at the lack of pain in the area of trauma itself.

The moist heat inside the large, plastic full-head mask she wore, now acrid and cloying with the smell of gastric fluid and fear on her breath, was unbearable. But the darkness the mask provided was in some way merciful, as it allowed Lisa to tell herself that the creeping blackness she saw was not internal – was not her mind shutting down. It was just the same cimmerian shade she always saw when she wore the Kit-E-Cat costume. It had to be . . . didn't it?

When Lisa started to doubt her own reassurances, she struggled to pivot her head in such a way that she might get a glimpse of the world outside the mask, to find out if she could still see. She gasped for breath, gagging on the salty, metallic taste in her mouth as she struggled to find the mesh eye-holes hidden beneath the chin of the cat face. She tried to pretend that she was seeking these vantage points on the outside world just as she had whilst on duty only minutes ago. Just as she had done every day for the last three months, when she needed to know whether the person approaching her was a child seeking an autograph, or a confused pubescent boy hoping to pull her tail, or a family who wanted to pose for a photo-graph, or a toddler who would come and snuggle into the soft fur of her costume and play with her rubber whiskers and plant a kiss on her plastic nose.

When she had started the job, she'd regarded every one of them with a certain coldly bemused detachment, like a lab technician watching baby rats trying to suckle from a hot-water bottle. Why the star treatment for a person in a furry suit? As a kid, Lisa had visited Universal Studios and Knott's Berry Farm and Disneyland in Anaheim plenty of times, and she had always been rather nonplussed by the wandering characters. But now, in her final moments, the raw humanity of these innocent strangers who lived in her memories and whom she would soon be leaving behind put a lump in Lisa's throat that she knew wasn't bile or gore.

Just as the waves of sudden altruism and self-pity threatened to engulf her, Lisa's desperately searching gaze found one of the mesh eye-holes, and the shock of what she saw through it made the waves shrink as abruptly as they had crested.

Her lips moved silently and the rasping from her gaping chest quickened and echoed even more loudly in the confines of the suit as Lisa involuntarily blurted out Leon LeGalley's name.

'Leon?'

She said it again, deliberately this time, and she also asked, 'Why?' And this time some sound came out, although it sounded slow and low and hollow and broken, like a busted tape machine or something from the pits of hell.

Leon LeGalley's face was grotesquely distorted as he stared alternately up at the cat head and down at the front of the suit, and the big cat paws that clutched it. Lisa guessed that it must look pretty horrific – all that venous blood, twinkling crimson on the stark white fun-fur.

As her knees finally buckled and she fell to the ground, Lisa heard the fibrous crunch of flesh being pierced – once, twice, three times. Not hers, she was sure. Then whose? It was followed by a revolting visceral slithering sound and a thud on the floor beside her. Then came Leon LeGalley's voice calling her name over and over, a voice wracked with torment and accompanied by a peculiar bubbling, reminding Lisa of both a very bad novelty record by Ringo Starr and the times when she used to try and amuse her little brother in the bathtub by trying to talk with her mouth partly submerged.

From her prone position, and the way her head lay, she now had a better view through the mesh, and although the blackness was for real now, and closing in fast, she caught a glimpse of the body beside her. Lisa looked on impassively, watching Leon LeGalley's hands fluttering ineffectually at the hilt of something buried in the lumpy red mess that was his stomach, until finally her field of vision began to recede.

Darkness bloomed at the corners and spread inwards, ringing the diminishing porthole of white light that was Lisa's final window on the world. The central circle shrank smaller and smaller as the darkness around it grew, until it was gone, just like the hole in which Porky Pig would appear at the end of Loony Tunes in order to pronounce, 'Th-th-th-that's all folks!'

It was an irony that Lisa Schaeffer might have appreciated.

Two

It was in the wide-eyed, sugar-addled rapture of one of her annual childhood visits to Dreamworld that Sylvia Avery first noticed there was something strange about Central Avenue. Even in a place like ImagiNation, a perfect, spellbound place like ImagiNation, streets shouldn't change length. That much she knew. But this one, the thoroughfare that ran from Fort Enchantment at the hub of the park to the turnstiles at the southernmost reaches of its periphery, appeared far longer when you arrived in the morning, aching to get into the park and onto the rides, than it did from the other end, when you were heading towards the exit.

Shortly after landing her rookie post on the Dreamworld security force – aged twenty then, but no less enthusiastic – Avery had guiltlessly basked in the confirmation that it had been her observational skills, and not her imagination, at work.

But that was half a decade ago. And now, as she hastened towards the turnstile, feeling the sweat begin to bead in her hairline and the thick, wet Florida air flood her respiratory system like so much scorching chowder, she watched with jaded eyes as the height and breadth of the buildings on either side of her subtly swelled from the scale of five-eighths to six-eighths and seven-eighths towards the life-size structures on either corner. She knew this architectural scam made the turnstiles seem far closer than they really were and, where once there had been wonderment, the magic of forced perspective was for the first time infusing her with a sense of frustration and impatience.

Around her, the visitors who had hurried to get into the park earlier that day fell blithely under its spell. No need to hurry now, plenty of time, they joined the gently bobbing human tide, ever ebbing away from the centre of the road, and forged onto the wide sidewalks to gaze at the artful window displays of the souvenir stores that lined the street. Through the triple-wide doorways of the stores – wide enough to accommodate many people who are holding hands with children and clutching thick, reinforced plastic shopping bags and pushing strollers crammed with toddlers and babies and plush toys and more shopping bags – they flowed, this dreamy, insistent current of tired, happy people. The men festooned with cameras and camcorders, the fathers among them carrying their sticky-fingered progeny on their shoulders, the teenage boys with their hands planted in the back pockets of their girlfriends' cargo pants, the women flagging beneath their ballast of waist-packs and back-packs and pocket books and diaper bags, calling the names of children and men who have left them behind.

Avery zigzagged the street like a savvy swimmer outfoxing an Atlantic rip tide, sights fixed on the guest-relations building to the left of the turnstiles, where her superior, Felix Perdue, was waiting for her. She hated disappointment, and fervently hoped that his unexpected and urgent-sounding summons might have something to do with the top-level emergency that everyone had been talking about for the last two hours.

When the code-11 call, intended only for the six most senior members of Dreamworld security, came through the walkie-talkie system on a burst of static at eleven-thirty that morning, Avery had barely noticed it. She had been too deeply embroiled in dealing with a noisy gang of Italian teens who had tried to get behind the souvenir photo-desk at the Niagara Falls Adventure during a fracas over their souvenir photo, which hadn't appeared on the bank of screens showing the last dozen barrelfuls of shrieking riders making the plunge.

Avery had known right away, just by looking at them, that one – maybe all – of the girls had hiked up their T-shirts for the camera, and that the picture had been pulled from the system immediately, as per standard procedure. Mostly, flashers didn't dare ask why their picture was missing, or accepted the explanation that the shot hadn't come out. But occasionally, like now, things would get out of hand, which was where Avery and her colleagues came into their own. Although Dreamworld's theme parks, water parks and resort areas are densely patrolled by teams of plain-clothes security staff, and still more who wear the same jolly themed costumes as the 'cast members' who work the attractions, uniformed security personnel deliberately keep a low profile, to maximize the psychological effect when one actually shows up – whether to intimidate a would-be trouble-maker, or placate an angry guest who has had something stolen and demands to see a 'real' cop, not a guy in a costume with a walkie-talkie. Few people realize that, just like Walt Disney World, Dreamworld is a bona fide municipality with its own de facto police force.

Avery had authoritative presence down to a fine art.

At first she'd feared that her relentlessly feminine appearance – the unusually long mahogany mane, the pneumatic build – would make her look like a 'sexy-cop' strip-o-gram when she donned the navy pants and fitted sky-blue shirt. But her air of unmistakable physical strength and quiet intelligence ensured that no one ever failed to take her seriously. As she had expected, the Italian teens called off their invasion of the souvenir photo-desk as soon as she approached them, and only resumed their formidable noise level when they were well out of the exit area and halfway into the gift store.

'Code-11 – that a violent crime or something?'

'I thought it was when a kid's gone missing – like, *really* gone missing.'

The exit-area attendants, gawky in their lumberjack costumes, had ambled over to stand near Avery, clearly hoping for titillating news from the world outside the Niagara Falls Adventure. College students on temporary hire for the high season, she felt sure. They looked at her hopefully. She held up her hands; shrugged.

'Far as I know, it's just a general call for the chiefs. Nothing specific. The only thing we're supposed to do is ignore it.'

The nerdier of the two boys licked his lips before speaking with what, for him, was probably considerable enthusiasm.

'But it's some big deal, right?'

She shrugged again. 'Apparently. I never heard them call it in three years.'

To Avery's relief, the next crowd of riders flooded the exit area, flushed and laughing, wringing out their clothes, allowing her to disappear into their midst and get back outside. The young attendants' salaciousness, their casual hunger for disaster, had left her feeling slightly wistful, serving as it did as a reminder that for every person who adored Dreamworld the way she did, there were plenty more who didn't. People who saw it as a symbol of cynical corporate greed or soulless, pre-packaged entertainment; production-line fun. People who sneered at Dreamworld's family values, political correctness, unflinching optimism. These people, their notions, frustrated Avery. Why didn't they see what she saw? Didn't they think it amazing that a place could be so beautiful and be kept so clean that visitors didn't dare litter or graffiti or vandalize? Or that every employee was smiling and friendly and helpful all the time because if they weren't, they'd be fired? Weren't they in awe of Dreamworld's free public transport system – the buses and trams, monorails and watercraft that were spotless and safe and ran on time without fail? Weren't they enchanted by the attention to detail, the love and effort put into the design and engineering of the place far beyond what was necessary to lure the paying customer? All those little details which ensured that anyone operating at a child's gentle pace and with a child's curiosity would be rewarded by delightful surprises – the secret passages and pathways and nooks, the hidden messages and pictures in the architecture and horticultural displays, the unexpected encounters with characters and entertainers who popped up as if from nowhere?

Certainly Dreamworld's utopian vision was an obvious one, but Avery couldn't understand why that made it any less ambrosial to experience or any more worthy of derision, and it depressed her that so many people rubbed their hands together in glee at the prospect of trouble in paradise. She didn't deny that bad things happened at Dreamworld now and again, but she was proud to be among the team who ensured that those things were dealt with quickly and quietly so as never to break the illusion for everybody else.

But perhaps, though Avery hated to concede it, there was something about perfection that made people restless. A small part of her could relate very well to Eve screwing up her chances in the Garden of Eden. And for the next few hours, that small part of Avery could think of nothing but the code-11.

While she dealt with the paperwork for a shoplifting incident at Fairyland Mercantile, walked an angry guest to the lost-and-found to retrieve his 'stolen' camcorder, and settled a tense exchange between a ride attendant and an indignant young couple who had parked their sleeping toddler in the stroller-parking area while they rode Journey to the Centre of the Earth, Avery listened out for any hint as to what was going on. But all she heard was conjecture.

At five twenty-five, Perdue's communication had come through, its nuances maddeningly unreadable, instructing her to meet him back at HQ right away.

When she finally reached the open-plan office behind the public windows, blinking as her eyes adjusted to the muted shade of the indoors and delighting in the icy air conditioning, Avery was surprised to find Perdue walking towards her, obviously on his way out.

'You wanted to see me?'

'Ah, Sylvie, here you are. Good.'

Perdue was the only person who called her that, the only one she'd ever allowed to get away with it since she was a child. Even so, it still grated sometimes, but not today. Today, she was too alarmed by Perdue's appearance for it to even register. He looked tense and vulnerable; younger, somehow, than his forty-eight years, although she noticed that his hair, which most people took for blond, now looked as grey as the grim pallor that leached the tan from his face. His pale eyes were full of – what? Whatever it was, it made her uneasy.

'What's up? You okay?'

Avery reached up and smoothed Perdue's collar, which was sticking out eccentrically. He crouched slightly to let her do it, nodding unconvincingly in response to her question.

'Better?'

'Yes. Perfect. You changed your shirt. That bad, huh?'

'Oooh, yeah.'

Perdue forced a smile. Despite his athletic appearance, he was a guy who sweated a lot, particularly when he was stressed out, and he kept fresh shirts both in his locker here at the main security office and in his car. It wasn't all that often that he needed them, but when things got bad, out they came. Back when they first met, Avery hadn't been sure whether to mention having noticed it or not, but Perdue had seemed relieved when she did. Now it was a little joke between them: on bad days, Avery would offer, 'Coffee? New shirt?' Or they'd refer to a particularly taxing situation as a 'three-shirt problem' – a riff on Sherlock Holmes's three-pipe thing. Today, however, Avery could see that Perdue was not in a jesting mood.

'You're not okay, are you? What's going on?'

'Tell you later.'

From the moment she'd arrived at Dreamworld, Perdue had recognized Avery as his equal in every sense but the rank assigned to her. She'd adored him immediately,

12

too, and not just because he'd said that she looked like Lara Croft. Now she was both Perdue's friend and his closest confidante, much to the chagrin of the rest of his subordinates. In the interest of keeping the peace, Perdue was always careful to avoid overt displays of their rapport, especially out here in the security bullpen. But now he leant down and rested his head briefly against hers in a good-natured show of exhaustion, a gesture that took her by surprise and disconcerted her further. She stood stiffly, focusing on him, not wanting to engage her peripheral vision and find out who, if anybody, was watching.

'But you called? You wanted me? No?'

'Uh-huh. Hayes asked me to get you. He's in my office.'

'*Hayes* did? Why?'

Felix Perdue shrugged in genuine bemusement, and forced another smile before starting off down the hall towards his rendezvous with whatever it was that had made him sweat.

'Avery. Grab a chair, honey. And shut the door.'

Hayes Ober was sitting at Perdue's desk with a cup of coffee in one hand and his cellular phone in the other. He nodded towards the empty visitors' chair and Avery realized with some bemusement that it was the first time in the entire fourteen-month period that she'd been dating him that she'd seen him in an office setting. It felt strange; incongruous. There he was, so smart and businesslike, and yet she knew every contour of the black Calvins beneath the chinos, knew what it felt like to curl her finger around the stray lock of brown hair that played on the back of the collar of the chambray shirt, knew the strength in the fingers that held the cellular and the coffee cup, and the way those deep-set, chocolate-coloured eyes could look burning from beneath half-closed lids. It took Avery a moment to regain her equilibrium.

'I need you to do something for me this afternoon. Do you mind?'

Avery leant forward in the visitors' chair, her mind racing. 'Of course not. Does Felix know? My shift isn't up for a couple more hours.'

'Sure, I squared it with him already. This thing, it's kind of sensitive, but with all this going on out there, seems like just about every bigwig in security is busy shitting his pants. So, naturally, I thought of you.'

Avery wasn't sure if she was supposed to be flattered. She searched Hayes's eyes and the not-entirely-relaxed upturn at each corner of his rudely generous mouth, and still she didn't know. He read her thoughts.

'Obviously you came to mind *first*, but we hate the "N" word, right? So it all worked out nicely to have this excuse.'

Avery dimly recalled having agreed with Hayes, one sticky night in bed back when they first got together, that nepotism was a tag they could both live without; she had the talent to get promoted in security without trading on his position as head of Dreamworld's elite team of Dream Technicians and the CEO's best-boy. But while a part of her had greedily accepted the implication of his apparent faith in her talents, another had been stung, had wondered if the converse were true. Hayes was the only person in the Florida arm of Dreamworld operations whom the mighty John Darwin trusted, and he guarded this privileged position with the ferocity of a man whose life depended on it. One word to Darwin and he could get her promoted tomorrow, but if she proved unworthy . . . His mere use of the 'N' word seemed to suggest this fear, the fear of being seen to fail in his own judgement, to make a bad call, to lose Darwin's trust. Which of her instincts had been correct, she still didn't know. Perhaps she was about to find out.

'So what *is* going on out there?'

Hayes fixed her with a steady gaze and grinned.

'Now, you *know* I'm not supposed to tell you that.'

Avery smiled back, faintly loathing the way that Hayes, like no one else – and despite having only twelve years on her – could make her feel like a little girl.

'It's pretty bad. I don't know why the hell I'm smiling,' he said eventually, putting down his phone and gesturing to Avery to close the door, which she'd forgotten to do when she came in. As it clicked shut, she noticed that mounted on the back was a framed copy of the *Time* cover that had featured a cartoon of Mickey Mouse and Kit-E-Cat towering triumphantly over Orlando like a benevolent Godzilla and Mothra, their conquerors' flags casting twin shadows over the cartoon rubble of crushed motor inns, chain hotels and independent tourist attractions.

Avery sat down again and watched as Hayes drained his coffee cup and wiped his mouth.

'Some nut followed Kit-E-Cat down into the utilidor from the Hansel and Gretel entrance, got Kitty in the chest with a nine-inch hunting knife. Went straight through the suit like butter.'

'Fuck. Fuck! You are *kidding*. . . Is he . . . ? Did he . . . ?'

'*She*. Some girl called Lisa Schaeffer. Twenty-three years old. Only been here three months. Emergency services pronounced her at the scene. Couldn't even find a pulse. The guy, too. Used the same knife, skewered

15

himself a few times. In the guts. Did a pretty good job of it. They said he might have made it if they'd been able to get in quicker, only – did I say this? – they were in the disabled restroom with the door wedged. Took the services fifteen-odd minutes to get it off the hinges.'

Avery felt sick; didn't know what to say. She watched Hayes trace his thin fingers over the ruggedly uneven flesh in the hollows of his cheeks, as he often did when he was thinking. She was relieved when he broke the silence.

'The D-man's really tied up over in LA, and word has come down that he wants me to take control, clean up the mess. Obviously I know jack about this kind of thing, but he needs someone he can count on to make sure everything gets taken care of, and I happened to be in the park this afternoon, so . . .'

Hayes threw a swift and obedient salute to denote the fact that no one says no to John K. Darwin, but Avery knew there was more to it than that. Hayes was relishing the compliment. Admittedly, it was well deserved. Hayes was Senior Dream Tech because he engineered attractions that people would stand in line for two hours to see, come torrential rain or one hundred per cent humidity. He manufactured environments that could make people nostalgic for a past that never was and hopeful for a future that would never be. He created themed resorts that painstakingly recreated other eras and other countries, authentic down to the finest detail, bar the fact that they were infinitely better than the real thing. If anyone had the imagination, skill and hubris to find a way of maintaining the glorious illusion that nothing bad ever happened at Dreamworld, it was Hayes Ober.

For her part, Avery felt a dirty thrill at the possibility that Hayes's unexpected presence in her patch might bode well for her: maybe a chance of getting a look-in on the investigation, the most exciting thing to happen in the history of the Dreamworld security force. Then came the stinging slap of guilt for the dual sins of embracing the 'N' word and thinking of herself when an innocent woman was dead. Avery ensured that her expression was appropriately grave.

'So what can I do to help?'

'With this? Oh, nothing. It's under control. Your big boss out there has got the investigation covered now. I already had a quick cup of coffee at the coroner's office and tomorrow the lawyers and I are going to start talking. See what to do about the families. Darwin knows it's not going to get out, so he's happy.'

Avery tried hard not to look disappointed. She tried to imagine what it would be like to know you were going to die and that the last thing you'd ever see would be the inside of a big, fibre-glass cat's head. She recovered convincingly.

'No, I meant the thing you wanted me to do. The thing you called me in for.'

'Oh, right.' Hayes didn't miss a beat. 'So, can you believe I've been dragged into another security issue, only this time I've got a vested interest. There was an incident over in Osceola County this morning. Nothing to do with us. The highway patrol were dealing with some accident on one of the state roads and found a dead guy in a picnic cooler – a fresh dead guy, that is. Some drifter. Only it turns out, can-you-fucking-believe-our-luck-today, that the guy'd done a few stints as a volunteer at the research centre, and that's where he was yesterday, apparently. That's what his buddies told the police. So now they want to talk to my people over there and they want to send a guy over to snoop around. So I'm, *over my cold, dead body.*

I reminded them that they don't have jurisdiction around here unless they have warrants and reasonable suspicion – whatever. The upshot is that I've promised them we'll get what they want, nice and official and everything to get them out of our hair. Gal in charge is called Lopez: She's waiting for your call.'

'Me?'

'Right.' Hayes fished a laminated pass from the back pocket of his chinos and shunted it across the desk to her.

'Clearance – expires tonight, though – and Daetwyler's expecting you. Talk to whoever, find out who saw the guy – you know better than I do what they need for these things, and call me on my cellular when you're done at the sheriff's office. We'll get something to eat.'

Avery still felt sick once more, and sicker at the thought of food, but she nodded as she picked up the pass and rose gingerly to her feet.

'And Avery?' It was Hayes speaking again, as she reached the door. He had just dialled a number on the desk phone and looked up at her with the receiver in the crook of his neck and an engagingly satanic smile.

'I'm sure I don't have to say this, but at the research centre? You're probably going to see some stuff you're not supposed to see.' Hayes winked and blew Avery a kiss. 'You know I love you, hon, but if it goes any further than it ought to, I'll have to kill you.'

Three

Dreamworld is larger than Universal Escape and only a shade smaller than its longer-established neighbour, Walt Disney World, which is to say that its sprawl is nearly twice that of Manhattan Island.

The highways that traverse it are straight and smooth, and all are impressively signposted, apart from the service roads which are sunk into the ground and flanked on either side by verdant berm, so that Dreamworld guests never see a delivery truck or an industrial vehicle. 'Think of this place like a big clock,' Perdue had told Avery on her first day at work. 'Everybody expects it to run to precision, but all they want to see is the face. The gears and cogs are cranking away behind it, know what I'm saying? But we keep those hidden.'

Avery took the service road whose entrance was hidden a few yards past the last exit to ImagiNation and followed its path behind the parking lots of the Outback Inn, past the twelfth and thirteenth holes of Cypress Fairways and the monorail depot and around the loop enclosing Emergency Services Plaza North, with its cartoon firehouse.

The Research and Development Complex did not appear on the map which Avery kept in her glove compartment, nor was its approach road clearly marked at the turn-off. But one night, after she'd given Hayes a blow job in his Lexus Coupé, he had talked her through the mosaic of Dreamworld parking permits on the windshield. The wordless sign ahead told her that she was on the right track – a faintly unsettling representation of Kit-E-Cat wearing a lab coat and wielding a test tube, one bulbous gloved finger held to his lips in a gesture of secrecy.

What Avery had not asked Hayes, neither that night nor any other, was what exactly got researched and developed at the Research and Development Complex. As far as she knew – as far as *anyone* knew – it housed several different groups from various walks of science, each working under generous grants from Dreamworld to develop technologies that the company hoped would keep them at the cutting edge of the leisure industry through the next millennium. But even when she and Hayes had dined socially with Richard Daetwyler, one of the project heads, the subject had been so pointedly avoided that Avery knew all she needed to about the level of secrecy involved.

The narrow road wound on through a dense thicket of palmetto and pine to a security checkpoint, where a woman wearing the same uniform as Avery scrutinized the laminate, tapped at a computer keyboard and waved her in with a standard-issue Dreamworld smile.

The complex was far larger than Avery had imagined, comprising several one-storey annexes in addition to the large, futuristic central building that she remembered seeing in Hayes's copy of the coffee-table book on Dreamworld architecture. The caption had identified it as 'an administration building inspired by the Georges Pompidou Centre in Paris' and it had looked like a real show-stopper, its silvery fascia panels burning gold where the sun struck them. Now, however, as the structure loomed ahead on Avery's approach, its bouncing reflections of light were as brutal and blinding as jail-house search beams, and the external network of red and purple pipes reminded her of a particularly unpleasant piece of roadkill she'd once seen on I–95.

The receptionist – sorority hair, coral suit, pussycat bow, perky yet officious – had kept Avery waiting for a seemingly interminable eight and a half minutes while she verified Avery's clearance. It wouldn't have been so infuriating, Avery concluded, if the woman hadn't spent so much of that time just staring at the laminate, as if doing so for long enough would furnish her with additional information.

After the last of several disappearances into a back office, the woman returned, tossing her blonde hair over her shoulder and smiling broadly as she proffered the visitors' book and invited Avery to sign in.

'You're clear! So, can I direct you where you need to go? Who do you need to talk to first?'

Although she couldn't hear all of the exchange, Avery thoroughly enjoyed watching the receptionist ask her superior in the back office for permission to leave her post in order to assist in a County police inquiry.

Four

Dreamworld property straddles two counties, and Dreamworld security enjoys a friendly and co-operative relationship with the police departments in both. Avery initially wondered whether someone had forgotten to tell this to Officer Serena Lopez, but soon came to understand the reason for the woman's spiky demeanour during their brief phone conversation.

Crime investigations are seldom neat, but the one into which Avery had roved was dirtier than most.

Until you hit the town of Melbourne on the Atlantic coast, State road 192 is an unlit, single-lane highway. It runs south through Kissimmee before veering due east towards the ocean, cutting a swathe through acres of glorious, humbling, almost animate antediluvian land-scape – the kind that jolts you into giddy comprehension of what Florida looked like for the fifty million years it took mankind to crawl from the primordial ooze and invent toll roads and strip malls and dinner theatre.

It was here, some time after three a.m. the previous

night, that a rented Harley carrying two accounting students from Michigan had collided head on with another vehicle.

By the time Officer Brett Toback of the Osceola County mobile patrol discovered the scene – three forty-six a.m. by the Chip 'n' Dale Rescue Rangers wristwatch his wife had given him as a rather ill-judged first anniversary gift – the other vehicle was nowhere to be seen. Whoever it was who had struck the cycle, scattering twisted metal across the highway, sending the driver soaring into the undergrowth and his female pillion rider skittering across the tarmac for some distance, had driven away.

Toback made an official record of this and radioed for paramedical back-up before violently expelling the two Taco Bell chicken gorditas he'd eaten a half-hour earlier.

Toback told the paramedics that he had been unable to find a pulse on either victim, although admittedly he had not even attempted to approach the girl. He didn't need no medical degree, he later informed his colleagues at the precinct and anyone who'd listen at O'Malley's sports bar in Winter Haven, to figure that he wasn't going to find anything. Hell, he'd have had trouble just locating a goddamn *limb* in that mess, let alone a pulse. He didn't tell them about the gorditas.

Bar the odd truck, the road had been virtually deserted, as was usual at that time of night, but Toback had remained at the scene for some time while the road accident investigation guys did their stuff, just in case any rubberneckers needed to be waved on.

In between making periodic checks in the wing mirror of his patrol car to see whether the blood vessel he'd busted in his right eye when he threw up had subsided any, Toback watched with interest as they took imprints of the skid marks on the highway, took measurements,

23

carefully bagged and tagged the loose car parts and
smashed glass, and began to comb the undergrowth for
debris that might provide further clues to the identity of
the second vehicle, the driver of which was probably
looking at charges of manslaughter and a generous
stretch in jail.

After an hour and three quarters, Toback noted that
the eye was looking somewhat better and, more importantly, the dry-heaving seemed to have stopped, even
when he gingerly allowed himself to think – by way of
a test – about glistening coils of intestine and Taco Bell.
There was a nasty moment when, climbing behind the
wheel, he had glimpsed the bone-white crescent moon
overhead and fleetingly been reminded of the girl's
exposed kneecap, and his aching ribcage had contracted
violently all over again. Fortunately, he was already halfway home when they found the picnic cooler.

By all accounts, it was an excellent place for a person
to hide something that he didn't want found: a shallow
stream of marsh, one of many which slashed open the
narrow ribbon of grass that bordered this stretch of highway. And the highway itself: a thoroughfare untrodden
by pedestrians, and steeped in inky-black shadow from
the towering undergrowth by night. Even if the hidden
item should rise or shift and become visible above the
water and through the swampgrass, and even if it should
be glimpsed in daylight by a curious individual in a passing vehicle, making a U-turn was barely feasible, and
the unchanging vista of the scenery, uninterrupted by
landmarks of any kind, would make it almost impossible
to find the intriguing spot on a return journey.

Presuming that the former custodian of this cooler and
its terrible payload had been aware of all these advan-
tages, this was a class act. If not, it was an extraordinarily

lucky burst of inspiration. Or, at least, it would have been lucky had the unfortunate motorcycle wreck not lured a swarm of keen-eyed police investigators to the scene.

Such was the general consensus among the accident investigation crew, and the newly arrived homicide detectives and forensic personnel nodded in agreement. Almost an hour passed before anybody mooted the possibility that luck – or lack thereof – may have had nothing to do with it: the driver of the fugitive vehicle might have had an extremely good reason not to stick around. Perhaps, somebody suggested, the driver was in a hurry to depart after dumping the cooler and, in his haste to hit the road, accidentally struck the cycle. Or maybe – fearful that his or her act of dumping had been observed – the collision was not an accident at all.

Certainly these hypotheses were not beyond the realms of possibility. The cooler, for instance, showed no signs of mildew or anything else to suggest that it had been submerged for any considerable time. And more importantly, it was immediately apparent to even the non-forensic members of the assembly that the occupant of the cooler had not been dead for very long.

Factoring in the preserving properties of the container versus the fact that Florida's heat and humidity tended to speed up considerably the onset and dispersion of the rigor mortis process, it was fair to guess that this man had been walking and talking as recently as the previous afternoon. When the lid was prised open, his body remained resolutely cooler-shaped; a visual gag straight out of Tom and Jerry, with a coldly macabre humour to it, even in real life. But no one was laughing.

Although the swamp water that had somehow leaked into the cooler had leached away much of the residual blood from the single gunshot wound in the man's chest, staining his dirty T-shirt and cheap shorts a delicate shade of pink, a great deal of gore, presumably from another injury, remained clotted around his mouth and his chin. It was thick and copious and almost black, and made the whites of the man's eyes – which were bugged out in a wildly unsettling expression of haunted panic – appear all the more luminous by contrast. If you looked closely, which no one did who didn't have to, you could see the blackened stump of the dead man's tongue, still suppurating, damp and open, where he had bitten it off.

Officer Serena Lopez liked things neat and tidy, and was grateful for the fact that situations like this didn't come up too often – cases which threw personnel from several different departments together, inevitably winding up with her having to nurse half a dozen metaphorical toes that had been stepped on. Besides the homicide and road accident divisions, she now had the guys from vice to deal with, since shortly after the deceased had been IDed, his distinctively dilapidated 1982 Pontiac Sunbird had turned up abandoned in the parking lot of a strip joint on Orange Blossom Trail that just happened to be under surveillance that week.

The last thing she needed right now was another officer on the case, and, worse still, one from a neighbouring agency, but by the time the call came through from Sylvia Avery, Serena Lopez had reached a state of ill-tempered acceptance. Bring 'em on. Bring 'em all on, she thought. At least there was no way this case could get any more tangled than it was already.

Five

Avery conducted her first three interviews – with the receptionist, the security guard and the admin clerk – in a corner of the Research and Development Complex's main administration office, carefully making notes by hand on a legal pad.

By all accounts, the demise of Jerry Lee Lucas at the age of forty-one years represented no great loss to society. The pool of occasional volunteers, mostly local students, was not excessively large, but the administrative staff remembered Lucas more clearly than any of the others, by virtue of his being older and infinitely more objectionable. Despite having visited the centre only three times, spending less than five minutes in the reception area on each occasion, he had managed to leave a lasting impression as a man who was rude, lecherous and foul-tempered.

'And I don't like to speak ill of the dead, but, oh my, he smelt bad, too,' the administration clerk had added, leaning towards Avery in a conspiratorial fashion, so close that Avery could smell the Aquanet in the woman's cotton-candy hair. The clerk had looked disappointed when she'd noticed that Avery made no move to commit this nugget to paper.

It all seemed fairly straightforward. Lucas had arrived the previous day at ten-twenty a.m., twenty minutes later than the other volunteers. He had signed the visitors' book at reception and two forms in the admin office – a standard insurance company release and a confidentiality agreement – before being taken by the security guard to the central waiting room, to be collected by the research team responsible for him. He had left the Research and Development Complex at six-thirty p.m., or so it was noted in the visitors' book, which had been transferred after hours, as per routine, to the unmanned back door.

According to Officer Lopez, Lucas had failed to return to his digs the previous night. The super at his building reported that three guys had shown up at nine p.m., bearing a six of Miller Genuine Draft and a poker deck. They had waited in the hallway acting rowdy for almost an hour before Lucas's neighbours complained and had them kicked out. They had spent the rest of the night playing pool at the bar down the street that was Lucas's regular haunt, but he never showed. No one had thought to report him missing, but all had thought his broken rendezvous odd. It wasn't so much that Lucas was a model of reliability, Lopez explained, more that nobody could imagine him having found anything better to do. The receptionist assured Avery that it was normal that Lucas's signature did not appear in the 'out' box opposite his name in the visitors' book. She had flipped to the clear pocket on the inside back cover and pulled out a typed sheet bearing the names of a dozen volunteers, a flurry of checks scribbled beside them.

'You're lucky. These get filed every few days. It would've taken me a while to find it. Standard sign-out sheet for a volunteer team. Whoever's in charge checks 'em off as they leave, signs the sheet and leaves it here on their way out. Someone updates the book the next day. Saves time.'

'Can I make a Xerox of this?'

'Uh-uh, I don't think so. I'm going to need to check on that.'

'You do that.'

Avery smiled as she wandered away, pen and pad in hand, writing down all the details she could remember. She managed ten names and four addresses and got a distinct rush from finally putting her exceptional powers of recall to some use other than memorizing her driver's licence number, social security and other people's birthdays. Moreover, she became conscious for the first time of her eagerness to ace the task set for her. And not because she wanted to please Hayes.

Dreamworld security force is authorized to handle situations and mount investigations relating to any incident that takes place on Dreamworld property. It has the authority, with a few caveats, to lawfully detain any individual who is under suspicion of committing a crime. Arrests and prosecutions, however, must be carried out by the neighbouring county's officials, hence the huge importance that was placed on co-operating with the local cops. Having your cheerleaders at the sheriff's office or with the D A was the fast track to promotion at Dreamworld, and Avery knew it. She returned to the reception desk with fire in her belly.

'I'm about ready to go through and see Dr Daetwyler now.'

'Okey-doke. I'll just need your autograph right here.'

The receptionist flipped open a four-page document that appeared, from skimming it, to be a declaration of confidentiality. Avery signed it, and was just about to ask for directions when a breathless young woman appeared at her shoulder.

'You're here to see Richard, aren't you? I'm just on my way back. I can take you through.'

She was in her mid-twenties, Avery guessed, clean-scrubbed and potentially attractive in a why-Miss-Jones-you're-beautiful kind of way, if only she'd worn spectacles that could be taken off or had long tresses that could be shaken down instead of the rather erratic and possibly self-inflicted haircut that made you think of eagle feathers. Now Avery came to think of it, there was something *generally* avian about the girl, despite the fact that she stood well over six foot and the lab-coat she wore over her jeans and MIT sweatshirt was almost comically short in the arms. Her build gave an impression of broad-shouldered strength, and yet the boney fragility of her handshake came as no surprise.

'I'm Catherine Homolka. Richard's assistant.'

'Sylvia Avery. Security.'

'Right. Richard's expecting you. Something happened to one of our volunteers, or something?'

'Uh-huh. Jerry Lee Lucas. You know the guy?'

'Sure. He was here yesterday. What do they think happened?'

Avery became suddenly aware that Catherine was staring intently at her, and when she looked up to meet the taller woman's eye, she found such an unexpected measure of fear in the searching gaze that she felt herself recoil.

'We don't know yet.'

Whatever had been there was gone, and Avery wondered if she had imagined it after all.

'Did you know him well?'

'Not especially well. Not at all, really. You won't need a statement from me, will you?'

'It won't be a formal statement. But, yes, if you saw him yesterday, I'll just need to ask you a few questions, take down a few details. That's all. That's not a problem, is it?'

Catherine Homolka shook her head and smiled, a nice genuine smile, as she led Avery towards the first set of heavy security doors and punched a six-digit code into the keypad mounted on the wall beside it. An awkward hush fell as Avery walked beside Catherine, striding to keep pace. Just the sound of their footfalls in the long corridor, now, and the hollow six-note sonatas at the next two keypads.

At the fourth and final set of doors, Catherine slipped her index and middle fingers into a narrow metal box mounted in an alcove and waited, leaning against the locked door.

'Very James Bond,' Avery remarked. Catherine seemed relieved that she had broken the silence.

'Everyone thinks it reads your fingerprints, but it's actually a biometric system: looks at your bone structure from different angles and generates a number. Everybody's different. Then you can set approved numbers in a security system like this, or put them on a metal strip on an ID card or whatever. Takes about fifteen seconds to make a match. Richard said they tried them out at one of the park entrances for a while – ImagiNation, I think – instead of picture ID, to stop people transferring those reduced-rate Florida residents' passes. Took too long, though, because loads of people got freaked out and wanted to know what the hell it was. Caused a real bottleneck, I guess.'

A click, and Catherine shouldered the door open. 'And here we are.'

To anyone who had ever set foot in a college science department or a corporate lab, Richard Daetwyler's plush and pristine research suite looked as jarringly unfamiliar as anything on TV or at the movies. Like everything else at Dreamworld, it appeared to have been conceived by a romantically inclined set designer with a bottomless budget, and stepping into its midst, Avery half expected Jeff Goldblum or Gillian Anderson to burst in wearing an anti-contamination suit, shouting, 'The DNA base-pairs don't match any found in nature . . . And they appear to be multiplying!' Any real scientist would have looked out of place in the midst of such a lavish set-up as this, and Richard Daetwyler was no exception. Rangy and boyish in his too-dark denims, plaid shirt rolled to the elbow and little wire-rimmed spectacles which threatened to slip down the curve of his aquiline nose, he looked more like a field reporter for *Rolling Stone*, Avery thought, than someone to be entrusted with a large research grant and several rooms full of expensive and possibly dangerous hardware. He beamed at her and extended his hand, the long poetic fingers parted, relaxed.

'Avery, hi, come in. I was so pleased when Hayes told me it was going to be you coming.'

Avery shook his hand. 'Just doing my job. Good to see you again.'

'Devon's here – Devon, honey, you remember Avery?'

Daetwyler's five-year-old daughter was curled up daintily on the buttercup-yellow sofa that stood against the far wall of the foyer. Avery felt mildly unsettled not to have noticed the child's presence when she first came in.

Devon stared at her. 'Uh-huh. I remember. Avery is dating Hayes. We all had dinner at the Japanese steakhouse with the drums the first time, and the other time was at the place with the great big fish tank.' The little girl tucked a hay-coloured tendril behind her tiny ear. Her hair was tangled and long, spilling into her lap where her little hands rested, partly hidden in the petticoats of her lilac nylon dress. As far as Avery could see, she appeared to be holding a small broadcast-quality tape-recording device. 'You wanted oysters for your appetizer,' Devon continued. 'But you were mad that they wouldn't let you have them raw, so you got ceviche instead. And after, you had lobster. But you didn't want to wear the plastic bib and then it all went on you.'

'Boy, you have a good memory,' Avery replied, genuinely impressed, though unsure whether the girl had intended the implication of foolish vanity to sting. Which it did. 'I forgot that. But I do remember that you were wearing the same pretty dress you're wearing today. Both times. I'll bet that's your favourite dress, huh?'

'It's my *only* dress. I have six of them,' Devon informed her. 'That way I don't have to think about what to wear in the morning. Like Einstein.' Devon sat up straight to show Avery the winsome cartoon woman embroidered on the bodice. 'It's Megara. From *Hercules*? Did you see that movie?'

'The Disney one? Are you allowed to wear that in here?'

Avery had intended the joke for Homolka and Daetwyler, but Devon didn't miss a trick.

'I can wear what I like. Daddy says I'm a maverick.' Devon stared at Avery and raised one downy eyebrow. 'Usually no one from Dreamworld comes here except Hayes and Mr Darwin. They're not allowed to. How come you're here?'

Avery was relieved when Daetwyler intervened with the suggestion that they talk in his office.

'The coroner's office haven't released their final report yet, but they're estimating time of death at some time yesterday evening.'

Avery measured her words carefully, afraid of exposing herself as someone whose only experience of this kind of law enforcement work came from watching *NYPD Blue*.

Daetwyler looked through her, thinking. He was leaning back in his swivel chair, holding his desk with both hands and swinging vigorously from side to side, like a hyper kid visiting his dad's office. Avery wondered how long he would keep it up.

'So it's going to be important for us to know exactly when he left the centre,' she continued. 'And who with, if anybody. They found his car at a strip joint on Orange Blossom, but we don't know if he went alone or what. So far, none of the staff there have given a positive ID, so it's possible that he never even went in. You see what I'm saying?'

Daetwyler carried on swivelling silently. But now he looked distracted rather than pensive.

'So you're certain he left the building at six-thirty?'

'They all left the building at six-thirty. All the volunteers. I checked off the sign-out sheet myself.'

'Did you see him get into his car? Drive away? Or wait? Anything?'

'Nope. I checked them off and came right back in here.'

Daetwyler shrugged apologetically.

'So he didn't necessarily drive off right away?'

'I guess.'

'Richard, we're playing for the same side here.' Avery gently met the scientist's gaze. 'If I can get everything the police need right now, they won't need to bother you again. Hayes doesn't want anyone from outside snooping round this place, and I'm sure you don't either. But if I can't sew things up for them . . .'

Daetwyler abruptly stopped swivelling and looked pleased. 'Right, hold on, you made me remember something: about ten minutes later, one of the other volunteers wanted to come back inside to call a taxi because his ride didn't show. And while I was out back doing that, I saw that the lot was empty. You think that'll do it?'

'So, by six-forty approximately, Lucas was gone?'

'Right.'

'Unless he was somewhere else in the grounds.'

'Uh-uh. Not possible. We have a twenty-four-hour patrol. With dogs. If one of our guys had been parked or was driving around, security would have let us know. Like a shot.'

'So what was his name, the guy who wanted the taxi?'

'Oh, you got me now . . . Hold on.' Daetwyler furrowed his brow and started swivelling again. Left, right, left, right. 'Nope. I'm sorry, I don't recall.'

'That's okay, I can check the visitors' book. You signed him back in, presumably?'

Daetwyler looked alarmed. 'Are they going to want a statement from him? Only thing is, I'm not sure if we're supposed to have some confidentiality thing with volunteers, like not giving their names out.'

Avery shot him a smile. 'Don't worry, if it comes to it, you can blame me. I'll say I got the name out of the book. Nothing to do with you.'

He didn't smile back.

'Richard, you must see that they're going to need to speak to this guy. And maybe some of the others. Find someone who can confirm when Lucas left, and who with – if anyone – you know? Obviously if Lucas gave one of the other volunteers a ride home or something, they would need to know that. If only to eliminate that person from the inquiry.'

Daetwyler's swivelling became more urgent. He thought for a long while before he spoke. 'Avery, this is between you and me, and I'm trusting you because I know you personally, okay? Off the record?'

Avery wanted to protest, but Daetwyler didn't give her a chance.

'There's a reason why it's not going to be helpful to get a statement from any of the volunteers who were here yesterday, and a reason why, if you did, it could be really difficult for me. And for Dreamworld. *Really* difficult.'

Richard Daetwyler took off his glasses and rubbed his left eye with the heel of his hand before putting them back on. The colour had drained from his already-pale features, and he inhaled deeply as if to steel himself.

'Not all the volunteers left at six-thirty last night. In fact, most of them didn't. Lucas did, genuinely. I swear it. You're going to have to believe me. The rest were supposed to – everyone was supposed to leave at six-thirty. But I had to keep a few people late. For observation. And that just *can't* get out.'

Daetwyler studied her face.

'Come into the lab,' he sighed, rising to his feet. 'I guess I'm going to have to show you what we're working on.'

Six

Richard Daetwyler led Avery into a cramped, antiseptic hallway, past a parade of heavy wooden doors. Their small observation windows, ruthless slices of tempered glass and security mesh, afforded limited view into the rooms beyond.

Daetwyler fumbled with an unfeasibly large cluster of keys at his hip, unlocked one of the doors and ushered Avery in. The meagre dimensions and sound-proofing panels reminded her of a radio broadcasting booth, and the furniture – two leather chairs and a bank of fitted metal closets that occupied the entire back wall – gave little clue to the cubicle's actual purpose. The two sat down.

'Okay, Avery, let me try and put this in a nutshell,' Daetwyler began. 'Stop me if you get lost. Let's start with . . . Okay, let me start by asking you: do you understand what's happening to you when you experience something?'

'I'm not sure I understand the question.'

'Okay.' Avery watched Daetwyler think; heard the careful patience in his voice as he changed tack. 'Do you understand what I mean when I say that all experience is brain activity?'

'Er . . . I guess you mean that if I'm seeing something, hearing something, feeling or whatever, all the information gets processed through my brain?'

'Right. Sort of. But processed isn't exactly the right word. The point is that it doesn't matter what external information your senses are gathering: the whole business of experiencing the world happens in your brain. You stroke a cat with your hand, but when you feel the fur – it's soft, it's fluffy, it's warm – that's all going on in your brain. Not in your hand. See what I'm saying?'

'I think so.'

'So let's say we're looking at your brain activity when you're stroking the cat. And let's say we can track the exact pattern – the firing, the electrical activity – and we have a record of it. You following me?'

Avery nodded.

'Now, what do you think would happen if we could generate exactly the same pattern in your brain, using electro-magnetic fields. What would you experience?'

'I'd feel like I was stroking a cat. I'd feel the same way, the same thing. Yes?'

'Exactly.'

'I see. But obviously, if there was no cat there, it wouldn't be exactly the same.'

'Well, no, but do you understand that it would feel exactly the same? *Exactly*. It would be no less real. Because technically, the *experience* would be the exact same one. Either way – cat or no cat – it's all happening in your brain. No difference.'

'Except the cat is invisible, I can't hear it, I can't smell it. I can only touch it.' Avery gave scant pause as her mind caught up with her mouth. 'Oh right, I see, but if you can log all the patterns for all the senses, you can pretty much recreate the whole experience of stroking a cat. Okay. I'm with you now.' She felt a flush of impatience as her mind raced further ahead. 'So you've figured out how to do this?'

'Not me, I'm afraid. Love to take the credit . . . Love to, but can't. It's just simple neuroscience. This kind of work has been going on for years. And there are plenty of people doing similar stuff elsewhere. The difference is in the funding. I've got it and they don't.'

Avery opened her mouth to speak, but Daetwyler pre-empted her.

'You're gonna ask about the applications? I'm personally interested in the medical side. Technically, there's no reason why we shouldn't be able to override a "pain" signal in an injured person with a "no pain" pattern. Get this set up in hospitals and you're talking about just unimaginable levels of benefit, especially where you've got a problem with using painkillers. Or if you want to get into a slightly murkier area, take the idea of a terminal patient. Right now, the only help people get with dying is being pumped full of opiates. What if we could give them a religious experience? Non-denominational, obviously. But a white light, a feeling of warmth and well-being; love. A bit of distant, gentle music. Maybe some kind of hazy, benign figures waiting with open arms, welcoming, c'mon over, don't be scared . . .'

Daetwyler studied Avery and, ever the scientist, out of his depth in the indistinct arena of human emotion, mistook her awed silence for lack of interest. He digressed quickly.

'But from the Dreamworld point of view, obviously it's the entertainment angle they've signed on for. Where do you go from where we are now? What's the way forward? Well, look around at what we've got. People come here to have experiences they can't get anywhere else – or, I should say, controlled, friendly versions of those experiences. They want to go over the Niagara Falls in a barrel. They want to see a bunch of ghosts. They want to go into outer space. But obviously there's a limit to what you can do. And here you are – potentially you've got the next stage. No limits. You can make people fly. Dive with dolphins and mermaids. Do a moonwalk. We're talking years down the line, but potentially . . . The potential is there. Beats the crap out of virtual reality. To say the least.'

'The very least. I'm impressed.'

Avery's mouth was dry, her mind open. When you're used to second-guessing people, it's a thrill to be taken by surprise.

Daetwyler unlocked two sections of the steel closet, opened the smaller of the two and brought out what appeared to be a lightweight yellow bicycle helmet, laced through with a few strands of coloured electrical cord. Avery found it impossible to hide her mild amusement and deep disappointment as Daetwyler handed the object to her. This time, he read her instantly.

'Obviously this is just what we're using right now in our studies. It's low tech, but it does the job. A couple of solenoids on here generate the electromagnetic field. The information – the specific patterns – *that*'s all in here . . .'

Daetwyler swung open the larger closet door to reveal an impressively hulking computer with double-tower drives and a flat-screen monitor.

'*This* is the important bit – the hardware. Down the line we'll almost certainly be able to focus the electromagnetic

40

fields – the ones with information in them – using methods that are, uh, less direct.'

'Like in a wall or something?'

'Right. Although bear in mind that if you had something that looked slightly more state-of-the-art, people probably wouldn't mind putting it on anyhow. So we might not need to go that way.'

'Like a virtual reality helmet.'

'Exactly. Only there's nothing virtual about it.'

Avery wrinkled her brow and winced in a humorous demonstration of bewilderment.

'You're going to confuse me again,' she laughed. 'Let's quit while we're ahead.'

This time Daetwyler smiled back, but the smile never quite reached his eyes. Avery remembered all at once why she had been made privy to these secrets.

'Richard, to be honest, I'd rather talk about this – I'm just blown away by it all – but I think there was something else you wanted to tell me. Why you don't want me to question the other volunteers . . .'

Daetwyler nodded forlornly and rose again, leading her silently back into the hallway and towards another door further along.

Looking down towards the lobby as Daetwyler fumbled with the keys, Avery could see Devon lying on the floor. She was on her back, her little feet playing idly against the wall, the sleek, expensive tape-recorder balanced on her chest. A wire snaked from it to the microphone she held in her hands, into which she was talking rapidly but deliberately, in tones too soft to be heard. Avery looked away again and inquisitively pressed her face to the observation panel of the door closest to her. She soon wished that she hadn't. From where she stood, she thought she could see Catherine Homolka hunched over a workbench, only there was something horribly wrong about the woman's crumpled posture. Avery felt a queasy lurch of unease and pulled away, suddenly afraid that Homolka might look up.

The room that Daetwyler brought her to next took Avery by surprise. With its rows of hospital beds, each with its own tangle of tubes and monitoring equipment, colour-coded trash cans and carts loaded with medical paraphernalia, it was as if they had wandered into a deserted ICU ward.

'What do we use this for?' Daetwyler raised one eyebrow as he pre-empted Avery's question. 'Okay, the short answer is that we occasionally use pharmaceuticals in our work. Not street drugs, obviousy. Nothing like that. Just standard, available compounds in safe doses appropriate to producing a hallucinogenic effect. We need to fine-tune our understanding of what makes the brain override the signals coming in from the outside world in favour of other signals. And nature is our best tutor. If we can pin down exactly what's happening to suppress the intrusion of reality when someone has a powerful hallucination, we can hopefully recreate that artificially when it comes to inputting our own data.'

Avery had tuned out. Her mind was elsewhere. 'Does Hayes know about this?'

'Of course he does. He's overseen the whole project from the beginning.' Daetwyler seemed impatient. 'And I'm sure you don't need either of us to tell you that this is exactly the kind of thing that really, really needs to be kept private. It's just a tiny part of our research, but if the press got hold of it, it would be . . . Well, like I said, you don't need it explained to you, I'm sure.'

Avery nodded.

'Police reports, anyone can look at them, right?'

She nodded again.

'If anyone – even you – talks to the volunteers from yesterday, it's going to be on paper for anyone to see. They were supposed to all leave at six-thirty, but we kept a few people back for observation in here because – well, just because we wanted to be sure that they were absolutely okay to drive before they left. We kept most of them until about midnight.'

'Lucas too?'

'No, not Lucas. I told you, he was fine, and we let him go, along with a few other people, between six-thirty and seven-thirty. We staggered it. So I'm afraid no one else saw him leave. But it also means that no one else from here left with him. And I'm very happy if you want to tell the sheriff's office that I personally watched him pull out of the lot. Catherine can back me up, if you like. Will that do?'

Avery's mind was racing. She knew that Daetwyler's final version of events didn't necessarily mean that Jerry Lee Lucas had left the centre alone. But the statement he'd told her to pass on to Osceola County would ensure that the investigation of the centre and its volunteers would be considered complete. Regardless, she never seriously considered any option but to concede to becoming complicit in Daetwyler's little white yarn. If the police thought there was any chance that Lucas had left with another volunteer, every member of yesterday's team would become a suspect in his slaying. Without the excuse of protecting the corporate secrets at the centre, Dreamworld security's involvement in the investigation would be over and no amount of wrangling or throwing around of weight by Hayes would change that fact. Osceola County would conduct the interviews, and Avery felt sure that few, if any, of the motley bunch who surrendered their bodies to science for cash had any loyalty to Dreamworld. Everything would come out, and it would all cruise down the healthy avenue of communication which had always existed between law enforcement and press. A press who would chase the volunteers and find out that they were more than just interns. That in itself would cause a stir. And they would find out about Daetwyler's project, giving Dreamworld rivals a good chance to play catch-up in the race to develop new entertainment technologies. Or perhaps they'd make the project sound so sinister that the whole thing would have to be scrapped, flushing a multi-million dollar investment down the drain, not to mention the lost revenue that might have been accrued in the future. Or it could be worse: they could pick up on the drugs – oh God, the drugs – or on the individuals kept back for observation, a situation which, Avery suspected, Daetwyler might be underplaying somewhat. *And it would all be her fault.*

Avery's skin crawled as she imagined Hayes's reaction to such disasters. The thought of losing him was unbearable, but over and above that – far, far over and above it – there was Dreamworld. It was her life, her family, the most important thing in her universe. In her childhood it had been her salvation, her visits there sweet sanctuary. Back then, it had been the only place where the horrors of her daily life disappeared – and not just metaphorically, but literally. The only place where she had ever felt truly safe, or been truly happy.

To live the rest of her life with the responsibility of

knowing that her actions had sullied, maybe even destroyed, this pure, glorious, joy-bringing Shangri-La . . . There was no doubt in Avery's mind: that was no life at all.

Seven

Most of Dreamworld's eighty-two residential homes are located on the outskirts of property boundaries, near the resort hotels, but not so near that anyone ever notices them.

Hayes Ober had been one of the first people invited to take their pick of the available lots, and he had chosen what was possibly the very nicest – one lying at the highest point of the elevated land behind the Hawaiian Village resort. From the back porch, you could clearly see Mount Kahuna with its roiling fibre-optic caldera and endlessly-gushing river of lava, and below it, the majestic sweep of Tsunami Cove, ringed with towering queen palms.

Sometimes, if Hayes didn't have to work late or see people for dinner, and if, like tonight, the weather was not too humid and not too hot, he and Avery would sit out here with a cold beer. Hayes would fetch a good Cuban cigar – usually a Montecristo No 2 – from the Tupperware box in which he kept them with a moistened piece of natural sponge, and they would play Scrabble, or do the *New Yorker* cryptic crossword together. It was during these gentle, familiar moments – much, much more so than when they were having sex, which they did frequently – that Avery's adoration for Hayes resonated most strongly, with a raging intensity that frightened her.

Tonight they sat in their usual seats on the porch, but Hayes had brought out only a large plastic bottle of Zephyrhills spring water and although Avery could see the outline of a cigar in his breast pocket, he had left his cigar-cutter and butane lighter on the counter indoors. He stared resolutely out towards the fake volcano and the thunderheads gathering low on the horizon without really seeing either, his concern and internal frenzy palpable despite his fixed expression.

In the distance, Avery heard the horn that signalled the hourly onslaught of giant artificial waves at the cove, followed, as it always was, by the excited shrieks of vacationers as they surged into the water with their bodyboards and inflatables, just a gaily-coloured swathe of tiny pin-pricks from where she sat.

'This security patrol guy, was he *sure*? Absolutely sure? Had he made any record of it?'

It was now the third time, in so many words, that Hayes had asked Avery this question since she broke the bad news to him. For a fleeting moment when she first told him she had thought that he was going to hit her, which was bizarre, because he never had and presumably never would. Now she chided herself for thinking it at all.

It had all gone so smoothly at the Research and Development Complex, right up until the last minute. Avery had used a spare terminal in the administration room to type everything up. She had printed it out on the blank inter-office report sheets that she had brought with her along with the fresh file into which she slipped the still-hot pages. On the way out, as Hayes had arranged, she had also picked up a slim ringbinder containing the gate attendant's master list of staff-car details – colour, make, model and plate. Hayes had already faxed Officer Lopez a copy of the attendant's records of the visitor vehicle details for the previous day, which was how they had confirmed that Lucas had been at the centre. Even so, the overzealous attendant had given Avery a hard copy, with the listing for Lucas's Sunbird illuminated by a gash of yellow highlight marker. Once back inside her own car, Avery had slipped these into the folder alongside her report. Only seconds passed before she got them out again.

According to Officer Lopez, the initial analyses of the accident investigation team were pointing to the hit-and-run vehicle almost certainly being a classic Volkswagen camper van, tangerine, at least twenty years old, but in a decent state of repair – or at least it would have been up until the moment of impact. Lopez had clearly been hoping that it belonged to a volunteer or a full-time employee at the centre, since this individual was currently the prime suspect in the case, and she'd seemed a little dismayed that this most obvious avenue of inquiry seemed to be a dead end.

Although Avery had seen a few VW campers on her last trip to Sebastian Inlet, when she'd watched Perdue compete in the annual 'Doctors, Lawyers, Weekend Warriors' tournament for veteran surfers, she couldn't remember having seen any driving around on Dreamworld property or in town at all, and her logic told her that the chances of finding one listed in the pages she held were reassuringly slim. Regardless, she failed to be reassured. Her breaths came shallow and fast as she skimmed the pages, and she felt a hideous swoop in her solar plexus on each of the three occasions that she briefly – mistakenly – thought she'd found a match.

She had checked both documents twice more, to be certain, and had just replaced them in the file when the uniformed patrol guard had knocked on her window.

He had held his hands up in apology as soon as he saw Avery's uniform and made as if to leave, but she wound down her window anyhow to tell him that she was just going.

'That's okay. Take your time.'

Call it instinct, call it fate, Avery was never sure afterwards why she said what she had said next. After all, her report was complete. The police could continue their investigation without any need to pry further into Dreamworld business. Avery's work was done. Everyone would be happy. But she said it anyway.

'Thanks. Could I ask if you were on duty last night?'

The man nodded. The hulking German Shepherd by his side sat down, as if it knew that its human colleague was not going to continue his patrol just yet.

'Yep, same shift. Five p.m. Till one.'

'Did anybody hang around at all? I'm thinking specifically of folks from one of the volunteer teams, from the main building . . .'

'Only one crew of volunteers in yesterday, ma'am.'

'You don't happen to remember a guy in a beat-up Pontiac Sunbird, do you?'

The guard shook his head quickly, thought a little, then shook it again.

'Sorry I can't be more help.'

'No problem.'

'There *was* one vehicle, around midnight. Volunteers. Guy and a gal. Sat in the lot just talking. Left when I moved them on.'

'But it definitely wasn't a Pontiac?'

'Right. It was a camper van. One of them old ones.

Pink, maybe, maybe yellow or orange. Hard to say. I keep telling them we need more illumination out here and they keep on promising, but it never happens.'

Avery drove back to Hayes's house on autopilot, her promise to call him forgotten, paddling hard against the cloudy swell of rising alarm. Twice along the way, her cellphone trilled – both calls from the sheriff's office, according to the readout on the LCD. Both times, Avery let it ring until it stopped.

A light, warm rain had started to fall, but if Hayes had noticed it, he had opted to ignore it. When Hayes concentrated hard on something, it was as if his mind became detached from his body, as if, at such times, his corporeal being was merely an inconvenient encumbrance to the exquisite and complex machinations of his sophisticated intellect. She remembered the evening, shortly after they first started dating, when they had sat right here on the porch and begun to talk about childhood road-trips – the shimmering, endless highway, the musty motels, the mystery spots and terrifying statues of Paul Bunyan, the dusty roadside attractions with their moth-eaten jackalopes and creaking carousels of dog-eared postcards, all pictures of factories and recipes for pie. At some point during the conversation, Hayes had been suddenly struck with the concept for the Americana resort, and had fallen into a sort of trance. Avery remembered the rest of the night vividly: the feverish scribbling, the motionless hours slumped zombie-like in the leather club chair, eyes glassy and darting like a channeller possessed by spirits. She remembered the ignored plate of food, the untouched glass of water, the animal yelp that came early the next morning when Hayes had been yanked from his fugue by a crippling pain in his lower abdomen. The frighteningly violent growl of irritation when it turned out to be merely a need to relieve himself that had failed to register for the last fourteen hours.

Now, Avery watched her lover's hair and face grow wet in the rain, feeling the same sense of isolation and nervous uncertainty that she had felt that night.

Hayes's reanimation was sudden and without warning. The seizing of her hands, the resolute tug that pulled her from her chair, the muscular arm that snaked round her waist and pulled her down onto his lap – all of this happened so quickly and caught Avery off guard.

Hayes rested his head on the soft swell of her chest and sighed, but his cadence, when he spoke next, was deep and rich and jarringly unmarred by fear or quandary.

'Avery, this is a fucking nightmare. That camper van: you know who it belongs to? Because *I* do. Had to get it moved out of the cast-member lot at ImagiNation today.'

Avery felt an icy charge climb her spine as she waited for him to continue. 'It belongs, or should I say belonged, to Lisa Schaeffer.'

'I don't understand.'

'Her boyfriend – he of the charming Othello stunt in the disabled toilet – was a volunteer at the centre. Name of Leon LeGalley. Presumably she went there to pick him up.'

Avery nodded because she remembered LeGalley's name from the volunteer sheet. 'But why wasn't the van registered on the printout?'

'Somebody up there likes us?'

'How do you mean?'

'I mean I'm not sure why. She had a cast member windshield sticker. Maybe they only log non-cast member vehicles. But the point is, *thank God*. Because officially Lisa Schaeffer and Leon LeGalley are alive and well. They've eloped. Jacked it all in. Withdrew all their money from their bank accounts, or should I say Lisa's bank account, Leon didn't have a penny to his name, threw a few things in a bag and hit the road this afternoon in the camper van. We were pretty pissed when Lisa didn't make it back from her coffee break, but hey, best of luck to them both. Lisa's parents – nice couple, Beverly Hills area code, spoke to them a couple hours ago – they would never have approved of a guy like Leon. Rap sheet as long as your arm. So there you have it. Love makes people do crazy things.'

'That's the official line, huh?'

'That, my honey, is what happened.'

The glaze of unmerciful threat that lacquered Hayes's mellow words and imparted a cold lustre to his gaze was, Avery noted with faint discomfort, something of a turn-on. She became suddenly aware of the points at which their bodies met: his arm around her shoulder; his chest against her back; his fingertips pressing into her bicep, a little tighter than necessary. Her haunches pressing into his lap.

Hayes, however, appeared oblivious to all this warm, rain-soaked proximity as he informed Avery that Lisa and Leon had joined the ranks of the four million US citizens who go missing every year, that the Schaeffers were planning to get a private investigator on the case if they didn't hear from Lisa within a week, and that he didn't have a problem with that.

Hayes didn't need to tell Avery what he *did* have a problem with, where this conversation was going. She understood as well as he did that if the Osceola County police had Lisa Schaeffer and Leon LeGalley chalked up as the fugitive perpetrators of a fatal hit and run, and prime suspects in the Jerry Lee Lucas homicide, they would begin looking for them immediately. And very, very hard. Maybe with the help of the federal authorities.

A web of deceit, like any web, is a fragile thing. Even a web spun with infinite delicacy and precision has its weaker threads. Pull on one, and the whole thing disintegrates. This was the unthinkable scenario.

'You didn't give the sheriff's office your report yet, right?'

Raindrops cascaded from Avery's hair as she shook her head.

'So you'll do it now. You didn't talk to the patrol guy. Every vehicle in the lot yesterday night is accounted for on the printout. Everything else . . . is between you and me.' Hayes smiled. 'Our little secret.'

Suddenly Avery was nine years old and the lap in which she sat was not Hayes's, but her stepfather's. Bile rose in her throat as the gentle, deadly words reached her ears, borne on a sour gust of breath. Pabst Blue Ribbon and Skoal Bandits. It was so real. So real. But now she was big. Tall. She didn't weigh ninety pounds any more. And she was strong enough to wrestle the arms away and leap from the lap. Only now when she whirled around she saw not her stepfather but Hayes. Hayes asking her to lie: for appearance's sake, for the sake of keeping it all together; the most important things. If you think they won't see that you're guilty too, guilty as hell, then you're crazy, Sylvia Avery. Just imagine what everybody would say.

When she started to cry, Hayes led Avery indoors and

sat her down before fetching a towel, with which he began softly to dry her hair.

Hayes Ober stayed silent for some time, waiting until his girlfriend's cheeks were dry and her hair only a little damp before he put to her the proposal that he knew would banish all other thoughts from her mind and buy her co-operation.

Eight

The character costumes worn at Dreamworld are made to be as lightweight as possible. If a bodypiece includes fur, the weft will have been looped with the tufts the maximum distance apart to allow for air circulation without looking threadbare. The headpieces are made of fibreglass over a metal frame and finished with a layer of plastic, and are at least twice the size of a human head to provide plenty of breathing space. But despite these best laid intentions, the combination of heat, humidity and costume is frequently too much for the cast members inside. Precautions are taken – shifts lasting only twenty minutes, an uncostumed cast member posted by the side of every costumed one – but they are not always enough.

Cast members whose jobs include costumed shifts fall within a specific height range – mostly under five foot three – and are of slim build. And not just because the characters they play look cuter that way. In high summer, loss of consciousness towards the end of a shift is so prevalent that there is even a common hand signal taught at Dreamworld to be enacted by costumed staff on the verge of fainting: arms crossed against the chest in an X. On seeing this, the character's uncostumed colleague, and any other cast member nearby of appropriate physical capability, has to move swiftly in getting the character to safety. Anybody tall and heavy would just take too much time and effort to move.

Even the daintiest person packed quite some heft when they were out cold, however, as Avery knew all too well. Her physical strength meant that she was often called upon to help in such situations, and the linking of her arm under a furry arm, the gentle lift, the brisk walk towards the closest utilidor entrance, the all's-well smile to theme park guests and the jovial remarks for their benefit ('Hey Kitty, where have you been? Kitten Caboodle is looking for you! Let's go!') – all this had become second nature to her.

The most important thing was to get the character inside fast, and get the headpiece off. Heat-related vomiting happened only rarely, but it happened, and, depending on the costume, it could pose a very real danger to the wearer. Billy Bug, with its small head-circumference, was the worst. Once a girl had lost her lunch so copiously in one of these that by the time Avery reached her the vomit was oozing through the eye-mesh in fine, worm-shaped threads, like oatmeal forced through a sieve, and despite the insulating properties of the fibreglass, Avery could clearly hear the frantic choking sounds issuing from within.

None of these experiences changed the way that Avery felt about the characters, however. To her, when she thought about Kit-E-Cat and his friends they were not the sweating, fainting, vomiting individuals who gave them physical motion. They were the big, benevolent, anthropomorphic creatures who every day cuddled a thousand children, who laid gentle plastic paws on the downy heads of babies in strollers, and put their arms around the shy young mothers and high-fived the awkward teenage boys. It was common knowledge within Dreamworld that each executive with the company was sent annually to the park to perform a shift in costume. The purpose was to remind them of what Avery knew already: the sheer delight that these mythical creatures brought the guests through playful interaction. A pure, unconditional offer of friendship in a tough world. It represented in a nutshell what Dreamworld was all about.

This notion was with Avery always, was one of the cornerstones on which her own world-view was built, and she had thought it unshakable. But right now, sitting in Perdue's office, holding a picture of Lisa Schaeffer – Lisa Schaeffer whose blood had been soaked up by the fur of one of these costumes, whose last breath had been drawn from the dark, close confines of its headpiece – now Avery felt these foundations begin to crumble.

'Sylvie, you okay?'

Avery nodded to Perdue, grateful for his perceptive concern. The brimming tears that she stabbed at with her thumb were the first she had shed in the forty-five minutes since they had begun talking about Lisa Schaeffer, but only because the reserves of emotional control that she had used to hold them back were now sapped.

'I just feel like . . . No, I'm fine, Felix, honestly.' Avery waved away the paper handkerchief that Perdue was offering her and finally laid Lisa Schaeffer's cast member ID photograph aside. It might have been the youthful prettiness of the girl's face, or her confident, hopeful expression, that had made Avery feel so sorrowful when she looked at it. Either way, she had been struck by an overwhelming sadness and had lost her composure. 'I'm just not used to anything like this. That's all.'

'I know. It's a terrible thing, Sylvie. I didn't last long over at Orange County, as you know. I guess that's why I headed for here instead. Never regretted it; never missed regular police work for a second.'

Avery nodded and gathered herself. 'I remember you saying. But I'm sorry, anyhow. It's unprofessional of me. And I'm fine now. I'm ready.'

She was grateful for Perdue's sympathy, but at the same time aware of his desire to get moving. It was nine twenty-five a.m. and although they had spent nearly an hour talking, their conversation had, in law enforcement terms, been something of a travesty. They had sat there, two raw, unhardened souls beneath their police-like uniforms, struggling to deal with the task before them and finding themselves mired in abstract discussion. They had talked about how unthinkable it was that a non-employee should be able to slip into the utilidor unnoticed, how some of the burden of guilt would cling to them for a long time, maybe always, because if they had been there, perhaps they could have saved this young woman who had died so horribly. And then they had spoken about the comfort that Lisa's parents might find in believing that their daughter was alive (although Avery felt certain that Perdue found this notion as hollow and impotent as she did). Finally, they had encouraged one another towards stoicism bolstered by the faith that to protect Dreamworld, as they were doing, was to preserve the happiness of the millions who flocked here annually.

At last, it seemed, both were ready to move ahead onto practical matters. And move ahead they did. But even when they began to work in earnest, planning their itinerary for the day, and scrawling notes onto the white board behind Perdue's desk, there grew between them the unspoken realization that neither one was going to raise the subject of Avery's unofficial promotion to the élite rank of investigative personnel.

Avery's accredited police college training had allowed her at least to skip the lengthy tour of duty that most entry-level recruits served manning the crash-barrier booths at the hotel entrances (*Are you staying with us tonight? Checking in? Okay, you're going to follow this road straight ahead, and we do have complimentary valet parking for resort guests.*) Regardless, she could reasonably have expected at least another four years, minimum, of foot-work in the parks before having the merest sniff at an investigative post. It wasn't that she was unworthy of such responsibility, just that the pyramid structure of the force meant that opportunities for promotion were rare. They depended on somebody from up top leaving the company, and few ever found a good enough reason to wave goodbye to the Dreamworld perks and kudos. But for Avery, it had turned out, none of this mattered. She had leapfrogged convention not through nepotism so much as – what was it? Emotional handcuffs? Friendly blackmail? These jumbled phrases had tumbled from her imagination, but neither rang true. All she knew was that she had felt a certain sourness soiling her initial thrill at Hayes's proposition the previous night, his suggestion that, as his most trusted ally, he wanted her on the case. He had crouched at her feet and clasped her hands in his, in what struck Avery as a weird burlesque of a man about to propose marriage.

'Will you do it?' Hayes had whispered, and Avery had said that she would. She would join Perdue in initiating the newly necessary second stage of Hayes's clean-up operation. And here she was.

Nine

It didn't take long after the opening of Walt Disney's first theme park in Anaheim, California, for the opportunists to move in and mop up the tourism overspill. Tacky gift stores, low-grade motels and all-you-can-eat restaurants mushroomed around the park, barking their crude come-ons to the passengers of every car heading for Disneyland and sullying the great man's vision of a pure and whole-some escape from everyday life. Having learnt the hard way, he built his second dream within a garrison of heavily forested land and when John K. Darwin planned his neighbouring utopia, he did the same. Whether you pick Disney, Universal or Dreamworld, it is possible to spend a two-week vacation in central Florida without glimpsing reality. But, of course, reality is never far away. It lies just beyond the boundaries of these properties, and it flourishes. It flourishes in the gridlock beneath the financial district tower blocks, and along the wide strips lined with girlie bars and factory outlets and fast food joints, and in the convention centres crammed with name-tagged salesmen hoping to cheat on their wives. See the tangle of highways, the dark alleys, the pawn shops and guns 'n' ammo stores. See the walk-in medical centres where tourists sit on plastic waiting-room chairs beside the homeless, the drunks and every other representative of disenfranchised humanity, and make no mistake: reality is alive and well and living in Orlando.

Any time that Sylvia Avery could, she would avoid straying too far outside Dreamworld property lines. Her own condo was the closest to it that she could find, but Hayes's home, well within the magical boundary, was better yet, and so, despite occasional misgivings about pushing too fast for the cohabitation thing, she rarely went home at all.

This morning, as she drove further and further from her adored haven and into a world that seemed to her so loud and fetid and dangerous, she felt a not entirely pleasant sense of being Dorothy in some nasty, macabre inversion of *The Wizard of Oz*: an innocent, wrenched from an enchanted dream to topple into a pigsty.

Perdue was spending the morning at the Church Street Station complex in downtown Orlando, where Leon LeGalley had occasionally taken shifts at a bar, mostly when a regular member of staff called in sick. Avery had secretly wished that she could have switched with Perdue and taken this task for herself, instead of calling on Leon's roommate Shannon Reilly. Not only was the dead man's abode in Sanford, which was a district she had been to only once and that had been quite enough, but when Avery had phoned to arrange the meeting, the woman had sounded sharp and unfriendly, bordering on downright hostile.

Sanford's historic main street was prettier than she had remembered it, if a little self-consciously 'olde tymey', and many of the avenues beyond were equally picturesque, all crumbling colonial whiteboards and ancient cypress trees hung with Spanish moss. As she neared her destination, however, the scenes outside her window gave way to housing that made the whiteboards look pristine, and all the usual vignettes of life just below the poverty line: the hulking skeletons of old cars rusting in front yards, kids who should have been at school listlessly shooting hoops, a grubby toddler, apparently unattended and clad only in an undershirt and drooping diaper, wandering dangerously close to the road, guys with mullets and moustaches, tanktops and too-tight shorts, sitting on their stoops drinking cans of beer, though it was barely ten a.m.

As Avery slowly cruised the wide, dirty streets, peering hopelessly from the not-detailed-enough map lying open on her passenger seat to the window, where she sought a friendly face to ask for directions, she became gradually aware of a slightly built young man on an orange moped, travelling some distance behind her. Was she being followed? Avery chastised herself for being so paranoid, but now she came to think of it, she began to wonder if she hadn't seen him a couple of streets back, too. By the time she reached her destination, however, there was no sign of the man, and Avery felt mildly embarrassed for what now felt like a hugely egotistical delusion.

The large house in which Leon LeGalley had roomed must have been quite handsome at one time, Avery thought as she pulled up outside, but it had fallen into a state of neglect which was probably irreversible. She parked her car, locked it – something she hadn't done for some time – and climbed the splintered wooden steps to the porch, which was crowded with boxes, old furniture and an odd assortment of broken leisure items, including a busted trampoline and a plastic rocking horse suspended on rust-encrusted springs.

The front door was open, and as Avery stepped into the hallway she noted that a TV sound-man looking for a suitable wild-track for a drama set in a seedy tenement would have rubbed his hands together in glee to find this place. It was all here, every trite cliché: the crying baby, the barking dog, the argument taking place in Spanish in some distant room on an upper floor.

'Who you looking for?'

The woman who stood before Avery, eyeing her uniform with some suspicion, was tanned and weary-looking and spoke loudly to be heard over the wailing infant in her arms.

'Shannon Reilly?'

'I think she went to work already. What did she do?'

'She didn't do anything, ma'am. I spoke to her this morning. She's expecting me. Are you sure she left already?'

The woman ignored the question and instead addressed a few words of placation to her baby, but she made no move to leave the hallway and allow Avery ingress. The stand-off was interrupted, however, by the appearance on the stairs of a pair of slim, tanned legs in sneakers. The owner of the legs continued her descent until she saw Avery. She stopped.

'You from Dreamworld?' The girl was heavily made up and wore denim Daisy Dukes and a white cut-off T-shirt bearing the logo of the Hooters restaurant chain. It barely covered her breasts, which were almost certainly enhanced by surgery. She was in her early twenties, Avery guessed, but looked older and harder than anyone of that age should.

'Shannon?'

'Uh-huh. You can come up, but you can't stay long. I gotta be in work by eleven.'

Shannon Reilly stared at Avery and at her neighbour, and brushed back her dry curtain of peroxided and permed hair. The other woman looked up expectantly.

'It's okay, Patty. It's about Leon.'

The woman stepped aside and narrowed her eyes at Avery as she passed. 'You find him yet?'

Avery shook her head.

'Men, they'll do it to you every time.'

Avery wasn't quite sure what the woman meant, but couldn't help feeling a flush of irritation. Maybe she'd been dumped, abandoned, left to look after a bevy of kids, but it didn't really compare with what Leon LeGalley had inflicted on Lisa Schaeffer.

Avery was still smarting as she followed Shannon Reilly up the stairs, trying her hardest to suppress her hostility towards the girl's former roommate, who was, she reminded herself, an innocent man. Just a love-struck downtown guy who'd run away with his uptown girl, never to be seen again.

Shannon Reilly brushed a pile of dirty crockery into her sink and hopped up to sit on the counter space she'd cleared. She gestured for Avery to sit on the bed, which stood not more than a few feet away from the kitchenette range. It was unmade and strewn with rumpled clothing, but the platoon of plush toys that lined its far edge stood neatly regimented in fuzzy, candy-hued pack-drill.

The walls were bare but for a framed photograph of a Labrador retriever. It was flaxen and vacant looking, and reminded Avery of its owner, who was currently fixing her with a sharp stare.

'So listen, I don't get why Dreamworld is so bothered about where Leon and Lisa have gone. You can get someone else to do Lisa's job anytime, right? So what do you care?'

The girl stared directly at Avery, who noticed for the first time that beneath the copious eye make-up were the clear signs of hours of crying. Avery measured her words carefully, speaking softly and slowly.

'Lisa's parents are worried about her, think it's out of character for her to do something like this, and they've reported her missing. So for now it's a missing persons case and it falls under our jurisdiction. So, we have to look into it. This is our job.'

Shannon said nothing, continuing to stare at Avery. Her face was still set, still hard, but now her eyes were filling, and she dabbed at them with the tips of her fingers, the kohl-stained tears leaving inky traces on the shiny blue surfaces of her long acrylic nails.

'He wasn't just your roommate, was he?'

'No shit, Sherlock.'

Avery swallowed hard. She had known it right away. But now what?

Shannon fished a packet of Virginia Slims from her purse and sparked up. The eye make-up was running freely down her face now, and her eyes glittered with a terrible fury.

'I'm sorry.'

'It's okay. He'll be back.'

'I hope so.'

'Yeah, he will. He'll be back. He didn't take none of his stuff with him. It's all here. Maybe I'll keep it, and maybe I won't. Haven't decided yet. But he'll be back. Stuck up bitch drove him nuts most of the time.'

'Lisa?'

'Yeah. She had him round her little finger. He said there was nothin' going on. But he always came back to

65

me. We been together like, four years, on and off. Always came back. I'm the only person who'd ever put up with him. Only this time, maybe I had enough. Fucking asshole. Maybe they deserve each other. You push someone too far, y'know?'

Avery nodded, although from the little she knew about either of them, Leon LeGalley and Shannon Reilly appeared to be ideally suited. She brought out her notebook, keen to get the entire encounter over with.

'So tell me again, Shannon, about when you last saw Leon? The morning he went missing?'

Shannon looked testily at Avery, clearly reluctant to switch from unburdening herself to dealing with the pragmatic aspect of the visit.

'I told you everything on the phone. He got in real late from the centre the night before, said they kept him late. He seemed in a real bad mood, but I didn't really care. I was in bed. I told him to shut up and go to sleep.'

'And this was about what time?'

'Like I said, I was in bed. Asleep. I don't know.'

'Approximately?'

'I don't know. Really have no idea. Maybe two, three. Four, even? Maybe later. What's the difference?'

Avery ignored the question and finished making notes before speaking again.

'You said he left before you the next morning. Did he say where he was going?'

'He was going to the centre.' Shannon stared at Avery. 'He was supposed to be done there for a while, but they called him in at short notice, said someone else had dropped out. Call came through about eight-thirty. Woke me up. I went back to sleep, he left. That's it.'

Avery clucked in a business-like expression of sympathy while secretly heaving a sigh of relief. Even if – in some worst-case scenario – the County police were to speak to Shannon, it seemed that there was nothing to her account to back up any suggestion that Leon had been in the car wreck involving Lisa's car. Her uncertainty about the time of his return even provided an alibi of sorts regarding the murder of Lucas, and there was certainly nothing in her tale to challenge the one so expertly spun by Hayes. Her task as good as done, Avery itched to leave, but was aware that it would look odd to do so without asking any more questions. She wracked her brains for something appropriate.

'Did Leon ever do anything like this before? Leave town without telling anyone?'

Shannon brightened, and leant forward as if the better to unleash her stream of vitriol. 'Are you kidding? You'd have known about it if he did, because I'd have fucking killed him. And he knew it. But anyways, he wasn't that into Lisa, that's why I don't buy it. He used to bitch about her all the time to me. Thought like she was using him or something.'

'Using him how?'

Shannon Reilly shrugged. 'Like she maybe had it too easy, she was bored. You know that old song by those English guys? It's called "Common People"? It reminded me of her. She had a real nice apartment, but she thought it was cool to hang out in a dump like this. And she was really into meeting all the scumbags from the centre, you know?'

'Are we talking about the song, or about Lisa?'

'About Lisa.' Shannon looked irritated. 'The song is, like, about a rich girl who wants to hang out in shitholes and screw blue-collar guys. Pissed me off. Not the song. Song's pretty good. Lisa. She pissed me off. Big-time.'

'You were saying she wanted to hang out with the

people from the centre. You mean the Research and Development Complex at Dreamworld? The volunteers?'

'Right. She was really into it all. Thought it was really cool, fuck knows why. Didn't get that if we didn't have to do it for money, none of us would've.'

'You worked as a volunteer too?'

'Used to. That's how I met Leon. Not at the centre – other places. Mostly the big pharmaceutical companies over in Tallahassee. They pay real well. And it's mostly the same people all the time, so you get to know everybody. And you do one, then you get hooked into the circuit and you hear about the other jobs when they come up. I don't do it no more, though. Got real sick one time – it was a trial for, like, a migraine tablet or something? I was, like, seeing all this stuff. And throwing up. I was in bed for a week. Wasn't worth the money. That's when I took the job at Hooters. Worst thing'll ever happen to you there is some guy grabbing your ass.'

Avery laughed in genuine amusement at the joke. But Shannon wasn't smiling; she was staring off into the distance.

Shannon Reilly was, in fact, wincing inwardly as she remembered the place in Tallahassee. The trial had been bad, certainly, but worse had been the humiliation of seeing the advert on the pinboard in the lobby that said 'good homes needed for lab puppies', thinking it meant dogs that had been used in scientific tests and, overwhelmed by tearful empathy, getting one only to find that 'lab' had been short for Labrador. She'd just wanted to give love to a needy creature, only to find that it didn't really need her after all and she'd been made to feel a fool. Just like what had happened with Leon.

Now, Shannon looked back at Avery, glad that this woman who was not too much older than she was and was sitting on her bed with her nice uniform and nice shiny hair and nice life didn't know this, couldn't know what she was thinking.

The dog seemed to be looking mockingly, accusingly, down at her from the photograph, and it made Shannon nervous. And suddenly she was sure she heard a whimper coming from the wall, muffled at first, then getting louder and louder, and she wondered if Avery could hear it. Wondered if Avery knew about what had happened to the dog in the end, too, how she'd eventually had it put down because it was a constant reminder of her own stupidity, and besides, dog food was just so expensive. If maybe, somehow, Avery knew everything. Then, suddenly, a new fear emerged: a fear that she might scream out a confession. If Shannon Reilly knew how to read, and if she'd ever read Edgar Allen Poe, she might have been reminded of *The Tell-Tale Heart*, and it might have tipped her off that this was all in her head. But she didn't and hadn't, and so she just sat there feeling scared, biting her lower lip, tasting the whale fat in her cheap pink lipstick.

'Shannon?'

Shannon Reilly held her breath, waiting to hear what Avery was going to say next.

'Shannon, are you okay?'

Shannon nodded, relieved. The whining from the wall subsided and she told herself that of course the woman sitting on her bed didn't know. She didn't know anything.

'Shannon, this circuit, you're talking about clinical trials, that kind of thing?'

'Exactly.'

'Shannon, I need to ask you something. There's another guy, a guy who worked at the centre, and I need to know whether Leon or Lisa knew him. It could help. His name is Jerry Lee Lucas.'

Shannon wrinkled her nose in disgust. 'Sure. Old guy. Smelt real bad. And he was a real jerk-off.'

'Did you know him well?'

Shannon shook her head and looked at Avery with some derision. Avery ignored the look.

'Did Leon?'

'No. Mostly, those people you wouldn't want to hang out with them. You'd just run into them on this or that job. That's all. Why, what did he do, Lucas?'

'It's not my investigation, but I know he was found dead the same day that Leon left town. Murdered.'

Shannon looked genuinely startled and Avery was unsure that her disclosure had been a good move. She quickly decided that she'd rather know Shannon's reaction, however – after all, it was what the County cops would hear if they ever got to her.

'What are you trying to say?'

'I'm not trying to say anything, Shannon. You asked me a question and I answered it.'

'You think Leon had something to do with it?'

The girl laughed, a bitter laugh that creased her eyes and sent further tracks of blackened tears streaming down her face.

'No way would Leon ever . . . Is that what this is about? Is that why you're here? Because if it is, you've got it so fucking wrong it's not even funny. Leon never hurt anybody in his life.'

Avery wondered how you could know someone, live with them, for four years without really knowing them. But then, Shannon was not like her, she reminded herself. Not like her at all. Shannon saw what she wanted to see.

'You know, I don't give a shit if you don't believe me.' Shannon's voice was strangulated now, and had edged up to a level loud enough to drown out baby, dog and still-raging domestic disturbance in the room down the hall. 'Don't matter. *I* know it's true. And Leon don't even know Lucas, hardly. Maybe you should be asking about Lisa. She's the bitch. Doesn't care who she hurts. Yeah, maybe you should be asking about her. Maybe she knew Lucas better than she said.'

The simplistic machinations of Shannon's mind were so hopelessly apparent that Avery cringed inwardly at the girl's lack of guile and, for the first time, felt genuinely sorry for her.

'You mean hurt emotionally? Like the way she hurt you? Leon? It's inexcusable, Shannon, but it doesn't make her a criminal.'

'Yeah well, I'm sure I don't need to tell you your business,' Shannon said, smiling enigmatically and hoping that the remark sounded cutting, but noting to herself that, damn, it actually sounded like a compliment. She wondered if Sylvia Avery would retort that she didn't need to tell Shannon *her* business, either, but then she remembered that her business was serving chicken wings and pitchers of beer to guys who wanted to look at her tits, so that was unlikely. At least, she told herself, she was skinnier than Sylvia Avery, and so Avery wouldn't look as good in the Hooters uniform, although that bastard manager would probably point at her and say, 'Ladies, for those of you who've forgotten, this is what real ones look like,' like he had once before with some other new girl.

Sylvia Avery probably wouldn't want to work at Hooters anyway, Shannon mused. Not when she had a nice job going round snooping into other people's business.

Avery regarded Shannon with some concern. The combination of burning eyes, catastrophic make-up meltdown and self-satisfied grin, the incisors smeared with pink lipstick, made her look quite terrifying, and she suddenly couldn't wait to get out, and get away from her.

'You need to get going, don't you, Shannon? Don't want to make you late. Thanks for making the time . . .'

Avery's gentle tone took Shannon by surprise, made her wonder why she didn't want to hear more about Lisa.

'Well, yeah, I gotta fix my face and go, but like I say, you should be looking out some stuff about that bitch. Whatever you find out about her, it wouldn't surprise me.'

'Right. Thanks. If I hear anything, or I have to ask anything else, I'll call you.'

Shannon looked confused. 'I guess. But don't you think I might hear from Leon before you do?'

'Uh, sure. Then call me. Please. Obviously. Here's my card.'

Avery felt the first flush of self-consciousness. Conducting a convincing missing persons investigation when there was no missing person was a quite tiring exercise in deception, even when the person to be fooled wasn't too smart. And even, Avery reflected with grim irony, for one who had spent most of her life mastering the art of guarding secrets and keeping up appearances.

Avery had never been so glad to get into her car. She sat for some time feeling the sun-baked cloth of the seat beneath her and inhaling the hot, stagnant air and relishing the solitary silence. Then she fired up the engine and drove fast through the squalid streets of Sanford, back towards Dreamworld, where the business of playing at make believe was oh-so-very-much easier.

Ten

Between Disney World, Universal and Dreamworld, visitors to Orlando and its environs can find a themed hotel to suit every pocket and every fantasy. Given what was on offer, Avery couldn't understand why anyone would choose to stay *off* property, and the majority of tourists were of like mind. Others, however, were prepared to trade off the benefits of the official resorts – proximity to the parks, full theming and the less-quantifiable X-factor that Disney came closest to pinning down when they spoke of 'being part of the magic' – in exchange for more space per dollar. And these travellers had plenty of choices available, from all-suite hotels and resorts to vacation villas and condos of all descriptions.

As far as Avery could tell, the Buena Vida apartment complex, located just a few miles south of Dreamworld property lines, was typical of these enterprises. This realization had taken her somewhat by surprise, given that it was the place that Lisa Schaeffer had called home. Although the prices were competitive in terms of vacation rental, they were far from economical if one was talking about permanent residence.

Wandering through the courtyard, past a fountain whose centrepiece appeared to depict two dolphins vomiting into a giant conch shell, Avery tried to calculate just how much it would cost to live in a place like Buena Vida for a year. The first total she arrived at seemed absurd, and her subsequent attempts at a recount, as she climbed the cool concrete steps to the upper storeys of the apartment block, were consistently interrupted by the noisy yells of the children who swarmed the place, heading for the pool or the arcade or back to their digs, buzzing with the thrill of being allowed to roam unsupervised.

The frontage of the building was open and Avery realized now, as she started down the length of the third-floor walkway, that the colourful bunting she had noticed from the ground, festooning each stretch of balustrade, was in fact damp bathing apparel and laundry.

Though she tried to continue her calculations as she walked, Avery found herself periodically distracted by one thing or another: here a tiny pair of Hunchback of Notre Dame underpants (what exactly would Victor Hugo have made of this?) there a floral swimsuit that could feasibly have accommodated a compact car (what on God's green earth did the owner look like? Could she actually swim? Could she even walk?). By the time Avery reached Lisa Schaeffer's apartment, she had decided that the young woman's monthly rent demand, however big, was probably irrelevant. Certainly it was now irrelevant to Lisa Schaeffer.

The door was on the catch, and as Avery stepped into the eerie silence of the large open-plan apartment, she was mildly surprised to see Perdue seated at the dead girl's kitchen counter, daintily picking at a take out carton of Chinese vegetable stir-fry. Initially, she was struck by the disrespectfulness of this act, but there was something about Perdue's innate tranquillity and dignity that lent it a certain air of reverence. She found herself remembering a story Perdue had told her about his teenage years, about a surfing buddy who drowned down at Spanish House, and how after the boy's burial service, Perdue and his friends had driven directly to the same spot, left their funeral clothes on the sand and stayed on into the night, riding the same waters that had devoured their friend. That act, like this one, seemed like a simple gesture reclaiming the joy of life from a place stained by death, as if celebrating the honour of being sentient, conscious, alive, in deference to those who no longer had such privileges.

Perdue looked up from his lunch.

'I'm nearly through here, Sylvie. Then we can get started.'

Avery nodded in agreement – Perdue always said he found it hard to focus if he skipped lunch – and stood silently absorbing her surroundings.

The apartment was still resonant with life, Avery felt, as if its occupier might walk in at any second, and although Lisa Schaeffer had lived here for only four months since her move from the West Coast, the degree to which she had stamped her personality on the place was considerable. The kitchen alone was a shrine to a certain facet of generation-X pop culture, from the large Pixies poster on the wall and the cluster of kitsch fridge-magnets, to the shelf that housed a set of South Park wind-up toys, a collection of novelty salt-and-pepper shakers and chilli pepper sauces. Avery idly perused the bright labels: flames, devils, mardi-gras masks, exploding volcanoes. Liquid Lava. Hellfire and Damnation. Bayou Butt-Burner. Cajun Rush Down-On-Your-Knees Hot Sauce. This last one had a little cartoon of Monica Lewinsky wearing kneepads and proudly proclaimed that it was a collectable limited edition.

Avery found herself wondering whether Shannon Reilly, so blithely unhip with her big hair and plush menagerie, had ever visited Lisa's place, and if so, what she made of it.

At one end of the kitchen counter was a neat stack of magazines, which Avery began to leaf through. The first few were all surfing titles.

'Good taste in reading matter, our girl,' said Perdue, covering his mouth which was still full.

'I'll take your word for it.'

At the bottom of the pile were mostly twenty something lifestyle glossies – *Details*, *Swing*, a couple of others that Avery had never heard of.

'You know, Felix, I'm beginning to see why Lisa's parents are having a hard time believing that she'd run away with a guy like Leon. You said they told you she'd never mentioned him? And they just seem so . . . different. Lisa and Leon having a relationship, I'm just starting to have a hard time buying it.'

Perdue shrugged. 'Yeah, well, exactly. A guy puts a knife in you and kills himself, that's a pretty clear sign of a bad match. Don't need to be Dear Abby to figure that out.'

Avery smiled, despite the sour taste in her mouth. 'I know, but . . . What I meant is, I'm starting to wonder if she really was with him at all. Maybe that was the problem. From what Shannon Reilly said, maybe it was all in Leon's head.'

'Maybe so, but Sylvie, don't forget that what we're looking for is the angle on their involvement with Lucas. Chances are, that's going to be the key. Whatever they were mixed up in, that's what was holding them together, is my guess.'

Perdue cleared the table and threw all evidence of his

meal into Lisa Schaeffer's steel flip-top trash can, after first removing the cluster of scented candles that were set upon the lid. He set them back down and regarded them with some amusement.

'These things are like the lava lamps of the nineties, don't you think? In twenty years time kids are going to sit around going, "Hey, when I was a kid we had a shit-load of scented candles everywhere, did you have a shit-load of scented candles everywhere? Yeah! Whatever happened to those things?" That and those navy blue sofa-throws with moons and suns on them.' He chuckled at his own observation, composed himself and rubbed his hands together in a gesture of getting down to business. 'So, let's do it. I'll take this main room, you take the bedroom.'

'I don't get what exactly we're looking for.'

'Essentially, just anything that links Lisa, or Leon, to Lucas. For our investigation, and also as a fallback. The VW ownership papers have been transferred to another name – false name – and backdated, but we've got to imagine the unlikely eventuality that County find out that it was hers anyway and come looking round in here. Anything we wouldn't want them to see, we'll take with us.'

Avery nodded and began to walk towards Lisa Schaeffer's bedroom, but as she did so, a dormant question began to stir in her mind and although she didn't yet know exactly what it was, she felt a cold stab of fear and discomfort as it grew. She pushed it away, resolutely determined to focus on the task at hand. Whatever it was, she would try not to think about it; deal with it later.

The bedroom was untidy, but it was small and contained only a clothes rail, a futon on a pine sofa-bed base, and a small matching chest of drawers whose surface was crowded with cosmetics. It didn't take long for Avery to find a few things that made her glad they had got here before Lisa's parents.

The clothes were the first thing. They were balled up and stuffed into a holdall under the bed, and Avery had recognized the smell of blood right away, even before she opened the bag. There wasn't much of it, admittedly: it was mostly on the left shoulder of the preposterously small tanktop bearing the Pokémon logo and a dinky animé creature. Avery studied the stain and noted the patterns, which were vaguely reminiscent of brush-strokes, no large drips. She felt safe in guessing that Lisa had sustained a head injury in the car accident, which had bled enough to saturate one side of her hair but was not a real gusher. Lisa's brushed-cotton combats attested to that: the dark spots on the left thigh were obviously from the same source, but they were small, and few. As Avery unfolded the pants, however, she noticed another smell – acrid – and realized with a mixture of revulsion and poignant sympathy that it was urine.

Avery called for Perdue to come in. 'Those old vans, they didn't have airbags back then, right?'

'Right.'

Avery nodded soberly, replaced the clothes in the bag and handed it to Perdue. He took a cursory look at the contents although it was clearly more out of a sense of duty than necessity. Presumably, Avery thought, his mind was concentrating on the most efficient method for their secure disposal.

The nasty thought, the one that Avery had been trying to ignore, was more than stirring now. It was yawning and stretching out languidly in her subconscious, its sharp claws snagging on the protective walls of her mind as it did so. And then it was gone again, Avery's awareness of it usurped by her sudden and total focus on an unexpected discovery. As she passed her hands through the space under the bed, Avery felt something brush against the back of her wrist, a thin cord or strap of some kind that appeared to be hanging from the underside of the bed itself. She tugged at it hard and felt its length extend until it hit an unremitting point of resistance. Leaping to her feet, Avery grasped the futon and braced herself to heave it from the bed. Perdue stepped forward to help, but she had completed the task with little effort.

'Remind me never to get into an arm-wrestling match with you.' Avery ignored Perdue's remark, her mind focused on what she had found wedged between the slats of the bed-base.

'That a camera, Sylvie?'

'Yep. Good one, too. Expensive. Wanna take a look?'

Avery passed it to Perdue and replaced the futon. He stared at the camera, again seemingly unsure of the purpose of his study.

'Is there any film in it?'

'Good point, Sylvie. Let's see . . . Yes. Twenty shots used up. We should get this processed.'

'Want me to handle that?'

'Where are you thinking?'

Avery told Perdue about a guy she'd known for years, a sweet young guy who had worked on the attractions at Atlantis when her regular patrol was there, and had been transferred to the main photographic centre at Atlantis a couple of years back, about the same time as she got transferred over to ImagiNation. He was fantastically well endowed, too, Avery remembered, but she didn't tell Perdue that part.

Perdue clicked off the last few shots, waited for the film to rewind, removed it from the camera and handed it to Avery.

As Avery continued her search alone, the black, formless thought became harder to ignore, scrabbling insistently now, bleating for attention, slamming itself against the barriers she'd thrown up, wearing them down. It was a question, she knew that much now. And something told her that she didn't want to know the answer to it.

She busied herself hunting through Lisa's closet, her breathing raggedly uneven, her hands trembling lightly, her heart in her throat, a strange terror of – what? She wasn't sure. But it reminded her of watching a horror film, watching some teenage scream queen edging blindly through the darkness, knowing from her own impotent vantage point in the audience that something dreadful was out there, but not what, nor when it would reveal itself.

The pedestrian nature of the things Avery found in the closet seemed only to increase the tension. The clothes hanging neatly, some still encased in dry-cleaner's cellophane. Nothing hidden in the pockets. The little hill of shoes, two pairs deep, on the floor. Nothing underneath. The shiny white Black Fly purse bearing the FlyGirls insignia. Avery dumped the contents onto the floor with trepidation but found only screwed-up receipts, a few cents in change and a L'Oreal colour-endure lipstick in Fawn Fatale, its lid missing. And here a plastic shopping bag containing a movie rented from Blockbuster, no doubt long overdue for return. Avery lifted the box and looked at the title, fear mingling with an indistinct and perverse hope that the movie would be something nasty, something horribly portentous, but it was 'Bottle Rocket', a gentle, clever, offbeat comedy she herself had seen and loved years ago, on some forgotten date.

She recognized then that she was yearning to find some gruesome artefact, to recoil from some terrifying discovery, as one yearns for the moment when the killer appears on screen, the screeching score shattering the silence, breaking the tension, making the crowd jump in their plush velveteen seats. Nervous, grateful laughter here and there in the theatre, marking the exorcism of the most unbearable of all fears: the fear of the unknown and the unseen. If anything, it was the very absence of the macabre in Lisa's closet that increased Avery's own, cold dread, because she knew now for certain that she would find no sanctuary from it. Its stalking ground was her own mind: a place from which escape was impossible.

By the time she was certain that there was nothing else of importance to be found in Lisa Schaeffer's bedroom, Avery was sweating freely, though whether from the physical exertion of the search or the mental exertion of controlling the burgeoning dread, the dread of the question, she wasn't sure.

Avery rejoined Perdue in the main room and sat down on Lisa's sofa, which, she noticed, was the same futon unit as the one in the bedroom. She raked her fingers through her damp hair and looked up at Perdue.

'Well, I'm done. You?'

'Yep. Didn't find anything. Went through her photographs but there's definitely none of Lucas.'

'Are we sure? Do we know what he looks like?'

'No, but we know he was forty-whatever. And besides, they're mostly of buildings, not people. And the rest are of Leon.'

'Of buildings?'

'Uh-huh. Dreamworld buildings. And some inside shots – the canteen, the utilidors.'

'The utilidors? Bad girl!'

'I know, it's strictly *verboten*, huh? Guess she was one of those people who couldn't resist breaking rules, probably couldn't wait to show 'em off to her buddies in LA – *"Look what I got away with."* I think it's kind of pathetic, actually.'

Perdue pulled two envelopes of pictures from his back pocket, sifted through them and showed one to Avery. It was of a young guy with a bad haircut and bleach-job, sitting in the passenger seat of a vehicle, grinning at the camera as he absentmindedly picked the label off a bottle of Molson Ice.

'This is Leon?'

Perdue nodded.

'Any of them together?'

'No, just him on his own. And the only other person in here is another guy.'

Perdue flipped through the photos again, picked one out. Avery scrutinized it. It was of a dark-haired boy – mid-twenties, Avery guessed – sitting at a restaurant booth before what turned out, on closer inspection, to be a Denny's breakfast menu. His countenance was mock solemn and he was bowed down, hands aloft, as if praying to Mecca. It took Avery a moment to realize that this expression of worship was being struck in reference to the legend on the bottom of the menu, which read, 'Behold the power of cheese'.

She laughed out loud. 'Who's this, do you reckon?'

Perdue shrugged. 'No idea. Better try and find out. Once you've dropped the film off, maybe that's what you can do. I'm gonna be stuck here the rest of the afternoon – got the parents coming in from LA. You could talk to the other gal who shared Lisa's shifts. Name'll be on the log back at the office. Don't show her the pictures, though, obviously. Leave them all here.'

'No, obviously. No problem.'

Avery shuffled through the pictures and looked at the one of Leon again. She jabbed a finger at the orange trim around the interior window in shot behind him. 'You can pretty much tell this is the van, huh? Glad you found these. We should definitely keep them safe, or get . . . rid . . . of them.'

And with a final slam the barrier broke between her conscious and her subconscious, and the thought – the question – loomed into ghastly entity. She heard herself give voice to it, her cadence oddly thick, oddly slow and hollow.

'Felix . . . Where is it? The van . . . And the . . . The . . .'

'Don't worry about that, Sylvie.'

He regarded her squarely, his eyes imploring her to drop the subject.

'But do you know? Did you . . .'

'Please don't ask me, Sylvie. Just trust me that it's taken care of, and let's get on with our jobs, yeah? I've got the Schaeffers arriving, and I've got to get in a mindset for that. Let's finish up here, and you can go and grab something to eat before you go to Atlantis. You didn't have lunch, did you?'

'No, but I'm not hungry. I'll get something later.'

'Will you, please? Promise me? Or you'll start feeling faint. Okay, Sylvie? Or I'll worry about you. Okay?'

'Okay.'

But it wasn't okay, nothing was okay. Up until now, Hayes's and Perdue's businesslike approach had been so soothing that the clean-up operation in which Avery had become involved had seemed nothing less than, well, clean. Sterile. Matter-of-fact. But now, in a hideous moment of clarity, this thought had invaded Avery's head, and it wasn't clean at all. It was visceral and grimy, and it spun her perception into a giddy 180 and made her skin creep. Now it would be there permanently, she realized, always at the back of her mind: the knowledge that somewhere, probably somewhere not too far away from where she stood right now, was a VW van and two dead bodies, concealed so as never to be found.

Perdue sensed her dismay and put a protective arm around her.

'This'll all be over soon, Avery, and we can start working at forgetting all about it. Getting on with our lives. You're doing a great job. Hang in there. It's all on track, all going so well. Even better than we could have hoped.'

'Yes?'

'Sure. The guys at the bar, they never heard Leon mention Lucas. And nobody thought it sounded out of character for the guy to leave town without telling anybody. No big surprise at all. I really don't think we have anything to worry about on either count. If they didn't know of any connection between Leon and Lucas, and Leon's roommate didn't seem to either – and you did buy that, right? – then we're halfway there.'

'The Shannon thing still made me nervous, though. We made one big oversight already: we didn't know that she was his girlfriend. It's pretty crucial. There have got to be other variables. There always are. And it's the variables that scare me. Don't they scare you? Aren't you scared of this blowing up in our faces?'

Perdue paused and thought carefully about the question in order to give an honest answer, and Avery loved him for it. Sometimes, Hayes's quick, slick, swaggering retorts scared her, because they had platitude and bluster written all over them.

'I think . . . I think, Sylvie, that the only thing I'm worried about is making peace with the fact that we may never know what happened. Eventually we're going to exhaust all avenues of inquiry, and we're going to hit a point where we've done everything we can do and our work is over, where we feel safe enough to close this case, and we're going to move on, and at that point we're still not necessarily going to have answers. All we need to know is that nobody else is ever going to get them either. I know I'm going to have to live with that, and it's hard. Whoever said, "Everybody loves a mystery," that's bullshit. Nobody loves a mystery. We all want answers. And sometimes we can't have them. That's all. That's all that bugs me. But I'll get over it.'

Avery felt small and fragile, and let herself nestle into Perdue's broad chest, breathing in the clean scent of his tanned skin. It was warm and comforting and sunny, somehow, a little like toast, or roasted peanuts. She remembered how he'd looked when she'd watched him at the surf tournament, how physically agile and unself-consciously abandoned, and she wondered exactly how horrified he'd be if she turned her face up to him right now, as if to invite him to kiss her. He ruffled her hair, but it was strictly paternal. Probably very horrified, she concluded. Very, very horrified.

'We're going to get through this, Sylvie, you and I, come out the other side undamaged. Like I said, it's nearly over now. And when it's over, a day will come when you never think about it again. I promise.'

And although she couldn't possibly have known it, somehow Avery did: Felix Perdue was wrong on all three counts.

Eleven

Even the most casual Disney enthusiast is aware that EPCOT – as in the Epcot Centre theme park – stands for Experimental Prototype Community of Tomorrow. But less commonly known is the fact that Walt envisaged the Magic Kingdom's neighbouring park as a real community, a 'living university' where scientists and engineers and thinkers would live and work, creating the technologies of the future in full view of the general public.

When Walt died, the idea died with him, but like all good ideas it was exhumed and cannibalized years down the line. Disney itself built the intricately planned city of Celebration on the outskirts of Disney property, although there is little there of interest to tourists, while Dreamworld utilized the other part of the EPCOT concept in creating *their* second theme park, Atlantis.

Though the bulk of attractions at Atlantis were comparable to those at any oceanarium – say, Sea World – the cutting-edge projects housed in the Ocean Pavilion, the vast water tank at the heart of the park, dramatically set the tone for the entire place, lending it an air of dignity that was tangible in its very atmosphere.

As Avery approached the Atlantis rear security

entrance, she remembered how much she'd loved it. How much she'd liked that slow pace and peaceful atmosphere, the almost subliminal New Age music – all pan pipes and ocarina, crashing waves and whale song – and the crowds that seemed to glide in quiet awe, never surging in a consumer feeding frenzy the way they did at other parks.

At the time, she'd been happy, but she'd always eulogized the fairy tale charm of ImagiNation and had never looked back after the longed-for transfer, never missed Atlantis a bit. Now, stepping within earshot of the piped music, waving in greeting to the old guy who had manned the security booth for the fifteen years since the park's inception, she felt a nostalgia for the place that had obviously been lying dormant all along.

'Sylvia Avery! We haven't seen you in a while! What a nice surprise!'

'Hi, Ray! How're things?'

Avery and her elderly ex-colleague exchanged pleasantries for a while before he asked whom she had come to see. Not wanting to get embroiled in a lengthy explanation of why she needed to visit Mitch Ducek in the photographic centre, she told him that she was on her way home and had decided to pay a social call to her friend Gwen Bissette at the Ocean Pavilion. Thanks to extensive and constant media coverage, Gwen and her élite posse of co-workers were practically royalty at Atlantis, and the old guy could barely contain his excitement.

'You send her my best, now!' he shouted as he waved Avery through – rather bizarrely, she thought, as Gwen would almost certainly have no idea who he was. 'Tell her to keep up the good work!'

She was still smiling to herself when her thoughts were

interrupted by the abrupt roar and splutter of an engine and the sound of gravel crunching and spraying a little way in the distance behind her. Avery turned round abruptly to see an orange moped making a sharp turn and accelerating rapidly away from the security booth and out of sight. Unless she was losing it big-time, Avery thought, that was definitely the same one she'd seen in Sanford. She was certain.

She began to stride briskly back towards the booth, calling out as she walked: 'Ray? What was all that about?'

The old guy looked nonplussed. 'Just some young fella. Came in the wrong way. Said he was looking for the main parking lot. Not a problem.'

'You didn't get his number, did you?'

'Nope. It'll be on the camera, though. I can zip back if you like, check it out.' His gnarled, trembling hands fiddled with the monitor before him. He looked excited. 'Someone you're looking for?'

'Maybe. Or maybe the other way round. I'm not sure. Could be nothing. But better to be safe than sorry.'

'Ayuh.'

Avery looked down, trying to strangle her smile as the old man squinted at the screen, then scribbled down a number on a scrap of paper. Besides good ol' boys who worked in garages in Stephen King novels, Ray was the only person Avery had ever heard saying, 'Ayuh,' and it had always made her laugh.

Avery thanked Ray, pocketed the scrap of paper and pulled out her cellular, punching the keys as she walked away. Perdue wasn't picking up, but she left the plate number on his voice-mail, asked him to check it out and call her back.

Once inside the park, Avery realized that although they e-mailed one another at least once a week, she actually hadn't seen Gwen in ages, and she began to wonder whether she'd have time to drop in on her after giving the film to Mitch. According to the log, Lisa Schaeffer's shift-partner wasn't due to finish up at ImagiNation until six-thirty, so it shouldn't be a problem to fit Gwen in between, if she was quick. She decided to try, and chose the shortest back-route to the photographic centre.

As was usual at the end of the day, the centre was crowded with tourists waiting to collect their processed prints and the souvenir portraits taken by the official park photographers who were posted in front of Atlantis's most recognizable landmarks. Scanning the counters, Avery was annoyed to find that Mitch was not on the shop floor, but the assistant manager directed her behind the scenes, where she found him sitting with his back to the door, working in the semi-darkness at a bank of computers.

'Yes, what it is, now?' Mitch Ducek wheeled round with a look of irritation on his face, which melted away when he saw that it was Avery and not one of his colleagues. 'Christ! Avery! I don't believe it. To what do I owe this honour?'

Mitch Ducek's nose was much larger than Avery had remembered (she was sure there was a joke in there somewhere) and sat in disharmonious concert, she realized now, with his greasy complexion, rubbery lips and overgrown eyebrows. Avery concluded with some dismay that she had probably never actually found him that attractive, and felt vaguely disappointed in herself for having patently been blinded by his physique at the time. Was she really that shallow? And that good at duping herself into thinking otherwise? The notion worried her.

'Hey, Mitch. It's good to see you. But it's kind of a business call, I'm afraid. I need a favour.'

Ducek tried with little success to hide the bruise

blooming on his ego as Avery explained that she needed a roll of film processed for a sensitive investigation she was working on.

'An investigation? So you got promoted? Congratulations. Mind you, it was only a matter of time, no?' He regarded her with a smug grin. 'You certainly covered your bases, screwing your boss *and* one of the Dream Techs. One of 'em *had* to pay off eventually, right?'

Avery was not violent by nature, but she struggled to contain a rising urge to punch Ducek's big, shiny, self-satisfied face.

'I've *never* slept with Perdue, if that's who you mean. And I would have thought that if screwing around had any bearing on getting promoted round here, you'd be CEO by now.'

'Obviously I'm screwing the wrong people.'

'Obviously.'

Avery felt mildly depressed at the level of petty sniping to which the conversation had plummeted, but acknowledged wearily that she didn't know anyone else she could call on instead. She inhaled and exhaled slowly.

'Let's start again. Hi, Mitch. How are you doing?'

Ducek considered the offer of a second chance and, much to Avery's relief, accepted it. 'I'm okay. Sorry, I was just a bit pissed that you hadn't been in touch in – what? two years? and I have to put up with hearing about you from other people all the time, and you know what they're like: couldn't wait to tell me that you'd moved in with that Dream Tech guy and all.'

'I haven't moved in with him. But I'm sorry, too. I should have called.'

'Nah, it's okay. *I* could have called *you*, I guess. I'm just having a seriously bad day. Some fucking family lost their souvenir picture and guest services are making me print up a replacement, only they've got no idea of the code number, obviously, they just remember it was outside The Abyss, around lunchtime, two Tuesdays ago . . .'

Ducek swivelled round to face the monitor in front of him, and jabbed at it with his index finger. It showed four smiling Japanese teenagers embracing Skipper the Dolphin in front of a tunnel formed by many thick, powerful jets of water. He clicked the return key on the keyboard. Now the image displayed was essentially the same, but with a young couple and their toddler in place of the teens. Ducek struck the screen again to emphasize his point.

'. . . which means I've got to go through approximately ninety billion pictures until I find a family with an eight-year-old in a Spice Girls T-shirt and a baby with – and I quote – unusually long black hair. Please shoot me now.'

'With pleasure.'

Ducek flipped Avery the bird without looking up from the screen, and called up a couple more images. Avery moved closer and put her hands on his shoulders.

'I know it's a pain in the ass, but that's a really decent thing you're doing, Mitch.'

He continued to stare at the screen.

'I don't really have any choice.'

'I know, but even so. Did I ever tell you about one time when I came here on vacation as a kid and I lost my Kit-E-Cat purse on the last day?'

'I don't think so.'

'Well, when it didn't show up in lost and found, and my stepdad said we had to go home anyway, I burst into tears, and there was a guest services guy there who asked if we could give them another hour to try and find it. My mom persuaded my stepdad to stay and wait, and while we waited, the guy took us up to the balcony on

91

top of Fort Enchantment – this was at ImagiNation – to watch the fireworks, which is where they take VIPs to watch the fireworks, and he got us funnel cake and popcorn and soda. And when the fireworks were over, he came back and you know what he had with him?'

'Your purse. Obviously.'

'No. Another Kit-E-Cat purse, a new one, exactly the same. And he'd read the description we'd given to lost and found and he'd replaced every single thing in there – my five quarters, my Rapunzel bobbypin, even my Dreamworld autograph book, and he'd gone around and got all the autographs of all the characters.'

Avery studied the reflection of Ducek's face in the monitor. He was smiling. 'Okay, now at last I understand why you're so rabid about this place.'

'Whatever. The only reason I told you is because when the family with the long-haired baby get their picture, they're going to feel like I did. They won't believe that someone went to all that trouble just for them. It'll change their outlook on human nature. That's no small thing.' She paused for a moment. 'I don't think I like the term "rabid", by the way.'

Finally, Ducek turned around. He grinned broadly at Avery, no trace of hostility remaining, leant back in his chair and stretched elaborately. She forced herself to avoid seizing this prime opportunity to look at the contours of his pants.

'So, Ms Avery, now I'm in the business of changing people's outlook on human nature, what's the favour you wanted? Better ask me quick before I go back to being my old uncharitable self.'

Having calculated that she probably had roughly an hour to spare, Avery decided to hazard a visit with Gwen. It had been a while since she'd done so, and although Avery knew with all certainty – the kind of certainty that comes only with true friendship – that Gwen didn't mind, wasn't counting, she felt a sudden sense of urgency in her desire to rectify the situation.

Since the park was still open and Gwen still on duty, she would have to take the official route into Ocean Pavilion along with the park guests, but she was irritated to find that she'd forgotten how lengthy the journey was.

She'd been able to jump all the lines with a friendly but authoritative air of purpose to her stride, but waiting for the first two elevators that took visitors into the depths of the structure had taken far longer than she'd remembered, as had the descents themselves, with their interminable piped spiel about the size of the artificial water tank and the number of breeds of marine life it contained. In fact, by the time she reached the final holding pen for the tour around the Biodrome, almost twenty minutes had passed, and frustratingly, the clipboard-wielding, lab coat-wearing Barbie doll who arrived to take the next departing tour was entirely unimpressed by Avery's status. Even when Avery spun a fairly convincing yarn about needing to see Gwen about an important personal matter, she stolidly refused to do anything until she'd completed her introductory talk to the tour group.

'Biodrome is a completely enclosed eco-system,' barked scientist-Barbie. 'And at three-and-a-half acres, it's the second largest in existence. Does anybody know what the largest one is?'

Avery put her hand up. Scientist-Barbie shot her a dirty look. A chubby, pre-pubescent boy in a Spawn

T-shirt piped up loudly, suggesting Biosphere Two in Arizona.

'No, it's Planet Earth. Ha ha, kinda fooled you there, didn't I?'

The woman paused before continuing, as was obviously directed in her script. 'Biodrome is the largest *artificial* self-sustaining eco-system, however, and it was constructed by the world's leading engineers, chemists, biologists, botanists and ecologists. We also hold another world record: our current fifteen-person mission crew has now been living inside Biodrome for five years, six months and seventeen days. That's nearly three times longer than the previous record.'

The woman paused again, and this time the assembled crowd broke into polite applause.

'Apart from functioning as an experiment in the possible future colonization of the oceans here on earth, and of other inhospitable environments – other planets, for instance – Biodrome also provides the scientific community with a unique opportunity for exploration in a huge number of different fields.

'Now, if you'll step this way, we're going to find out about just some of the exciting projects currently under way here before we take a walk through the observation tunnel that runs through the heart of the Biodrome. And we do have a special treat for you today: you might have heard, as of this morning our orang-utan colony in the rainforest area has an adorable new addition, which is great news, and mother and baby have been out and about this afternoon, so hopefully you should get a chance to see our new arrival.'

After fielding a question from a little girl about the baby monkey's name, the tour guide asked the group to wait before muttering into her walkie-talkie and impatiently beckoning Avery to follow her through a door at the back of the holding pen.

The communications room, designed for use by visiting students and by the media, was sparse but comfortable, comprising three computers, an office chair at each one and a row of benches at the back of the room to seat any overflow of visitors. Today, however, the room was empty.

'I patched a message through and Dr Bissette will be with you as soon as she can,' the woman told Avery. 'Presumably you know how all this stuff works?'

She responded to Avery's words of thanks with a chilly murmur of acknowledgement before stalking out briskly, shutting the door behind her. Down here, several fathoms beneath the water tank, the hum of the computers, the sound of her own breathing and even the ambient silence itself were eerily thick, and Avery was relieved when Gwen's face flickered onto one of the screens. She settled in the chair before it and pulled the tiny microphone towards her.

Gwen looked concerned, and the collar and shoulders of her red cotton boilersuit were polka-dotted with drips of sweat that had fallen from her long blonde tangle of hair.

'Oh God, please tell me it's not Scully . . . is she okay?'

'Scully? Oh, your *cat*? For a minute I thought they'd stopped your weekly delivery of *X-Files* videos and you were, you know . . . Anyway, I have no idea. I assume she's fine. I just stopped by to say hello. I didn't mean to get you worried.'

Gwen laughed, relieved.

'God, they're such jerk-offs out there. They made out that you had some vital news.'

Avery pulled a sheepish face. 'My fault, totally my fault. I'm sorry.'

'That's okay. It's great to see you. I've only got about five minutes, but I'm desperate to catch up. You haven't mailed me in eleven days, eh?'

'I know. Oh God, I don't know where to start. How are things with you, Doc?'

'Apart from being absurdly hot in here today, well . . . Generally, very tedious. *Really* tedious. No one's been injured or fallen ill for weeks, unless you count Jenny Otomo's delightful ongoing yeast infection, so I haven't had much to do. Mostly I've just been doing the Johns Hopkins research stuff – the blood tests? Two a day for the whole team. So everybody really hates me right now. And that, good buddy, is my news in its entirety. Now, give.'

Avery brought Gwen up to date as best she could whilst using only the official story; she included as few details as possible, so that it wouldn't feel like she was lying. She wished she could have told Gwen about Daetwyler's weird research and his weird kid with the tape recorder, and the lab assistant with the haunted eyes. Or revealed that Lisa Schaeffer and Leon LeGalley were not on the run, but were dead. She would have liked to have appealed to Gwen's medical knowledge to ask about the world of pharmaceutical trials, or to her natural wisdom to ask if she had any ideas as to how the hell Lisa and Leon might be involved with the late, odious Jerry Lee Lucas, or where Leon's crazy, brain-dead girlfriend might fit into the frame. But she couldn't. She didn't dare. Not now. Not yet.

It felt weird holding back from her closest friend like this, but Avery really had no choice, and fortunately Gwen seemed to understand, and she moved on swiftly.

'What about Hayes? How are you getting along with him?'

Avery thought carefully for a moment.

'Well, this situation complicates things, that's for sure. But I realized something this afternoon. I realized why he's probably the right person for me. Something that hadn't occurred to me before.'

'And that was?'

'There probably aren't that many people who feel the way I feel about Dreamworld, what it means to me. But Hayes does. And I hadn't realized how important that was. I don't think I could be with someone who was cynical about it, who didn't see what I saw, didn't get what I get from it.'

Gwen Bissette nodded thoughtfully and squinted at the screen, scrutinizing Avery. 'So why aren't you happy? You're not, are you? Something doesn't feel right. What is it?'

Avery looked at her watch. It was ten after seven. 'I don't know. I'll think about it and mail you.'

'You *do* know. Try me.'

Avery sighed. 'Okay. It was just that last night I had this horrible flashback. About my stepfather? And, to a lesser extent, my mom. About the way that I grew up believing that making things *look* right, making things look perfect and flawless, was the most important thing. If you tried to actually *make* it right, you'd end up destroying the thing you were trying to protect. Do you get what I'm saying?'

'Of course. But I don't get where Hayes comes in. Please don't tell me he's beating up on you, or I'll be out of that air-lock so fast it'll make your head spin.'

'No, no, it's nothing like that. It's just that I saw those same beliefs in Hayes, in the way he feels about

Dreamworld. Everything has to look right, and if something is wrong, actually setting it right is out of the question, because it risks destroying this sacred unit. So he'll tackle whatever's wrong by brushing it under the carpet. Making it look right. And seeing that in him made me realize that I'm the same.'

'Of course. That's what your job is all about. Surely you knew that all along?'

Avery put her head in her hands. 'So essentially, I've turned into my stepdad.'

'Bullshit. I think you're torturing yourself, here. I know you can't tell me exactly what's going on, but obviously it's nasty and it's upset you, and so it's stirred everything up. Just the fact that you're saying this to me is proof that you're not someone who sweeps everything under the carpet, eh?'

'So you don't get a bad vibe about this? You don't figure I'm doing the wrong thing? Being in this job, I mean.'

Gwen gave a playful faux-frown.

'I don't do vibes, Avery. If you're asking me what I *think*. . . I think it's not for me to judge. Only you can know that kind of thing.'

'But is it fucked up to want to protect Dreamworld the way I do? The way Hayes does?'

'I don't know about Hayes. All I know is that Dreamworld is your family now and it's natural to want to protect it. And if you choose to protect it the same way you protected your original family, then it's legitimate enough. But if you feel you did the wrong thing back then . . .'

'I don't.'

Avery was surprised at the force of the words as they tumbled into the dead air of the communications room.

'I don't. I know that much. I had the power to destroy my family and I chose not to. It had nothing to do with any coercion – although God knows, there was plenty. It was in my hands and I made a decision and saw it through. How could I live with myself if I thought it was the wrong one? I can't go back and change it.'

Avery swallowed hard, afraid that if she started to cry, she might not be able to stop.

'I have to go, Gwen. I'm going to be late. But . . . thank you.'

Despite the slightly jerky, pixellated quality of the image on the screen before her, Avery was sure that she could discern a certain wistfulness in Gwen's smile as she kissed her fingertips and pressed them to the screen.

'Go get 'em, Avery,' she said softly.

Avery stood up and kissed the tiny spherical camera mounted atop the monitor.

'Thanks, Doc. I will.'

And one by one the pixels dissolved until the screen faded to black and Avery was alone.

Twelve

Though it all depended on your taste, of course, most Dreamworld employees were in agreement that Cleo's Barge was just about the nicest place to eat and drink on property. Housed in the rectangular concrete base of the Sphinx beside the artificial Nile that ran through the heart of the King Tut's Palace resort, its interior was a glorious symphony of gold leaf, lapis lazuli and cool marble, the beverage menu included 200 different beers from around the globe, and if you got a window seat, you could enjoy watching the kids playing on the slippery rubber croco- diles that infested the sparkling waters outside. If you came later at night, the same windows afforded a great view of the nightly firework display over Atlantis, which, it was generally agreed, was superior to the displays at ImagiNation and Dreamworld Studios, Dreamworld's third theme park. Best of all, Cleo's Barge was one of those best-kept-secret kinds of places, far quieter, even at busy times of year, than the other good bars and res- taurants on property.

Avery was idly asking herself, as she sipped an ice-cool tankard of Belgian Gouden Caroulus and watched a little boy trying to give his older sister a leg-up onto a crocodile, why she hadn't been here for so long – since her transfer, in fact – when her reverie was interrupted by the intrusion of the thought that she might have done something really stupid by coming here instead of heading back to ImagiNation, as she had originally intended.

Avery's cellular had no service in the depths of the Ocean Pavilion, and when she'd got back outside and above sea level, Perdue's message had been waiting, with the information that the moped she'd seen was registered to someone by the name of Lloyd Clowes III.

Apparently, the name hadn't checked out with any Dreamworld records, neither employees nor volunteers at the centre, but Perdue had called an old buddy at Orange County who'd checked the DMV records and given him the salient details from that, which Perdue had now passed on to her. He had signed off by reminding Avery to get something to eat. As she climbed into her car, turned on the stereo and pushed in her favourite Barenaked Ladies CD – quiet enough that she could still hear her walkie-talkie but loud enough to make her smile – she realized she was feeling better and was just beginning to consider taking that particular piece of advice when she saw something that made her forget about her appetite.

Pinned under the wiper on Avery's windshield was a note. She could see, even before snatching it up and scanning it, that the signature scrawled at the bottom read 'Trey Clowes'. She balked for a minute before remembering that third-generation namesakes often got called Trey. It was him.

The rest of the note was economical, to say the least:

NEED TO TALK TO YOU ABOUT LISA OFF THE RECORD.
MEET 7:00 AT CLEO'S BARGE?

Avery read the note through twice. The physical description and date of birth on Clowes's driving licence made him a very likely candidate for being the guy from the 'behold the power of cheese' photo, and if she was right, it would mean that she wouldn't need to go back to ImagiNation to quiz Lisa's colleagues and face their unbearable questions about why Lisa wasn't there any more. That was tempting. So was the idea of going to Cleo's Barge, Avery had to admit. She liked it there, and, besides, Hayes was over on the West Coast for the night and she had nothing to do and the idea of a cold beer and some stuffed jalapenos was sounding very good about now. She knew, of course she knew, deep down, that Perdue wouldn't be terribly impressed with the safety aspect of her decision to go for a rendezvous with someone who had been tailing her all day and had somehow managed to sneak into the Atlantis security entrance parking lot to leave a note on her windshield. But at least, she told herself, he'd be glad that she was finally getting something to eat.

Avery was just wondering whether she was a fool to be feeling so safe, to be sitting here sipping her beer and chowing down on the plate of stuffed jalapenos that had just arrived, and buying wholesale the lie that nothing bad ever happened on property – the whole damn masquerade that it was her job to maintain – when she heard someone say her name. She looked up to see a figure standing beside her.

'I wasn't staring at your breasts, by the way, I was

reading your name tag. I'm Lloyd Clowes. But, uh, most people call me Trey.'

Avery looked at the person on the other end of the hand that was extended towards her and became unexpectedly flustered. Black skateboard shorts, a black cotton bowling shirt bearing two large embroidered Chinese dragons. Broad shoulders. Great legs . . . All of the above were very much to her liking. But it was his face, more than anything else, that really threw her.

Clowes looked like his picture, and yet he didn't. Avery was surprised, although she shouldn't have been because she was the same: one of those people who photographed as either quite pleasant or just ordinary, but in real life, in motion, exuded a deep complexity, wisdom and charisma that rendered the same features captivating. In Trey Clowes's case, it was almost disconcertingly so.

She stood to greet him, meeting his gaze. His eyes were so dark as to appear almost black, as was his hair, which was closely cropped and stood to spiky attention, yet apparently not as a result of the application of any grooming product: it looked silky and thick, like the pelt of some small wild animal. Avery found herself wondering what it felt like, and as they shook hands, she noticed that Clowes was pretty much exactly the same height as her, and was inexplicably struck by the realization that it would probably be really easy for them to have sex standing up – something she felt she'd missed out on, always having had partners taller than herself. Obviously, Avery noted, the heart-to-heart with Gwen had restored her back to her old self again.

'So, Sylvia, I tried to call you, but your mother said you were busy, and the operator kept cutting in . . .'

'Excuse me?' Avery stared at Trey Clowes, blankly and slightly anxiously.

'You know –' Clowes took an audible breath and, with not inconsiderable gusto, belted out the first verse and most of the chorus of 'Sylvia's Mother' by Dr Hook. His voice was lousy, but Avery only admired his lack of inhibition the more for it.

'Sorry. I'll bet people do that all the time.'

'Actually, no. That was something of a first for me.'

'But you are named after that song, right?'

'Exactly. Yes, I assume I'm kind of named after it. But the song's not really about the girl, though, is it? It's more about her mother, no? Which says a lot more about my mother than she'd probably like.'

Avery was struck suddenly by an uncomfortable awareness of how abruptly the conversation had reached a certain level of intimacy which didn't tally with her picture of herself as someone who was guarded and mysterious and professional, and also by an irrational fear that Clowes had somehow picked up on her brief carnal fugue. She drained what remained of her beer and pushed the glass away in an attempt to punctuate the conversation, to declare this particular paragraph closed. It was clumsy but it worked. He seemed quite intimidated.

'I guess you want to know who the hell I am, why I asked you to meet me. And I – I'm sorry about following you, I just, I was going to Leon's place to find out what was going on, and I saw you driving around in the Dreamworld security car and I knew you must be going there about Lisa. I was worried about her. I'm, I'm kind of a friend of hers. But I didn't want to call the security office and like I think I said, I . . .'

Avery suddenly felt a little sorry for Trey Clowes. She didn't have the greatest record as a judge of character, but he really did seem harmless, and she felt she should speak, interrupt his awkward soliloquy, put him out of his misery.

'It's okay, Trey. Sit down. Do you want a beer?'

He looked relieved and a little surprised.

Despite Clowes's cloak-and-dagger shenanigans, it now seemed that he was looking for information, rather than offering it. The 'off the record' thing was, Avery guessed, probably due to some bizarre fear of authority, as if he thought that anything he said, including, 'Do you know where my friends are?' would be taken down and used against him in a court of law.

Clowes sat down a little too quickly, fixing her gaze as he did so and smiling a little too broadly, making her wonder briefly whether her sympathy had been misguided, her judgement off. Or maybe it was just that he liked her. Anyway, she told herself, she had her beer and her jalapenos and a feeling that he might actually be pleasant enough company to make the half-hour or so she'd have to spend with him – for the sake of politeness – quite bearable.

'I'm definitely not supposed to drink on duty, but technically it's after hours, and I'm guessing that you're not going to rat on me.' She handed him the beer list. 'What would you like? Do you prefer light beer or dark?'

'I usually have Asahi, the Japanese one? But it's kind of pricey. Is that okay?'

'Sure. So, you come here a lot?'

Clowes nodded.

'I'm surprised. Not many people know about this place unless they're staying here at the resort or they work on property. Did you used to work here or something?'

'No. I used to work at Disney, though. Summers.' He stroked his chin. 'But I got sick of having to lose the facial hair.'

Avery laughed, slightly bewildered.

'Uh, *what* facial hair?'

Clowes laughed awkwardly, a peachy-hued wash of embarrassment rushing to his cheeks.

'Oh yeah . . . No. I know. Well, no actually I forgot. But, no, sometimes I like to wear a goatee. I like to have the choice.'

Avery could have teased him further but decided to let it drop. There was something about Trey Clowes that brought out her maternal side, although she was sure that he was only three or four years younger than her at the most.

'No. I knew what you meant. I knew it was against Disney policy. Same deal at Dreamworld, even for temp workers.'

'Exactly. So I got sick of that. That and not being allowed to point with one finger. I never could figure that one. You guys have that too, right? You have to do the two-fingered point when you're showing someone directions or whatever?'

Avery nodded. 'We do. So come on, how come you know Dreamworld so well? You didn't answer my question.'

He tapped his forehead lightly in chastisement for his forgetfulness. 'I've been spending a lot of time on property for what I'm doing now. It's kind of a college project.'

'*Kind of* a college project?'

'Well, it *is* a college project. My senior thesis. It involves me talking to a lot of employees here and at Disney and Universal. So I talk to a lot of people, and most of the Dreamworld guys, if I offer to buy them a drink, they always want to come here.'

Their server arrived and Avery ordered their beers quickly, keen to continue the conversation. She knew she should be getting briskly down to business and heading home, but she was intrigued.

'So what's the subject?' she asked.

'Of my thesis? Urban legends.'

'Like the lady who put her poodle in the microwave? And the couple with the guy with the hook for a hand and he's bouncing the head on the roof of the car and the cop says: "Whatever you do don't look back'?" All that stuff?'

'Uh-huh. Except the last one you said, that's two different stories. But, yeah, that's the kind of thing. All those anecdotes that happened to your friend's hairdresser's babysitter. But my thesis is on theme park legends.'

'Really? What's your major, exactly? Not that it doesn't sound legitimate. I'm just curious.'

'Folklore. Urban legends are contemporary folklore: the modern oral tradition. Or so my tutor tells me.'

'Sounds completely fascinating. But I don't get the theme park angle.'

Clowes looked slightly weary, as if he was about to say something he'd said many, many times before. 'It's just: what are the stories that spring up around theme parks? What are the different categories, who tells them, how long do they take to spread, how do they mutate, why are they told? Are they true or not? But that's almost irrelevant, whether they're true. The real key thing that studying folklore is all about is really looking at what function the various stories serve. They all serve one function or another.'

'Like what?'

'Oh God, I can't go into it now. There're so many. Ask me another time.'

Avery smiled, unable to tell whether his intimation that there may *be* another time was arrogance, guilessness

107

or just a figure of speech. He interrupted her thoughts.

'I didn't mean to be rude. It's just we'd be here all night, and I'm trying to remember these days that other people have lives to get on with, even though I don't. I sometimes forget.'

He smiled at her and she smiled back, warming to him.

'I'd love to hear about it some time, Trey. Honestly.'

'Sure you would.'

'I would! I'd love to hear some Dreamworld stories. I don't think I've ever heard any.'

'Are you kidding? There are hundreds. I've never met a cast member who hasn't heard at least some of them. How long have you worked here?'

Avery bristled slightly. 'I don't know, a long time. I'm losing count.' She thought back to her early days at Atlantis: helping wrangle the Biodrome crew through the crowds and the media. The day she'd met Gwen. When was that? How long did Scientist-Barbie say they'd been in there? 'Five years. Not far off six,' she told Clowes, riled further by his single raised eyebrow. 'Obviously I've heard *some* stories. Obviously.'

'Like?'

She strained to think of something. 'Well, I mean, there's stuff like, everyone tells this story about a guest comes up to them and asks, "What time does the three o'clock parade start?" But it always happened to someone they work with, never them. It's almost certainly apocryphal. And not the kind of thing you'd bother remembering, particularly.'

If Trey Clowes had picked up on her dig, he'd chosen to ignore it. 'Yeah, that's a popular one. They tell it at Disney, too. But that's quite a simple example – in terms of the story itself being short and also the function it serves: makes the cast members feel superior to the guests, boosts morale. The stories I tend to focus on are more detailed and you can disappear further up your own ass interpreting them. Which is what writing a thesis is all about, of course.'

'Of course.' Avery nodded and smiled knowingly and noted that, although Clowes was a wise-ass and clearly nowhere near as smart as, say, Hayes, she still hoped that he couldn't tell that she hadn't actually been to college, apart from law enforcement training academy.

'Anyway, now I've bored you to death, I guess we should talk about Lisa?'

Avery was mildly surprised by the reluctance she felt at the proposition of segueing back into work, the actual purpose of her meeting, and the sudden, not unrelated yearning she felt at remembering that this drink with Trey Clowes was not a social occasion.

'Sure. There's not much I can tell you, though. I'm guessing you know that she and Leon seem to have gone on a little impromptu road-trip or something?'

'Okay. You see, I don't think so. I don't think that's what happened.'

'Right. What *do* you think happened, Trey?'

Clowes looked at Avery and hesitated nervously before speaking again.

'I – I guess the first thing I should tell you is that actually Lisa is kind of more than a friend. She's kind of my girlfriend.'

Avery wasn't sure what was worse: the fact that she hadn't seen it coming, or the fact that she now had to come to terms with having spent the last five minutes drooling over a dead girl's boyfriend. That the dead girl was a two-timing dead girl didn't really make it any more palatable.

Avery was used to having colourful thoughts about just about every guy she met – she prided herself on her ability to find something appealing in nearly every single one – but it had been a long time, perhaps not since she'd met Hayes, since she last found herself thinking thoughts that were not just bed-centric. But in the last five minutes, she'd been thinking how much she'd like to go out to dinner with Trey Clowes and ask him things like what was the last movie he saw and when did he lose his virginity and how did he get that little scar above his eyebrow. This level of personal distraction irritated Avery, particularly when she was keen to do her job thoroughly, and she became further frustrated when she felt faint pangs of what could only be described as envy when he started to tell her how worried he was about Lisa Schaeffer.

Trey Clowes had met Lisa at the Bamboo Lounge in Kissimmee, a premier after-hours hang-out for theme park workers from Disney and Dreamworld; a place where cast members could bitch about their jobs and tell dumb-guest stories and get drunk outside of the cloistered on-property atmosphere which some felt had shades of Big Brother. Avery, not being one of them, didn't frequent the place, but she knew it nonetheless. Everybody did. Lisa and Trey had got talking, and he had told her about his thesis, and she had asked him if he knew any cool stuff about the Research and Development Centre, because she was really intrigued by it. She said that all her buddies back in LA had been begging to hear the weird stuff – the dirt – about Dreamworld and she confessed that she'd taken some pictures in the utilidors and nearly got caught out, so she needed some good salacious gossip to pass on that wasn't going to get her into trouble. Trey had told her some of the stories he'd collected, and she'd wanted to know if they were true or not, and he'd explained that, for his purposes it didn't really matter, but that probably some were and some weren't. She had gotten really fired up by the stories, particularly the ones about people volunteering to be human guinea pigs, which was something she said she'd never heard of before, which was not surprising, Trey noted, since she'd obviously never been strapped for cash. She'd become quite obsessed by the concept, and eventually asked Trey if he knew any volunteers; he told her he knew one or two, people he'd grilled for stories in exchange for a few drinks. Lisa had said no more that night, but she'd asked him out on what he grudgingly described as 'kind of a date' and had started up again, grilling him about the volunteers, eventually asking if she could meet them. Trey had echoed Shannon Reilly's assessment that Lisa seemed to like the idea of tasting the seamier side of life, which he thought was sort of crass, but he'd been quite taken with her, and he'd dug out Leon LeGalley's number and arranged for them all to go out, mostly because Lisa was very insistent, but also partly because he'd once mistakenly promised Shannon Reilly that he'd take her to a Red Lobster one day and he really wanted to get it out of the way.

Trey had, he admitted, been a little put out when Lisa had spent the entire evening talking to Leon, and although he'd been prepared to tolerate the couple of occasions that Lisa had unexpectedly invited Leon along on nights that were supposed to be dates, he'd been very unhappy when he'd started to suspect that Lisa might also be seeing Leon on the side, and had decided not to call her for a little while.

It was a week before she called him, but then they'd spent twelve glorious hours together – breakfast at Denny's, a tour of Orlando's tackier attractions like Splendid China and Terror on Church Street and finally dinner at the Medieval Times dinner show, in homage to their favourite scene in *The Cable Guy*, which they both agreed was Jim Carrey's most underrated movie. They'd had a great time – 'really connected again' was how Trey had put it – and so he'd been particularly surprised when the date was followed by only sporadic attention from this person whom he now considered to be his fully-fledged girlfriend.

Three days ago, though, they'd been to the movies. And that, Clowes said, had been the last time he'd seen her. Avery felt an odd mixture of sympathy and something else entirely less altruistic when she noted to herself that it would in fact be the last time he ever would.

'So you said you were worried about Lisa?' Avery asked. 'I don't get why.'

Clowes looked distressed.

'Messing around with a guy like Leon . . . It's a bad idea. He's an old-fashioned guy – I'm putting it nicely, here. What I mean is, it was okay by him cheating on Shannon, but Lisa didn't want to be with him all the time, and he wouldn't put up with that the way I did. He's the kind of guy you can bet probably never had anything like that happen to him before. Served him right. But it scared me.'

'What are you saying, Trey?'

'I'm saying, well, no, it was after the phone call that I got worried. She called me the night before she disappeared. She was in a weird mood, half elated, half scared, it seemed like, and she told me something terrible but really wild had happened, and she wasn't going to be here much longer, she was going to go back to LA really soon. Like, in a few days.'

'Are you sure?'

'That's what she said. Why?'

'Because it sounds weird. You know she hadn't even quit her job? Even temporary workers need to give two weeks' notice, I think. It might even be three. Else they don't get their wages for the previous month.'

'I don't think she needed the money. Her folks are loaded.'

'Even so, she'd have been blacklisted. She wouldn't have been able to work here again.'

'Right. I know. That wouldn't have mattered to her. Take my word for it. That didn't worry me. It was this: she said that she was surprised about Leon's reaction when she said she was leaving. She said he was angry.'

'Was she worried about that, about his reaction?'

'No. *I* was worried. I grew up around here. I've known guys like Leon all my life, unfortunately. So I was worried. And I still am worried. Which is why I wanted to see you and tell you this. Because I don't believe for a second that she's run away with him voluntarily. So, no, she didn't seem concerned at all. But that's what she was like: she figured that anything that involved getting round people, that's what she was best at. This Leon thing that came up, it was just a mild inconvenience to her that she'd have to deal with before she left. I don't think she even understood why he was so pissed. She's good at getting what she wants out of people, but she's bad at reading them. If she was better at it, she wouldn't have told him what she told him – the thing that made him mad.'

'And what was that?'

Clowes closed his eyes and rubbed at them hard with

the heels of his hands. When he'd finished he sighed and looked up at Avery earnestly, in silence, his searching gaze appearing to have a distinct sense of purpose to it, as if he was trying to gauge something from her, trying to make some decision. Afraid of influencing him, Avery said nothing. The silence was long, yet not awkward, and eventually he sighed once more before beginning to speak again.

'When I came here, I wasn't sure if I was going to tell you this. I was just going to tell you enough to try and get across this horrible feeling I have that this isn't a missing persons case you're looking at, and that was all. God knows I don't have a lot of trust or respect for Dreamworld, and I figured that the spin this thing puts on everything, they might not bother to keep looking for Lisa. But I really like you, Sylvia, and it doesn't mean much coming from me because I'm a really crappy judge of character, but I *trust* you. I think. Tell the truth, I don't know if you'll judge Lisa for what she's done, but I think I'm going to risk it and tell you anyway.'

'Tell me what?'

'About Lisa's secret.'

Avery caught her breath, afraid to speak lest Clowes change his mind at the last minute. She cocked her eyebrow to signal her readiness to listen. He regarded her carefully and spoke slowly.

'Lisa Schaeffer isn't exactly who she said she was.'

Thirteen

Like Walt Disney World's Magic Kingdom, ImagiNation is built atop a catacomb – wide concrete tunnels, 'utility corridors' or 'utilidors' designed to ensure that no visitor will ever see a trash can being emptied, a food delivery, a brinks truck collecting the day's haul, a headless cartoon character chugging a coffee or sneaking a smoke.

Felix Perdue's comparison of Dreamworld to a clock – the unpolished cogs of everyday necessity ceaselessly clicking beneath the clean regularity of its face – is just one analogy. Others prefer to use the image of a duck propelled by unseen legs, churning madly. And although Avery had always felt that neither entirely captured the essence of Dreamworld, she had always favoured the latter because it spoke more eloquently of the toil and mayhem that kept the operation running smoothly, and that in the case of ImagiNation, took place quite literally beneath the surface.

This morning, however, as she moved briskly through the utilidor system in her haste to reach Perdue, Avery found herself reminded of something else entirely: a stomach-flipping moment in her childhood when, luxuriating on the newly laid lawn of St Augustine grass in her back yard, she'd inquisitively pulled up a corner of the turf and lain frozen in awe-struck horror at the seething multitude of earthworms and weevils, earwigs and beetles that writhed in the sod beneath the perfect green shag-pile.

It was the first time that Avery had been in the utilidors since Lisa Schaeffer and Leon LeGalley had died, and she now realized the irony in the sheer convenience that this abomination should have taken place down here. It was as if murder and suicide were just two more factors of practical life that might offend the tourists and had therefore to be relegated to these discreet, concealed walkways; as if offensive weaponry and bleeding cadavers were just two more entries on the long list of distasteful items to be concealed from the paying customer, along with pallid frozen hot dogs, drums of canola oil and empty character costumes.

Although it was still an hour before official park-opening, the utilidor was alive with noise, layer upon layer of aural clamour that somehow today made Avery feel hot, panicky, like she had when she'd peeled back the grassy lid of the little hell beneath her back yard. Besides the echo of footfalls on concrete, hollers of greeting and instruction and the hum of golf-carts and mini-forklifts, there was the periodic tumult issuing from the wide metal tubes of the AVAC trash disposal system that ran along the low ceiling; the whoosh, rumble and rattle of a trash bag sucked through a vacuum at ninety-eight miles an hour just above your head, loud enough to blot out a fragment of your conversation or make you jump if you weren't expecting it. And this morning, Avery found herself jumping every time. But most disturbing to Avery right now was the incessant piped music above it all, a different signature piece in each sub-section of utilidor, playing on an endless loop. It was a concept typical of Dreamworld's politically correct approach, introduced so that visually impaired cast members – who could not make use of the signage and colour-coding – could tell at all times which section of the park they were currently beneath.

Avery had planned to walk swiftly past the disabled rest room where Lisa and Leon had died, and to this purpose she quickened her step and lengthened her strides as she passed the stairwell and elevator that led from the utilidor up to the Land of Make-Believe section of the park, via a discreet door located in the exit area of the Hansel and Gretel ride. But despite her velocity, Avery found it impossible to avoid thinking about what had taken place here. Being just one of several auxiliary access points located within a relatively small area, this sector was, as usual, far quieter than the main thorough-fares, and it was immediately – chillingly – apparent just how easy it must have been for Leon LeGalley to follow Lisa Schaeffer down the stairs and bundle her into the rest room without being seen. Avery was just beginning to think that it was actually surprising that intruders – well meaning or otherwise – didn't penetrate the utilidors more often, when she focused on something else, some-thing much worse. The music. 'My Home is Your Home', the signature tune for the Land of Make-Believe; the bright, tinkling voices of the dolls from the Global Village Cruise, their too-sweet harmony and innocent sentiment in terrible juxtaposition to the dark horrors haunting Avery's mind. 'My Home is Your Home', seemingly louder here, in the near-silence of this stretch of utilidor, reverberating around the stairwell and bouncing off the concrete walls, tumultous now in Avery's head, making her ears ring, and making it impossible to avoid the dawn-ing realization that this was the soundtrack to Lisa Schaeffer's slaughter.

Avery didn't stop running until she reached the next sector, when the walls changed from candy-pink to Halloween orange, and 'My Home is Your Home' was replaced by the thundering classical strings of 'The Hall of the Mountain King'. Avery had never been so pleased to reach October Country, and not just because this was where she knew she would find Perdue, and finally be able to share Trey Clowes's astonishing revelation, which she was bursting to do. Right now, even more than this, Avery simply wanted *out*. Out of the utilidors. Out from under the water with the churning webbed feet, back to the smooth surface of the lake where the ducks glided without apparent effort.

So although Avery knew that Perdue was by the midway, and that there was an exit further down the utilidor that would bring her out right by the gateway to the Shadowood County Carnival, she had no hesitation in bounding up the first flight of stairs that she came upon.

Avery burst out into the pale morning sunshine. The air was dewy with evaporation from the freshly sluiced walkways, and Avery took deep, grateful gulps of it as she started her hike across October Country.

The women in white voodoo-priestess robes peered out from behind the counters at Baron Samedi's Curiosity Shoppe as Avery passed, and the ride operators taking their positions at The Legend of Sleepy Hollow stopped what they were doing to watch where she went. Strolling past the Witch's Hat and Jack O'Lantern's Tavern, it was the same story. In order to ensure that the majority of park visitors will never see a member of uniformed security personnel, Avery and her colleagues were expected to use the utilidors to get from A to B, popping up as if from nowhere to deal with tasks as they arose and disappearing just as quickly on their completion. The sight of a security uniform on a public thoroughfare is rare, and usually the sign of something out of the ordinary, and so always generates mild curiosity. Avery felt the eyes upon her, but she didn't look back as she strode on, cutting across the pumpkin patch, her sights firmly fixed on the hulking black skeleton of the carnival's artfully foreboding Ferris wheel. All this staring – she knew that it was something she was going to have to get used to. Because as of five minutes ago, she had made up her mind: she wasn't going to go down into the utilidors again unless she absolutely had to, and if anybody had a problem with that they could go kiss her ass.

Shadowood County Carnival was Avery's favourite corner of ImagiNation, possibly her favourite place in the whole of Dreamworld, and almost certainly, she mused now, responsible for the key moment when she knew she'd fallen in love with Hayes Ober.

Even on this bright morning, it was as lusciously alive with creeping menace as always, the perfect, macabre representation of a carnival from nowhere, part classic seventies *Scooby Doo*, part *Something Wicked This Way Comes*, everything that had touched something deep in Avery's childhood imagination. Scary, but safe-scary. The kind of scary that you could dip into and out of whenever you wanted. The kind of scary you could control, that made you feel strong and intrepid because you could.

Back when she'd only spoken to Hayes a few times, in the first two days of the Dream Techs' conference in Los Angeles to which she'd been posted, she'd had a strange instinct that he might have been the creative force behind the Shadowood County Carnival. Sure, she'd already been captivated by his air of calm swagger hiding tenuously constrained volatility and his slightly seedy, pockmarked good looks, but she'd told herself that if her instinct was right, then she'd know for sure that he was the one, the 'lid for her pot' that her mother had always said was out there in the world somewhere. Part of her almost didn't want to know the answer. If she was wrong, then she'd have to consider that *all* the things she'd felt about him were just the product of deluded projection. If she was right, then she'd know that she had to have him. Both possibilities scared the hell out of her, and when she'd found out the answer from one of the other conference delegates – an affirmative – her relief was still delicately spiked with alarm. She had never wanted someone as badly as she now wanted Hayes. He was *hers*, and she had suddenly understood how stalkers felt. She knew that if he wasn't interested, if she couldn't have him, she'd be tempted – hypothetically, at least – to kill him instead, just to hear him screaming her name.

A fresh dusting of fake cobwebs had been applied overnight to the charmingly rickety midway stands, and the beautifully rendered forced-perspective here made them appear to loom, bear down on the visitor venturing along the walkway between the two rows. Unable to locate Perdue immediately, Avery paused on the path, taking advantage of the absence of crowds to stand just for a moment, drinking in the delicious sense of cold threat. Few people ever noticed this engineered effect, appreciated it the way that Avery did, and when she'd complimented Hayes on it that night in the bar as her opening gambit, she'd watched in delight as the other delegates became invisible to him, as he became inflamed, bewitched by her. It had taken him about seven minutes to invite her to his room.

Avery was still lost in prurient reverie when Perdue appeared at her side, looking mildly concerned.

'Sylvie?'

'Hey, Felix – I was looking for you. I found out something incredibly weird yesterday. About Lisa. Where can we go that's quiet?'

The room behind the Haunted Fun House which housed the security monitor screens was cool and dark, and since the park was still half an hour away from opening, the ride attendant hadn't minded too much when Perdue chucked him out temporarily.

Avery watched the monitors, the little fun-house passenger carts eerily empty as they trundled in and out of vision, while Perdue stared at the magazine that Avery had spread open in front of him.

'I don't know what I'm supposed to be looking at here, Sylvie.'

Perdue looked up at her, puzzled, and flipped the magazine closed to look at its cover, keeping his hand in the page that Avery had presented him with. The cover featured a picture of Christina Ricci wearing what appeared to be a child's party dress, trampling on a pile of squashed jello and cupcakes. She was holding a cigarette in one hand and a small automatic weapon in the other. Perdue stared at the picture before reading the title aloud.

'*Click*. What the hell is *Click*?'

'It's one of those twenty-something lifestyle things.

Apparently. Comes out of LA. I had to go all the way to Waldenbooks in the Florida Mall. None of the regular places stock it.'

Perdue flipped back to the page Avery had first opened. This time she jabbed her finger at the headline and sub head above the text.

'*Lap Dancing Uncovered? A month in the life of Hollywood's fastest growing industry,*' he read aloud.

'Look at the byline.'

'Well, fuck me backwards . . .'

Perdue gazed incredulously at the spread, and back to the name of the article's author. He looked up at Avery again, a slightly baffled expression on his face.

'Are we sure this is the same Lisa Schaeffer?'

Avery nodded, and began to tell Perdue everything about Trey Clowes and what he'd told her, leaving out the details about how she'd gone to meet him after-hours despite the fact that he'd been tailing her all day. When she'd finished, Perdue raked his silver hair back from his damp forehead, revealing the dark patches that had bloomed in the underarm area of his shirt. He rubbed his temples as if to dispel a headache and did not look at Avery as he spoke.

'So you're sure she was here to write one of these undercover pieces she does? She didn't maybe just decide on a change of career?'

'Well, according to Trey, yes. I mean no. I mean, yes, she was definitely here on assignment. That's why she was living at Buena Vida. She wasn't planning on staying long. In fact, Trey said she'd only been planning to stay six weeks in the beginning, but she hadn't been able to find enough dirt about Dreamworld to make a good piece, so she'd hung out a little longer. She was definitely pinning her hopes on the Research and Development Complex, but her editor told her she'd have to stay until she got something solid. Everyone knows how litigious Dreamworld is. I guess he needed more than what Trey had told her, more than just hearsay.'

'Which is why she was screwing Leon.'

'Exactly.'

'*Nice* girl.'

Avery flinched slightly. Having her own sentiments reflected back to her by Perdue made Avery suddenly uncomfortable. They seemed a little skewed, she had to admit. Frigid. Sordid. After all, Lisa was dead now; no matter how marked the polarity between the girl's values and Avery's own, the punishment could hardly be said to fit the crime.

Perdue rubbed his head again.

'So Leon found out that Lisa was using him to get dirt on the Research and Development Complex and got pissed?'

'According to Trey, yes.'

'And that answers a lot of our questions, right? At least we know why he killed her.'

'Yes, but . . .'

'I know. It doesn't really help us. It doesn't explain what happened with Lucas.'

'Yeah. But we can be pretty sure now that there's no way Lisa had anything to do with the murder.'

'Why? Because she's some snot-nosed, so-called journalist?'

Avery was momentarily startled by the venom in Perdue's voice, had to work hard to hide the indignation and irritation in her own.

'Look, Felix, I'm not saying . . . Well yeah, I am. It just seems very unlikely, now that we've got a clearer picture of who Lisa was, what she was about. It just seems very unlikely that she'd be involved in something like that. I'd be very surprised. I'm sure you can go with me at least part-way on that.'

Perdue brushed his hair back again. Avery noticed that the sweat patches at his armpits had gotten bigger.

'Oh, *sure*. I *would* have said that. It's just the small matter of she was driving her van on the highway in the middle of the fucking night right about where they found Jerry Lee Lucas stuffed in a picnic cooler. Not to mention the fact that she killed two folks on a motorbike and drove right off without reporting it to the police. Apart from that, I'd say she was the very picture of high-tone decorum.'

Avery and Perdue sat in silence for some time, Avery hoping that Perdue might use this period to simmer down. She studied him carefully before she spoke again. His whole face was glistening with sweat now, but he looked like his rage had subsided; like he was thinking rather than stewing.

'Look, Felix, you want to know what I think? It's just a guess, but I think maybe there was something else going on.'

'Like what kind of thing, Sylvie?'

Avery was relieved to hear him using her name again, even though it grated slightly, as it usually did. She rearranged herself in the ride attendant's swivel chair, and took a breath.

'Like something that was nothing to do with Dreamworld directly. Something that Lucas and Leon were maybe involved in together. Drugs or something? Some scam. I don't know. And maybe Lisa found out about it, and decided to make her article about that instead. It wasn't what she came here for, but she couldn't find much that was really worth exposing about

Dreamworld – I mean, the utilidors, the research centre . . . Big fucking deal, right? But if she could write about something else, something really squalid and illegal and play up the fact that it was going on under Dreamworld's noses – we make a big deal about being so clean-living and family values and all – and that people who volunteer at the Research and Development Complex are involved . . . That's a big deal for her. Plus it gets her out of the thing hanging over her that she's going to get sued by Dreamworld, and her boss is going to make her personally responsible. Which Trey said is what the guy had said. Made her sign some contract saying the article she delivers is all going to be true to the best of her knowledge and *she'll* be liable for any legal consequences arising, blah blah blah, not the magazine. So she's looking for something else, she finds something else. And then it all goes wrong, Lucas gets killed by someone who's involved, maybe even by Leon, and when Leon finds out that Lisa's not on his side, she's a reporter, they're not all in it together like he thought, then *that's* why he gets pissed, and he's scared that she's going to turn him in and split back to LA. So he reacts the only way people like Leon know how.'

'And then he feels so bad that he kills himself too?'

Avery shrugged. 'Maybe. It's just a theory. But it makes a lot more sense to me. I hardly think Leon was such a delicate flower that he'd kill Lisa because he was hurt that she was using him. And it explains where Lucas comes in.'

Perdue thought for a while, hunched forward, occasional beads of sweat running down his face, dripping onto his thighs. Finally he gave Avery a strained smile and spoke softly.

'Okay, I buy it. For now, I buy it. So, what we have

to do is find out if Lucas was involved in anything. And for God's sake let's do it fast, because the police are going to have a far better chance at it than we are. This is their patch, not ours. If you're right, Avery, we'd better get to work, because I have a nasty feeling that they're going to get there first.'

Avery gathered up the magazine, shoved it back into her bag and stood up. Perdue stood too and turned to open the door, revealing the vast dark stain on the back of his shirt, between the shoulder blades. He spoke to Avery over his shoulder.

'I'm going to head over to Lucas's digs. You check out the bar by his house, soon as it opens, talk to the people who work there. From what Officer Lopez told you, sounds like they know him pretty well. That okay? Or you wanna do it the other way round?'

Avery shook her head. 'Uh-uh. If it's okay by you, you do both, Felix. I'll go down to County HQ. I still didn't give them the hard copy of the printout from the research centre, so I have a good excuse to stop by. I want to get some idea of what they know. Figure out how long we have left.'

Fourteen

On reflection, telephoning Officer Serena Lopez on the way to the sheriff's office had been a mistake. What she should have done, Avery mused, as she sat, still smarting, in a booth at the Taco Bell across the road, was just showed up and asked to see Lopez or someone else on the case. She should have pretended that she didn't know whether it was okay to simply hand the vehicle registration list over to the attendant at the public counter, that she thought maybe it needed to be done in person. Then she'd have had a chance to get talking to someone, ask a few questions. As it was, Lopez had been as chilly on the phone as the first time they spoke, and had told her that there was no hurry, it would be fine to drop the document in the mail. It was just for the files. It wasn't important.

Undeterred, Avery had driven over anyhow, told the counter clerk that she happened to be passing, that she thought she'd drop it off personally. But to no avail; she'd had no choice but to leave the envelope at the desk. She'd blown it.

Partly, Avery had come into Taco Bell to get a coffee and gather herself. Partly, she'd figured that maybe, just maybe, this was where members of the mobile patrol coming off the graveyard shift would stop for their morning sustenance before heading home. Whoever found Lucas's body must have been on that shift, and that someone had surely been sidelined when the homicide department took over. Just the kind of someone, she figured, who might jump at the chance to get involved again. And as it turned out, she was right.

She'd turned on the charm for the first pair of uniforms who came in, found out who'd been on the 192 that night. She'd paid for their breakfast burritos by way of thanks.

It hadn't been hard to find Officer Brett Toback after that – he'd been the only cop sitting in the Subway three blocks down, and although he seemed reluctant to explain his aversion to Taco Bell, Avery sensed immediately that he'd probably be more forthcoming in other areas, especially if he thought he might get a freebie for his troubles.

'So, you guys, you get unlimited admission to the parks, or a bunch of tickets for the year or what?'

Toback emptied another sachet of Sweet 'n' Low into his coffee, stirred it, then set about cleaning under his fingernails with the coffee-stirrer.

'Depends on your seniority. Me, most people my level, we get entrance on certain days of the week, up to a certain limit, I think.'

'You use 'em all? You must get sick of the sight of the place!'

Toback flashed her a cheesy smile. Avery smiled back. This was going to be easy.

'Not really. I love the parks. But even if I did, I couldn't pass those entrances on, it's like a cast member ID. I could get you some passes though, probably. For you and your family.'

Toback acted surprised, as if this were not what he'd been driving at. 'Really?'

'You bet. My boss, if someone has a bad experience at the park, he's authorized to give them passes for a return visit. So we have plenty back at HQ. We have line-jumping cards, too. Give 'em out to people who've been waiting to go on the big attractions and then it breaks down and stays out of commission for the day. Next time they come, they can just show the pass and we backdoor them. They don't need to stand in line. They give those to VIPs too. I could get you a handful, no problem.'

Toback's eyes shone. 'You're kidding.'

'No. I'm sure I could work something out.'

'You could? That'd be incredible! It'd be just me and my wife. We don't got any kids yet.'

'Sure. And maybe you could do me a favour in return?'

'What's that?'

Avery leant in conspiratorially.

'I have a friend who works at the Research and Development Complex. On reception. Knew Lucas from when he used to come in there a lot. Said he was quite a charmer.'

Toback looked doubtful, and Avery realized that he had probably read, or at least heard about Lucas's rap sheet. She recovered masterfully.

'You know how some girls are. They go for the bad guys. I don't get it myself, but anyhow, she was pretty cut up about what happened. She keeps asking me if I know what's going on with the investigation, whether they got the guy who did this yet. And I only wish there was something I could tell her.'

Toback nodded sagely. 'Ain't much to tell right now, I'm afraid.'

Avery's heart leapt. *Thank God.*

129

'No? From what Lopez said, I thought you had the vehicle, the suspect's vehicle details? It was a Volkswagen or something?'

'Yeah well, that's a dead end, for now. So, as I understand it, we're a little stuck. But I'm sorta out of the loop. Keep on looking out for that van on my shifts, but I'd say they blew town.'

Avery silently acknowledged what Toback had said, and watched his face carefully to see how long it would take him to twig. It took a while, but as he raised his coffee cup to his lips, Avery could see clearly that the lightbulb had come on. He replaced the cup on the table without taking a sip.

'Say, your friend, you think she might know anything that could help us out?'

Avery pretended to look surprised and inspired by Toback's suggestion, and slowly put down the chocolate chip cookie she'd just bitten a chunk out of. She chewed thoughtfully before responding.

'Well, like I told you, it was me who did the intra-office report, talked to everyone at the centre. And all I was told to ask was whether Lucas had left with anybody else, and what time and all. Now, if you had more to go on, anything new, I could always go back and do a second round of inquiries. Might turn something up. Why don't you have Lopez call my boss? Name of Felix Perdue. Do you want me to write that down for you?'

Toback looked crestfallen. Just as Avery had hoped, he was clearly keen to find himself a way back onto the case.

'Else we could do something maybe less formal, I don't know . . .' Avery raised one eyebrow at Toback, watched his face light up.

'Uh-huh. That'd work.'

Toback nodded slowly, his grin more inappropriate than ever. The guy seemed to have very little control over his facial expressions, Avery noted, trying not to laugh at the image that had just popped into her head: Toback playing poker.

'So listen, Brett, tell me what you've got, and I'll see what I can do. Scope things out my end, report back. If I get anything, it's all yours. I'm not in the investigative department, so it's no skin off my nose. I'm just patrol.'

'Me too. But I'm hoping to . . . Hold on, so how come you were doing the intra-office stuff? Sounds like investigative.'

Avery hadn't planned to show her cards, but after a moment's reflection couldn't see any reason to hold back. 'My boyfriend. He kind of works at the Research and Development Complex. So I know people there. And the kind of stuff they do, they'd always rather deal with folks they know. They're kinda picky about who can visit. So my boss sent *me*.'

Avery fixed Toback with a look that told him that she wasn't prepared to elucidate on the nature of the afore-mentioned 'stuff'. She watched him struggle painfully to subdue his curiosity.

'Sure. I can understand that, I guess.'

'Right. So you gonna tell me what you got?'

Toback drew an eager breath; a man with nothing to lose and everything to gain. 'Okay, so you know that Lucas's car, we found it outside this strip joint on Orange Blossom? It's called Emanuelle's. Well, as luck would have it, vice had the place under surveillance that night. Some bust they're working on. Not the club, just some guy, I think. Dealer maybe? But anyways, they were there. And they got the Volkswagen on tape. Arrived just after Lucas's Sunbird. We only got a partial on the plate, but we narrowed it down some. In fact, I think we got it.'

'You did? I thought you said it was a dead end, the vehicle?'

Avery held her breath.

'Right. Registered to a fake name, fake address, far as we can tell.'

She exhaled hard.

'But at least now you'll know when you see it, huh?'

Toback shrugged. 'They gotta have new plates by now. But we'll know it anyways. We got authority to pull over any Volkswagen – any orange one, any one that looks like it's just had a respray. Pull it over, take a look in the back, that'll do it.'

'Look in the back for what? Blood?'

'Nuh-uh. Bullet hole. The guy was already in the cooler when they put a bullet in him. Exit wound in his back, put a hole right through the bottom of the cooler. Carpet fibres stuck in the burnt up plastic round the hole. Analysed it: said it's definitely the kinda carpet they use inside a vehicle. What do you call it? I don't know. Car carpet. But anyways, means the bullet's gotta be lodged in the back of the van. Means that's where they did it. So as for blood, there won't be much from the gunshot wound. Might be some from, uh, whatever else, though, but if they got any sense they'll have cleaned that up by now.'

Toback paled slightly at whatever image had entered his head.

'What else? Lucas had other injuries?'

'I didn't see the final autopsy report – like I said, it's not my case no more. Never really was, from as soon as they found out it was hit and run and homicide. But word going round is whatever they did to him before they killed him, it must have been pretty bad. Guy bit his own tongue off. Fact, it might have been the bleeding from that was what killed him, all told. Figure they just shot him to, like, make sure . . .'

For a fleeting moment, Toback's cheeks bulged as if he were about to vomit. Avery studied him with concerned fascination. She and Perdue might be soft compared to most law enforcement agents, but at least they'd had the sense to know their own limitations and follow a realistic career path. Toback, on the other hand, seemed to have chosen a job quite unsuited to his constitution. She felt it would be prudent to change the subject.

'Brett, you keep saying "they"? You reckon there was more than one person involved?'

Toback looked relieved and grateful at the turn of the conversation. The colour began to return to his cheeks.

'Looks that way. The vice footage? You can see there's at least two people in the van.'

'Right. So what else?'

'Not much. Far as I know, that's pretty much the full story so far. But vice have finally turned all the footage over to homicide now they're done with it, and they got stuff from inside the club. In fact, it's mostly from inside. So what they're hoping is that you can see who Lucas is with. That's the next stage. And they're pretty confident. So what I'm thinking is, when they get the pictures, maybe I could contact you, sneak you out some copies, have you show 'em to your people at the research place. We've had Lucas's drinking buddies down to the station twice now. They're saying they don't know jack about that night, and Lopez says she believes 'em, says she thinks it's gotta be something to do with his other pals, guys from the centre. Whaddya call 'em? Volunteers.

That's why she was so pissed when the Volkswagen didn't show up on your printout. Apparently someone at your office says she can't send any of our guys down there unless we've got some new evidence or something. You know. Reasonable suspicion, whatever.'

Avery scribbled the number of the ImagiNation security HQ on a paper napkin and handed it to Toback.

'Yeah well, that's the way they operate over there. Corporate secrets, it's a big deal. But call me when you get those shots. As soon as you get them. We wanna help, really. If there's anyone involved in something like this working on Dreamworld property . . . Well, jeez. We wanna get all this fixed as much as you do. Quick as possible. So I appreciate the update.'

'No problem. You tell your buddy at the centre we're onto it. It's looking good.'

'You bet.'

Avery smiled as she rose and offered Toback her hand. He stood up, took it.

'Pleasure to meet you, Brett. I'll be sure to get those passes fixed up for you.'

She looked at the young officer's wrist as they shook hands. 'And I tell you what, I'll see if I can get you a Kit-E-Cat watch, too.' She flashed Toback her most winning smile. 'Can't have a good buddy of Dreamworld's wearing Chip 'n' Dale.'

Officer Brett Toback was still beaming as he sat down and watched Avery leave Subway and start back down the block, fishing her Star-tac from her pocket to check her messages as she strolled.

He saw her stop dead in her path for a moment, and looked on, slightly puzzled, as her arms dropped limply to her side, her shoulders rising and falling heavily as she stood in contemplation. But Toback thought little of it and went back to the more immediate business of draining his coffee, head thrown back, eyes fixed on the bottom of the styrofoam cup, which prevented him from noticing that Sylvia Avery had broken into a run.

Fifteen

No matter how quiet the parks are at Dreamworld, you'll never be the only shopper in a store. And no matter how long you spend browsing or buying, there's always another tourist who'll take longer than you. He'll still be there when you leave, strolling the aisles, picking up an item here, perusing a shelf there. Fiddling with his camera, rifling through the pockets of his shorts looking for who-knows-what, tinkering with the screw on the arm of his sunglasses. This is because he's not a tourist at all. He's what's known as a fox, a plain-clothes member of the security team. He may look like he's busy enjoying his vacation, but he's working for the cat, and he's watching your hands, because, as they told him on the first day of his training programme, that is what people use to steal with.

A fox's cover is his greatest – and only – weapon. He'd be no more likely to risk blowing it in the middle of a busy store than a regular cop would lay down his piece in the middle of a bust. He won't talk to the clerk. He won't talk to his fellow shoppers – unless he's spoken to, or he's making an arrest. And he certainly won't talk to his uniformed colleagues. But despite the considerable number of shoppers present, the fox working the photographic centre at Atlantis rushed over to Avery as she burst in and asked if she was okay.

She hadn't noticed until then how fast she'd been running, to get from the lot and across the park to the centre. And it dawned on her now, judging by the fox's reaction, that she must look pretty harried. She felt a stab of dismay as she realized that she could get into trouble if this got back to the office. Looking panicky, running, giving anybody the impression that something urgent or worthy of concern was going down – this was a strict no-no. Foxes were lower in rank than investigative but above patrol, and this guy would be well within his rights to file a report back to ImagiNation HQ. It might wind up with Perdue, or it might wind up with any of his five peers. Pot luck. Not good. Avery tucked her hair behind her ears, touched the back of her hand to her burning cheek and smiled calmly at the fox, trying to affect an expression of puzzlement at his concern.

'I'm fine, it's just a little hot out there.'

The man's concerned look turned to one of mild hostility. She'd made him blow his cover and now she was spinning him some unconvincing line. Her safest bet, she figured, was to try and help him regain it, and hope that he'd let the whole thing drop. She raised her voice slightly, affecting her best Dreamworld perky tone.

'Is there anything I can help *you* with, sir?'

The fox glared back, and replied through gritted teeth.

'No, *ma'am*. But thanks all the same.'

He turned away, picked up a Skipper the Dolphin picture frame and raised it close to him as if to study the price sticker, whilst making sure that Avery could see that he was actually taking a good look at her name tag. She pretended not to notice and threw him a friendly wave as she made her way to the processing room.

'Jesus, Avery, you look like shit.'

Mitch Ducek was sitting in the same chair he'd occupied the last time Avery had seen him, only now, instead of being draped over it in his usual laid-back sprawl, he was scrunched up, one foot on the chair, the other beneath him, as if ready to leap up, or at least go in for some prolific fidgeting.

'Thanks. You don't look so great yourself. That was some message you left me. What's the matter? I came as fast as I could.'

Ducek sprang to his feet, scuttled to the doorway and said something to the clerk behind the desk before closing the door and locking it behind him.

'I don't know what this is about, Avery, but I don't like it. Gives me the creeps. You've dragged me into this, didn't tell me anything about it, and now I – I just feel, I don't know. I don't want anything to do with it. You shouldn't have given these to me. You should have given them to the police. I haven't wanted to leave the fuckin' room since I processed them, and I can't leave them in here. I don't want them in my locker, I shouldn't even have them. I don't want them, it's . . .'

'Why? What? What's in them?'

Ducek reached miserably into the back pocket of his pants and passed the slightly bent envelope to Avery, holding it at arm's length, between thumb and forefinger as if it were something putrid.

Avery stared at the envelope. It was the glossy, standard-issue type: a photograph of a smiling toddler bathed in sunlight, face smothered with ice cream. A cartoon picture of Kit-E-Cat holding a camera, a speech bubble blossoming from his lips that read, 'Say cheese!' The legend, *Your memories from Dreamworld*. Avery had a nasty feeling that, in a few moments' time, all this was going to seem disgustingly ironic. She opened the envelope and took out the prints.

The first few were of her, taken by Perdue in Lisa's apartment when he had finished off the film. Ducek watched as she moved these to the back of the pile.

'Are these out of order?'

'Yes. Sorry. I was looking at them. And I, I guess I was worried in case someone else found them, opened the envelope. I put those at the front.'

'So the rest are in order?'

'Yes. No. Well, just about. Apart from the last two are mixed up. Whose pictures are they, Avery? Why are you in them?'

Avery laughed nervously at the painful gravity etched into Ducek's face, wondered what he had imagined.

'Perdue finished off the roll, that's all. Belonged to someone else. Someone I don't know. Nor do you.'

She gave Ducek a pointed, quit-asking-questions look before returning her gaze to the photographs.

Next up were several pictures of the Research and Development Complex in darkness, sinister and looming, the moon and clouds trapped in its reflective walls. Now a shot, taken at a distance, of the security booth at the centre, the guard tapping at her computer unawares. Two shots of the uniformed patrolman and his German Shepherd, walking across the deserted lot, away from the photographer.

Then five images that were so dark as to appear completely black, save for a few chinks of orange light here and there. Avery squinted at the one on the top of the pile, held it at arm's length and turned it from landscape to portrait, but could make out nothing. After these came a picture that appeared to be of the ceiling of a vehicle: Lisa's van. A mistake, Avery guessed. She looked up quizzically at Ducek, who flicked his hand impatiently, *keep going*.

'It's at the back, the one that . . .' Ducek's voice was hollow as it tailed off. 'I put it at the back.'

The last picture was mostly black, too, but here you could make out a few different shades within the gloom; night sky; dense black tree-tops against it. And here some low light source from out of range had brightened the foliage enough to pick out in silhouette a little part of the scene that was taking place in the foreground. The image took a few moments to register, and when it did, Avery felt like she was being hosed down with hot treacle. Instinctively, she turned the photo over, away from her. She took a deep breath before turning it again to take a closer look, make sure she'd really seen what she thought she'd seen. She had.

If she hadn't known about the cooler, Avery might not have known what the angular shape near the lower righthand corner of the picture was. The angular shape that was partially poking out of the dark silhouette that had to be the back end of some vehicle. But she would have recognized right away that the thing looming over it was a human figure. It was neither obviously male nor obviously not; the hunkered-over position made it hard to get any sense of build or height, and the head was almost entirely devoured by the shadows. But the cooler and the right arm were cleanly picked out in chiaroscuro, as was the hand. And in it, the gun. Pointed at the cooler. Avery looked up at Ducek, not knowing what to say. She wasn't sure what she'd expected, but this wasn't it. She was glad when he spoke first.

'So you're going to give these to the County police, I guess? You guys don't . . . deal with this kind of thing, right?'

'I'm not sure.'

Avery put the photographs back in the envelope, tucked it into her bag and planted a kiss on Ducek's cheek.

'Thank you. I really appreciate you doing this. And, obviously, don't say anything to anybody please, yeah?'

He reared away from her. 'What, that's it? *Thanks, Mitch*? You're not even going to tell me what this is about? You drag me into this and –'

'Mitch, I can't. You know I can't.'

Avery started walking towards the door. Ducek shook his head in frustrated resignation. Then a thought struck him and he called after her.

'Avery? One thing: the police, they'll probably figure it for themselves. But tell them just in case: you could probably get a bit more detail out of those black ones. With the right hardware.'

Avery stopped and turned back to face Ducek. 'Really?'

'Probably.'

She opened her bag and took out the envelope. Ducek raised his hands in protest.

'Oh, no. No way. Forget it.'

'You could do it, couldn't you?' She gestured around the room. 'The stuff you guys have in here –'

'I said *forget* it.'

'Couldn't you?'

'I could maybe do *something*, but . . .'

'Please, Mitch?'

He studied her face, trying to figure what, if anything, might be in it for him. Avery walked up to where Ducek sat at the bank of terminals and threw the envelope into his lap. She ruffled his hair. It was a cheap trick, but there was no one else, no other way. Maybe in some respect she was more like Lisa Schaeffer than she cared to imagine.

'Tell you what, do it for me, and when all this is over, you can buy me a beer.'

'I can buy *you* a beer?'

'Uh-huh. And breakfast is on me.'

Ducek's leering grin, which he seemed unable to contain as he fished two slivers of negative strip from the pouch and wandered to the other side of the room, compounded Avery's encroaching depression. She slumped heavily into the nearest chair, as if some great weight had descended on her. A few years ago, she'd have slept with someone just to get him off her back, no question about it. She'd never used sex as a bargaining tool as such, but only because, she reflected, the opportunity had never arisen. If it had, it wouldn't have seemed like a big deal. But now she had no intention of fulfilling her promise, no intention at all, and the self-disgust settled on her shoulders, a dense, punishing ballast that she longed to cast away.

Back at her side, Ducek tapped at a few keys, glanced at the screen before him, manipulated the cursor and tapped again with a theatrical flourish. He seemed, Avery noted, to have recovered remarkably quickly from his I-feel-sullied distress, and now appeared to be relishing the chance to make believe that he wasn't just some dweeb who worked at a theme park. Avery realized that, under his breath, Ducek was unnecessarily muttering strings of numbers and words like 'enhance' and 'modify'. She felt a pang of irritation.

'I'm sorry, are you auditioning for *Bladerunner Two* or something?'

Ducek ignored her and carried on tapping and keying. Avery watched his forefinger as it danced across the trackpad with the verve and velocity of Gretsky on the ice. She sighed and sat back. It was going to take a lot to burst this particular bubble, and frankly she didn't have the energy.

Finally, Ducek swivelled away from the terminal, looking delighted with himself, and beckoned her to move closer. She stayed in her seat.

'I'm watching.'

'Okay. This is how you saw it, right?'

Avery looked at the black rectangle on the screen, nodded.

'And this . . . Is about the best I can do.'

Ducek highlighted something on a pop-down menu, hit return and sat back, smugly expectant, as the two of them watched the contents of the black rectangle change magically to a mass of greys, forming a coherent image.

The interior frame of a wide windshield and passenger window. The black night sky, roadside underbrush outside. And inside, the silhouettes of two heads. One of the heads – the one closest to the lens, disastrous haircut, weaselly jaw – belonged to Leon LeGalley, for certain. And at first nothing seemed out of the ordinary, Avery thought: *two people; Lisa and Leon*. And then she realized that someone, most likely Lisa, had to have taken the photograph.

Avery stared at the other head.

'There's someone else in the van.'

Mitch Ducek said something in reply, but Avery didn't hear him. She was looking at the shadowy outline of the second passenger in Lisa Schaeffer's Volkswagen. Looking at the little spikes of thick hair, the jut of a cheekbone, the perfectly straight line of the elegant, pointed nose. In her intense state of focus, she didn't recall having spoken out loud. But she must have, because Mitch Ducek's response to it yanked her out of the suffocating inner space into which she'd been sucked and back into the processing room. She looked up at him, slightly dazed.

'What did you say, Mitch?'

'I *said*, who the hell is Trey Clowes?'

Sixteen

Rows of Portakabins; swarms of leather-skinned men and roving herds of menacing machines; scattered quarries of varying depth and treachery; iron rafters jutting from the mud-like remains at a robotic-elephants' graveyard. The signs posted regularly along on the high, solid fence that surrounded the construction site read, 'PARDON OUR FAIRY-DUST', which made you think: well, that's one way of putting it. But, oddly enough, Avery noted as she squelched her way from her car to the nearest cluster of activity, there *was* something rather magical, rather enchanted and beautiful, about the way that the Americana resort was beginning slowly to rise in all its glory from the soupy, barren clay beneath her feet.

She had stopped for a moment to admire the scene at a distance – the vivid hues of the newly completed crazy golf course, the angular skeletons of the nascent structures that would house the guest rooms – when she noticed that Jim Desmarais, the chief site engineer, was bounding over in her direction, waving cheerfully as he approached.

'Hey, Avery! Long time no see! I guess Mr Ober doesn't want you down here too much, all these good-lookin' shirtless guys around, huh? He been keepin' you locked up, huh?'

Desmarais guffawed heartily at his own joke while Avery grinned politely and tried not to stare at the alarming diamond of milky-white beer-gut exposed where one of his shirt buttons had popped open.

'Yep, that's it, Jim, that's it. Shackled to the kitchen sink.'

Desmarais gave a generous booming laugh and thumped Avery on the back. 'What can I do you for, sweetheart?'

'Jim, did someone come in on a moped in the last twenty minutes or so? A guy? Young guy?'

Desmarais scratched the protruding wedge of stomach. 'Uh-uh, I don't think so, but then I been mostly in my office. Did you ask over on the west side already?'

Avery shook her head.

'Any idea who he was coming to see?'

'Nope, no idea. He might have been unauthorized.'

Desmarais looked concerned, his forehead crumpling into deep furrows.

'A young guy, you said?'

'Right. Early twenties. About my height. Black hair. Nice-looking.'

Relief smoothed his forehead like a shot of botox. He began to nod enthusiastically.

'Woah, Avery, you had me going there for a minute: thought we had a trespasser on site an' I didn't know about it. No, I know the guy you mean. He was here talking to some of my men. Called yesterday, asked if he could come up today. College student. Real nice young man. Polite. You said moped and I didn't click. Didn't see him come in. He a friend of yours?'

'Not exactly. I need to talk to him, though. Pretty

urgently. I know he's on property quite a lot so I got one of the girls back at HQ to feed his plate number into Big Brother and it turned out apparently he's here.'

'Big Brother, huh? That's all science fiction to me, that stuff. That's when you know you're gettin' old. Mr Ober was tellin' me about it, and I was just – *phew*. Bet it comes in handy for keeping track of your old man, though, huh? You just do your thing on the computer and boom! *Hey honey, I know where y'are, you said you was comin' home! Your dinner's gettin' cold!'*

Avery forced another smile, despite her rising sense of urgency, not to mention the slightly irritating implication that she was some rolling pin-brandishing harridan whose primary delight at having access to a multi-million dollar piece of traffic surveillance software was the opportunities it offered in the field of hi-tech henpecking.

'*Right*. Yes. Jim, the guy, is he still here?'

'I'm guessing. It was only ten minutes, thereabouts, and he wanted to talk to the guys over on the west side once he was done with my fellas here. Should be there still. I'll tell ya – you'll laugh – I nearly threw him off site first of all when he said what it was about.'

'Why? What *was* it about?'

'Oh, I assumed you knew about this college project of his?'

'No, I do.'

'So, he was trying to explain it, but it was kinda – whoosh!' Desmarais gave the universal hand gesture for *it-went-over-my-head*.

'Yeah? What was he asking?'

'About a story he'd heard. Supposed to have happened here on site. And first off I'm: *I don't know who you are and why you wanna know this, but either you better watch who you say that kinda stuff to or else you better have a damn*

147

good attorney. One or the other. Well, I didn't actually say that, but I'm *this* close. But then he's explaining he knows it's not true, he's just interested in how people tell stories in the workplace and whatnot. Like Chinese whispers or something? In the end I'm, like, *Look, I don't know what the hell kind of things they study at college these days, kid, but you speak to whoever you need.'*

Avery hadn't meant to seem rude, but instinctively she'd started walking away, towards the opposite side of the site, afraid of missing Trey Clowes before he left, and Desmarais, faced with the alternative of continuing his rambling account without an audience, had begun to trot alongside her.

'What was this story then, Jim?'

'Oh, some tomfoolery, I don't know. Guy getting his arm blown off by the airless paint-gun. You know what – you'll laugh – last job I worked on, it was supposed to have happened there, too. Supposedly some guy's changing the gas canister, the nozzle's in the crook of his arm, he hits the trigger by accident and – bam! – his arm fills up with three gallons of paint like some goddamn balloon and bursts over everybody. I mean it's possible, yeah, sure. But nobody's that dumb. Far as I know, ain't never happened to anyone. You get a bunch of guys together, everybody wants to top the next guy's story at the bar: *Think that's bad, well lemme tell you what happened to this Joe at the job I'm on . . .'*

Avery smiled genuinely this time, amused by the fact that Desmarais had instinctively grasped many of the salient points that some college professor was making a living out of teaching to people like Trey Clowes.

'What's an airless paint-gun?'

'Oh, it's like a high-pressure spray gun. Gas propelled. Use it on big areas, whatever. I think some of the guys a bit further along are using 'em . . . To your left there where they're doing the big Florida Orange stand. Up there? Yep, there, that's one.'

Avery glanced over and upwards to where Desmarais was gesturing. She observed with mild interest as a woman standing on a hydraulic platform aimed a large spray gun at the surface of the vast spherical structure some distance away. As she squeezed the trigger, a thick, solid jet of fluorescent paint was forcefully expelled from the muzzle, exploding onto the concrete in a vast starburst of colour. It made Avery think, in passing, that she could understand why such a powerful tool might inspire fear, but mostly it made her think of Jedi light-sabres.

'Cool! Looks safe enough, too.'

'Oh, you bet. Wouldn't use 'em otherwise, sweetheart. Very safe. Line it up, turn it on. You use the safety catch when you're changing the whatsit, and . . . I mean, that's what I told your friend: I said, *You'd have to be pretty dumb, you'd, like, have to try pretty hard to have an accident with one of these things.* It's just silly talk. Silly talk . . . Avery, you okay?'

Out of nowhere, an unwelcome thought had struck Avery like an uppercut to the jaw, and she'd stopped dead in her tracks.

'Jim, did he show you any student ID?'

Desmarais's forehead was once again a mass of fleshy dunes and valleys. 'No. I mean, he offered to right at the end actually, but like I said, he seemed like a good guy, so I said, *No, it's okay.* 'Sides, I figured with all that mumbo jumbo about the modern oral thingamabob and whatnot, he's *gotta* be a college student.' Desmarais chuckled nervously. 'Am I right or am I right?'

Avery stared into the near distance. At the elevated point they'd reached she could see down into a nearby quarry where four well-built men were standing, engaged in relaxed repartee with Trey Clowes, who appeared to be demonstrating to them his not-inconsiderable skills with a hacky-sack. He was wearing shorts and sneakers and a Beck T-shirt and appeared to be having an impressive run – four hits on the ankle, two on the knee and another on the ankle before the small beanbag finally eluded him – and Avery wished that the butterflies that she'd felt in her stomach were real butterflies, so that she could trample them violently into the mud. This was the last thing she needed.

Her silence had unsettled Desmarais even further.

'I mean, he *is* a college student, isn't he?'

Avery didn't take her eyes off Trey Clowes. 'Truth is, Jim, I don't know. And I don't know why I didn't wonder before. Especially seeing as I just learnt it first-hand yesterday: fact that people aren't always who they say they are.'

'You don't know?'

Desmarais paled.

'No, Jim, I'm afraid I don't. But believe me, I intend to find out.'

When he first saw Avery striding towards him, Trey Clowes had broken into a huge, uncontrollable grin, black eyes shining, delighted to see her. It had saddened Avery, just a little bit, to watch him clock the cold expression on her face, watch the smile melt away and be replaced by a look of cowering dismay, like a puppy who had just pissed on the sofa. She had forced a professional smile as she greeted the construction workers before asking Clowes if she could speak to him when he was done. Now they were walking away from the group, Avery moving briskly as if she knew where she was taking him, although in actuality she was desperately looking around for somewhere suitable, somewhere quiet. She kicked herself for not asking Desmarais if she could borrow his office. And now he was nowhere to be seen.

Clowes pocketed his hacky-sack and regarded her nervously.

'Avery, what's this about? Is it Lisa?'

'Like I said, let's find somewhere we can talk. Then we'll talk.'

'Did I do something wrong?' Clowes's eyes pleaded with her.

'I don't know. Did you? You tell me.'

He looked away, exasperated, apprehensive.

Not knowing where to go, not wanting to let on or to stop walking, Avery eventually led Clowes to the northern tip of the site, to the deserted crazy golf course. It was hardly very professional, but at least, she consoled herself, the informality of the surroundings might lull Clowes into some kind of relaxation. She needed him to trust her, to tell the truth. After all, it hadn't been very hard to intimidate him, and he seemed distressed rather than defensive. Avery tried to chase away the other D-word that had occurred to her. Trey Clowes couldn't be dangerous, could he? Was she really *that* bad a judge of character? She looked around. There were plenty of big guys within shouting distance. It was broad, blazing daylight. She'd be okay, surely? At the third hole, she sat down on a bench in the shadow of a twenty-foot fibreglass hotdog and beckoned Clowes to sit down next to her.

151

She looked at him steadily. 'So, Trey, tell me. Do you work for *Click*, too?'

Clowes reacted as if Avery had slapped him. 'For, for *Click*? Are you *serious*?'

'Why are you snooping around? Talking to cast members? Asking all this stuff about people having accidents? Is that how you really knew Lisa?' He shook his head in disbelief. 'Avery, I can't believe you're saying this. I told you everything. Why would you suddenly –'

'Show me your student ID,' Avery interjected briskly.

Trey Clowes stood and dug a well-worn Black Fly surfers' wallet from the back pocket of his shorts. The rip of the Velcro as he tore it open echoed harshly in the silence of the golf course. He thrust a laminated card at her.

She glanced at it: Lloyd Clowes III. Born on the eleventh July, four years later than her. She could tell right away that it was kosher, but studied it anyway before she handed it back. Clowes stared at her, eyes burning with hurt and indignation.

'Is that it? Is that what you wanted? Don't you have anything better to do? Like looking for Lisa? Or maybe you don't give a shit about her. She was just some scumbag journalist. And Dreamworld's reputation is what really matters, right? I thought you were different, Avery, but I guess I was wrong. I guess you're just like everyone else here.'

She exhaled slowly, deliberately, trying to stay calm. 'Oh, believe me, Trey, I want to know what happened to Lisa. I can think of *someone* who seems to be more interested in covering his own ass, but it certainly isn't me.'

A small thrill of panic flashed across Clowes's face. 'What do you mean by that?'

'I think you know *exactly* what I mean. Why don't

152

you tell me what happened the night before Lisa went missing? Or if you don't want to talk to me, maybe you'd rather tell someone down at the Osceola County sheriff's office? There's a highway patrol guy I know who'd just kill to get a chance at meeting you. Works the 192 grave-yard shift. I think you know what I'm talking about.'

Trey Clowes buried his face in his hands for a moment, then ran his hands through his hair and closed his eyes. 'I'm in trouble, aren't I?'

'I don't know, Trey. Are you? Should you be? What did you do?'

'I guess you know already. Else you wouldn't be asking.'

Avery shuddered. Was he really talking about Jerry Lee Lucas? He couldn't be. This was all wrong. Not what she signed on for at all. For a moment, Avery considered getting up and just walking away. Going back and telling Perdue: fuck it, I quit. Going back to park patrol, letting Perdue and Hayes deal with this. She'd never breathe a word of it to anyone. Hayes would understand, forgive her, wouldn't he? The scenario filled her with relief, hope.

Avery's mind raced. *What now?* She should have spoken to Perdue first, she knew that. But seeing Lisa's pictures had been like a lit match tossed onto the crack-ling tinder of her need to know what had happened, her need to know the truth about Jerry Lee Lucas, Lisa Schaeffer and Leon LeGalley, about the inciting event that had turned her life upside down. She'd wanted it so badly that she hadn't been able to think straight. Shit, she thought, what have I done? She was still searching for what to say next when Clowes began to mumble in the soft tones of defeat.

'I know. I know I should have gone to the police right

away. But I had no idea what kind of trouble I'd be in
. . . by association. I was scared, Avery. I still am.'

His voice grew louder and less controlled and he buried
his face in his hands again, hunching forward this time,
curling up.

'Oh God. Oh *God*! I don't know what to do. Are you
going to make me go?'

'I'm not going to *make* you do anything, Trey.'

He looked up at her, confused. 'You're not?'

'No. Well, it's hard for me to say whether you would
need to if I don't know what happened. But, besides,
going to the police, it's not necessarily . . . I don't
know . . .'

Avery couldn't bring herself to finish the sentence, to
speak words out loud that so starkly paraded the gaping
chasm between her own agenda – Dreamworld's agenda
– and the accepted, prudent course of action.

Clowes fiddled with the lace on one of his Gazelles and
stared studiously down at the hot-pink, poured-in-place
safety rubber on the ground beneath them. His voice was
quiet once more, cracking slightly.

'This is what I'll do, Avery: I'll tell you exactly what
happened. And then . . . Then maybe you can tell me
what I should do? And whatever it is, I'll do it. I swear.'

Without thinking, Avery slipped her arm around
Clowes. His back was warm and broad under the soft
cotton T-shirt, and she could feel him breathing, shallow,
sporadic little breaths like the light, desperate fluttering of
a rain-battered dragonfly, beating its waterlogged wings.
And now she was this close to him, Avery could smell
his hair, this boy who might or might not be about to
tell her that he had been involved somehow in murdering
another human being and dumping the bloodied cadaver
in a picnic cooler. And his hair smelt good.

Name's Avery, Sylvia Avery, she thought. The most screwed-up law enforcement agent in Central Florida. Pleased to meet you.

Seventeen

Apart from the more obvious events, the thing that Trey Clowes remembered most clearly was that it was one of those days when he felt like everybody in the world hated him. First it had been that nice girl from Dreamworld Studios, the perky little hostess from the animation tour. She'd seemed fascinated by his thesis, leapt at his offer of an early evening drink at the Bamboo Lounge and given him some really great material, including a new variation on the Unwelcome Prize which he'd never heard before. (In her version, the recipient of the lucky-numbered entrance ticket who receives unwanted national publicity is not a Mormon who has abandoned his divine work for a sneaky forbidden vacation, but a fugitive criminal whom an FBI agent watching the TV news recognizes from the most-wanted files.) She even swore blind that she had actually *met* the guy from the TV advert with the aerial shot where Kit-E-Cat is seen standing atop the parapets of Fort Enchantment – the guy who supposedly was so keen to get chosen for the job that he didn't mention his fear of heights, and had notoriously – when deposited into place 300 feet up by a cherry-picker – crapped inside the suit. Trey didn't bother to tell her that the famous advert had never even existed. He got the feeling that, even if he had, she wouldn't have believed him. He surreptitiously made a note at the top of a fresh page in his pad: *People appropriating legends as personal anecdotes: a potent new method of vectoring old stories? Increases belief etc, falsely renews chain of credibility etc.*

It was time well spent anyway, and more so for the fact that the girl seemed to like him, and that always made him very happy. He had just been wondering whether maybe he'd put his notebook away, start asking her some stuff about herself, see if she wanted to go get something to eat, when Lisa Schaeffer had beeped his pager. When he'd called her back, she'd asked if he was free for the evening and he'd said that he was and instantly loathed himself for it. Especially when she said, 'Good. I'm outside now. Finish your beer, ditch the bimbo and get your ass out here. And I can see you, by the way, from where I'm sitting, so wipe that look off your face before I change my mind.'

To his dismay, the girl had insisted on leaving the Bamboo Lounge too. He had told her that he had to meet somebody, but hadn't said that it was here or now. He'd felt so bad for her when she'd clocked Lisa, beautiful, saturnine Lisa kicking open the passenger door of her van. Lisa in her tiny, tight Pokémon T-shirt and the brushed-cotton khakis that revealed a glimpse of flat, tan belly. Lisa, hands on the steering wheel, not deigning to acknowledge either of them, just staring straight ahead, Frank Black and the Catholics cranked up high, singing along, delicately enunciating the words to 'Western Star'; waiting for Trey to get in.

He'd stood at the open door, staring her out. Thinking, for some reason not unconnected with wanting to claw back a little self-respect: if she doesn't speak to me, I'm not going to get in. Lisa Schaeffer had stared back, her eyes chilly and as coldly shiny as her lip gloss, still singing.

She'd sung a few more lines with laser precision, including the Spanish bit, before patting the seat beside her and breaking off to speak.

'What are you waiting for, Trey? Jump up.'

He'd clambered in, slammed the door behind him and said, 'How high?' Lisa Schaeffer had thrown her head back as she laughed. 'Now you're learning, Trey. Now you're learning.'

If he'd thought the look on the girl-from-Dreamworld-Studios' face was bad, it was nothing compared to the look of pure hatred he received when Leon LeGalley stumbled out of the Research and Development Complex at nine p.m.

Climbing grudgingly into the seat beside him, Leon had ignored Trey and leant forward to address Lisa directly.

'What the fuck is *he* doing here?'

'Nice to see you, too, LeGalley.'

'When you haven't just left me sitting in a parking lot for two and half hours, Leon, *then* you can bitch about who I bring with me. Till then, if you don't like it, you know what? Get a ride home from somebody else.'

Trey sat back as Lisa and Leon sniped at one another across him, and had to admit that he'd been asking himself the same question. What *was* he doing here? He knew that he was weak, and that, regardless of her mind games, he liked Lisa's company. That was two reasons. But what did *she* want? She'd arranged to pick up Leon LeGalley

158

from his volunteer shift at the centre, presumably with a view to going out afterwards. And judging by the fury and impatience that he'd watched germinate in her, she hadn't expected Leon to keep her waiting. So it wasn't about wanting company. Maybe she enjoyed the chance to mess with two people's heads in one go; a mind-fuck *ménage à trois*. Or was it because there was a part of her that didn't want to be alone with Leon? Trey guessed at the latter.

The last couple of weeks, Lisa said, she'd been suffering a growing urge to tell Leon the truth about what she was doing in Orlando. The deception was making her weary, and besides, if she didn't do it soon, it was going to be a case of: I'm going back to LA in two days, tomorrow, today – have a nice life. She had no idea what Leon's reaction would be, and – she'd admitted as much – that was not a feeling she relished. As far as Trey could see, she had a secret back-up plan: turn down the heat on her relationship with Leon, wind him up enough to make him go away. Then she'd never have to tell him at all.

As he tuned back into Leon and Lisa's conversation, however, Trey gathered quickly that Lisa had a new agenda tonight: something that had taken her mind off everything else. She had switched from ball-buster mode to cute-but-determined. Her speciality.

'Well, Trey doesn't mind. You don't mind, do you, Trey?'

'Don't mind what?'

'Waiting. Until the last guy comes out. I want to ask him what was going on. Why everybody got kept late. There's only one guy left inside, we think. That car over there, that belongs to Jerry Lucas, you figure, right, Leon? He'd have to know what happened. Leon doesn't know.'

Leon stared ahead, muttering darkly about how he didn't care *why*, he'd been there since eight that morning, felt like crap. Wished Lisa would just drop it and drive. But Lisa wasn't going to drop it. *Couldn't* drop it, any more than a snake could drop a rat once it had dislocated its own jaw and started to swallow.

'I waited for you, Leon, now you can wait for me. The guy *can't* be in there much longer. I just wanna hear about what was up, you know? If I don't, it's gonna drive me nuts all week. You know what I'm like.'

Trey, knowing Lisa's true motivation, knew that there was no point in trying to change her mind. He climbed into the back seat, sat back and decided to butt out, say nothing, listen to Frank Black instead. *Pistolero* was the only cassette Lisa had in the van tonight and this was its third cycle, but Frank was the man, and besides, it was infinitely preferable to hearing another volley of Lisa and Leon's verbal jousting, which was the oral equivalent of watching Lennox Lewis square up to a ninety-five-pound guy with no arms.

The security patrolman who asked Lisa to move-it-along-please hadn't noticed when she grabbed her camera from the glovebox and fired off a couple of shots of him as he retreated. Nor had he noticed that, once out of the lot and past the security barrier, she had pulled over her van onto the grassy verge and killed her engine and her lights.

'Now what in hell are you doing?'

The edge in Leon's voice, which was beginning to frighten Trey, had no noticable effect on Lisa.

'What does it look like I'm doing?'

'It looks like you're still waiting.'

'*Very* good. Correct.'

'*Jesus Christ*, Lisa.'

'We were waiting in there, Leon, and now we're waiting out here. What's the difference?'

'You're a fucking crazy woman, you know that? What are you taking pictures for?'

'What's it got to do with you?'

LeGalley looked stumped. And furious. In a feeble cover-up, or perhaps to bait him further, Lisa picked up the camera off her lap, held it to her eye and pointed it at him.

'I just like taking pictures, I guess. Say cheese. You get in too, Trey.'

Trey leant forward wearily as Lisa reclined against the window to fit them both into the shot. The shutter snapped several times in quick succession.

'Flash didn't go off.'

Trey heard the peculiar stodginess in his own voice, realized it was the first time he'd spoken in a while. Lisa cursed quietly under her breath.

Now Leon chipped in. 'Must be busted.'

She glared at him. 'Nice going, Herb Ritts. Thank you for that.'

A sour, crackling silence followed, and lasted – how long? Trey wasn't wearing a watch, couldn't figure out exactly how many excruciating minutes – hours? – ebbed away before Jerry Lee Lucas' battered Pontiac Sunbird finally sped past. When it did, Lisa fired up the ignition and hit the gas with such force that both Trey and Leon, unprepared, were flung back in their seats.

'You're gonna follow him? Are you serious? He could be going anywhere. How far you gonna drive?'

'Until he stops. Cheer the fuck up, Leon. We waited this long. What's the point in quitting now? Don't you wanna know what happened back there?'

'No. And to tell you the truth, I'm starting to wonder

what the hell is up with you tonight, the hell you really want. You got something going on with Jerry Lee too?'

Lisa howled with laughter. 'Leon, you are *such* a fucking loser! You wanna come with us or you wanna get out right here? Your choice.'

Trey Clowes noted with grudging admiration the way that Lisa had gouged a dual purpose out of the night's events. If she was lucky, she might get something for her *Click* piece *and* piss Leon off so much that he'd be off her back for good.

'What's the matter, Leon? I woulda thought you liked strip joints.'

For the first time that evening, maybe ever, Lisa seemed genuinely thrown. Having followed the Sunbird for a while – Trey told Avery that he guessed it was about twenty minutes give or take – the three of them were now sitting in the parking lot outside Emanuelle's, a vast, characterless box of a building set back from the crawling traffic of Orange Blossom Trail. A building that might just as easily have been a Sports Authority or a Best Buy or a Ross-Dress-For-Less, if it weren't for the brightly lit sign above its entrance.

Leon avoided Lisa's eyes, staring instead at the sign, at the poorly drawn cartoon woman reclining ecstatically in a martini glass as if it were just about the most delightfully comfortable place anyone could ever wish to sit.

'I just never been in with a girl, is all. I don't know why you'd wanna go.'

'Oh, for Christsakes, Leon, you know why. We don't have to stay long. I'll just find Jerry Lee, ask him what happened, then we can go somewhere else. Finished. End of story.'

'You ever been in one of these places before, Lisa? Ain't a place for girls.'

'Yeah, as a matter of fact I have. Worked in one for a month in LA. Bottomless as well as topless, not like here, so believe me, I've seen it all. Okay? So can we go in now? Else we'll never find him in there. It looks big. And busy.' She glanced around the teeming parking lot and noticed, to her great irritation, that she'd lost sight of the Sunbird.

Glowering but defeated, Leon heaved open the passenger door.

Despite Trey's protests that he didn't know what Jerry Lee Lucas looked like, wouldn't be much help and might even impede her search, Lisa insisted that he come into Emanuelle's too. Grudgingly, however, she'd agreed that he could wait for her and Leon at the bar, if that was what he really wanted.

Now, nursing a swampy-tasting draught beer and grimly looking on as a skinny chick – with breast implants so large that they looked painful – writhed around in front of him, Trey wondered yet again what the hell he was doing. He could have been having a nice meal, a nice talk with the nice girl from Dreamworld Studios. And she would have still liked him, instead of hating him, like she surely did now. Trey wondered what exactly was wrong with him, why he always seemed to choose people, situations, that made him feel like a turd in a swimming pool.

By the time Lisa returned, alone and even more surly-looking than usual, Trey had cheered up somewhat. The crappy old dance track that had been playing when he first sat down had been followed by The Butthole Surfers'

'Pepper', and the skinny chick had been replaced by a much more voluptuous girl with porn-star lips and intelligent eyes whom he would be reminded of two days later when he met Sylvia Avery for the first time. When he told her that, Avery looked alarmed, unsure whether to be flattered or not, but mostly she looked agitated, keen to skip ahead to what happened next, what happened when Lisa returned.

'Can't find him. Come on. We're going.'

'Where's Leon?'

'Waiting for us. Come on, quick. Maybe he decided not to come in after all.'

'Who, Leon? I thought he was with you?'

'No, schmuck. Jerry Lee.'

Trey had hoped that Lisa couldn't tell that he was trying to buy enough time for his minor hard-on to subside before he stood up. He told Avery that part, too, just to see how she'd react. Trey was glad when she laughed. It was something Lisa wouldn't have done, he was sure.

As it was, Lisa – whether she could tell or not – was having none of it.

'Will you just shift your ass, Trey? Parking lot's pretty jammed. I'm hoping we might still catch him.'

Lisa grabbed Trey's arm, tugged him to his feet and shoved him towards the door. As he glanced back over his shoulder, the pretty stripper smiled wryly yet sympathetically at him, thinking – Trey supposed – that Lisa was his jealous girlfriend. He smiled wistfully back, musing on how happy he would be if that were the truth.

It hadn't taken long to find the Sunbird in the lot outside. They'd been driving round the east side of the building towards the exit, and there it was. Parked. And empty. Lisa started cursing again.

'Maybe he was getting a lap dance in the back,' Leon offered helpfully.

Lisa ignored him and wound down her window to flip the bird and hurl abuse at the guy who had pulled up behind her and was honking his horn for her to move.

'Eat me, motherfucker!'

Trey leant forward, laid his hand gently on her shoulder. 'Easy, Lisa. We don't wanna get in a fight, here. Either let's park up again, or let's just go.'

'Asshole's got a point, Leese, there's cops over there, look. And I'm on probation. I don't need this.'

Lisa ignored both of her male companions, angrily yanked the gearshift into drive and floored the pedal. But no sooner had they recovered from being flung back again than Lisa stepped hard on the brake and they were thrown violently forward. Trey, who had steadied himself just in time, tried not to laugh at the somewhat comical *bonk* noise that Leon's head had made when it hit the windshield; tried not to laugh while he gently berated her.

'Lisa, Lisa, what the hell are you doing? Take it easy!'

Lisa was pointing at the rear-view mirror, gesturing frantically back to the spot where the Sunbird was parked.

'Did you see that? Did either of you see that? Look – no look, now she's gotten into that other car, that one there, they're driving off! Shit!'

'What? What are you talking about?'

Leon rubbed his head with one hand and with the other grabbed the sleeve of Lisa's T-shirt to get her attention, a little too hard, getting a handful of Lisa's flesh, too, and not by mistake. Trey looked at Lisa's arm, watched three rosy ellipses appear on it where Leon's fingertips had been. He swallowed hard, not liking the

165

way this was going. Lisa, meanwhile, in her breathless excitement, seemed impervious.

'There! Back there! Someone just got out of that car next to Jerry Lee's car and opened up his door and got something out. Got back in, wait, now they're driving off. He must be in that other car now, fuck – they've gone the other way!'

The scramble to catch up with the second car – some kind of sport utility vehicle as far as Trey could tell – involved more erratic accelerating and braking, the running of two red lights and a near-miss with an MPV. Leon's temper simmered gently throughout, bubbling into a raging boil when Lisa cut across three lanes of traffic to follow the sport utility onto the slip-road leading to the 192.

'Crazy fucking bitch! What are you doing?'

He lunged at her, gripping her arm again, twisting the sleeve of her T-shirt in his fist, harder this time. Lisa screamed out in pain.

'Get off me! You want me to crash? They went this way! Didn't you see?'

'What, you wanna go on the freeway? How far you gonna go? I've had it. I wanna go home. Stop the fucking van. I'm getting out.'

Lisa stared resolutely ahead, jaw set, ignoring Leon, even when he hit her hard across the back of the head. Trey shrank back in his seat, glanced into the rear-view mirror. Lisa's mascara was streaking and she was chewing at her lower lip, but she didn't take her hands off the wheel, or her eyes off the road.

It was nearly fifty minutes, Trey estimated, before any of the three spoke again. Then they all spoke at once, each uttering his own expression of astonishment as they passed the car they had been following.

It was pulled over at the side of the highway, on the grass. The rear hatch was thrown open and someone was beginning to pull something white and large, very large, from the trunk. The figure stopped trying to pull it, then threw its lid open instead. And then the jarring vignette was gone, shrinking into the distance as Lisa, Trey and Leon sped past.

Lisa craned her neck round, eyes wide, to look at Trey in the back seat.

'That was them, wasn't it? Wasn't it them?'

Trey nodded, and Leon, his fury temporarily forgotten, mumbled, 'The hell is he doing, you reckon?'

Lisa ignored them both, driving steadily on for a little way, deep in thought. Without warning, she threw a sharp, impulsive U-turn. Leon swore some more while Trey just sat there breathing hard, one hand over his heart, feeling its frenzied movement beneath his fingers like some little creature struggling to escape from his ribcage.

At this point, Trey told Avery, he saw Lisa pick up her camera again and he said, 'Lisa, don't, don't, keep your hands on the wheel.' At least he thought he had said it, but he may have just started to say it, and then stopped when he saw what he saw when they approached the sport utility vehicle again. Or maybe it was when he heard what he heard.

First there was the click of Lisa's camera shutter in the black silence. The gunshot came a split second later, the quick flash of fire momentarily illuminating the open picnic cooler, half out of the car's trunk, and the arm of the figure standing over it.

And then Trey had perhaps started to say something else, something about how Lisa had veered into the oncoming lane, something about the thing he saw

167

coming towards them so fast, but then again, perhaps he hadn't. He couldn't recall. It was all too quick. The sickening smash of metal dashed against metal, the sparks, the thump on the bonnet, the girl's face as velocity yanked her high into the air, the smell of gasoline and heat and blood. Then a sliver of hideous silence before the splash as the cooler punctured the surface of the thin ribbon of swamp at the roadside, the slam of a door, screeching tyres, the sport utility vehicle driving away. And finally the splutter of the Volkswagen's own engine as Lisa started back towards Orlando.

Eighteen

'Is all that true?'

Avery felt terrible, just terrible, that it was the first thought to enter her mind; she felt even worse for the fact that she blurted it out. And worse still when she looked over at Trey Clowes and saw that his eyes were bloodshot, the eyelashes damp.

He stood up, hands in pockets, staring at his shoes again, kicking lightly at something imaginary on the ground.

'That's what they're going to say, isn't it? The police.'

'Well . . . Obviously you're opening a pretty big can of worms, *two* big cans. Hit and run, homicide . . . They're going to question you, pretty thoroughly, if that's what you mean.'

'But would I come under suspicion? And what about the fact that I didn't say anything before? I mean, how much trouble am I in?'

Avery found herself torn between dearly wanting to comfort him and knowing that she had to deter him from going to the sheriff's office at all. She decided to hedge around, buy herself a little time to think.

'Well, tell me what happened next. Did Lisa plan to turn herself in, or . . .'

Trey Clowes laughed. 'Not exactly. There was just more fighting. Driving back through Kissimmee, I said, "Let's stop at the lounge, get a drink, calm down, talk about what we should do." We didn't even get into the bar. It started in the parking lot, the fight. Leon wanting to know why she was taking a picture, why she had got us all into this.'

'He felt bad for the guy and the girl on the bike?'

'Hardly. No, it was more like, he couldn't get his head round – well, I guess he thought that she took the picture to show the police or something, like evidence. And even though he and Lucas weren't big buddies or anything . . . Look, Leon's attitude is *keep your nose clean*. You see something happening, you butt out. Last thing Leon would ever do is help the police.'

'Even if the victim was someone he knew?'

'The *victim*?'

Clowes stood motionless, his brain ticking over, the colour draining from his face, and with it most of his semblance of control, of holding it together.

'Hold on, Avery, what are you saying? You mean . . .'

He really doesn't know, Avery thought, thrown unexpectedly off balance. Either that or Trey Clowes was quite the most convincing liar she'd ever encountered.

'Jerry Lee Lucas. In the cooler. Yes.' She scanned his face, found nothing but the same bafflement and dismay. She spoke gently. 'You didn't read the paper? It was in there somewhere.'

Clowes shook his head. 'I don't tend to . . . Jesus, I can't believe it. I mean, I didn't know the guy, but from what they were saying about him afterwards, I don't know. All this time I just figured it was him we saw . . .'

'Nope, he was at other end of the barrel. The wrong end.'

Clowes visibly brightened somewhat, although it was the false brightness of attempted self-reassurance. Wasn't it?

'So I'm not in as much trouble as I thought? Like, I can't actually tell the police who did it. I thought maybe knowing the perpetrator and not saying anything was like harbouring a known criminal or whatever the charge is.'

Avery shook her head. 'You have no idea who the other car belonged to, then? No idea at all?'

'Well, look, I thought that maybe I remembered seeing it at the Research and Development Complex that night. Thought that maybe it was still there when we left. But it might not even be the same one. Hell, I don't even know what make it was, what model. No idea. I thought it looked familiar, but, you know . . . I couldn't say it with my hand on my heart. No.'

'I see.'

'But Lisa, Lisa was sure. Said it was at the centre when we left. And on the road, following Lucas's car just like we were. That's why she noticed it. But she could have been wrong.'

'Okay, so what happened next? Leon asked what the hell Lisa was doing, and she said?'

'Well, like I kind of said when we first met? That was when she told him. About who she is, what her job is, whatever. And he *freaked*. With a capital F. Started beating up on her. That's when I jumped in. Haven't had a fight since fourth grade, so I was pretty pathetic. And I have the bruises to prove it.'

Clowes turned to face Avery head on and lifted his Beck T-shirt to expose his torso. She concentrated as hard as she could on the enormous clouds of purple and blue that she'd been invited to look at, rather than anything

171

else; rather than the soft flesh or the not-notably-worked-out but nicely defined musculature. But it was difficult.

'Boy . . .'

'Yeah, I know. Guess Leon's had a lot more practice than me.' Clowes dropped his T-shirt again; shrugged. 'Didn't get any thanks for it, either. Lisa got really pissed. Just had enough of the whole thing, I guess.'

'What did she do?'

A hint of bitterness seasoned the philosophical good humour in Clowes's laugh. 'Got back in the van. Told us she never wanted to see either of us again. Said she was leaving for LA the first flight she could get and don't bother trying to get in touch. That's when Leon stopped punching me, started trying to open the door of the van. Threatening her.'

'Threatening her how?'

'Like saying, "I'll go to the police, I'll tell them what you did. See how your boss likes that for a story." Some crap like that, anyway.'

'Christ. What did she say?'

'Said: "Not if I get there first, tell 'em you were the one driving." Then she drove off like a crazy woman.' Clowes gave a nervous barking chuckle. 'Nearly hit someone else on the way out of the lot. Sorry, I shouldn't laugh . . .'

Avery smiled a little, and Trey sat down on the bench beside her again and for a while the pair sat without saying anything.

'Avery, I feel bad that I lied to you the first time. I really do want to help. I want to do the right thing. I – I was scared. Like I said, I hope you understand.'

'I do. And you told me now. So forget about it.'

He smiled briefly, but there was clearly something else, something gnawing at him.

'And, and . . . I need to ask you something. But I don't think I want to hear the answer.'

'Try me.'

'How did you know I was with Lisa and Leon that night?'

Avery weighed it up momentarily, but she knew that she was going to tell him. About the camera. The pictures. Keep it simple; she had enough lies to remember already. So she told him.

It was impressive, Avery thought, just how fast Clowes's mind had worked, extrapolating from that single piece of information. How he'd realized that if Lisa had not taken her camera – not to mention its explosive contents – it seemed increasingly unlikely that she had blown town of her own accord. He wracked his brains for some permutation, some reason that she would have left without it, and could think of none. All told, it was a bad sign. Very, very bad. His mouth struggling to keep up with his brain, Clowes clumsily conveyed his fears to Avery, whose expression couldn't hide the fact that he was barking up entirely the right tree.

She didn't know exactly why she decided to tell Clowes the truth about what had happened to Lisa. As hectically as her trust for him had veered from one uncertain extreme to another, so now did her feelings about every supposed constant in her life: Dreamworld. Her place in it. Herself. It was as if nothing was certain any more, and then this in itself – the total absence of logic and rationale – demolished the keystones of her self-image. If she wasn't the straight-thinking, uncompromising defender of Dreamworld, then who was she? Avery didn't know. Didn't know what she thought, merely what she felt. And even this she merely *knew*, but did not understand. Didn't understand, and couldn't begin to, why as soon as she had told Clowes the truth, she felt sweet relief flood into her, like air filling her aching lungs after drowning for so long in a sea of lies. It made her feel heady, drunk, anaesthetized, so that she barely felt Clowes's raw pain, barely heard his animal howl. And then she held her breath, submerged herself just one more time, to tell Trey that Dreamworld security were quietly and efficiently taking care of the case themselves, and that she would liaise with the County police about the other matters, ensuring that – in exchange for his silence – his conscience would be cleansed without any chance of finding himself in trouble with the law.

High on victory and self-satisfaction, Avery grabbed Clowes by the arms when she said goodbye to him and kissed him on the cheek, tasting the salt from his tears, the fresh ones that hadn't yet dried in the searing after-noon sun.

Avery flew across the construction site and into her car. Not once did she look back at the little figure still sitting, head in hands, beneath the fibreglass hot dog, nor doubt for a moment that the case was well on its way to being closed.

Nineteen

'How can you be so sure?'

It was something like the fifth time in ten minutes that Perdue had queried Avery's trust in Trey Clowes. And every time he asked, it further shored up her sense of relief that she had not told Perdue absolutely everything, not told him that Clowes now knew what had really happened to Lisa and Leon. She *did* trust Clowes, no question, and she trusted her instincts. Didn't she? If she did, that was enough. And if it wasn't enough for Perdue, then it was better that he didn't know, didn't have to worry about it.

Once Avery had persuaded Perdue that, given the time frame, Lisa and Trey must have been right about seeing the sport utility vehicle at the centre, all that remained – they thought – was to ID its driver; Lucas's killer. Once they knew, they could ensure that he was struck from the Research and Development Complex's volunteer pool, distancing him from Dreamworld, should the police find him – through the vice-squad footage from Emanuelle's, the bullet that would still be lodged in the back of his car – and charge him for his crime.

Avery gazed through the window of Perdue's office, down at the teeming streets of Dreamworld, the happy faces of the visitors, and felt a surge of pride at having played a vital role in preserving the integrity of the place. Despite Perdue's implacable countenance, she couldn't stop herself grinning.

'Hey, Felix, quit worrying. We did it. *We did it*.'

'I don't know. There's something that doesn't feel right. Maybe it's just me.'

'I think so.'

'Look, Sylvie, this has been . . . .My God. When I speak to Hayes, when he says it's over, when he says he's happy, Darwin's happy, then I'll be pleased. Then I'll be able to celebrate.'

Avery reached forward to where Perdue sat opposite her and squeezed his leg reassuringly.

'So I'll see you both about six-thirty, Hayes's place? I'll bring the MGD and Chex-mix.'

A dense, late-afternoon shower had begun to fall by the time Avery and Perdue set out, he to see Hayes Ober, she to the centre, to ID the sport utility vehicle and its driver. In her excitement, Avery barely noticed her hair dripping into her eyes, her clothes clinging to her skin and soaking the car seat.

The menacing appearance of the main Research and Development building, its reflective panels alive with the muddy clouds of the swirling squall above, gave her pause for a moment, but only for a moment. She looked down, watching her feet instead as she scurried through the puddles towards the security booth, thinking only of completing her task and of six-thirty, of celebrating with Hayes and Perdue.

She had been disappointed, yes, when the attendant told her that their daily vehicle records were kept on file for only a few days at a time before the cache automatically erased itself. But not terminally disappointed – after all, she realized, it might have been hard to figure out which vehicle was the right one. Looking around the lot now, sport utilities seemed to be fairly popular, and she would have had to cross-reference with the volunteer records anyhow. It would be far simpler, she saw now, to get just those records instead. She should have thought of it before.

The receptionist had initially seemed astonished that Avery should dare to show up without a security clearance laminate, but after some intensive wheedling on Avery's part sent a message through to Daetwyler's research suite. It was ten minutes, however, before Catherine Homolka, who seemed more confident – and yet more distant – than she had before, appeared at the first set of security doors.

'I'm sorry, did you have an appointment with Richard?'

'Uh, no. I didn't think . . . If he's busy, though, I don't need to see him. I just need the volunteer lists. I need to check the vehicle details of the volunteers who were here the last time that Lucas was.' There was a long silence. 'Is that going to be okay?'

Homolka stared at her again, saying nothing, making no move to touch the keypad that would open the door behind them.

'I . . . I don't know if there might be a confidentiality problem there or something. I'm going to have to check. And, yeah, Dr Daetwyler *is* pretty tied up right now.'

'But you'll try?'

'Uh, sure.'

Homolka reluctantly operated the pad before walking quickly ahead and through each ensuing set of doors, her long legs making broad strides, not once looking over her shoulder to see if Avery was keeping up with her.

When they arrived at the lobby of Daetwyler's suite, Homolka gestured to Avery to sit down and told her that she'd be right back.

Agitated, Avery stood up as soon as Homolka left; began to wander around. The television on its wall-bracket overhead was blaring CNN, the on-the-hour headlines, but before Avery could register exactly what they were, she was startled by a small voice coming from behind her. She wheeled round, to see Devon Daetwyler – Megara dress on, tape-recorder in one hand, microphone in the other – sprawled out in the armchair in the corner.

'Hey, Devon. Didn't see you there. How you doing?'

Devon Daetwyler looked up, slightly irritable, clicked a button on the tape-recorder and looked at Avery as if to ask what the hell she wanted. The absurdly dour expression, so incongruous on a child's delicate features, made Avery laugh.

'Woah, I'm sorry, am I disturbing you?'

'I was kind of in the middle of a letter, yeah. But I can do it while you're here. If you don't talk to me.'

'A *letter*?'

'Yes. Dictating a letter.'

Avery tried not to smile, tried not be patronizing. 'Who for?'

Devon's eyebrows knitted like two fuzzy little caterpillars squaring up for a battle to the death. She enunciated her words slowly and with biting mock-patience: 'Do you mean who is the letter being written *to* or who is going to type it out?'

'Um . . . Both?'

'You sure ask a lot of questions.'

'It's good to ask questions, Devon. That's how you learn stuff. That's what science is all about, huh? I'm sure your dad told you that.'

'No, mostly science is about coming up with a hypothesis and then doing controlled experiments to find out if you were right or not. It hasn't got anything to do with being nosy.'

Avery couldn't believe she was getting into such a confrontation with a five-year-old, it was absurd.

'You don't have to tell me if you don't want to, Devon. I won't talk to you. You carry on. Have fun.'

The little girl scowled at her, then sighed.

'If you really want to know, Catherine types my letters. Daddy says that if *he* says it's part of her job, then it *is* part of her job. And I write them to anybody I think should get one. People make a lot of money off kids, and that gives us a right to say what we think. So that's what I do.'

'Don't you go to school?'

'I have a tutor in the mornings. Okay? Now, do you mind if I carry on?'

Avery shook her head no, and then shook it again in quiet disbelief as she wandered back to the couch and sat down. Now Devon was talking into the microphone again.

'Letter to Mattel Toys. Date. To whom et cetera. I saw your advert for Talk-To-Me Barbie and it looked good. My first problem is that I could only see ones in Best Buy that were for Windows and we have a Mac. Why can't you make it dual platform? It's not very hard. But then when I looked at the box, I decided I didn't want it anyway, because all she can talk about is parties and dating and shopping and weddings. These are the four things. You probably know that. I am a girl and . . .'

Grimly fascinated by the venom in Devon's tirade, Avery barely noticed that Catherine Homolka had returned, silent and uneasy, with Richard Daetwyler by her side, smiling and controlled by contrast.

'Hi Devon, baby. Avery, you wanna come on into my office? We can talk there.'

Devon blew a kiss at her father before returning to her rant, whilst Avery stood to greet the lanky young scientist.

'Well, sure. I mean, I don't want to disturb Devon any more than I have already. But there's no need to take time off whatever you're doing. Did Catherine explain what I was after? I just need to see the volunteer files. I can go through them here, I don't even need to take them out.'

Although his brows were thicker than his daughter's, Richard Daetwyler looked very much like her when he frowned.

'Avery, I think we might have a problem here.' He gestured to his office, and, more insistently this time, suggested that she step inside. Avery was beginning to feel uncomfortable.

When Catherine had left the room. Daetwyler sat down and Avery did likewise. He began to swivel on his seat almost immediately as he laboured to get his words out.

'Look, Avery, we have a problem, I think,' he repeated.

'Which is?'

'Which is, I can't give you the files, I'm afraid.'

Avery's jaw dropped and she emitted a laugh of disbelief. 'Excuse me?'

'I just can't do it, Avery. It's part of the agreement we

enter into with the volunteers. Those files are confidential. No exceptions.'

'Maybe I should explain: we now have a pretty clear idea of what happened to Lucas. And we know what kind of car the perpetrator was driving. And, I hate to say it, but whoever it was, his car was here. So I need to go through the files in order to ID him. And when we ID him, we can make sure that if and when he's caught by the County cops, there's no link between him and the research centre. And then it's all over and we can all breathe a sigh of relief and go back to our business. You get me now?'

'I get you, Avery, but I can't do it.'

Daetwyler shrugged, held his hands up, smiled apologetically. Still swivelling. Right. Left. Right. Left. Avery felt her anger brewing, fought the urge to climb across the desk, grab his skinny shoulders and make him stop. Maybe shake him a bit, too; watch his spectacles slide down his nose and hear his teeth clattering together. Instead, she stood up and made to leave, eyeing him coldly.

'Whatever. It would've been nice to get this tied up tonight, but tomorrow will do. I'll go speak to Hayes now, and you can bring the records over to us yourself. I'm sure he'll be a little pissed about the delay, but I'm pretty good at calming him down. I'll put in a good word, tell him to go easy on you.'

Daetwyler stopped swivelling. 'Look, I just . . . Yes, if Hayes tells me *go ahead*, then the files are all yours.'

Avery walked into the hall, speaking without looking back at Daetwyler. 'Oh, I know they are, Richard. I know they are.'

Avery yanked the door hard, heard a whoosh of air as it swung to, and a thud as the fire-exit door behind

Daetwyler's desk – which had been ajar – was sucked back into the jamb with the abrupt change of air-pressure in the room. Then she heard the thunderous crack echoing down the linoleum hallway as the main door slammed shut. The only way it could have been any more satisfying was if Daetwyler's fingers had been caught in it.

Twenty

The rain had persisted and grown heavier while Avery had been inside, and although she'd wanted to drive away from the Research and Development Complex as soon as possible, get as far as she could from that menacing structure whose every surface crawled with reflected storm clouds, she thought it better to remain parked while she talked to Perdue on her cellphone.

He had shared her frustration at Daetwyler's lack of co-operation, but she could hear Hayes, who was at Perdue's side, giving reassurance that they wouldn't have to wait much longer. As soon as Avery heard his voice, when he took the phone from Perdue, she began to feel better.

'Avery, honey? Did you hear what I was saying? I said to Perdue that you and I, we'll go back and see Daetwyler in the morning, first thing, and get those files. It's not going to be a problem, I assure you. So don't worry about it, okay?'

'Sounds good. I was just disappointed. I guess . . . I guess I just so wanted it all to be tied up tonight.'

'I know you did. But it's fine. It'll be tomorrow instead. Listen, Avery, it's actually just as well, because there's one more thing we should probably follow up on before we tie things up. A call that came in. It's probably nothing, but . . . Hold on, I'm going to pass you back to Perdue. He'll explain.'

Avery's heart sank when Perdue told her that Shannon Reilly had called the office, asking for her urgently. All Avery really wanted to do was go back to Hayes's place, take a nice hot shower, get something to eat and go to bed. But it looked now like she was expected to drive all the way across town to Hooters to catch Reilly before she started her evening shift. Avery tried not to sound too sullen, not to render her sigh of resignation audible as she took the address from Perdue.

'Okay. Got it. I'll see you tomorrow, then.'

She was happy to note that Perdue sounded vaguely apologetic.

'Thanks, Sylvie. Good luck. I'm sure its nothing, too, but we can't take any chances. And Hayes has got an eleven o'clock phone call booked with Darwin tomorrow, so he wants to be able to tell him that we know exactly what's going on. No loose threads. I would have done it myself, but she asked for you specifically, and she sounds like kind of a tough customer.' Perdue paused briefly while Hayes muttered something in the background. 'Hayes says he's getting takeout from Wolfgang Pucks at the marketplace on the way home and do you want the usual?'

Avery told Perdue that she did, switched off her phone and drove away towards the heavy swell of rush-hour traffic, dreaming of tortilla soup and Chinese chicken salad; hoping that whatever Shannon Reilly wanted, it wasn't going to take too long.

Avery had driven past various branches of Hooters, many times, but had never been into one. As she approached the main entrance and saw the throngs of stag-night guys and beered-up tourists waiting for a happy-hour table, she thought how very much she'd like to have kept things that way.

While she waited for the manager to let Shannon know that she was here, she tried not to look at the sad-eyed, crispy-haired girls in their tiny shorts and tight Hooters logo T-shirts, tried to tell herself that she'd just imagined the acrid smell of male body odour that threatened to overpower the more agreeable aroma of spicy hot chicken wings.

The first thing Shannon had said was, 'Not in here, let's talk outside,' but when she saw the rain and the blackening sky, she'd become agitated, as if her brain might short-circuit with the taxing task of cooking up an alternative plan. She'd seemed both relieved and tragically impressed when Avery suggested they sit in her car, and as Reilly shucked on an outsize candy-pink sweat-shirt over her skimpy uniform, she kept mumbling, 'Good idea, good thinkin', uh-huh.'

Shannon Reilly used the long acrylic, French-manicured nail of her forefinger to doodle delicate spirals in the condensation on the passenger window, and she looked at these, and not at Avery, as she began to speak.

'I got something to say, okay? And I want you to tell it to that guy you work with. And that's to lay off talking like Leon killed somebody. You get me? Because he's in enough trouble already, breakin' probation, without you guys going round talkin' out of your asses. Okay?'

Avery stared at Shannon Reilly incredulously. For this she was letting her soup get cold? Letting the strips of fried blue-corn tortilla go soggy, the sprigs of fresh cilantro wilt, the blob of sour cream melt away into nothing?

She tried to reply as slowly, patiently, as she could. 'Shannon, I was told that you needed to see me urgently. Is this what you wanted to say?'

'Damn right I did. That guy you work with, he was down talking to some people I know today, makes out like he wants to know about Lucas, but he's asking all these questions about Leon, acting like Leon killed him. They called me right away, told me. So yeah, damn right that's why I called you.'

Abruptly, Avery stopped thinking about soup. 'Hold on, Shannon, you never mentioned that you knew Lucas . . . His *friends*. You said you hardly knew the guy. Now they're calling you up. Am I missing something here?'

Shannon Reilly curled her lip and gave Avery a filthy look. 'Don't go turning this round, puttin' it on me. I done nothin' wrong. It's you guys are out of line. This ain't about me.'

Avery sighed. 'Look, Shannon, you need to get to work, I need to get home. My colleague is just doing his job. That's not out of line. If it makes you feel any better, I can tell you that since he visited your friends this morning – the ones you forgot to mention – we've received some other evidence and it's taken the heat off Leon. He's no longer under suspicion. So unless there's anything else you want to say to me, can I suggest –'

'Yeah, well how do I know that's true? And, yeah, there *is* somethin' else I want to say, and you ain't kickin' me out of your car till I said it.'

Now it was Avery's turn to look angry. 'Fine, well, since you're insisting on talking, maybe I should ask you a few questions about how you knew Jerry Lee Lucas? And how well you knew him? You know, Shannon, as

186

of this afternoon, we really didn't think there was *any* link between him and Leon. Now, from what you've just said, I'm not so sure.'

Shannon Reilly slapped her hands onto her bare thighs in exasperation, screamed, 'Fuck you!' and then, rather incongruously, burst into tears. Avery watched her with grim bemusement, trying to make out the strangled words of protest that slipped out in between the great snorting sobs.

'He didn't! I swear! He only knew them a little . . . through me . . . the lab rats, everybody knows each other. That's what it's like. That's all.'

'But you stayed in touch with these guys? Even after you stopped guinea-pigging?'

'Noooo! It's not like that. It's not.'

'What is it, then? Something else? Drugs?'

'What, now you're gonna bust me?'

'Listen, Shannon, I don't care what you get up to. Sanford's not under our jurisdiction and we're not really connected with the County forces unless they ask for our help. So I can assure you, I really don't give a shit.'

Shannon Reilly stopped crying and stared at Avery. 'You don't?'

'Not really. Lucas's homicide, that's being handled by County, not us. But you can bet that if Leon was involved in something with Lucas and his buddies, they're going to find out. And they're not going to be anywhere near as easy-going about it.'

Reilly stared again at the spirals she'd drawn on the window. Her voice was softer now, her imploring tone almost a whine. 'I just want to protect Leon, that's all. I don't care what he did, I love him. Maybe you can't understand that. Those guys, if he knew them, he knew them because of me. It's my fault. I'm not sayin' it *was* because of drugs, okay, I'm not saying that. And I'm not sayin' that there was never any fights between those guys, I mean, that kind of person, they're in disagreements all the time, you know, but it's no big deal. The thing is this: I just want you to know that Leon didn't do nothin' wrong. Deep down, he's a good guy.'

'Why didn't you tell me all this before? About Lucas, about –'

Reilly slapped her thigh again, this time in melodramatic disbelief. 'Hello? Why do you think? Look, you might think I'm dumb, trying to protect Leon and all, but he's all I got. I know it looks bad that he ran away the day after Jerry Lee got it. I know what it looks like. But I want you to know he didn't hurt no one. When he comes back, I want him to be with *me*. I don't want him in jail again. I don't think I could stand it, all on my own again, the waiting, I . . . Look, why I called you here is to say that I know, I really, really know that he could never, ever kill anybody.'

The anger and the pity and the image of blood on white fun-fur and the sound of 'My Home is Your Home' and the echoes of Lisa Schaeffer's empty apartment made Avery's head spin. She rested her hand lightly on Shannon Reilly's arm.

'Shannon, I think it's very noble of you. And I *do* understand. Sometimes you can want to protect something so much, something you've got that means a lot to you because it's your life . . . The only life you've got. Even if it isn't perfect, you want to protect it, and that feels like the right thing to do. No matter what doubts you have, you still want to –'

'I know what you're sayin'.'

Avery studied Shannon's tear-stained face and felt guilty at being so surprised that Shannon really *did* seem to have understood what Avery was driving at.

'I know what you're sayin', and it's true,' Reilly continued. 'But I really, really do know for sure that Leon is innocent. I wouldn't say it . . . Well, yeah, you know, I probably *would* say it otherwise. But the truth is, I really do know it. For a fact.'

'Is there something else you want to tell me?'

'Yes, there is. But I hope it's true that you don't care about the drugs, that you won't do anything. Or talk to County?'

'If you want it, you've got my word. I won't. So what is it?'

Reilly dabbed daintily at her eyeliner and stared straight ahead at the torrents of rain beyond the windshield. 'When I said Leon couldn't have hurt anybody, killed anybody, I meant he actually *couldn't* have. He's got arthritis. One of the guys, he says it's the coke, too much coke. Does something to your joints. And it's getting worse all the time. Since the beginning of the year, he can't even hold a pen. He could hit someone maybe, kick someone, I'm not saying he couldn't do that. Or that he wouldn't. But he couldn't use a gun, like with Jerry Lee, they said he was shot? No way. No way at all.'

Avery fought the urge to tell Shannon that Leon had seemed perfectly adept at holding a knife when he killed Lisa. She nodded sympathetically instead. Perhaps Leon LeGalley had suffered some pains in his hands, sure. Reilly's lie must have been inspired by something. But that was all it was: a lie. A waste of time. She was starting to think about the tortilla soup again.

'Okay, Shannon. Thanks for telling me that. I'll make sure that the information gets passed on to my boss, the rest of the department. Whoever. I'll even see to it that County lay off him. Okay?'

189

Reilly smiled briefly before dismay clouded her face. 'Do you have to tell the centre?'

'Um . . . I don't *have* to, no.'

Avery started a little as Reilly threw her arms around her neck and hugged her, enveloping her in a sickly sweet cloud of Vanilla Fields and hairspray.

'Ohmigod, *thank you*. He really needs that work, you know? That's why I didn't say this when you first came. You gotta have a clean bill. He didn't think they'd have him if they knew about the arthritis. Or the drugs. So he lied on the medical questionnaire. But then, *everybody* does. Everybody lies about somethin'. I wanted to tell you, clear his name, but I was like, if you told the centre and he came back and found that he didn't have a job there no more because of me, he'd have broken my neck.'

Or sliced your chest open with a hunting knife, Avery thought.

Before Shannon Reilly got out of the car, she squeezed Avery's hand, gave her a scrap of folded paper which she'd taken from her purse and said, 'Call if you need to. Listen, I'm sorry about how I was. Before. And tonight. I had you all wrong, I guess.'

It wasn't until Avery hit some traffic on the I–4 halfway home that she thought about the scrap of paper, which she'd flicked onto the floor by her feet. She already had Shannon's number. Shannon knew that. Avery swooped down, picked it up, opened it, read it. And after that, even the thought of Wolfgang Puck's tortilla soup couldn't rekindle her appetite.

Twenty-One

It took a lot to put Sylvia Avery off her food, and even more to put her off sex, but by the time she climbed into bed that night, she no more felt like either than she felt like taking a bungee jump off the top of Mount Kahuna.

Shannon Reilly's note, the carefully rounded letters and numerals revealing not her own contact details but the name and telephone number of Leon LeGalley's doctor – raising the possibility that there might be truth in the story – had taken care of her appetite. And about forty minutes after she arrived home, Perdue had telephoned, returning her panicked call, saying that he'd checked out the doctor, verbally confirmed the report, *and* seen a faxed copy of the relevant page of Leon's medical records. That had put paid to her libido.

Now Avery lay in bed wearing one of Hayes's outsized Kit-E-Cat T-shirts and the pants from a pair of brushed-cotton Brooks Brothers pyjamas she'd found in his drawer, which appeared never to have been worn. She stared through the floor-to-ceiling windows at the darkness beyond, watching the lights that punctured it: flickering pinpricks from the burning torches that ringed Tsunami Cove; the fireworks in the west, above World Expo, and much, much farther away, the klieg lights and lasers from Disney's Pleasure Island, ripping through the pregnant grey clouds that hid the moon and the stars.

'You cold, honey? Shall I turn off the AC?'

Hayes had come in and was regarding Avery with some concern.

'Nope. It's fine. Just right.'

He stared at her oddly and she realized that it was the first time in her adult life that she'd worn clothes – *proper* clothes, anyway – in bed. Back at home, when she was a kid, she'd worn her pyjamas like armour, or the filthiest, most shapeless T-shirts and huge men's longjohns, or, her favourite, a kind of giant Babygro that she'd found in a thrift store and wore with the poppers done up all the way to the neck. It had never made any difference, of course, but she'd done it anyway. Her nocturnal nakedness as an adult, now she came to think of it, was her show of bravura, her reclaiming of her own body. But tonight, for the first time since leaving home, she had instinctively sought out night-clothes, and she knew exactly what it meant. A few minutes after Hayes climbed into bed, after pawing her for the third time and finding himself presented with her back, as she rolled over and away from him, he figured it out too. He clicked his bedside light on and sighed.

'Avery, you have got to stop letting things get to you like this. If you want to talk some more, we can, but how much more reassurance do you need? If I have to say it again, I will: as far as I'm concerned, *nothing has changed*.'

Avery sat bolt upright, drew the covers up around her chest and stared straight ahead. The curtains were closed now, no view to gaze on, so she watched the gentle syncopated swish of the Polynesian palm-leaf wall fans instead.

'But what if Leon didn't kill her? I mean, have you

192

thought about that? What if *someone else* killed them both? It makes much more sense. Why would a dumb idiot like Leon LeGalley kill himself? I doubt he ever felt an ounce of remorse in his life.'

'Avery, I don't mind talking, but I'm not going though *this* again. The rest room was locked from the inside, wedged shut. No one was in there but Lisa and Leon. No one else came in, no one else went out. Paramedics saw it, I saw it, couple other people saw it.'

Now she turned to look at him. 'Who? Who did?'

'Couple of cast members who are now enjoying a nice vacation courtesy of Mr Darwin, getting a taste of all the other nice vacations they're going to have every year until they drop dead, providing they don't blab. I took their statements myself, Avery. There's no confusion, no room for doubt, believe me.'

'So do you have any other explanation for how a man with chronic arthritis managed to do what Leon did to Lisa?'

'Listen, maybe he was having a good day, maybe he held it in his fucking teeth, I don't know, and to tell the truth, I don't care. It's the least of my worries, believe me. Goodnight.'

Hayes clicked the light off again and slumped down heavily. Avery lay still in the silence, her mind ticking over. Ten minutes later she turned over and gingerly touched his shoulder.

'Hayes? Are you asleep? I just had a thought.'

He sighed deeply as he turned over towards her.

'What?'

'Leon had been at the centre that morning, right? Well, what if they gave him something? In the tests? Drugs?'

'Yeah? And?'

193

'And what if it was something that, I don't know, *affec-ted* him, somehow. Made him violent, irrational. Made him do what he did. But also did something physically, numbed him, overrode the pain in his hands. It's possible, isn't it?'

'Maybe.' He thought for a moment. 'Doesn't make much difference, though, does it? He's dead, she's dead, it's not one of the things we have to worry about. If you mean I should be feeling guilty that it might be our fault, indirectly, then ask me again in a couple of days, when it's all over, and maybe I will. Right now, I'm just concerned about getting this all tied up by the time I speak to Mr D tomorrow. Okay? Can we go to sleep now?'

Avery snarled in the darkness. 'Great. And then next time they use this drug, whatever they were using, and another volunteer goes nuts and kills someone, then we can clean that up too. That'll keep us all *nice* and busy.'

'This is crazy, Avery. You're getting all worked up about something non-existent. Something you've got no proof of.'

'No? What about the guy who killed Jerry Lee Lucas? Looks like he was a volunteer, too. And Trey Clowes said how aggressive Leon was being all night. Don't you think it might be worth looking into?'

Hayes digested Avery's words and sighed again, less testily this time.

'Okay, so when we talk to Daetwyler tomorrow, we'll find out what he was using. If there are any possible risks, we make sure he stops using it.' Hayes put his arm around Avery. 'Sound good? Feel better?'

Avery didn't really feel any better, but she told Hayes that she did.

194

The sex was, Avery concluded, probably the worst she'd ever had.

Bu benim evimdir . . . This is my house . . . Won't you come on inside . . .

The dream started with the little Turkish boy, the little doll from the Global Village Cruise, only in Avery's dream he was far more animated than the real dolls in the ride, with moving lips, frantically waving arms, feet that struggled to free themselves from where they were nailed to the floor. And his invitation to enter the portals of his mountain cave home was tinged with a certain desperation, as if perhaps some unspeakable disaster had taken place inside and he required the assistance of a responsible adult to tell him what in God's name he should do next.

We may live far apart, but never forget it . . .

There was a nasty discordance about the playback of 'My Home is Your Home', something distant and sluggish and low and sticky about it, and as the sense of unease began to envelop her, Avery tried to scramble out of the little boat. The ride was darker than in real life, and although the song was definitely running far too slow, the boats themselves were running much, much faster, skimming along the murky foam like lightweight canoes on a white-water run.

At first, Avery's main concern was squinting into the darkness to find the dimly lit emergency exit signs above the maintenance tunnels, and noticing with dismay how rapidly these were flashing past, but as she sank into bleak acceptance of her situation, she realized, her chest tightening, that much of what now made 'My Home is Your Home' such a horrifying tune was the faint sound of children's screams in the background.

As her boat hurtled around the next corner, Avery tried to close her eyes but she couldn't, and as the heat became almost unbearable, the sweat flowed into them from her hair and stung like acid. The screams were far louder here, and they came from all quarters. They came from Avery's left, where the Brazilian children stood rooted to the spot as they shrieked, 'Esta casa é minha!' over the crackle of burning thatch and wood. And from the Mexican dolls – 'Esta es mi casa, Avery!' – helplessly looking on as their adobe homes buckled and crumbled under the heat. The screams came from the right, too, from the New Guineans who waved their little arms at Avery and shouted 'Dispela emi haus bilang mi!' and stared fearfully at the rising water while they clung to the roofs of their partially submerged wooden stilt houses.

Avery flew past, gawping impotently at the burning moss roofs of the Norwegian houses, and the remains of Mali mudshacks that had been washed away in the same tides that had sunk the Thai houseboats.

'Dette er mitt hus, Avery!'

'Ni yen'ka so' ye!'

She tried to block out the cacophony, but it was hopeless, for wherever the water carried her, there were more cries, more scenes of destruction. The boat slowed a little as Avery attempted to reach out to the little Bolivian dolls crushed beneath the rubble of their collapsed stone cottages. She managed to grasp the cold plastic hand of a little girl, her heavily lashed doll's eyes closed, her rosebud mouth moving slowly as she whispered, 'Akax utaxawa,' over and over. But the boat sped up again, and Avery was left holding the little severed arm that had been torn from its socket, the quivering red sinews at the shoulder dreadfully human.

The final room of diorama on the Global Village Cruise represented the United States, Avery knew that, but tonight it was nothing like it should have been. Instead, it was a perfect miniature version of ImagiNation, a precise recreation of the place Avery knew and loved so well. Identical, but for the fact that it was ablaze and was teeming with thousands of dolls, all yelling and crying and running in every direction, trampling over one another in the panic.

The ride exit was looming into sight, when Avery felt something dripping into her lap and onto her hair. All at once the boat slowed almost to a stop and Avery looked up to source the liquid. Blood spattered onto her upturned face as she found herself staring into the shiny glass eyes of Kit-E-Cat. He was aboard a little dinghy and wearing a jaunty sailor's cap, just like the last animatronic model in the real Global Village Cruise, but instead of sitting in an anthropomorphic position and waving good-bye to the riders, this Kit-E-Cat was crouched on his haunches like a real cat, using his paws to hold down the writhing thing he was gnawing at. The white fur around his mouth was drenched with blood.

Avery looked away in disgust, and rubbed frantically at her wet face. She willed the boat to keep moving, but it came to a complete halt, and now the tortured howl coming from above pierced Avery's eardrums, forcing her to look up again, where she saw that in Kit-E-Cat's drooling maw lay a lifeless little doll that looked exactly like Lisa Schaeffer. The drooping legs were clad in low-slung combats and, on top, the doll was wearing a Poké-mon T-shirt, although much of this had been chewed up by Kit-E-Cat and was obscured by a glistening heap of tiny internal organs and ribbons of sticky intestine no wider than pipe-cleaners.

The doll's eyes were closed, its mouth frozen in its last distorted grimace of pain. As Avery stared at the face in mute horror, the background noise receded into giddy silence and now all she could hear was 'My Home is Your Home', playing so slowly as to be little more than a crawling baritone blur.

Rising gingerly to stand in the now stationary boat, Avery reached towards the Lisa Schaeffer doll. As her hand made its slow approach, the eyes snapped open, and the doll's mouth crept into a grin.

'Esta casa é minha,' said the doll in a mockingly cute tone. Dispela emi haus bilang mi!'

The minute row of perfect white teeth were stained red, and the little mouth was filled with blood, which bubbled in time with the doll's words: 'Esta es mi casa! Dette er mitt hus! Ni yen'ka so' ye!'

The doll-voice grew higher and higher and faster until the horrible mantra sounded almost like a spool of tape on rewind.

'Akax utaxawa! O lou fale lenei! Ça c'est ma maison! Bu benim evimdir!'

But the final words were slow, regular and clear, Lisa Schaeffer's own bright West Coast whine: 'And this?'

The doll gestured casually at the scenes of apocalypse below her, then raised her voice slightly to be heard over the sound of Kit-E-Cat tearing mouthfuls of gore from her abdomen, and over the screams, and over the noise of the miniature Fort Enchantment crashing to the ground.

'This is *your* home, Avery.'

Twenty-Two

Avery had shot up into a sitting position as she woke, and now, as she sat blinking in the darkness, sweating freely, she realized that she must have cried out, too, because she had woken Hayes.

'What? What? What is it?'

'Just a dream. I'm sorry. I had a bad dream. Go back to sleep.'

Hayes Ober, still half dozing, reached over and stroked Avery's hair. 'Okay. S'okay.'

Avery listened to the swish of the fans, gathered her thoughts.

'Hayes? Can I ask you something?'

The lump in the bed beside Avery stirred, grunted and turned over. She asked again.

'Yeah, I'm listening. Go on.'

'It's about Daetwyler. Been bugging me. It's just: if my theory turns out to be true, I think I'm going to find it very hard to . . . Put it this way, I'm not going to feel that it's enough just to make sure it never happens again. What happened to Lisa Schaeffer . . . To Jerry Lee Lucas . . . How hard we've all had to work to protect Dreamworld . . . If it's Daetwyler's fault, I don't know how easy I'm going to find it to just let it ride. I know we can't go to the police, can't prosecute him, but – '

Hayes had sat up and now he snapped on the light and stared at her. 'But what?'

'I don't know. I'm just saying, I – well, don't you think? Doesn't it seem a bit rich that you can screw up so badly, screw up people's lives and just get off scot-free?'

Hayes looked genuinely puzzled, and not a little testy. 'I don't know what you're driving at, Avery.'

'I'm not sure, either . . .'

'Tell you what: you think about it, we'll talk in the morning. It's an important day, and I don't know about you, but I *need* to sleep. Okay?'

'I don't need to think about it. Okay, here's what I figure. I don't know if it's right that we should let Daetwyler carry on his work. If we find out that he's responsible – for these deaths, for jeopardizing everything we stand for . . . perhaps Dreamworld should make a stand? Do the right thing.'

'And get rid of him? Ditch the project? Avery, do you have any *idea* of the potential his work has?'

Avery sneered. 'What, financially?'

Hayes Ober's hackles rose. 'I'm not talking about our investment. Or future revenue, okay? I'm talking about bringing joy to people, bringing them new experiences. Escapism. Liberating them. I want to be able to do that. That's why I'm here, doing my job. You know that. And that's my priority.'

'And you don't have a problem with the fact that this wonderful invention of Daetwyler's might have cost three lives? Maybe more, by the time it's finished? That's not going to be a problem for you? It's not gonna be on your mind, just a little bit, when you do the grand unveiling to the public?'

Ober paused for a moment and responded calmly.

'Avery, history is full of worthy inventions that have had a high human cost, a moral cost. And people have had to ask themselves if it was worth it. Treatment for frost-bite, that was discovered in the World War II death camps in Japan. Unit 731. They used to stick little kids, babies, out in the snow. And what about animal experiments? We wouldn't have antibiotics, blood transfusions, organ transplants. The road of progress is pretty bloody, Avery. You can't condone it, not in a million years, but surely it would be more of an insult to those who died to reject the only positive thing to come out of their deaths?'

Avery gawped at Hayes, thinking, I don't really know you at all, do I? 'I'm sorry, let me get this straight: you're saying that it's okay to torture and kill if something good comes out of it?'

'Oh, will you fucking grow up? Don't put words into my mouth. Of course I'm not. I'm just saying that in our society, it's – oh, will you look at your face, Avery, for Christ's sake! I can't talk to you if you're going to look at me like that. I wish the world wasn't this way. I wish people weren't cruel, didn't devalue life. I wish the real world were more like Dreamworld. But it isn't. That's why I chose to live here instead.'

Avery snorted loudly. 'But you don't care if you're responsible for dragging Dreamworld down to the same level as the rest of so-called civilization? And we're not talking about saving lives. I mean, Daetwyler's stupid gadget: what's that about? Attempting to let people make believe they're somewhere fantastic, doing something great, stepping out of this world for a little while before they have to go back to their crappy lives? Escapism. *You* said it. Did you ever think that Dreamworld could spend some of its money on actually making the rest of the world better, instead of creating a little utopia here, just to give them a taste of how their town might be if they had this kind of money to spend on their roads and custodial people and maintenance and policing?'

Hayes smiled fondly – patronizingly? – and embraced Avery, who remained stiff and unyielding in his arms.

'Honey, I agree. Of course I do. But you've got to remember, I had all these conversations, these thoughts, back when I was at college. Everybody does. And I still feel the same way, I'm just aware now, as you are when you get older, that you can't save the world. If you can make a little corner of it better, do just a little, then you're lucky. And I feel lucky, believe me. What we do here is not nothing, you know? When people come here, you're right: they see how their town could be, how their lives could be. No crime, no litter, people in stores who smile and treat you like a human being. We're keeping those values alive. What we do is no small thing. We bring families together. We show people tolerance and equality at work. We encourage people to remember what it was like to be a kid, to be full of wonder and curiosity and respect for the world and the other people in it. We show people how things *could* be. And if just one person who visits here is changed by that, gets inspired to change things in *their* little corner of the world, we've done good.'

Gradually, while Hayes spoke softly into her hair, while more of his sentiments began to hit home, to make sense to Avery, she began to relax, to return the embrace. But now he was gently holding her shoulders, easing her away from him, so that he could look into her eyes.

'Please don't get cynical on me, Avery. It doesn't suit you. Please? Promise me you won't change?'

And then Hayes Ober kissed Avery lightly on the forehead and told her – for the first time – that he loved her. But her mind was racing, wondering whether it was too late, whether the sense of disillusionment growing within had begun to change her already.

But there was something else, too. Something hanging in the air between them as they gazed at one another. Something unsaid. She couldn't be imagining it.

'What?'

'What "what"?'

Hayes affected a puzzled look, as one might when faced with a question from left-field. But Avery could tell he was faking.

'You know what "what". There's something else, isn't there? Something you're not telling me.'

Hayes made a perfunctory gesture towards suggesting that he wasn't sure whether to tell her what was on his mind or not, but this too failed to ring true. Clearly he was aching to share this information with her, whatever it was. She sat up in bed, attentive and encouraging.

'It's Daetwyler, Avery. Devon's mother has petitioned the courts for custody.'

'So if he *has* done something wrong, he loses her.'

'Exactly. And not just that. If there's even an *inquiry*. . . You see?'

Avery curled her hair around her finger, around and around, unsure of how to feel. 'I think so.'

'Look, hon, it just means that I would need to be absolutely sure of my suspicions before I did anything. Or it'll be on my conscience for the rest of my life.'

'So this isn't just about the park?'

Hayes smiled at the relief on Avery's face, relief she had wanted to hide but couldn't. 'No, I guess not. Does that make you happy?'

'I think so. Yes. I think it does.'

Fifteen minutes later, Hayes Ober was asleep, deeply asleep. Avery watched him doze for a little while, studied his face and prayed that they were going to get through this, together. Then, resigning herself to the fact that there was now no chance of slumber, she crept from the bed and wandered into the sitting room.

The curtains were open, and through the window Avery saw that the sun had begun to rise behind Mount Kahuna, sprinkling the calm waters of the cove with sparkling jewels of pale yellow light that were brighter and more beautiful by far than the glittering artificial inferno that erupted from the volcano.

Twenty-Three

What with the shambling line of students and wasters in the lobby, and the troupe of white-coated junior lab techs bustling up and down the hall, it was the busiest Avery had ever seen Richard Daetwyler's research suite. She'd been disappointed to note, however, that her own deliberately frosty and ominous presence in this mayhem, with Hayes at her side, didn't seemed to have fazed Daetwyler at all.

'Hayes, buddy. How's it going? Avery. I'll be with you guys in five, is that okay? I just need to get the volunteers checked in, and then I can let my team get started on the prepping and I'll be with you, yeah?'

'Good man. We're here. Take your time.'

Avery hoped that Hayes had intended this last remark in a snide way, to imply that he'd rather Daetwyler took his time in order to avoid screwing up on whatever he planned to do with today's team of human lab rats. But if he had, Daetwyler certainly hadn't picked up on it. Avery couldn't make out the merest flicker of concern cracking his brightly focused demeanour, and it annoyed the hell out of her.

Catherine Homolka appeared suddenly from a side door,

and sidled up to Hayes Ober, ignoring Avery altogether. 'Hayes, I'd really appreciate it if while you're waiting I could get a quick word with you? About something else?'

'Not a problem.'

Avery gritted her teeth and felt a pang of annoyance that despite her above-average height, both Hayes and Homolka towered over her. It almost seemed as if she could feel the soundwaves of their exchange ruffling her hair as they passed overhead.

Catherine led the way from the lobby towards Daetwyler's office, her hand resting firmly on Hayes's elbow, keeping him at her side. Avery strode behind, determined not to let on that Homolka's deliberate exclusion tactics had got to her.

Homolka pushed open the door to the office, the door that had made such a great slamming noise the previous night.

'We'd better talk in here – Devon and her tutor use my room in the mornings.'

Homolka sat down in Daetwyler's chair and gestured for Hayes and Avery to sit, still without acknowledging Avery directly.

'Actually, this is *about* Devon.' She gestured to Devon's tape-recorder and a stack of paper and envelopes that stood beside Daetwyler's computer terminal. 'The transcribing . . . It's not part of my job description, and it's not like I don't have enough to do here without –'

'Hold it, hold it, Catherine. Transcribing? I don't know what . . .'

'Richard makes me transcribe Devon's letters. She dictates all these letters, all day. Stops when the tutor gets here at ten, starts right in again as soon as he goes. Then I have to type them. I graduated top of my year at MIT. If I wanted to do clerical work, I'd've –'

Avery was pleased to note the faint irritation on Hayes's face as he interrupted. 'Catherine, I really have a lot on my mind right now. Have you tried talking to Richard about this? It's really not my – '

Homolka's voice was raised as she interrupted right back. 'And I can't even hear what the hell she's saying, so it takes me hours, hours I could be spending doing . . . I mean, she does this in the lobby, and she's, like, muttering into the microphone and there's CNN cranked up God knows how loud because Richard likes to be able to hear it from the main lab, and there's people coming and going and she's got this little voice like . . .' Homolka scrunched her face up in disgust.

Hayes Ober rubbed his forehead briefly. 'I'll mention it to him, okay? Maybe we can get someone from the typing pool in the main building. But right now . . .'

'Have you ever tried transcribing a tape, Hayes? Let alone one where you can't hear what you're supposed to be transcribing? It's shit work. Really shit work. The kind of thing you wouldn't even subject the volunteers to.'

Avery laughed out loud, spoke far more brashly than she'd intended to. 'And from what I gather you put the volunteers through, that's really saying something!'

Hayes looked almost as annoyed as Homolka as he shot Avery a look and got up. 'I *really* don't have time for this right now. Where the hell is Richard? Catherine, can you get him for me please? I have a meeting with John Darwin, he's come all the way from LA, I . . .'

'I'm here, I'm here. All yours. And we can make it as quick as you like. I don't want to keep you.'

Richard Daetwyler had walked into the office and began to rummage in the top drawer of his desk. Homolka stood aside to allow her superior better access.

'Thanks, Catherine. I have the file you wanted, Hayes, the one Avery asked me for yesterday? The volunteers file. Like I said to her, if it's okay by you . . .'

Daetwyler sat down, leaving Homolka standing, stewing, at his side. Hayes reached across the desk and took the file being proffered.

'Good man. Avery, is there anything else we need, d'you think?'

'Yes, there is.' She spoke quickly and directly to Daetwyler, not allowing Hayes to catch her eye. 'I need to ask you about the drugs you've been using in the tests.'

Daetwyler looked pleadingly at Hayes. 'What about them?'

Now Avery looked at Hayes, too. He appeared restless, but nodded at her, giving the okay for her to continue.

'We need to know if there was anything you used on the last day that Jerry Lee Lucas was here which could have, firstly . . . could have had a physical effect, like an *anaesthetizing* effect. Physically. If someone had, say, a medical condition which gave them pain, badly enough to restrict strength and movement, could any of the things you used, I don't know, *override* that?' Daetwyler seemed less thrown by the question than Avery had expected. 'Uh, let me think. I think . . . I think the answer is yes, maybe, yes.'

Avery and Hayes looked at one another, and then Avery gestured for Daetwyler to continue.

'I mean, there's not much else I can say, really. Except, yes, it's a possibility. We were trying out a substance, it's not a million miles from scopolamine, which is . . . Do you know what that is?'

Avery shook her head.

'It's like, well, it's a pharmaceutical – legal, of course

– that in minute doses is used to treat motion sickness, plus a few other things. And in slightly larger doses it causes quite powerful hallucination. But its very safe, so it's pretty useful for us. I think I said, we're currently examining the neurological process of brain-generated experience usurping external sensory input?'

'Yes, you mentioned that.'

'So that's why we're using it. But we've not had any problems. The effects last four to six hours at most. By the time everybody goes home, it's all metabolized. Not a trace left. We're very careful. Why?'

Avery looked at Hayes again, but this time his face was harder to read. She answered carefully. 'I'm not really at liberty to say. That would be up to Hayes. But you can confirm that if someone left here perhaps before it had had a chance to metabolize, one of the side-effects might be a certain physical . . .'

'Yeah, a person would be pretty unaware of much physically. That's what I mean by external sensory input. That would include signals coming from the body. I know that doesn't sound like what you'd classify as external, but it is. Like I think I was telling you, all your body stuff – whether it's touching something –' Daetwyler patted the desk in front of him, '– or feeling pain in the body itself, that's all external. Your brain processes it and you experience it. Unless those signals are shut off. Which is one of the things that this drug does. And that's why we're using it. But that's not a harmful thing, in itself. I mean, you wouldn't want to do any cooking or, you know, you might burn yourself and not know it . . .'

Now Hayes spoke, his languorous, confident cadence balm to Avery's ears after Daetwyler's nervous babble.

'That's okay, Rich, that's all we needed to know. Isn't it, Avery?'

Avery avoided his gaze again. 'Just about. Except for one thing: this drug, could it make someone violent? I know you said it's safe, but, I mean, what if they accidentally got a wrong dose? A higher dose. Could it affect someone's behaviour? Incite –'

Daetwyler shook his head vigorously. 'Not a chance.'

'You're quite sure?'

Daetwyler looked at Hayes, apparently stung to hear any doubt from the lips of the man who had mentored the project from its inception.

'Yes, I *am* quite sure, Hayes. Of course I am. Look, first, there's no chance of fudging the dosages. Let me say that. But if we're speaking hypothetically, then actually I can assure you that an overdose would have the opposite effect. It would make someone pretty passive. Very passive, actually. Okay?'

He looked at them with haunted eyes – pleading? – and Avery found herself registering a strange mixture of emotions, sympathy at first which mutated into a blatant awareness of a *lack* of sympathy plus a weird sense of guilt. It was none of her business, she knew, but she couldn't help wondering whether Devon would be better off with her mother. There was something desperate and unclean about Daetwyler's desire to cover his own ass. Was it that? Where she now believed she understood Hayes's delicacy around the matter of indicting Daetwyler, she felt herself thinking about how Daetwyler behaved with his daughter, treating her like a little adult . . . But no, that wasn't it, either. He treated her like a little *experiment*. A lab creature; a hobby; something to be trained and tinkered with, allowed to develop unnaturally in unnatural surroundings. Under Daetwyler's care, Devon had turned into an urgently weird kid, and now it was impossible to hold back the tidal wave of pity she inspired.

Avery wasn't listening as Daetwyler talked to Hayes about the project and how it was coming on. Just watching. Watching the way his face became animated, the way his eyes became bright behind the little glasses. There was something faintly disgusting about the raw passion on his face simply by virtue of the fact that it *hadn't* been there whenever Avery had seen the man's dealings with his own child. And then she knew it for sure: she didn't trust him, didn't approve of his screwed-up priorities. No, more than that, she didn't *like* him. Not one little bit. If Richard Daetwyler had done something wrong, he was going to pay for it, and Hayes could go to hell and take his bleeding heart with him.

'Many thanks, Rich. I think that clears everything up.'

Daetwyler had finished talking about whatever he'd been talking about, and Hayes had nodded decisively before glancing at his watch and speaking. Now, he rapped his knuckles on the file that Daetwyler had handed him, before handing it to Avery.

'We might need to talk about scratching someone in here from the records, but I'll bring you up to date later. For now, I think we're about done. Shall we?'

Avery rose, hugging the file close to her, and said a terse goodbye to Daetwyler and to Homolka, who appeared to be struggling to keep herself from saying something she might regret.

While they waited for the air conditioning to cool the interior of Hayes's car enough to make getting back inside bearable, Hayes and Avery leant up against its scorching bonnet, he scanning the contents of the volunteer file, she watching the windsock at the perimeter gate of the Research and Development Complex, flaccid on its pole, untroubled by even the merest breath of wind.

'Gonna be a hot one.'

Hayes looked up from the file, impatient. 'You say?'

'I said, it's . . . Never mind. Sorry. Carry on.'

He furrowed his brow, not really listening.

'There are quite a few sport utilities in here. We're going to need to go through a process of elimination, I think.'

'Shit.'

'Uh-uh, it's okay. Won't be too hard. And I've got enough to tell Darwin it's all under control, at least.'

But now it was Avery whose mind was elsewhere. 'No, I said shit because . . .'

Her eyes were fixed on a distant figure approaching. Although still too far away to make out any features, Avery knew, from the height, the build, the blur of black hair, exactly who it was.

And now he'd seen her, too, and he had begun to run towards her. She wasn't sure why she felt such a terrible sense of foreboding, such a sense of impending doom infusing the idea of Trey Clowes meeting Hayes Ober, and she was no closer to figuring it out when Clowes arrived, breathless and grinning before her. He paused awkwardly for a moment, then threw his arms around her in a friendly but heartfelt hug.

'I found you! I just wanted to say thank you, for the other day, your support . . . For trusting me.'

Clowes stopped, perhaps catching a glimpse of Hayes Ober's icy countenance from the corner of his eye as he disengaged himself from Avery. He held out his hand. 'Trey Clowes. You must be Avery's boss. I've gotta tell you, she's one in a million, this –'

Hayes shook Clowes's hand, a little too firmly, didn't smile. 'Hayes Ober.'

'He's not my boss, actually, Trey, he's –'

'Hayes Ober? No way! The Dream Tech? You know, I was at the Americana site the other day and it looks *amazing*, I mean . . .'

Avery held her breath, praying that Trey wouldn't ask Hayes about the airless paint-gun story. Trey had clapped his other hand over Hayes's and was shaking it vigorously.

'Oh, man, it's an *honour* to meet you, it really is, I can't begin to tell you . . .'

'Trey, Hayes has an important meeting right now, so we'll have to shoot, but it's good to see you. And really, there's no need to thank me. You've been very helpful.'

Clowes dropped Hayes's hand, looking slightly wounded.

'No, I want to thank you, really, in fact, that's why I was looking for you: I remembered I owe you a drink. You bought me one when we first met at Cleo's Barge, remember? Could we maybe meet up? I'd like to . . . Thank you properly. I know it's what Lisa would have wanted.' He gave a bitter little laugh. 'Well, no, actually, she wouldn't have, she always got pissed if I went anywhere with a girl, but I guess . . .'

Avery steeled herself to glance over at Hayes and was alarmed to see him climbing into his car and snapping on his seatbelt. She began to back away from Clowes, to make her way hastily around the car to the passenger side. She shouted to him across the roof.

'Trey, call the office, yeah? And maybe we can –'

Hayes had slammed the driver's-side door and started the engine, and now came a low, hollow *thunk* as he engaged the central locking. Avery, having raced around the car in ungainly haste, rattled desperately at the passenger-side door handle. Hayes cracked open the window and stared at her testily.

'What?'

'I . . . I'm coming with you!'

'I'm late, Avery. I'm not going to have time to drop you off.'

She watched him punch the gearshift smartly into drive with the heel of his hand, then she rattled the locked door handle all the more desperately.

'Wait! Hayes . . . That's okay, but . . . Where shall I? I'll see you at home, later, or . . . ?'

He turned away from her and shouted a curt goodbye to Clowes before turning his gaze back to Avery, his clear, expressive brown eyes polluted with anger. 'Not tonight. Got a lot to do. I'll call you.'

And with that, Hayes Ober drove away, leaving Clowes and Avery staring at one another through the gravel dust, across the space where his car had been.

Twenty-Four

Long before Dreamworld, or Universal Escape or Disney existed, there was Coney Island. And yet in the evolution of the American way of pleasure, one key ingredient was lost: the element of sexuality. Where modern parks encourage innocent – possibly infantile – delight, in an environment of clean, spacious, civilized safety, there was something risqué about Coney Island, something insidiously bawdy in the way that the cramped lines and violent rides forced close physical contact, and encouraged the indecorous and blatant display – in the company of strangers – of wanton exhilaration. It was a place where the very absence of safety and comfort, the very stripping away of decorum, created a frisson of delicious and slightly dangerous sexual excitement and humiliation, like a dream in which you find yourself naked in public.

Avery had never been to Coney Island, but she had read all this in one of Hayes's books on the anatomy of the twentieth-century leisure industry, read it one night when he was working, in the throes of one of his fugues maybe, or perhaps while she was waiting for him to get home, she could not remember.

Right now she was thinking of it only because that particular passage had suddenly, vividly become illuminated by personal experience: riding behind Trey Clowes on his moped, her hands lightly clasped about his waist, her legs spread on either side of his thighs, her breasts brushing against his back as he threw corners and accelerated on the straights. In the context of this innocent, functional purpose, absolved of all guilt and responsibility – how else can one ride pillion after all? It's unavoidable – these points of contact seemed so illicit, so surreptitiously and bewitchingly filthy, that Avery found herself becoming quite overheated. And it had nothing to do with the admittedly searing ambient temperature.

By the time they arrived at ImagiNation, in the cast member parking lot behind the security building, Avery dismounted to find her legs unsteady and her palms clammy. She hesitated to remove Clowes's spare helmet revealing what she was sure was a visible flush to her cheeks, but she took it off anyhow, wiped her hands on her pants, hoped that he wouldn't notice.

'Kinda hot under there, doesn't it?' He grinned. 'You get used to it after a while. Best way to get around, anyway.'

Avery nodded enthusiastically. 'Fun.'

She looked at the little orange bike and saw for the first time that it had 01 stencilled on its side. She laughed as she realized it was styled after the General Lee.

'I hadn't noticed that before. Nice touch.'

Clowes smiled shyly. 'Thanks.'

An awkward silence followed; a what-now? silence, which Avery took it upon herself to break. 'Thanks for the ride, anyway.'

'Well, I could hardly leave you stranded there, could I?'

Avery's face fell as Hayes's horrible departure came

flooding back. 'Yeah – I'm sorry about that. He's kind of . . .'

'Was it something I said?'

Avery patted Clowes on the shoulder. 'God, no. Christ! Don't worry about it. Hayes has a lot on his mind, that's all. Forget it.'

He looked at the ground, nervously tossing his Ren and Stimpy keychain from one hand to the other.

'You said . . . About seeing him at home . . . Are you . . . ?'

'Uh, yes. Yeah. But that's not –'

'Should I not have said you took me for a drink? I didn't realize . . . God, I guess I dropped you in it. Oh, man . . .'

'No, forget it, really. It wasn't that, anyway. Like I said, today's a really bad day for Hayes. He just decided to take it out on me. It's not your fault.'

'Can I take you for a drink to apologize anyhow?'

Avery smiled slowly, suddenly aware of a burgeoning desire to throw Clowes up against the wall of the security building and kiss him, while trying very hard to remind herself that a lot of it had to do with feeling pissed off with Hayes, with wanting to claw back some ego points.

'Yeah. You can. Or how about a coffee? Like, now?'

There was nothing much that she and Perdue could do until Hayes had seen Darwin anyway, she figured. And even if there was, she was in some measure of shit already.

This time when she climbed onto the moped behind Clowes, Avery reached right around him and locked her hands above the warm steel of his belt buckle, snuggling into him, beaming in the private darkness of the motorcycle helmet. She was feeling better already.

In this atmosphere of wilful misbehaviour, it seemed to

fit perfectly that, despite the pre-noon hour, they should order beer instead of coffee at Cleo's Barge. And it seemed appropriately devilish – not stalker-like or sinister – when Clowes confessed that he'd hunted Avery down at the Research and Development Complex by calling security HQ pretending to be from the Osceola County sheriff's department; and by talking one of Avery's colleagues into using Big Brother to track Hayes's car.

As Clowes talked and the alcohol went to her head, Avery found herself fighting the urge to study his forearms, which lay lightly crossed on the table before him as he fiddled with his beermat. Aesthetically, this was her favourite part of the male anatomy, and whilst she was happy to enjoy looking absent-mindedly at any particularly fine examples belonging to passing strangers, she had always been more reticent in checking out those of people she suspected she might be seriously attracted to. Perhaps she feared disappointment; she wasn't sure. It wasn't so much the fear that a low-grade pair would destroy the attraction. If there was a fear at all, it was that a particularly impressive forearm might deepen the attraction to the point where she felt dangerously out of control – lured irreversibly by a mere physical detail to a point where she might not want to be.

What the hell, she thought. And she looked.

The sleeves of his T-shirt were long, almost three-quarter-length – Avery's favourite. And her stomach lurched gently when she noted that the forearms also adhered very much to her tastes: slim, yet not spindly; muscular, yet definitely not pumped up, and furred with a medium-density covering of hair that was downy, not coarse and not too dark.

Whilst always happy to accept a little variety, Avery tended to judge all forearms against the first set that had made her melt, the set to which she could trace the inception of what she supposed she had to admit was a fetish. They'd belonged to a young musician, one half of a quirky duo that a boyfriend had taken her to see playing when she was back in high school. She couldn't even remember the boyfriend now, nor the band's name, but she certainly remembered the arms. At some juncture in the gig the lankier of the two had produced a piano accordion. And that was when she'd first noticed them. The intense power within their distinct delicacy and slenderness. The slight pallor and lack of unnecessary adipose tissue that revealed sapphire veins beneath the flesh. The surprising, graceful swell of muscle and sinew beneath the flesh as he played, languorously teasing the heavy instrument apart before driving the button-studded segment home again while the slender fingers of his left hand danced over the keys. Time had not faded this vivid image whatsoever, and now that she had steeled herself to make the inevitable comparison, she reluctantly admitted that Trey Clowes's forearms compared very favourably indeed.

Her scrutiny had not gone unnoticed. Trey looked down at his arms and hands, brushed away an imaginary piece of fluff on the hem of one his sleeves, and looked up at her perplexed.

She was already in that place she had dreaded going, she knew that. And when their eyes met, she knew for sure that there was no going back. It was physical attraction, yes, but she felt something else, too. When Hayes had driven away a chilly cloud of isolation had descended over her, and now it was gone, replaced by a sense of having an ally again, someone she felt something for and who, she was pretty sure, felt something for her. Someone she could trust. She had been like a sleeper, awoken in the dark to find her sheets missing: naked, frozen and miserable. Now she was covered again, cosseted beneath the plushest comforter, and she began to feel the warmth return, the liberty to move freely, to stretch out like a cat and relish the security, the sense of relief.

She waited for him to speak but heard her own voice first, slow and controlled. 'Trey? If you want, I'll tell you what's going on right now. With the investigation. I shouldn't, but if you want . . .'

He looked pleased, yet unsure. 'You don't have to – I mean, I don't want to get you into trouble.'

Avery took a large swallow of beer and smiled. 'I'm already in trouble. And I want to.'

Trey Clowes listened intently, silently, as Avery brought him up to date, not speaking until she came to the latest part. She had not expected any feedback from him, not really, so it took her by surprise when his black eyes widened and he leant forward excitedly in his seat, waving at her to stop.

'Wait, wait, wait! Hold on, what did you say the drug was called, the one they were using?'

'I don't know, whatever I just said. Anyway –'

'No, wait – did you say scopolamine?'

'Yes, something like that. So anyway, I was saying that Daetwyler said that, yeah, it *could* have blotted out whatever Leon suffered from enough for him to –'

'No, no but, scopolamine – is that definitely what he said?'

Avery paused to think about it, curious now. 'No, wha

220

he actually said was that it was similar to scopolamine. Why?'

'Because . . . Look, I know this sounds stupid, but it's a thing I know a bit about from one of my courses. And it's given me this thought that's – no, it's pretty far-fetched, I mean . . .'

Avery leant forward, interested. 'Go on. Tell me anyway.'

'Okay, well, we were doing a project on how genuine news stories mutate into legends, and one of the examples we had to look at was all those categories where someone meets someone else in a bar and wakes up with no memory of what's happened to them. Then they discover something horrific like their kidney's been removed. Or they've got the sperm of fourteen different men inside them, that kind of thing.'

Avery rolled her eyes, though she hadn't meant to seem rude. Trey looked sheepish.

'No, I know, they're ridiculous stories. They're myths. But you can trace them back to a few cases in New York, and a lot of cases in Colombia, where scopolamine – or a similar substance – has been used in crimes. And actually, those stories are pretty outrageous, too.'

'People having their kidneys stolen? Ya, right.'

'No, not that. In New York it was mostly straightfor-ward thefts. A gang of women targeting businessmen in the airport hotels. I swear this is true, I have an FBI report, I can show you it.'

'No, I believe you. I'm just not getting the connection.'

'I'm getting to it. Okay, the crimes in Colombia, those are mostly gang rapes – in Bogota they get four or five cases every weekend, women showing up at the Kennedy Hospital and they don't have any idea what happened to them, which is probably merciful. But the weirder cases

221

are *really* weird. Like, there was one where a bunch of guys dosed this wealthy couple with this drug – in Colombia they call it burundanga – and they drove them round ATMs and had them withdraw all the money from their accounts. Then they got them to empty their safe and help them load up pretty much all their other valuables from their house into the gang's van. This is totally true, I swear. The couple had no idea how the gang had gotten their safe open or how they'd got their pin numbers until they saw the bank's security footage and found their own fingerprints all over the safe.'

'I don't buy it. That sounds like a myth as well.'

'I know. But it isn't. On my life.'

Avery shrugged. 'I still don't get –'

'Why I'm telling you this? Look, the thing about this kind of drug is that it makes people compliant. Completely conscious and able, but without any ability to exercise free will. Suggestible. In other cases some of the victims were made to courier drugs from one place to another. Some got used in armed robberies, or to carry out hits.'

'Sounds like bullshit to me, like some kind of convenient defence in a court case: *I didn't know what I was doing, I'm innocent, I must have been drugged and told to do it.* Just doesn't ring true, Trey.'

Now he was mildly annoyed. 'Whatever.'

'So, what are you saying? That someone might have drugged Leon and got him to kill Lisa, and then kill himself?'

'It just seems odd that one minute Leon was at the Research and Development complex getting dosed up with scopolamine –'

'It wasn't scopolamine.'

'Okay, *a similar drug.* With similar effects, we assume

222

And then next minute, he's together enough to gather up some kind of weapon and sneak out and find his way to ImagiNation and find Lisa. You want far-fetched? You've got it right there. Not to mention that from what I knew of him, he really didn't seem like a suicide type of guy. He wasn't exactly a tortured soul. He was a pretty straightforward, common or garden asshole.'

Avery had to admit that Clowes had a point there, and one she'd not considered before. She drained her glass of beer and contemplated ordering another.

'Let's say you're right. Who told him what to do? Why would someone want to do that?'

'Whoever killed Jerry Lee Lucas, maybe? Whoever it was, they saw us. Saw us in the van, watching. If it was someone from the centre, they'd have known Leon. And they'd have recognized Lisa, maybe seen her with him before, maybe even knew her too. And they knew that they'd been seen. That's a pretty solid motive.'

'But Trey, that would mean . . .'

His face clouded over abruptly as he stumbled on the same possibility as Avery.

'Oh, man. I hadn't thought of that.'

Suddenly, despite the four rather poky Belgian beers, Avery was stone cold sober. 'Trey, I've got to get back to HQ, tell Perdue about this. If there's even a chance that you could be in danger . . . We've got to do something. And in the meantime you should maybe, I don't know, I mean, be careful.'

Clowes instinctively looked over both shoulders, scanned the almost entirely empty bar, then felt slightly foolish.

'Calm down, Avery, it's okay. Look, you said you have the volunteer files now, you're going to be able

223

to find out who drove the sport utility, who killed Lucas. Most likely, yeah? I mean, once you know, you'll take him in right away, won't you? And that'll be, what? Today? Tomorrow? 'Less he's left town. Right?'

Avery bit her lip. How could she possibly tell Trey that all Hayes and Perdue intended to do was to strike the suspected murderer from the Research and Development Complex records so that the County police – if they ever found him for themselves – couldn't link the homicide to Dreamworld? How could she tell him that her job, in this instance, was essentially not law enforcement but public relations? She couldn't. She spoke without meeting his gaze.

'Of course. Well, I mean, *we* won't take him in, we don't have jurisdiction, but we'll liaise with County and *they* will. Okay? So don't worry. But I have to get back there now, make sure it's being taken care of. I shouldn't really be here.'

Avery had leapt up from her seat and was rifling through her wallet, looking for cash. Clowes stared at her, unnerved by her obvious sense of urgency.

'It's okay, I said I was buying.'

Avery kissed him on the cheek and stood hesitantly as she prepared to make a dash for the door. It was going to take her at least twenty minutes to get back to ImagiNation without her car. She'd have to walk back to the King Tut's Palace reception building and take the monorail, and she didn't want to waste a second.

'Will you call me in a couple hours, like, let me know you're okay? And I can give you an update?'

'Yes. Look, take it easy, Avery. Even if we're right about this, I can only guess that whoever it was didn't know *me*. Or didn't see me in the van. I was in the back, remember? Else he'd have found me before now.'

Avery forced a smile. 'I know, I know . . . I'm just . . . I want to get onto this. Right now.'

Twenty-Five

Avery was relieved at first to find Perdue absent from the office – perhaps he didn't even know she'd been gone – but this peace of mind wasn't to last long. The note on her desk informing her that he was out on call in the park, demanding to see her urgently on his return, was beyond terse, and the four hours that Avery spent nervously awaiting his return seemed interminable.

She had guessed that he was going to be angry that she'd gone missing. But the way he greeted her gravely and without words, the way he clicked the door of his office closed behind her, and gestured for her to sit down – all this told her that whatever reaction she had prepared herself for, she'd made a gross underestimation.

Perdue remained silent and staring directly at her for some time, occasionally opening his mouth as if to speak, and then closing it again, as though none of the words coming into his head was sufficient to express what he felt. Eventually, the suspense killing her, Avery spoke first, telling Perdue that she was sorry. Sorry to have gone AWOL. But now she was back and she needed to speak to him urgently.

Perdue shook his head, his frustration written vividly

226

on his face. When he finally spoke, his cadence was irritatingly low and controlled. 'I talked to Hayes.'

Perdue's accusing tone turned Avery's contrition into indignation.

'So presumably he told you that he just fucking left me at the Research and Development Complex? How was I supposed to get back here, huh? Trey Clowes offered me a ride, so I said yes. And then I needed to cool off. Because I was so mad at Hayes. So I grabbed a coffee before I got back here. It's not like I was gone *that* long.'

Perdue rounded on her, his voice becoming quieter and more controlled as his ire grew. It was a habit that she'd heard other people talk about, but never observed for herself; he'd never been angry at her before. And it was just as bad as they said, just as intimidating, and yes, it did make you yearn for him to shout at you instead. Anything to stop that delicately poisoned murmur.

'Trey Clowes knew that Lisa was dead. Hayes said he told him: "It's what she would have wanted." You told him, Avery.'

She swallowed hard, decided to brazen it out. 'Yes, I did. I did tell him that. Because it was the only way that . . . Look, Perdue, he's not going to say anything to anyone. I wouldn't have told him if I thought – '

'Do you have any idea how serious this is, Avery? Any idea at all?'

'He's in danger, Felix. I think whoever killed Lucas knew that Lisa and Leon saw him, I think he killed them to protect himself.'

'The hell are you talking about? Daetwyler told you that whatever Leon had been given that morning would have made him able to handle a weapon. There's no doubt any more about who killed Lisa. Subject closed, Avery.'

And then, since she figured she was already in a whole heap of trouble, Avery decided to tell Felix Perdue about Clowes's theory. And as she laid it out for him, carefully, intelligently, she realized that she was beginning to buy it herself.

Perdue listened intently, without looking away and, when Avery was done, he continued to look at her, even while he reached into his drawer and pulled out what Avery recognized as the folder she and Hayes had collected from Daetwyler that morning. He tossed it across the desk towards her.

'Great theory, Avery. Only problem is that whoever killed Lucas obviously wasn't a volunteer. Check it out for yourself. None of the volunteers who owned sport utilities has worked at the centre for months. Two of the guys don't even live here in town any more. So that blows that one right out of the water, doesn't it?'

'Does it? I don't think it proves anything, myself. What, people can't borrow someone else's car? Or get a ride from someone else? I mean, Leon had Lisa pick him up. Probably a lot of them do that. Think they might feel crappy at the end of the day, the tests, whatever, don't want to drive . . .'

Perdue smiled patronizingly and made a show of trying to stifle a laugh which was so melodramatic and exaggerated that it made Avery's hackles rise.

'And that proves this crazy theory of yours, huh? You're just clutching at straws now, Sylvie.'

At the sound of her name, the name that she loathed so completely, Avery balled her hands into fists, her fingernails biting into the palms.

'Yeah? Well, how's this for another straw? Say the car is irrelevant, and our suspicion is on whoever was at the centre on the morning that Leon LeGalley skipped off to

ImagiNation. Who's to say that it was a volunteer at all? Who's to say that it wasn't someone who worked there full time?'

Perdue leapt to his feet, flailing his arms in exasperation as if he was so irritated that he didn't know what to do with himself.

'Now what the hell are you talking about? What, you're suggesting that – who? Daetwyler? That assistant girl of his? One of *them* did this? Avery, I think maybe you should go home. Lie down. Come back when you can think straight.'

The blare of his voice stoking her own ire, she reared sharply forward across the desk towards Perdue, like a cobra going in for the strike, the hiss in her voice equally reptilian.

'I *am* thinking straight, thanks. For the first time this whole stupid situation is actually beginning to make some sense to me. And if you thought about it more carefully, you'd feel the same way.'

Perdue sat back down, visibly dismayed that Avery had managed to get him so riled; managed to force him right past the stage where he could do his icy-cold domineering whisper and into a position of perceptible wrath. Avery revelled in it. Wondered if she could get him to raise his voice again. But now he was onto it. Controlled, sitting again, collecting himself. And so infuriatingly quiet that she had to strain to hear his words.

'So, would you like to tell Hayes about your marvellous new theory, or shall I? May I get this straight, are we accusing Daetwyler of murdering Jerry Lee Lucas too, or just Lisa Schaeffer? Oh, and Leon LeGalley, of course. I'd hate to get this wrong when I tell Hayes, who will be delighted to hear it, I'm sure.'

'Look, I didn't say Daetwyler, necessarily. Or Homolka.

But there are other people there. Lab techs, and juniors. Plenty of them. And I'm just saying: we should check them out too. Not just the volunteers. And I think you're doing Hayes a disservice here, frankly. If there's a chance that one of our own employees, someone *that* closely affiliated with Dreamworld, has done something this serious, I very much doubt that Hayes would want to ignore it. Wait for the whole thing to blow up in his face. Think about it. What if I'm *right*? You think you and Hayes are gonna have an easy time clearing up a mess like that? It gets out that some loser kills his girlfriend at ImagiNation, we can maybe weather it. Eventually it'd blow over, get forgotten. But some lunatic working under the auspices of Dreamworld screws up, goes nuts, you think you can put a positive spin on *that*? Good fucking luck.'

Perdue shook his head in disbelief. 'You're serious about this, aren't you?'

'Damn right I am. And I think you should be, too. And what about Trey Clowes? Don't you think we owe it to him to not just stop looking? What if I'm right, what if he *is* in danger? You wanna wait until something happens to him and then tell me: "Oops, you were right"? You wanna cover up another murder? Who knows where that one'll be? Maybe the guy won't have the decency to do it in the utilidors this time. Maybe he'll do it in the middle of Central Avenue, in the middle of the fucking three o'clock parade. *That'll* be fun.'

'Avery, you're really letting your imagination run away with so many *whatifs* here. I mean, why would anyone from the centre . . .'

'Look, Daetwyler said himself that something went wrong the day that Lucas died.'

'No, he didn't. Not exactly.'

'Well, he hinted at it, right? What if Lucas knew, saw

whatever it was? Threatened to go tell someone? Blow the lid off it? Or what if he was involved, threatened to sue? Daetwyler, Homolka, someone else from the lab, why the hell *wouldn't* they consider taking things into their own hands? Did you know that Daetwyler stands to lose custody of his daughter if there's any kind of slur on his name? Did you know that? Huh? It's amazing what lengths people'll go to when they want to protect themselves, Perdue. I know you know *that* much at least. Maybe better than most.'

Perdue massaged his temples. She waited for the explosion, or the killer whisper, but neither came. Now he sounded genuinely exasperated, and genuinely alarmed – dismayed? – by the growing realization that their relationship was collapsing under his nose.

'Avery, *stop it*. Just stop it. This is insanity. I told Hayes that I thought you were ready for investigative, but now I figure I was wrong. This has obviously . . . got to you. I don't know. You've got to get a grip, here.'

Avery studied her palms, the little red crescents where a couple of her nails had punctured the skin.

'Oh, I'm ready for investigative, believe me. The only thing I can't deal with is the fact that we don't really seem to be doing any investigating. I'm ready for investigative, I'm just not ready for a job that seems to consist mainly of advanced level bullshitting, advanced level sweeping-everything-under-the-carpet and hoping it stays there and that nobody notices the lump. I'm not ready for it now, and I don't think I ever will be.'

Perdue stared at her, and the complete coldness of the stare put out the fires of anger and reminded Avery of the last look that Hayes had given her. It filled Avery with an overwhelming sadness, a suffocating sense of loss and regret, of mourning.

She stood up to leave. 'Look, Felix, I'm just saying that I can't believe you're prepared to hope for the best. I can't believe that's what Hayes would want, either. If there's even a chance that I'm right –'

Felix Perdue slapped his palms loudly onto the desk before him. 'What the hell do you want to do?'

Avery regarded him calmly, feeling the thrill of control regained drenching her like the first blast of a hot shower after a skinny-dip on a cold night.

'I want to get access to the bodies.'

His silence encouraged her to continue.

'I mean, we have private forensics people we use, don't we? Well, we could run tests. See if there are traces of this drug in Leon's body, what levels. The dose that Daetwyler was using for the tests was small. If we only find a small amount, then we'll know that I'm wrong, and we can just forget about it. If it's significantly bigger . . . Don't you think it's worth doing? For peace of mind, at the very least?'

Felix Perdue dabbed the beads of sweat that had sprung up at his temples. 'No way. Not possible.'

Now the shower was gooseflesh cold and stung like a deluge of tiny, relentless needles. 'Not . . . Not *possible*? Of *course* it's possible. You know where the bodies are. You –'

'We can't get access to them. Okay? End of story.'

'No. *Not* okay, Felix. Not okay. I don't believe you. I think you just don't reckon it's worth the effort.'

Now Felix Perdue was angrier than Avery had ever seen him before, struggling to modulate his voice, struggling to control his limbs and his sweat glands, his very being. He moved slowly, stodgily, as if under water, as he leant across the desk towards her.

'You wanna get access to Leon LeGalley's body, Sylvie? You wanna do that? You wanna dig him up? Be my guest. All you have to do is knock down the new amusement arcade at the Americana resort. No problem, huh? You'll find him under about nine foot of concrete. Lisa Schaeffer, too. Knock yourself out.'

Avery sat motionless in the chair. 'You disgust me, Felix.'

The hurt in Perdue's eyes had carved a deeper slash in her heart than the venom it had replaced. 'In that case you'll be relieved when I call Hayes and tell him that . . .'

It had spilled into his voice, too, that intolerable pain; a great, terrible tidal wave of it that diluted his malice to nothing, and stung and burnt like alcohol poured over Avery's seeping emotional wounds.

'Tell him what?'

'Tell him that I want you off the case, Avery. As of right now.'

She walked slowly as she left Felix Perdue's office, closed the door gently behind her and maintained a dignified pace and a stoic expression as she moved through the security bullpen, ignoring the stares and the roaring silence of her colleagues. And she walked with silent grace across the parking lot in the dying evening light to her car.

It was only once she was inside that she let the tears come; let them stifle her breathing and soak her face and blur her vision as she sped down the tree-lined service roads, through the wide, unirrigated plains of undeveloped Dreamworld property and into the bruised carmine sunset, towards the final resting place of Lisa Schaeffer and Leon LeGalley.

Twenty-Six

Which part of her reconciliation with Hayes was the hard-est, Avery wasn't sure. It was *all* hard – the apologies, the elaborate verbal portrait of Trey Clowes-as-feckless-idiot, and of herself as contrite, blundering ingenue, prostrate and desperate for forgiveness at the feet of one older and wiser. It was hard and it hurt. Hurt her sense of honesty, of pride, of righteousness. Her psyche ached an ache that was worse than any physical pain she could remember.

That she was soothed by Hayes's forgiveness – a for-giveness she had earnt by duplicity and dishonesty and self-betrayal – only made things worse. And the genuine love she still felt for him and the gratitude for his under-standing were at hideous odds, she reflected, with her overriding feelings of victory in the name of her own agenda. Avery realized this now as she lay in Hayes's bed, in his arms, listening to the swish of the fans and the nightsong of the cicadas beyond the window.

But even as she admitted how hard it would have been to spend a night alone in her echoing apartment, a place that belonged to someone else, some single woman, an Avery who no longer existed, she looked at Hayes as if through the eyes of a stranger. And in a way, that's what she was. She was happy to be here, yes. And she remembered how it felt to love Hayes and to be in love with him. But the joy she felt at being here was the joy of yet another Avery. A new Avery, a spy, a crusader. The loyal mortal envoy of Lisa and Leon and Jerry Lee, the guerrilla defender of Dreamworld and impassioned protector of Trey Clowes.

Some time after leaving the security HQ that afternoon, on the drive to the Americana resort construction site, the new Avery had begun to emerge. It was she who had confidently jangled her own doorkeys at the security guard as she lied about being sent by Jim Desmarais to retrieve something from his Portakabin. She who had strode bravely through the deserted gloom, untroubled by the black, black shadows of the towering concrete tanks. And she who had silenced the old Avery, the one who caught her breath and clutched her pounding chest and wanted to avoid passing through them, reminded of something she'd read as a child in a book about ghosts, about towering rocks in Tibet whose shadows would suck the soul from those who strayed into the pools of darkness they cast on the ground.

This was the Avery, however, who yanked the bunches of weeds and wildflowers from beside the fetid portable toilets that stood like great rusting coffins against the electrified perimeter fence. Who held her tangled bouquet to her breast, gliding towards the games arcade like some spectral bride.

This Avery, the old Avery, had knelt on the rubble and rested her forehead on the bright new glass doors, tenderly placing her offering before them. Had wondered how properly to pay one's respects in such a macabre situation, but had done it anyway, with grace and reverence.

And when the moment of lucidity, the ghastly, almost

unfathomable reality of it all, had hit her like a freight train, she had closed her eyes and instinctively controlled her ragged exhalations like a woman giving birth. The innocence, the idealism, the blind faith – some little part of her essence began to leave her, and she could feel it as tangibly as if it were bleeding from her eyes in the tears that she wept.

The Avery who stood up and walked slowly away, the Avery who winked her thanks at the security guard and drove off, knowing just what she had to do and where she had to go – this was the new Avery.

And later in Hayes Ober's bed – after they'd fought and protested and talked and finally made love to one another – this Avery tumbled into the chasm of exhaustion that had opened before her and slept the deep, urgent sleep of a new-born creature.

Twenty-Seven

Avery awoke, groggy and blinking, to find Hayes gone. He had opened the drapes before he left, and the sun was streaming in, bathing the bed in a yellow wash of heat that made her want to stay there. She glanced at the bedside clock and then looked again, squinting in disbelief at the digital readout. Had she really slept until eleven-thirty? She rolled over, wide awake now, and picked up the phone.

Finding Hayes's voice-mail activated on both his office line and his cellular, she decided to call Trey Clowes instead. It took a while before it clicked that she didn't actually have his number, and she heaved herself out of bed and padded across the room to the walk-in wardrobe.

Having slipped on a fresh set of underwear from the bottom drawer of Hayes's dresser – *her* drawer – she now stood by one of the hanging rails in a state of mild confusion, trailing her fingertips over the clothes that were hers. Most of her weekend clothes were here, and nearly all of her evening wear – the DKNY separates and little Anne Klein dresses and suits that Hayes had bought her to wear to the endless roster of dinners with his colleagues. It occurred to her in passing then that she never went out with anyone *but* Hayes. But if she was honest with herself, she had to admit that her social life pre-Hayes used to consist solely of dates and more dates. Or, if she happened to be in one of her many short-lived relationships, cosy nights in with takeout and a rented movie. A Blockbuster night. Her favourite. There was Gwen, too, of course. They often spent hours online, instant-messaging one another, which sort of passed as a social evening, Avery figured, as much as anything could that involved typing and wearing a bathrobe.

Here at the end of the clothes rail were the components of Avery's spare security uniform pieces: the indigo pants and sky-blue shirts still hanging in their light plastic sheaths from the Dreamworld dry-cleaning department. She stared at them and frowned. Did she still have a job to go to? This one? Her old one? She wasn't sure. Her old patrol had been taken over by a new recruit, she knew that much. It meant that Perdue's mobile division was fully staffed, and if she was to go back, it would be under someone else's' auspices. Were there even any other posts free? And could something have been found for her so quickly?

Certainly Perdue had remained true to his threat and called Hayes to request her demotion. But Hayes had merely reported this to her without comment, and she hadn't dared ask him to elucidate. Hayes had forgiven her, though, that was certain too. And he had met her new theory – Trey Clowes's theory – with unexpected calmness and interest, and with a promise that he would take care of it himself, see Daetwyler and Homolka first thing this morning. If they had something to hide, he explained, it would be in their best interests, and in the best interests of Dreamworld, to tell him, so that he could decide the prudent route to take. Hayes's angle of approach was blatantly clear, however: if he could find a way to preserve the integrity of both Dreamworld and Daetwyler's project he would do it.

This dual aim now clashed more violently than ever with her own morals, but Avery had to admit that if there were dark confessions to be made, then Hayes – with his apparent desire to continue research and maintain the status quo – would be the most likely person to obtain them. This was not only Avery's *best* hope of finding out what had happened, but her *only* one, she felt. And once she had been assured that Trey Clowes was not under threat, there was nothing to stop her, she told herself, from coming up with some new way in which to use the information. Some plan that would protect Dreamworld whilst serving some measure of justice, too. The events of last night had convinced her that Hayes was more easily swayed by her opinions than she'd thought or hoped, and she had a good feeling that she could swing things her way, the *right* way, providing she could keep herself close enough to the investigation. There again, perhaps just staying close to Hayes was not enough. Why take a chance?

Avery tore away the plastic film from a pair of her uniform pants, yanked them from the hanger and pulled them on.

Avery had planned to grab a cup of coffee before steeling herself to knock on the door to Perdue's office. She hadn't planned, however, to run into him at the coffee machine. This, and the fact that he held not one but two cups in his hand threw her somewhat.

What to say now? Her mouth was dry and she'd hoped

to have a little more time to think over this particular rapprochement, but she forced herself to do some mental cheerleading. If she'd reconciled with Hayes – who'd had the added dimension of sexual jealousy over Trey Clowes to deal with – she could do this too. Of course she could.

'Replaced me already, Felix? Boy, I know you work fast, but . . .'

He looked at her, uncomprehending. She gestured at the cups and his face softened.

'I was just going to call you, Sylvie. I spoke to Hayes, but when you didn't show this morning I wasn't sure if you were coming in. Wasn't sure what was going on.'

Avery smiled shyly. 'Me neither. But here I am. Any word from Hayes yet? About his meeting at the centre?'

'Not yet. They couldn't see him until later, weren't in this morning. So I guess he's there about now. But I think I owe you an apology anyhow.'

This she hadn't expected. 'Why?'

Perdue carefully transferred one of the coffees into the crook of his arm and used his free hand to open the kitchenette door and his foot to hold it there.

'Come into my office. You can see for yourself.'

Trey Clowes was wearing some kind of navy-blue, long-sleeved T-shirt bearing a picture of a fifties-style robot and the Mambo surfwear logo. Avery was particularly relieved to note the length of the sleeves, because it reduced the risk of her getting inappropriately lascivious over someone who looked so shattered, so drained, so utterly haunted.

'Trey! What the hell is it? What's happened?'

Clowes looked at her dumbly, then at Perdue, who

had gently put his own coffee down on top of his filing cabinet before handing the other to Trey, who reached for it with trembling fingers.

'He thinks he was maybe followed home yesterday. After he was with you at Cleo's Barge. He's not sure, but he thinks so. And then this morning he found this on the seat of his motorbike.'

Perdue pointed to something lying on his desk, something that Avery couldn't see from where she stood in the doorway. She walked in, closed the door behind her and froze again when she heard Clowes's voice, vibrant with fear.

'I came here right away to find you, Avery. I'm scared.'

She looked into the unfathomable black eyes and quickly looked away again, unsettled.

Perdue had moved to his desk and beckoned to her to come over.

'The forensics contractors are on their way over. Glad you got here now.'

Avery took a breath and looked down to where Felix Perdue was pointing.

The note had been written on a piece of paper torn from a legal pad using something ruby red – ink or paint, not blood, although that was certainly the desired impression – and the writing had been executed using some crude instrument. A twig, Avery mused. Or maybe a key? The thick pools of ink forming the letters had warped the paper dramatically, and you could see that even now there were areas amongst the dry ones that still glittered with a dense, awful moistness.

TOO BAD
I FOUND YOU
SEE YOU SOON

The words were unarguably disturbing, as chilling in their simple threat as the author had obviously intended. But their psychological impact was increased a hundred-fold by the scratchy, jagged and dripping style in which they'd been written. This the author couldn't have planned, Avery was certain. But should he or she choose to market this font commercially, the designers of slasher-movie posters and horror novels and scary theme-park attractions would surely come running from every corner of the globe, open chequebooks in hand.

She stared at the note again, mesmerized, in awe at its raw power. No wonder Clowes looked the way he did.

'Did you get a look at the person following you?'

She glanced up at Clowes, who was now sitting back in the chair with his knees curled up towards him, feet firmly on the edge of the seat, clutching his coffee cup in both hands. He shook his head, and Perdue expanded for him.

'Uh-uh. Not even sure what kind of car, except it was light coloured, new-looking. And not a compact car. Bigger.'

'But not a sport utility?'

Clowes shook his head again, and, again, Perdue answered.

'Definitely not.'

'But it's the same person, presumably. I mean, it has to be.'

Perdue shrugged. 'I would guess. Looks like maybe when I was making those calls yesterday, trying to rule out the sport utilities on the volunteer list, I might have struck pay-dirt after all. Tipped someone off that we were onto them. And so they know that we must have talked to the only survivor – the person they want to get hold of.'

Perdue gestured to Clowes, who seemed to shrink even further into himself and the chair in which he sat.

'And then, Sylvie, I have a horrible feeling that they found *you*. At the centre, and saw Trey with you. Followed you both. Then followed him home.'

Avery was confused. 'Found me how? And how would they have known that I had anything to do with the investigation?'

'Everybody I called, I gave them both of our names. Said, if you think of anything, remember any volunteers who maybe got a ride from someone with a car fitting the description, to call either one of us.'

'Yeah, but how would they find me?' she reiterated. 'I don't get it.'

Perdue shrugged. 'I have no idea. But it's not impossible.'

Avery couldn't help glancing over at Clowes, who looked momentarily sheepish. No, it *wasn't* impossible for someone with a bit of cunning to find her, that was for sure.

Perdue continued his concerned musings. 'Or maybe they've been watching you for a while, following you too, I don't know. Hoping that you'd lead them to Clowes. You've been around a few places – over to Leon LeGalley's girlfriend's home, what's her name? Shannon Reilly. Over to where she works. Down at the centre a lot. You said it yourself – this volunteer circuit is pretty tight. They all know one another. Word would get around.'

Avery tried not to scowl at Perdue. 'So we're back to thinking it's a volunteer? Wouldn't it make more sense if it were someone who works at the centre? They know me already, they also know I'm on the investigation. Did that not occur to you, Felix?'

Perdue's voice dropped a few decibels. Not quite a whisper, but definitely quieter than normal. Avery tensed a little.

'Look, Avery, Hayes seemed to be prepared to take your theory – *Trey*'s theory – on board, and so am I. Okay? He's going to talk to Daetwyler and Homolka, and if nothing comes of that, we'll check out the junior lab techs and all the part-time workers. Obviously someone has it in for Trey, and, given that, then yes, I'll have to not rule out foul play at the centre on Leon LeGalley's death as well as Lisa Schaeffer's. I'm on *your* side, Avery. So don't harangue me, please.'

Avery tried to ignore the nagging memory of Perdue's horrible pig-headedness the day before and concentrated on feeling simple relief at his volte-face. She decided not to acknowledge his chiding, either.

'What about Trey?'

Clowes and Perdue looked at one another.

'We already talked about this, didn't we, Trey? I called Hayes for advice, and he suggested that Trey stay right here, at least for now, until we can find somewhere that's safe for him to go and provide him safe escort there. And in the meantime, we get right onto this and try to eliminate the danger altogether. And . . . Trey, would you excuse us for a moment? Avery, would you mind stepping outside?'

The pair stopped in the corridor outside Perdue's office and Perdue closed the door behind him. His voice was lowered again, but now only in the name of secrecy.

'Hayes said that supposing – just supposing – that Daetwyler and Homolka *did* turn out to know anything about this, he's going to need to fix things from *that* end, come to some arrangement. So he'd rather that Trey was with us. Said he might need to speak to Trey himself, do a little negotiating. A propos of what he . . . saw.'

The distaste must have registered on Avery's face.

'I mean compensate him, Sylvie. Something like that.'

'You mean buy him off.'

She had to strain to hear Perdue's low hiss of a reply, whose volume now had less to do with secrecy and more to do with rising temper.

'I mean *compensate him*. Got that? I'll make sure he's safe, Sylvie, that much I promise you. But don't kid yourself that I don't know why you're so desperately concerned. You might have been able to convince Hayes otherwise with some crap, but not me. And don't forget your priorities, either. You work for Dreamworld. We're your family. You put your family first.'

Much to Perdue's chagrin, Avery burst out laughing. 'I'm sorry, did I just walk onto the set of *Goodfellas*?'

She was relieved to hear his cadence returning to a normal sound level. But its sobriety sent a chill right through her. 'Look Sylvie, never mind your private life, that's not my business. But the accusations you're making towards people at the centre, towards the research projects, towards our security policies, you're scaring me. I want you here Sylvie, I *need* you here. I never had any kids, and you're the closest thing to family that I've got beyond this place. And you're the same, we both know it. Here's where you belong. It's in your blood. I just don't want to see you hurt. And I think that out there, in the real world, you *will* get hurt. And you're strong, I know. After everything that's happened to you, you could take that, deal with it. But God knows, Sylvie, *I* couldn't.'

Twenty-Eight

As she waited to hear from Hayes, it seemed to Avery that Perdue's office was teetering on the event horizon of some gaping maw in time and space, where the minutes crawled past at a far slower rate than they did elsewhere. Outside, far, far below, beyond the window where she now stood, she felt she could almost see the moments rushing past, by-passing her, moments through which she and Trey Clowes would slowly pass later, at some delayed point in time.

It was a crowded day in the park – comparable almost, though not quite, to the swarms expected at Easter or Thanksgiving or Christmas – and many wiser individuals had clearly decided to forgo the hell of the long lines at the attractions in favour of simpler pleasures. Dreamworld, like many other theme parks, is built in the 'hub and spoke' design conceived by Walt Disney. John K. Darwin's twist, however, was to turn his central hub circle into a commodious yet intimate 'marketplace' built around a peachy copper monolith – an effigy of Kit-E-Cat – encircled by a wide walkway and occasional 'lay-bys' containing charming diversions. These diversions were some of Avery's favourite things in the park, and from her vantage point she watched others enjoying them, greedily assimilating their joy. The joy of the shrieking children who chased the fat sparkling bursts of water issuing from the interactive fountains and giggled at the clown who blew soap bubbles so huge that he could step inside them. The joy of the teenage couples, forgetting to be cool as they marvelled at the man who could write both of their names on a grain of rice before suspending it in a tiny vial of oil hung on a pendant. Now, switching her gaze to the northern end of the marketplace, closest to the top of Central Avenue and to Avery's vantage point, she lapped up the anticipation of the crowd around the pearl-in-the-oyster stall. And she delightedly held her breath with them as they watched a woman plunging her hand into the salty barrel and craned their necks to see the treasure revealed by the shucking of the shell. Now and then a huge cry would go up – audible even here, three storeys above street level – when somebody got a particularly large pearl, or a rare one: pink or, better yet, black.

Avery turned away from the window with a smile which melted away at the sight of Clowes's grim countenance. This didn't escape his notice and he looked away, guilty perhaps at bringing her down.

'You really do love this place, don't you?'

'More than anywhere else in the world.'

'Even now? After all this? Everything that's happened here?'

Avery thought about it. 'Yes.'

Perdue had left the room to use one of the main terminals in the computer room in order to access various employees' records, and now Clowes glanced nervously at the door, as if checking for his imminent return.

'It's weird, Avery. You and me, we've got nothing in

common, and yet I feel so . . . This sounds stupid . . . In tune with you.'

Avery smiled helplessly. 'I don't know what to say to that.'

'You don't have to say anything. It's just weird for me is all. Like, Lisa? We liked all the same things. And yet we didn't really get along at all. I guess I always thought – like, until now – that . . .'

'Yeah, I know. It's propaganda. It's movies. Movies and TV that does it. Always pisses me off, you know. You always have this scene where someone goes: "Ohmigod! You put mayonnaise on your fries?' I put mayonnaise on *my* fries!!!" Then they find out that they both like some book or some song and it's always something really obscure that nobody's ever heard of. It's just lazy, isn't it?'

'*Lazy?*'

'Yeah: lazy writers' shorthand, for "these two are perfect for each other".'

Clowes thought about it and nodded. 'Yeah. But, I mean, in real life. Sometimes . . . I don't know. I mean, you and your boyfriend, I bet *you* like the same things. You both like this place, that's for sure.'

'True. But I've always thought that *hating* the same things is much more important. You don't hate the same things, that'll get you in trouble every time.'

Clowes laughed. 'Hating the same things. Right. You're pretty smart, you know that, Avery? I guess that's why it still surprises me that you like it here so much. That you work here. I didn't think anyone like you ever would.'

She wasn't sure whether to be flattered or not. 'What's not smart about wanting to spend your time someplace nice? Someplace that's friendly? A little city that's as close to perfect as you're ever gonna get in the US. I always thought that was a pretty astute move of mine.'

'But it's *not* perfect, is it? Not really. It just looks like it is. On the surface. Because you and everyone else, you work very hard to keep it looking that way. Me, I find that kind of creepy.'

Avery stared at the door, willing Perdue to come back in. He didn't, and she stood up instead. 'I'm going to get coffee. Want one?'

'So, now what?'

Perdue arched back in his chair, locked his hands behind his head, stole a quick glance at the damp armpits of his shirt and hastily put them down again.

It was three p.m. and Hayes, finally done at the Research and Development Complex, had called en route back to the office to report what he'd found.

Avery, who had been sitting on the visitors' sofa beside Clowes before the call came through, had transferred herself to the chair opposite Perdue's desk when it did, and it was here that she now perched in a state of intense agitation.

'These alibis, Felix – we're sure they're watertight? I mean, has Hayes checked? Or should *we*? Or what?'

Perdue shook his head. 'He did all that while he was there. I mean, he's bringing everything back with him, but there's nothing to check. It's kosher, Sylvie. Face it. We need to think of something else.'

She would have none of it.

'So there's what? Testimonies, from members of staff at the centre, the lab techs, saying that Daetwyler and Homolka were at the centre all morning the morning Lisa and Leon died?'

'Right. Hayes took them himself. Individually. They all tallied. And while we're at it, Daetwyler and Homolka's statements tallied too.'

Avery looked unconvinced.

'Big Brother's log backs it up, Sylvie. They *did* leave the centre very late the night before, but they both left Dreamworld property by the south exit. If they'd been going to Orange Blossom Trail, they'd have gone north, by the closest exit to the centre.'

Avery stood up suddenly, started pacing the room. 'They're intelligent guys, Perdue! You know that! They know about Big Brother. They might have driven round the long way on purpose!'

'Even if they had, the times barely tally with what Trey saw, the time that Trey got to Emanuelle's. And, as you know, neither of them drives a sport utility.'

She sat down again, exasperated.

'What about the next morning?'

'Big Brother says they arrived first thing, blew at the regular time that night. Neither one of them left the centre all day.'

'How do you know that? They wouldn't maybe take somebody else's car instead? Did that not occur to you? This all – well, to my mind it proves nothing.'

Now Clowes chipped in. 'Yeah, and also what if the log got tampered with? My first roommate at college, he could get into just about any system. I mean, these guys, Avery says they're, like, MIT grads. They'd know how to do it, probably.'

A shadow of doubt passed briefly over Perdue's face. 'I don't think anyone could get into Big Brother. I mean, we had experts set it up. They protect against those things. It's very secure.'

Clowes gave a snort of derision. 'Sure. Right.'

Perdue thought for a while. 'Is it possible to tell if the system had, I don't know, been *tampered with*?'

Clowes shrugged. 'Possibly. I think so. I mean, I know a little bit about computers myself. My roommate taught me a lot. I could take a look, if you wanted.'

'I don't know. We should maybe get someone in from our computer department.'

Clowes looked a little hurt. 'Whatever. I just thought maybe for the sake of secrecy you wouldn't want to. Like, if you had to explain exactly what you were looking for to whoever did it? Also, I'd like to help. I feel like kind of a spare wheel around here.'

Perdue shot Avery a look. 'I don't think Hayes would approve, but I'm gonna say yes. Right now we need all the help we can get. And Trey's right: I guess the fewer people get involved, the better.'

Just moments after Perdue had returned from settling Clowes in at a terminal in the computer room, Hayes Ober arrived back. A pretty blonde security junior was by his side, and as soon as the two walked in, Hayes's eyes searched urgently around the room.

'Where's the Clowes kid?'

Avery and Perdue looked at one another. She was relieved when Perdue answered.

'I sent him off to, uh, sit in another room. So Sylvie and me could go through some stuff in private.' He looked at the security girl, who was hopping from foot to foot, then back to Hayes. 'What's up?'

Hayes closed the door behind him and gestured to his companion. 'Kym here, she got a call – what was it, honey? About ten minutes ago? Someone on a cellular. Wanted to know whether the owner of the moped in the security lot was still in the building. Right?'

The girl nodded enthusiastically.

'Did they say anything else?'

The blonde ignored Avery and addressed her reply to Hayes instead. Avery felt a prickle of annoyance.

'They asked, like, where. What department?'

'But you didn't tell them anything, honey, right?'

The girl looked aghast. 'Of course not. I said: "I'm afraid I can't give you that information." And I tried caller-ID after he'd gone, but he'd blocked his number. Is there anything else I should do?'

Hayes patted her on the shoulder. 'No, you're fine. Thanks for your help. You can go now.'

After she'd left the room, Hayes, Perdue and Avery agreed that Clowes ought not to leave for now, and certainly shouldn't return home.

'I've stepped up security outside, but I don't want you running around either, honey,' Hayes told Avery. 'Whoever this guy is, there's a good chance he's seen you with Trey. If there's even a possibility that . . . Well you know, I want you to be careful. When you're ready to leave tonight, call down to security, ask for Nelson. I've told him you're gonna leave your car here, and I want him to drive you back to my place, see you in. I've gotta take the execs from Nathan's Famous down to the Americana site, talk to them about running something outta the giant hot dog. But I shouldn't be home too late. Sound okay?'

Avery crossed her fingers mentally. She already had her own plans, and they weren't going to fit in with Hayes's at all.

'Yes. Got it. Fine.'

He must have sensed her trepidation. 'I'm serious, Avery. I'm not having you taking any risks. You're too precious to me.'

Perdue smiled at her, then at Hayes, like a proud father, and Avery beamed back at them both, trying her best to look honest.

'I know. I promise.'

Hayes clapped his hands together, then rubbed them vigorously. 'So, Perdue? You know what you're doing?'

'Uh-huh. The junior lab techs. The volunteers again. Get proper statements this time. Who was coming, who was going, everything.'

'Thank you.'

Avery looked indignantly from one man to the other. 'So Daetwyler, Homolka . . . We've just scrubbed them off the list?'

Hayes strolled over to behind Avery's chair, put his hands firmly on her shoulders and leant down, his smoothly shaven cheek pressing against hers. 'Avery, I trust you, I trust your judgements. I think you're a great investigator. On your say so, I just went and accused two professional scientists, whom I engaged on a multi-million dollar project, of premeditated homicide. And I was glad to do it. And if some more evidence comes up, I'll go talk to them again, but for now we're on very thin ice. *I'm* on very thin ice. So I'd appreciate it if . . .' His tone of voice made finishing the sentence unnecessary. Avery stiffened.

'Fine. Understood.'

Hayes ruffled her hair. 'Good. See you at home later. And be careful.'

After Hayes had left, Avery decided to share her thoughts with Perdue, tried to convince him not to rule out Daetwyler and Homolka. Hayes may have believed their story, but he was someone who wanted very, very badly to believe it. And her own feelings hadn't changed. They could have seen her at the centre with Clowes. And since neither were at the centre first thing this morning, according to Hayes, either could have left the note for him. The call had come through *after* Hayes left them, too. And they could easily have accessed Big Brother from the centre's main computer system in order to find out whether his bike was on property today. Moreover, she reasoned – as Perdue listened impatiently, obviously gagging to weigh in with his protests – whoever left the note must have known that Trey would run to safety; the safety of Dreamworld security. Why would an outsider do that? Warn Trey that he was in danger and send him running for cover? It would only make the stalker's job harder. Unless – Avery figured – that stalker was someone who wouldn't contemplate making an attack in public. Someone civilized, a professional person. And someone with contacts, who knew her and Perdue and Hayes, and who knew that he could get into the security building on those pretexts. Late maybe, when everyone else had gone. Whoever it was had Trey Clowes trapped like a lab rat in a maze. Perdue took all this in with an air of caution. As much as he respected Avery, he'd always been in thrall to Hayes, and seemed determined not to rock the boat. So Avery set about obediently joining Perdue on his round of calls to the volunteers and other Research and Development personnel, none of which yielded anything to lend support to Daetwyler and Homolka's claims. Admittedly, none corroborated her own theory either, but this didn't surprise her. Whoever was behind all of this was a very slick customer indeed: cunning, intelligent and careful. He or she would never have allowed themselves to be seen leaving the centre, of that Avery was certain.

At seven-forty, Avery said goodbye to Perdue; told him that she was going home.

'Did you call Nelson?'

Avery bit her lip before lying. 'Yes, I'm meeting him by the door.'

'Okay. I'll be here if you need me. All night. Hayes wants Trey here, still. We don't really know where else to put him. And obviously we can't leave him alone.'

Avery felt suddenly sorry for Perdue. 'All night? Oh, man . . .'

Perdue smiled. 'It's all right. Double pay. And I'm taking tomorrow off.'

'Even so, isn't there someone here on night duty anyway?'

'Well, yes, but they need to be going in and out to the park dealing with the graveyard shift people and what-have-you. We can hardly expect them to stay here and babysit.'

'Babysit?'

'Right. He's a nice guy, Trey, but like I said, we can't leave him here on his own.'

When it hit her that Perdue hadn't been referring to matters of safety, Avery hardened a little. 'What, he's gonna steal something? Snoop around? For Christ's sake, Felix, he's put his life in our hands! He's not going to . . .'

Perdue rolled his eyes. 'C'mon, get real, Sylvie. Comes down to policy. Anyhow, I don't mind doing it.'

She shrugged. 'You say so. I'll call you tomorrow.'

He grinned at her in a reconciliatory fashion. 'Not too early, huh?' She smiled back weakly. 'And be careful

Lock the doors when you get home. Don't let anybody in. Oh, and have Nelson stop off on the way back, get you some takeout. He won't mind. You skipped lunch again. Don't think I didn't notice. Okay?'

Now she was overcome by genuine fondness for him and her smile broadened. Before she could stop to think she found herself leaning forward to deliver a small kiss to his forehead. 'Whatever you say, Dad.'

The computer room was dark, lit only by the hard white glow of the terminals, and Clowes was the only person left inside.

Avery cleared her throat loudly to alert him to her presence, not wanting to make him jump. Her swivelled his chair around to face her.

'I'm going now, Trey. You all right?'

'Fine. Perdue said he'd stay with me. That was nice of him.'

He rubbed his eyes, which were blurry from staring at the monitor for so long.

'You find anything?'

He shook his head. 'No, but tell the truth, I'm not all that *au fait* with this exact system. It's pretty state of the art. I'm just trying all the different things I can think of and maybe I'll find something eventually. Good to have something to do, anyway. Keeps my mind off stuff.'

Avery was about to leave, say goodbye, when she made a sudden decision. 'Trey, I need your help, need to ask you something. If you can keep a secret.'

He sat up, interested. 'For you? Of course I can. Shoot.'

'The other day, when you found me at the centre? How did you get in there without a pass?'

Trey Clowes looked at the floor. 'Oh, I kind of snuck in.'

'Snuck in how?'

'Should I tell you? I don't know. Are you gonna set Kit-E-Cat on me?'

A chill ran through Avery as Trey's light-hearted quip inadvertently triggered a flashback to her nightmare. To Kit-E-Cat's scarlet maw, the Lisa Schaeffer doll's tiny little intestines. Avery faltered slightly.

'Set Kit-E-Cat on you . . . no. Obviously not. I won't say anything.'

'Sure?'

She looked him squarely in the eye. '*Yes*, Trey. I'm sure because I'm asking you because I want to know how you did it so that I can go and do it right now myself. *Okay*?'

He looked slightly taken aback. 'Okay.'

After Clowes had told her and she had said goodbye, he turned back to the screen and pushed up the sleeves of his sweatshirt. Avery caught her breath, unable to stop herself from looking at the arms, and at the face reflected on the screen in the darkness. Not a perfect image, just a greyscale ghost over the strings of letters and numbers. A high, smooth white brow; charcoal shadows in the eye sockets and beneath the cheekbones; and here, where the mouth parted slightly and here again beneath it, a horizontal smudge cast by the fullness of the lower lip in repose. Avery hovered awkwardly, wishing she could have dived in and kissed Clowes as effortlessly and unself-consciously as she'd kissed Perdue moments before. Only perhaps not on the forehead. Perhaps, more specifically, about four inches south.

Twenty-Nine

The emergency lay-by to the side of the service road was
easy to find, and Avery pulled in, killed her engine and
watched the sky impatiently. It took a good half an hour
for the benign pink cotton-candy puffs to mutate into
angry purple welts that finally turned grey when the sun
set. And at last Avery climbed from the car and began
carefully to make her way along the narrow grassy belt
that flanked the tarmac.

Overhang from the pepper trees and palmetto brushed
her face as she crept by, now and again rebounding as
she passed, tapping her lightly on the shoulder or the
back of the head, making her jump and look behind her,
though she knew that she was entirely alone.

The gap in the foliage was just where Trey said it would
be – at the point where, if one searched the night sky,
the ears and trident belonging to Atlantis's monolithic
ten-storey Kit-E-Cat-as-Poseidon appeared to be directly
behind the silhouetted turrets of Fort Enchantment.

Getting into the thicket had been as easy as Trey had
said. But forging *through* it, or indeed finding viable egress
at the other side, was a much trickier business altogether.
Branches and palm fronds sliced at Avery's face and arms
as she pushed through, and at the densest part, she found

herself squinting helplessly into the blackness, trying to ignore the tiny mystery rustlings around her and wondering if she might, in fact, have got it wrong.

Eventually, just when panic and claustrophobia threatened to engulf her altogether, she caught sight of a chink of weak orange-sherbet coloured light clenched between the thick roots at floor level. As she dropped reluctantly to her hands and knees, there was a sudden outbreak of scurrying sounds nearby and Avery froze momentarily before reminding herself that it was most likely to be Dreamworld's little brown rabbits. And, even if she were mistaken, the snakes and racoons that she feared would be running *away* from her rather than the other way round.

She emerged from between two roots somewhat bedraggled, stood up stiffly and noted with relief that the parking lot was almost empty and the patrolman and his dog were nowhere to be seen. She paused to survey the personal damage before continuing: a snag in the knee of her pants, a small tear to her shirt. Plus a fairly unpleasant-looking gash on her arm, which fortunately turned out to be little more than a scratch once she'd rubbed away the dirt and the initial streak of blood. And having smoothed her hair and straightened her clothing, she began to make her way across the lot to the centre with as much speed and stealth as she could muster without looking suspicious.

The back door, the one leading directly into Daetwyler's research suite, was the first hurdle. To Avery's great annoyance, she realized that its function as an exit was guaranteed exclusivity by the lack of any handle on its exterior face. Kicking herself for not remembering this, for not thinking of any plan beyond how to get into the grounds unseen, Avery began to edge her way round the side of the building, with a vague thought about Daetwyler's office forming in her mind.

The door. She had slammed the door that day, and there had been another thump, an outside-opening door responding to the change in air-pressure. She remembered it clearly. And this, the anonymous grey firedoor she had now reached, this must be it. She tried the handle, but to no avail – it was locked fast from the inside. Now, crouching low, she peered through the keyhole, and the darkness that met her eye told her that the key was in there.

The parking lot was almost pitch-black – the patrol guy hadn't been kidding about the meagre lighting – and although she was glad of the cover it provided, it made her current task all the more testing. Working blind, Avery fumbled to dismantle the silver pen that she'd taken from her breast pocket. Holding the lid between her teeth, she struggled to unscrew the body of the thing, and finally to extract the slim refill tube that channelled the ink. Holding her breath on occasion so that she could more keenly hear the silence – which she kept imagining broken by human movement, both within the darkened office and in the lot behind her – she tried to control her fumbling fingers.

The tube removed, the pen reassembled and placed back in her pocket, Avery now jabbed the tube hard into the keyhole, and the key fell to the floor with a metallic chink. She held her breath again.

Lying on the cold concrete, she could see through the gap at the bottom of the door, could see the key lying there, and tried to use the tube once again – to little effect – to sweep it out. Lying prone as she was, she felt the vibrations of the patrolman's footsteps a few seconds before she heard the hollow slap of shoe-leather on tarmac and the scrabble of the dog's claws. She leapt to her feet, and waved at the patrolman in civilized greeting.

'Evening!'

Her voice wavered a little in its attempt to sound casual and he regarded her with some uncertainty and did not speak. So she addressed him again.

'Sorry if I startled you.'

He nodded soberly, still unsmiling. 'You didn't. Is there a problem?'

Avery thought quickly. 'I don't know, is there? I was going to ask *you* that. I was just on my way home and I got a buzz on my walkie-talkie. Central command said one of the alarms had been tripped back here – Professor Daetwyler's suite? And no one had got to it yet? Just figured you might need some backup.'

The patrolman frowned, plucked the walkie-talkie from his belt and held it to his ear to see if it was working. It was.

'I didn't hear anything.'

Avery shrugged. 'Weird. Still, I told central I'd check it out.' She gestured towards the door. 'Shall we?'

As soon as the patrolman had disappeared into the main lab, Avery made her way to the door of Homolka's office, silently turned the handle and stepped inside. Her fellow security guard would, she knew, be following procedure, slowly navigating the premises, back to the wall, as per standard law enforcement training. This would take a while, she convinced herself, so although she would have to work reasonably fast to find what she was looking for, there was no point in succumbing to panic, which would only hinder her progress.

Working without switching the light on – which would have contravened procedure and alerted suspicion – made things a little harder. But fortunately for Avery, Homolka was obviously the anal-retentive type, and had everything neatly filed and marked, including the bounty that Avery sought.

Rifling through the slim coffin box marked 'Devon's tapes', Avery shouted out to the patrolman in an attempt to cover the noise. 'Nobody in the professor's room! Moving into the next office!'

The reply came from a reassuring distance away. 'Roger that. Nobody in the labs, either.'

The shadows within the box, however, in combination with Homolka's spidery handwriting, made it hard to see the dates marked on the side of each cassette, and Avery was pulling them out ever more frantically when she heard the man's footsteps approaching.

Closer, closer, closer. And then nothing.

Outside the door, the guard stood silently, listening. He poked his head into the office, a suspicious look on his face.

'Everything in order here?'

Avery jumped and followed his eyeline to the open box in her hand. 'Yes. Fine. Box fell on the floor. I was just putting the stuff back.'

He raised an eyebrow. 'Uh-huh.'

'Probably there before. Doesn't look like anyone's been here.'

'No?'

'I don't think so. You know, maybe that was what they heard. Box falling.'

'I thought you said an alarm had been tripped.'

Shit. Avery chastised herself and silently counted to three, tried to look as unruffled as she could.

'Did I? I don't know. Maybe whoever called it got the code wrong.'

Yeah, nice going you fucking idiot, she told herself angrily. They accidentally called the special code for 'box falling off shelf'.

The patrolman looked understandably confused. 'Sounds like the whole thing was a mess up. Me, I didn't hear anything.' He watched her fingers, frozen inside the box as they had been when he walked in. He eyed her coldly. 'Which division you from, anyhow?'

'ImagiNation. But I'm a friend of Dr Daetwyler's. I guess I just thought if I could be any use here . . .'

'Yeah, well, next time . . . I've had this site under perfect control very well up until now, and I can't imagine that I'll need any back-up in the future. Okay? Let's go.'

She hovered uncomfortably. 'I'll just put these back.'

'Nobody's supposed to be in here, Miss – what did you say your name was?'

'Avery. Sylvia Avery.'

'Sylvia Avery. Well, can I suggest you put the box down where you found it, Miss Avery, and let's go.'

She shrugged, again struggling to look casual, and walked slowly behind the guard towards the exit and back out into the balmy night air.

'Where is your vehicle, Miss Avery?'

She gestured vaguely towards the opposite side of the building.

'Staff lot. Sorry. I used my boyfriend's space. I figured in an emergency it would be . . .'

He nodded sourly. 'And your boyfriend is?'

'Hayes Ober. From the Dream Tech division.'

The man nodded again, bid her a still-wary goodnight,

and began to walk away. Avery began to walk in the opposite direction.

As soon as he was out of sight, Avery broke into a run and forced her way into the underbrush. With no time to select a decent gap, breaking through to the other side proved to be a particularly unpleasant and gruelling test of her strength and valour – a matter of simply pushing against the sturdy branches in one direction and then another until something gave. When she finally emerged she was draped with cobwebs and leaves that stuck to her hands and face, but she didn't hesitate for a moment, instead breaking into a run towards the lay-by and her car.

Nor did she bother to clean up once inside. Instead, she unzipped her pants and began to fish down inside them. Having retrieved the cassettes that she'd stuffed down there in the split second before the patrolman had burst into the office, she threw her precious haul into her lap, thrust the engine into life and the gearshift into drive, pausing only briefly to raise her bloodied middle finger in the general direction of the Research and Development Complex before she sped away.

Thirty

'. . . eighty-thirty on this morning of June thirtieth . . .'
   '. . . I was disgusted to see that . . .'
   '. . . just joined us . . .'
   '. . . When Jerry shut Tom in the fridge . . .'
   '. . . in the next hour . . .'
   '. . . dangerous . . .'
   '. . . further update on the big trial . . .'
   '. . . My daddy says . . .'
Catherine Homolka hadn't been kidding. It *was* hard
to hear Devon Daetwyler's tiny voice over the boom of
the CNN anchor. Damn hard. But for Avery's purposes,
it was just the confirmation she needed that the tapes
had been put into the correct boxes, and that one of the
three she had filched had been recorded on the day of
Lisa Schaeffer's death. And listening to this confusing
cacophony, waiting for what she could only hope she
would hear, knowing that it was a long shot anyway,
Avery felt almost sorry for the long-suffering lab assistant.

   It *was* a long shot, but right on the mark. About twenty
minutes into the tape, the moment came. Avery stopped
the car, pulled over to the side of the road and hit rewind.
Now she sat, tapping her nails on her teeth and keening
her ears, praying that she'd heard right.

CNN announcing the date again. And the time. The right time.

Devon calling a halt to her latest diatribe.

A creaking door, a pair of footsteps. Two people, certainly. One walking more slowly, more heavily than the other. And then Homolka's voice.

'You set?'

The reply too faint to hear in the din of the lobby, or maybe even unspoken. Maybe a nod. Then some more shuffling.

'See you later.'

Daetwyler speaking, without a shadow of a doubt.

'Bye-bye.'

Devon, now.

'Bye.'

Homolka.

Avery played it again, twice, just to be sure, and then once again from further back, this time counting the minutes that elapsed between the last CNN time-bulletin and the verbal exchange between Daetwyler and Homolka. Then she called Perdue.

Her fast, heavy exhalations echoed into the mouthpiece of her Star-tac as she listened to the ringing tone, jiggling her knees, urging him to answer. The ringing stopped, replaced by the infuriatingly calm voice of the voice-mail lady and the beep.

'Perdue? The hell are you? Call me as soon as you get this. I think I've got something. I think I might be able to prove that Daetwyler took Leon LeGalley out of the centre at pretty much exactly the right time. The time he'd need to have left the centre to arrive at ImagiNation at the time we know that LeGalley did. Should I call Hayes, or what? I don't know. I'm gonna wait for your call, okay? Don't be long. Bye.'

She was about to hit the memory access number for the security HQ when she noticed a missed call sign on the LCD of her phone. She pushed another key.

'You – have – two – new – messages. Message – left – at – nine – o – five – p.m. – today . . .'

'Sylvie?' It was Perdue. 'Me. You sitting down? Because I think I've got it. I know exactly how I can find out for sure whether Leon was alone at ImagiNation that morning, or whether somebody was with him. And if so, who. Now, I told Hayes already, and we can't do it now, but he's setting up everything we need for tomorrow morning. I think it's over, Sylvie. I think it's really over. Hang in there. Call me.'

The second message was also from Perdue, still sounding excited, though this time a little more harried with it. 'Sylvie? I've gotta leave the office right now because the guard at the Americana site called here and said he needed backup. Possible trespasser or something? So that's where I'll be, but I'll keep my cellular on, obviously. Now the HQ night guy is out in the park, so I'm gonna take Trey with me.'

A muffled noise in the background.

'Trey says to say hi by the way. Okay. We'll be back here ASAP. Call when you get this, can't wait to bring you up to date. I'm pretty fired up.'

Perdue hesitated a moment. 'You know, just now and again, this damn job of ours is almost as good as surfing. Not quite, but almost. Almost.'

Filled with fondness for Perdue, Avery dialled his number once again. And once again, it rang and rang.

Thirty-One

Felix Perdue was standing alone in the dark when his cellular began to trill, the blackness of the shallow quarry itself compounded by the soul-sucking shadows cast from above by the concrete tanks at its perimeter.

Perdue thought he'd switched the phone off when it had rung the first time a few minutes before, interrupting his silent progress through the construction site and – he feared – putting him at a disadvantage to the elusive interloper that he sought. So when it now burst into life again the electronic melody gave him a sharp start, and he fumbled at his belt, his lightly trembling hand first hitting his walkie-talkie in error.

Having found the smooth outline of the correct gadget in his pocket, he retrieved it and glanced at the readout. Avery calling. He began to raise the phone to his left ear, his finger ready to hit the green telephone key, to take the call, when he felt a presence behind him, and something else, something nozzle-like, jabbed sharply into his right ear.

Felix Perdue wheeled round, but the thing in his ear was being held fast, didn't budge. His eyes bugged out as he saw exactly who was at the trigger of the airless paint-gun before they blew from his head entirely and landed some fifteen feet away along with a splattering of paint, viscera, quite a lot of his left cerebral cortex and the cellular phone, which – remarkably undamaged – continued to ring.

Thirty-Two

When she saw the front door of Hayes's house open, and the security van in the drive and Hayes, there on the doorstep with that terrible, terrible haunted expression, Avery was overcome by a feeling of abject dismay. She'd gone missing again, she was home late, Hayes must have called out security to look for her. Even walking at a decent rate, her progress up the driveway seemed painfully slow, gave her time to think, *no*, it couldn't be that. Was it Trey? Oh God, oh God. Something had happened to Trey. She broke into a run but didn't have time to speak before Hayes caught her in his arms. The forcefulness of his crushing bear-hug constricted her breathing and it was a moment before she realized that his shoulders were heaving slightly and his face, which he had buried in her neck, was just a little damp. She pushed him gently away and looked up at him.

'Hayes, what's the matter? What's happened?'

The moments after he told her that Perdue was dead were almost total blank numbness, interspersed with flashes of elaborate emotion, an instant parade of the five stages of bereavement, only the floats were being piloted by Indy 500 drivers. Denial became anger chased down by bargaining, with depression hot on its tail. She waited for acceptance, but it had stalled at the starting line, and now denial came round again and stayed.

Avery didn't really recall going inside with Hayes, didn't recall moving one leg in front of the other nor the change in temperature and light between outdoors and in, but now she was sitting curled up on the sofa with Hayes's arms still around her, and she realized that she still didn't know exactly what had happened. When she asked, Hayes began to explain, and when he became too distraught to continue, the plain-clothes security officer took over.

The man, who sat awkwardly in the armchair opposite her, was heavy-set, middle-aged, and she recognized him from ImagiNation HQ, was pretty sure his name was something that sounded vaguely made up, like it should be in a book. Asch? Calum Asch?

His explanation was brief and succinct, professional and businesslike, aside from the part where he mentioned 'the mercy of the good Lord' in relation to the fact that Perdue would have been killed instantly.

Avery's voice was dry and crackly when she finally spoke. 'So it was a trap, yes? The person who called for backup – it wasn't site security, obviously.'

Calum Asch exchanged looks with Hayes before responding. 'Well . . . obviously.'

Avery thought for a moment before giving voice to what was troubling her. 'But . . . The guy wanted Trey. And Trey was there. Why did he –'

She couldn't bring herself to say the words 'kill' and 'Perdue' in the same sentence.

The men exchanged looks again and made some kind of unspoken agreement for Hayes to take over the talking. He tightened his embrace around her and spoke softly.

'Avery, he knew that Perdue was on the verge of getting evidence that would prove his involvement in the killing of Lisa Schaeffer. And possibly Leon LeGalley, too. He maybe didn't know that I knew, as well. He couldn't afford to let Perdue do what he was going to do tomorrow. So he killed him.'

Avery looked confused. 'But . . . Whoever it was – how could he have known that?'

Now Hayes realized finally that they were talking at cross-purposes. 'Avery, honey, there *was* no intruder at the Americana site. We checked the security video. Unless someone knew where all the cameras were, there's no way they could have avoided being seen. We have to conclude that there was nobody there . . . Except Perdue, *and Trey Clowes.*'

Avery felt the blood burning in every vein in her body, a cold, poisonous, creeping feeling that began in her chest and spread rapidly, like she'd been injected with Draino.

She felt herself leaping up, heard herself letting go some involuntary bark of protest and sat back down numbly as the parade in her brain began again. Finally she said quietly, 'I don't believe that.'

Hayes's reply was far more venomous in tone than she'd expected. 'Oh, you don't? Well, perhaps you'd like to talk to the Americana security guard who caught him, perhaps he could show you the bruises, huh? Would you like that?'

'They got Trey? Where is he?'

She realized at once that this was the wrong question, but it was too late. Hayes's eyes widened, swimming with a bitter soup of injury and ire, and he spoke slowly, with his face right against hers as if talking to a particularly infuriating child.

'I – don't – know. He – got – away.'

'But nobody saw him do it? I mean, maybe he was scared . . . How do we know that –'

Now Hayes just seemed weary. 'Avery, please. Who else knew about the paint-guns? You've got a good brain. Try using it.' She flinched as his hand approached her forehead. He tapped it just a little harder than he'd intended to. 'Your brain? Remember that? It's here. Couple of feet north of the part of your anatomy you seem to have been thinking with the last few days.'

She tried not to rise to his goading, although if Calum Asch hadn't been there she'd have been very tempted to slap him. Hard.

'So the threat Trey got – you're saying he wrote it himself? Made it up? And the phone call? What? He did it while Perdue was getting coffee or something? You *seriously* think that?'

'What better way to dump himself right in the middle of the investigation? Find out for sure if you'd bought his story, or if there was any danger of getting found out? He thought he'd sent you up a blind alley with all that stuff about Jerry Lee's death, the woman in the parking lot, the fucking non-existent sport utility, everything. But he didn't think it through. Didn't bank on you getting so worried, that *he* was going to be in danger. You were right – why would someone go to the trouble of wiping out just two of the witnesses and then forget the third one? They wouldn't, and they *didn't* because the third witness was the perpetrator. Only whatever the murder was about, whatever those guys were tangled up in, Trey didn't know that he couldn't trust Lisa. Didn't bank on her taking a photograph. So he had to get rid of her quickly, without getting himself into more trouble. The drug they had at the centre – he knew all about that. He knew from Leon probably beforehand, knew what a larger dose of the stuff could do. He had it all planned. And I have to admit, it's pretty impressive. The kid's got quite an imagination on him. If he wasn't a homicidal little toe-rag, I'd almost be tempted to offer him a junior position in my department.' *A homicidal little toe-rag.* Avery was finding it hard to adjust to thinking of Trey that way, and to seeing the whole case, all she'd discovered, refracted through this new and very different prism. Most of it had filtered through with ease, beside the tape, Devon's tape, the thought of which now sent beams of danger-signal-red bouncing into her mind's eye. For a moment, she'd almost voiced this theory to Hayes, about Daetwyler and Homolka's exchange in the lobby, but she found to her slight dismay that her excitement about it had now waned. It certainly wasn't what one would call hard evidence, and would never be admitted in a court of law. Leaving the centre at that time could all have been just a coincidence. After all, without knowing the exact time of Lisa and Leon's deaths there was a good-sized margin of error in the time window. She slumped back in the chair, crushed. Now her mind had begun working differently.

'But how did Trey get into the centre that morning?'

Hayes shrugged at her question, stumped, but Avery felt no sense of victory. She knew the answer herself, more or less. Trey had snuck into the parking lot at least once before with no trouble. The patrolmen didn't know one volunteer from another, and they depended on the front-end security to keep out trespassers. They wouldn't question somebody on the grounds during business hours. As long as Trey had hung out at the back waiting for someone to come out, he probably wouldn't have had any difficulty sauntering in, losing himself in the crowd of volunteers and lab techs and putting his scheme into action.

The atmosphere in Hayes's sitting room was thick and heavy, and the sound of every tiny movement seemed amplified – the snow-shoe crunch of the crushed-velvet sofa cushion as Hayes edged slightly further away from Avery, the clink of Calum Asch's coffee cup placed on the glass side-table. Avery listened to the hum of the silence in between these noises until suddenly she was struck by the absurdity of the notion that Felix Perdue was no longer alive. Where the hell was he? She put her face in her hands and screwed her eyes up tight, as if trying to squeeze this wholly unthinkable piece of information out of her mind. But it clung like a tick, rooted there, disgusting, sapping her.

'Look, Avery honey, I know you're feeling . . .'

Avery turned to look at Hayes. Ghost-lights blotted out portions of her vision as her eyes grew accustomed to being open once again, but between the bright coronas she could see that the hardness in his face was gone.

'God, Avery, I can't even begin to describe how *I* feel. Perdue, I . . .'

His voice cracked and her heart melted. She laid her fingertips on his shoulder very carefully, as if approaching a stray dog for the first time, unsure of whether it might turn and bite. And slowly, very slowly, he unfurled his arms and placed them lightly around her again and allowed her to rest her head on his chest.

'Oh Jesus, Hayes. I've been . . . What have I done? I am *so* sorry.'

'Avery, you don't have to be sorry. I'm just – my God, honey, it could have been you. When I think that the person who did this to Perdue, he was . . . you were . . . I can't even think about it. I can't even think about losing you.'

She nodded gratefully, opened her mouth to speak, but no words came out.

Calum Asch, presumably embarrassed to find himself in the midst of this particularly mawkish scene, rose to leave, blurting out his words with some considerable unease.

'Well, we have it all under control, Mr Ober. Clowes is on foot and we've got a good dedicated search team and everybody else is on alert. He's not going to get far.'

Hayes gently withdrew one arm from Avery and held his hand up in thanks.

'Great. You keep me posted, okay?'

The rest of the night was even more of a blur. Hayes seemed to have decided to treat Avery like an invalid, and she felt slightly embarrassed at how easily and gratefully she accepted the comforts he offered. The hot bath during which he sat at her side on the bathroom floor and talked quietly to her. The insistence that she go to bed, where he tucked her in, fussing over the pillows and comforter like a nervous new father. And later the huge portion of angel-hair pasta *puttanesca*, her favourite, which he brought up on a tray. And though she'd been filled with shame, as it seemed somehow disrespectful to Perdue, she'd had no trouble in polishing off the entire bowl.

Presumably, she thought, all this hard work at taking care of her gave Hayes something to focus on, some way to deal with his own grief.

The doorbell first chimed mid-evening. A second ring came later, and although she could now hear Hayes and a few other male voices in the living room, she was happy to snuggle down and listen to the distant hum of their discussion. It was only when, much later, Hayes brought her up a mug of cocoa with tiny reconstituted marshmallows in it – she hadn't even been aware that he'd had such a product in the cupboard – and hovered by the lightswitch with the suggestion that she try to sleep, that she suddenly got sick of playing this particular game. Where she had previously felt like a little girl intermittently napping on the back seat of her parents' car, comforted by the delicious sense of having all responsibility removed from her, now she was the kid who'd wandered downstairs in her nightgown to find a cocktail party in full swing. Avery sat up in bed and took the cocoa from Hayes, dizzy with the rising sense of feeling out of place, excluded. She pitched her voice at its professional, can-do setting, now desperately missing the equal footing they had been on. She wished now that she wasn't in bed, didn't have her face free of make-up, didn't have her hair tied back after washing it in the bath; wasn't naked.

'Hayes, what's the news? Any news?'

He shifted from one foot to the other, stared at the floor. 'Nope. Not yet.'

'What have you been doing? Have you spoken to Darwin? Does he know what's going on?'

Ober brushed his hair from his eyes as if to better study his shoes. 'Yes. I've got to see him tomorrow. It's complicated. It's a question of what we're prepared to see go to court and what we're not.'

He folded his arms, making it clear that he wasn't about to elucidate.

'But you'll keep me up to date, right?'

She hadn't been able to hide the edge in her voice and now he looked at her pointedly.

'Yes, Avery, I will. But let me get this clear: your involvement, it's over. Until we've got Trey Clowes in our custody, I don't even want you leaving this house. You've taken enough risks. This is where it stops.'

She was shocked at the panic she felt on hearing his words.

'You're not serious?'

He hadn't blinked once.

'Try me.'

She was dismayed to hear herself sounding tearful and not professional at all. 'I just . . . I'm in too deep already to be able to . . . This whole thing, I can't just walk away from it.'

'Your problem, Avery, is you've got this fucking teen-age sense of, I don't know, *invincibility*. I told you to be careful yesterday, I set you up with Nelson, somebody to look after you, and you scooted. *You* may not care what happens to you, but *I* do. And if you no longer have any respect for my personal feelings, can you at least take into account my professional obligations, please? I already have a public relations nightmare on my hands. I can't afford to lose another member of security personnel and I'm not going to let it happen.'

Avery looked away from him.

'Is that all this is to you? *A public relations nightmare*? I mean, what about justice? For Perdue? Doesn't that mean anything to you? And for Lisa? And Leon? And Jerry Lee Lucas? I mean, "what we're prepared to see go to court", what're you saying? You might not prosecute Trey for Lisa and Leon's murders because they happened at ImagiNation and it would *look* bad? Or Perdue's? But Lucas, *that*'s fine because it didn't happen on property? I mean, what are you saying?'

Hayes Ober threw up his hands in anguish. 'Oh, for

279

Christ's sake! No! Don't make me . . . Look, you can trust me. I *will* see that justice is done. And I *will* protect Dreamworld at the same time. The two aren't mutually exclusive. Problem solving is my job, Avery. It's what I'm good at. Just trust me, and let me get on with it.'

Avery leapt out of bed, pulled the covers around her and thundered over to Hayes in the doorway, her eyes blazing. 'No! Answer me, goddamn it! Is that what you're saying?'

Her sudden loss of composure only served to increase his own sense of control as it always did, and he spoke softly but tersely, as one might to a toddler throwing a tantrum in the middle of a supermarket.

'Avery, you have to trust me. I'll have a clearer picture when I'm back from seeing Darwin. Then we'll talk.'

She gritted her teeth. 'What about Lisa's parents? And Shannon Reilly? You're prepared to let them live out the rest of their lives tortured by not knowing what happened to the people they loved?'

Hayes brushed his hair back again, as he tended to when he was edgy. 'That's one of the things I need to talk to Darwin about. It's possible that we might, uh, release the bodies. Unofficially. Somewhere off property. Let County find them. Even if your theory is correct, which I'm not saying is impossible, forensic evidence is going to show that Leon killed Lisa and then killed himself. It's been too long for anything to show up in Leon's blood. It'll be ruled a murder-suicide, it won't be connected to Dreamworld, the relatives will be able to have funerals, et cetera, et cetera. But obviously it's an option that needs to be thought through. So –'

Avery, who had fallen into a shocked, puzzled hush, interrupted him. 'You're going to dig up the arcade?'

Now Hayes looked equally foxed.

'What arcade?'

'Isn't that where the bodies are? At the Americana?'

Now some distant network of cogs locked teeth in Hayes's mind.

'Oh I see, Perdue told you that? Yeah . . . He was very concerned about somebody discovering them, so I told him they were in the foundations of the arcade. With the VW. Took a weight off his mind. Didn't want to burden him with the truth. I wanted to protect him. And now I want you to let me protect *you*, okay? Can you just let me do that?'

Avery boggled. 'I'm sorry, I'm not getting you. "Protect" is now a euphemism for "lie to", or am I missing something?'

Hayes grabbed her suddenly by the shoulders and shook her lightly but firmly. 'No. *Protect* you. As in keep you alive. As in make sure that what happened to Perdue doesn't happen to you.'

While they'd been talking about Perdue, it had been as if he had never gone away, and this reminder was like finding out that he'd died all over again. It was this – more than the shaking or Hayes's stern tone – that silenced her eventually, and she nodded weakly in defeat. She wanted to protest as he led her back to the bed, wanted to complain when he turned off the bedroom light, wanted to say something else as he walked out of the door. But she didn't.

Avery lay there awake in the darkness for a while, thinking about the planet, this planet that was revolving like it always did, only tonight it didn't have Felix Perdue on it any more. And tomorrow morning, even though she'd have slept through the whole night, oh-so-patiently, he still wouldn't be here. And every morning now would be the same, no matter how long she waited. For ever.

The sheets beneath and above her felt cold now, clammy and unfamiliar, the pillow hard on her neck; the lonely discomfort of a stranger's bed. Avery knew this feeling well, better than she liked to admit. But this wasn't the lurching aftermath of a loveless one-night stand, not this time. This wasn't the yearning to leap from the pool of semen and sweat and self-loathing and into a shower and out to her car. This bed was Hayes's bed, the bed she'd shared with him for over a year. The stranger was Hayes. And what he had taken tonight was not her body but something that she had always guarded much more fiercely – her sense of control and compre-hension of her universe. Was it he who had changed? Or was it she?

And before she fell asleep, Avery thought about Trey, too. She groaned audibly as a great and bloody brawl took place, two figures fighting for supremacy, fighting to represent Lloyd Clowes III in Avery's mind.

In the blue corner, the sweet, smiling Trey wearing his shorts and Gazelles and Beck T-shirt. And in the red, the other Trey, a Trey she'd never met, wearing most of the contents of Felix Perdue's skull.

Thirty-Three

When Avery awoke, it was like she'd never been asleep. The knowledge of all that had taken place was there, right there as her eyes snapped open, and she jumped from Hayes's bed and ran to the wardrobe, not wanting to waste a second. Without hesitation, she climbed into a clean uniform and thundered down the stairs and towards the front door, where she was mildly surprised to find a young male security guard sitting on one of Hayes's dining room chairs. She fixed him with a determined look.

'I'm going out.'

'Uh, I don't . . . Mr Ober said you were to stay here. For your own protection.'

'You still haven't got Trey Clowes?'

'Not as far as I know.'

Her heart leapt. She was going to find him herself, bring him in. She was going to do it for Perdue and Lisa and the others and when she did, it was going to be oh so sweet. She turned on her heel without saying a word and walked towards the kitchen.

Avery had half expected to find someone posted by the front door, but she was somewhat thrown when she found two further members of security personnel at the dinette, drinking coffee. They watched her awkwardly as she strode purposefully towards the back door, exchanged uncomfortable looks as she tried the handle and found it locked. She glared at them.

'Um, Mr Ober ordered us to secure the house, Miss Avery.'

Avery stared down at the younger one, the one who had spoken. 'Give me the key.'

The older guard, realizing that his colleague had bottled out, took over. 'We have to follow our orders. He said nobody is to go in or out. Including you.'

Now the younger one piped up again. 'Like, *especially* you. He's really worried about you. Said that if anything happens to you, we're . . .'

The boy drew his finger across his throat and emitted a melodramatic gurgle. Avery's nostrils flared as she tightly wound a piece of her hair around her finger. Around and around and around until her scalp hurt. She had to stay calm, had to stay calm at all costs.

'I have to go out. I need to go out. Now.'

The younger guard failed spectacularly to read her; remained laconic. 'You need something from the store or something? I could go, if you want.'

And now he failed to read the meaning of the silence with which she responded. 'If it's, like, *ladies'* things you need, and you, like, don't want to . . . Uh, Officer Yee could go for you.'

He gestured behind him, bringing to Avery's attention for the first time the fact that a third officer was present in the kitchen, sitting at the breakfast bar in front of a medium-sized stack of black hardware. She was wearing a pair of headphones, which she now removed as she waved a sheepish greeting. Avery stared at the fiesta of lights and cables.

'And what the hell are *you* doing?'

'Monitoring the phone line. And the local cellular network. In case Clowes tries to contact you here or on your cellphone. Depending on where he's calling from, we might be able to use it to locate him.'

Avery gaped wordlessly as she looked around the kitchen one more time before running back upstairs to the bedroom and slamming the door behind her. A glance out of the bathroom window revealed two guards posted at the back of the house and a further four out front. Despite the fact that one of these was perched on the bonnet of Avery's parked car, drinking coffee from a Kit-E-Cat insulated mug, and another had just shouted something that concluded with the words, 'Really great old Seinfeld rerun last night,' the vague formation in which they stood made them seem thoroughly military, entirely domineering.

She picked up the phone and dialled Hayes's cellular, wiping angry tears from her eyes. He picked up almost instantly.

'Honey?'

'Tell them to let me the hell out of here!' Avery shouted as loudly as she could, relishing the mental image of officer Yee wincing downstairs.

'Avery –'

'I want to get back to work. I'm going nuts. I need to keep busy.'

'I know. I know. And you will. Next week, tomorrow, whenever you want, whenever you're ready –'

'I'm ready now.'

He ignored her interjection.

'– providing we've got Trey Clowes. Until then, you're going to sit tight.'

'So I'm under house arrest because – what? You don't trust me to look after myself?'

'Avery, I don't have time for this. I'm standing in the middle of LAX, I can't find my driver and I've got a meeting with Darwin starting in twenty minutes. When I get home tonight, we can talk.'

'You don't understand. I need, I don't know . . . *Closure*. To have been taken in by Trey . . . I've come so far down the line, been through so much and . . .'

'You want to lay it to rest. I *do* understand. If you feel you need to see Trey Clowes, then when we've got him, I'll make sure you get a chance to do that, okay? I'll take you to see him myself when he's in custody. And you can say whatever you want. I'll even give you some time alone with him, if that's what you'd prefer. I'll make it safe for you to do that. Just hang in there. Sit tight. I'm catching the first flight back. Okay?'

Gazing out of the bedroom window, Avery told him that it was, and tried not to let on that another plan was forming in her head even as she spoke. And as soon as she'd said goodbye, she locked the bedroom door and switched on her walkie-talkie.

Thirty-Four

The guards at the back door mobilized quickly, scrambling into the undergrowth in hot pursuit of the nonexistent Trey lookalike spotted by the non-existent mobile patrolman on the winding road beyond the bushes behind the house. As soon as she observed this, Avery sprang up from her crouched position by the open bathroom window and hoisted herself out onto the sill. The six-foot drop onto the arched roof of the carport looked daunting, yet she took it with admirable grace. Commending herself heartily but equally wary of becoming overconfident because of it, she took pause momentarily before prostrating herself and undulating, Gurkha-style, across the apex of the corrugated roof.

This part was not so easy, and Avery's breaths came short and fast as she tried not to imagine what might happen if she were to list to either side; tried not to think about sliding or rolling from the roof and onto the tarmac below.

Once she had reached the outer edge of the structure she scooted around ninety degrees and began to let herself slide. Her palms, now damp with fearful sweat, provided far less traction than she had hoped, instead skimming the surface and – was she imagining this? –

actually increasing the speed of her descent. Her attempts at slowing her progress by gripping a corrugation ridge with either hand made no difference at all – she was still slipping downwards with alarming rapidity, only now she was burning her fingertips and her palms as she plummeted. Eventually she felt the side of the carport fall away, her legs flailing vaguely below her in the noth-ingness, and prayed that when her torso caught up, she would find the support pole where she expected it to be.

Avery's relief when she succeeded in catching the pole in both hands was marred somewhat by the various star-bursts of pain she instantly felt – her shoulders wrenched hard at the sockets by the impacted velocity, her raw palms singing with vibrant agony as they gripped the sun-toasted steel. But she ignored this as best she could, as she did the jarring in her knees as she landed heavily on the ground. The guards were coming back, she could hear them, and any time squandered on physical recov-ery would cost her this single chance at escape.

Hayes's Cherokee, the one he used at weekends to tote his fishing gear to the lake or tow his jet ski to the Atlantic Intracoastal Waterway, was parked beneath the carport, as always. Noting with some dismay that the vast Yamaha jet ski was currently hitched to it, mounted on its trailer, Avery cursed softly as she dived into the driver's seat. But the key, thankfully, was where it always was – slipped above the sun-shield – and despite her trembling hands, Avery drove it into the ignition on the first attempt.

As she burst forth from beneath the carport and screeched onto the drive, the audacity of this part of the plan hit her and she began to wonder what the hell she'd been thinking. The surprised, almost hurt and slightly pathetic expressions on the faces of the guards – particularly the Seinfeld fan, whom she nearly clipped with the hood of the car as she sped past – sent a flush of shame running through her, but she drove on, and she didn't look back.

All eyes were on Avery as she walked into the bullpen, and almost immediately Calum Asch appeared, as if from nowhere, and stood nervously before her, blocking the path to her desk in the corner of the investigative department. Or what *had* been her desk. She'd used it very little in her short tenure at this division, having spent most of her time on the road or in Perdue's office, but she realized immediately, from the glimpse she was able to get past Calum Asch's considerable bulk, that the few things she'd kept there were now gone.

'What's happening? Where are my things?'

Calum Asch laid a meaty paw on her shoulder. 'Avery . . . Gosh. We weren't expecting you in so soon. I'm afraid your new office isn't ready just yet, but . . .'

'My new office?'

The heavy-set man shifted uneasily from one foot to another. 'Right. I'm guessing perhaps Hayes didn't have a chance to . . . You've been transferred. I think he wanted to tell you the good news himself. Oh, gosh.'

The sudden silence in the bullpen was almost funny to Avery, reminding her of those bad adverts or comedy sketches where someone makes a faux pas in the middle of some swanky social gathering and all conversation and music comes to an instant halt, accompanied by the jarring scratchy noise of a stylus pulled abruptly from a vinyl record. She smiled despite herself.

'The good news, huh? And that would be what?'

Asch, mistakenly relieved to see her smiling, relaxed slightly. 'Well, that you've been transferred. To VIP liaison.' He leant down slightly, and spoke in a conspiratorial stage whisper. 'Best damn job at ImagiNation. There wasn't an official opening, but they've been saying for a while that they could definitely use an extra person. Prepare for a little jealousy from some of these goons around here. But you've earnt it, no question. Congratulations.'

He offered her his hand, which she stared at rudely, and didn't take.

'I don't want it. I want to keep my job in investigative.'

A murmur ran through the bullpen, reminding Avery of those adverts once again, of people doing comedy double-takes and spitting out mouthfuls of Chablis in heavy-handed horror. She glanced around the room and raised her voice.

'What the hell are you all looking at? Don't you have anything to do?'

With excruciating embarrassment, Calum Asch retracted the rejected hand and raised it gingerly to Avery's shoulder again, applying gentle pressure intended to suggest that they walk in the direction of his own office.

'Perhaps we ought to discuss this in private . . .'

She continued to stare around the room in challenge to the rubber-neckers and told him that this was fine by her.

Perdue's replacement was to be Lynda Young. Avery knew her vaguely – knew that she was blonde, mid-to-late thirties, laid-back and affable, yet admirably blunt in a way that intimidated some, which Avery rather envied. She'd been in investigative longer than any of the others at her level, Asch explained, and was unquestionably the first in line for the job. Any official applications for an investigative post would now filter through her desk as well as those of the existing seniors, and Asch would be glad, he said, to take Avery through right now, introduce her properly.

Avery stared at the floor, unable to look him in the eye. 'I shouldn't have to reapply. I *have* a job in investigative already. I can't just be demoted for no reason.'

'*Pro*moted,' he reminded her.

Avery spluttered her words, barely able to speak. 'Babysitting a bunch of suits all day? Backdooring people onto attractions and making restaurant reservations and polite conversation? You call that a promotion? I'm a law enforcement official! That's what I trained to be, that's what I am!'

'Look, Sylvia, I'm sure there is some alternative . . .'

Sylvia. She slipped her hands under her backside, unable to trust herself. 'Oh yeah, what fantastic position are you gonna offer me now? I could put on a long blonde wig and play Rapunzel in the parade, maybe?'

'We could perhaps, I don't know, see if it's possible for you to have your old job back. But nobody thought you'd . . .'

Calum Asch looked like he was about to suffer a cardiac infarction.

'*My old job*? I guess you wouldn't call *that* being demoted, either! Somehow I think an industrial tribunal might disagree with you.'

'Avery, I think perhaps I'm not the person you should be speaking to.'

'This is Hayes, isn't it?'

Now Asch avoided *her* eyes. 'He cares about you deeply, Avery. I've never seen him so scared. When I was waiting with him for you to come home, he ... I ... I've never seen him like that before.'

'This is Dreamworld! Law enforcement here, it's ... Jesus Christ, its hardly the streets of South Central! What does he think's going to happen to me? I'm – what? – gonna get caught in a riot over someone cutting in line? Be trampled by looters at Fairyland Mercantile? Raped by a gang of Danish backpackers on a wilding spree?'

'Avery, I wish I could help. Please.' Asch held his hands up in a gesture of surrender. 'Don't shoot the messenger.'

Avery rose slowly from her seat, still snarling slightly. 'Okay. I'll take it. I'll take the job. Temporarily. Today. Then I'm going to see to it that I get *my* job back. Not my old job, *my* job. So don't you dare let anybody go near that desk. It's *mine*.'

Calum Asch nodded his hanging head with all the verve of a well-beaten heavyweight trapped in his corner by a haranguing coach. 'Second floor. Corner office. Your stuff's in a box on your desk. Your – uh, *new* desk. Debbie Kitchen's in charge. She wasn't expecting you till later in the week, but I'm sure it'll be fine. She'll take care of you.'

Avery was stalking out of Calum Asch's office, concentrating on her posture and holding her head erect, when he spoke her name again, said *Sylvia*. She looked at him unpleasantly. 'What?'

He gestured at her belt.

'You can, uh, drop your uniform by any time you like, but I do need you to turn in your walkie-talkie, kind of ... now.'

Initially Avery had only joined Little League as a kid as an excuse to hang out with the neighbourhood boys, but judging by the tears that sprang into Calum Asch's eyes as the blur of speeding black gadgetry alighted in his bloated hands, it appeared that her slider was as lethal as it ever had been.

Thirty-Five

Avery had coped very well, if she said so herself, walking through the utilidors with Debbie Kitchen – her first time back since she'd vowed never to go down there again. Stepping into the costume room, however, was much harder. She focused on the counter towards which they were headed, trying desperately not to look to either side as they made their way through the forest of hanging rails. Regardless of her efforts, it was almost impossible not to catch glimpses, here and there, of the furry costumes hanging amongst the others – the lumberjack shirts and lederhosen and carnival regalia. No matter how she tried one would sneak into view, its lifeless, sagging form making her think of poor, dead Lisa Schaeffer.

Debbie Kitchen had given Avery's shoe and dress sizes to the male attendant behind the counter and was now smiling warmly at her while they awaited his return. She was petite, snub-nosed, apple-cheeked and wore her thick, honey-coloured hair in a too-cute-for-words pixie cut. Avery would have been prepared to stake cash that at home, Debbie Kitchen wore slouchy socks and big fleece pyjamas and held her coffee cup with both hands and curled up in armchairs like she was waiting for Nora Ephron to write a romantic comedy about her in which she'd be played by Meg Ryan. She was one of those people you'd love to punch in the face, just to see whether anything would stop her from being so damn perky.

'I'll say it again, Sylvia, we are just *so* glad to have you on board.'

Avery smiled back, hoping that it looked like a real smile and not a baring of fangs.

'We'll have you fixed up and ready to start in no time.'

Her clothes changed, her security uniform poignantly handed back across the counter and bagged up, bound for the Dreamworld laundry division, Avery finally steeled herself to walk to the full-length mirror at the end of the costume room.

'Wow!' said Debbie Kitchen, appearing behind Avery's left shoulder.

'Wow,' echoed Avery.

She looked like an air hostess. She inspected herself again, from the bottom up – from the dainty scarlet court shoes with their chunky but kittenish three-inch heels, to the form-fitting, just-on-the-knee, red pencil skirt and matching tailored jacket, to the silky little white blouse with its too-high Peter-Pan collar which made her generous décolletage look decidedly show-stopping, if a little obscene. She averted her gaze, afraid that she might cry. It wasn't that she looked out of place. On the contrary, she looked perfect, and perfectly at home in the uniform, like she'd been wearing it for years. That was what scared her more than anything. Never before had she seen herself so far removed from who she thought she was, and never before had she had any doubt that this previous identity was anything but an immutable truth.

It had seemed like a good idea at the time, taking on this new role, just for today, *play along* as it were. At least she would have some legitimate reason to be in the security building and out on property. Screw Hayes and his over-protective crap. She could take care of herself. And she'd be able to keep abreast of the investigation and use the computers and other resources for her own means. But now she felt that her life had been stripped away along with her uniform, the memories of it distant, illusionary, delusional. It reminded her of something, a *Twilight Zone* episode? A book by Philip K. Dick? Some hideous morning where you wake up in another life and you're the only person who remembers who you were before and you have to ask yourself whether you imagined it all.

'Are you okay, Sylvia?'

For a split second Debbie Kitchen looked unperky, until Avery nodded vigorously.

'I'm fine. Ready to rumble.'

'Excuse me?'

'I mean: let's go. What's on the agenda?'

The two women, in their identical air hostess uniforms, began to walk back towards the utilidor, Avery sashaying somewhat on the unfamiliarly high heels.

'Well, we have four VIP tour parties coming in today, three for here, one not. Now, I'm told you know this place like the back of your hand, so let's give you one of those. There's a standard itinerary, which I'll give you, and you can modify it if there's something they don't want to see, or something else they want to see early on. And all you need to do to backdoor your party onto the attractions is show the attendant your pass and she'll have you skip the line, put you right on the ride. We'll pick up your pass in a sec, but also –'

Debbie Kitchen stopped walking and fished into the breast pocket of her jacket, proffering a small stack of cards. They read – in a jolly, cartoonish typeface – *We're sorry you were unable to ride just now!*

'They're line-jumping passes,' Debbie Kitchen began.

'I know what they are. They're the ones the folks near the front of the line get given when the ride breaks down. So they don't have to line up again.'

'Exactly. If you're running out of time, it's getting late, and your party wants to do different things, you can send some of them off with one of these. You mark on the back which ride it's for, and how many in the party. Do you have a pen?'

Avery tapped her own breast pocket and realized to her dismay that she must have left the silver ballpoint she usually carried in the security uniform she had just relinquished. She'd handed it over, she thought with a heavy heart, with the same casual recklessness as that with which she'd turned in her old uniform, her beloved career and her entire identity.

'No, I don't.'

Debbie Kitchen wagged her finger in cheesy mock disapproval before handing Avery a slim ballpoint. It was pink and featured a cartoon of Kitten Caboodle posing as a 1940s Forces sweetheart, all furry Betty Grable legs and industrially upholstered bathing suit. Avery wondered, as she slipped the pen and cards into her pocket, whether it was a deliberate parody of those saucy biros with a picture of a woman who got naked when you tipped the thing upside down.

'Right. So I'm all set.'

'Oh, wait a minute, do you know where to go? For backdooring? I mean, most of the attractions it's the wheelchair entrance or, if it's one of the newer attractions where the lines are wheelchair-accessible, then it's the exit ramp. Any doubts, ask an attendant. Now for the shows, ask which shows they want to see, radio ahead at least a half-hour before start time, and ask them to rope off the number of seats you need.'

Avery's ears pricked up.

'Radio ahead? I get a walkie-talkie?'

'Uh-huh. I'm gonna give that to you right now.'

'I didn't know you guys were issued with them.'

Debbie Kitchen seemed baffled by Avery's sudden interest.

'Riiiight . . . Uh-huh.'

'I mean, when I was on security, I never heard anyone but security on the network.'

'Oh, I see. No, we use a different channel. We have to, obviously.'

Avery's heart began to sink even lower. Of course they used a different channel. And she could bet, knowing Dreamworld's draconian efficiency, that it wasn't even possible to switch channels on the hardware she was about to be issued. God forbid there should be an accidental flip of a switch and some VIP should hear mention of shoplifting or a fight or an accident or any of the other bad things that never happened at Dreamworld.

'The other tour group – the one that's *not* for ImagiNation? – I was just wondering . . .'

'Oh, they need to see the Americana site. I was going to send Amber, who you met upstairs? She's the only one who's read all the bumpf all the way through so far, and –'

Now Avery's heart took flight from the basement, and she stopped dead and rounded on Debbie Kitchen, clapping her hands hard onto the woman's arms as if to shake her, startling her considerably although she hadn't meant to.

'I can do it instead! I know that place like – I mean,

my boyfriend *designed* it! I've been there a hundred times! I know loads of cool facts about it, I could . . . I could do a *great* tour. Debbie, let me do *that* one? Will you?'

Debbie Kitchen, reeling slightly from the unexpected desperation in Avery's voice, eyed her new colleague with mild concern.

'I – don't have a car for you yet, though. I haven't spoken to the fleet manager. I thought you weren't coming till later in the week. You can't use your security car, you need to give that back.'

'It's fine. I have my boyfriend's jeep today.'

'Well, I don't –'

'Don't what? *C'mon*, Debbie! I'd be perfect for the job! You *know* it!'

Debbie Kitchen wracked her brains, unable to discern exactly what it was that felt not quite right.

'I . . . I don't . . . I don't see why not. Okay! Sure!'

Her voice became perky again, marred by a dash of surrender and trepidation. It was not a particularly appetizing recipe.

Avery clapped the smaller woman on the back, sending her momentarily off balance, and accompanied her upstairs with great excitement to collect her walkie-talkie, clipboard and a freshly laminated ID pass.

Thirty-Six

Avery had her plan all worked out. She was to meet her VIPs at the west gate and commence the tour from there. She'd take them around the site as quickly as possible before questioning the construction workers and snooping around, see if she could garner any information about where Trey might have gone when he left the site the previous night. Then she'd return to her new office – which, as she figured it, should be empty with the other girls still out on *their* morning tours – getting a good half-hour clear to use the computer and bring herself up to date. Then she'd tell Debbie Kitchen that she wanted to familiarize herself with the backdoor attraction entrances, or something like that, and she'd split again, go on the trail of Trey, following whatever leads she'd picked up. She was so excited she could hardly breathe.

The tour itself was much less soul-destroying than she'd expected, and not just because of her gleeful anticipation of the rest of the day. The VIPs – executives from a small group of Chicago-based gothic-horror-themed restaurants – were entirely male, which certainly made life easier, and her jokes and tidbits of fascinating behind-the-scenes information found a very appreciative audience indeed. A couple of times she had that Philip K.

Dick feeling again, both of them when she was basking in the rapt attention and appreciation coming from her audience (one of whom wore a highly inappropriate black suit, narrow tie and shades and looked like he could easily be a slightly malevolent, amoral CIA agent who'd engage in extremely rough sex fully clothed and with an air of disinterest – a look that was a secret penchant of hers). At those moments, Avery felt entirely at home in her air hostess garb, began to feel she'd been doing this all her life, and wondered to which poor soul those dim memories of bereavement and betrayal belonged in the back of her mind.

They had just arrived at the far-northern tip of the site, and the dazzling masterpiece of engineering that was the Americana resort's very own mystery spot. Avery stopped walking and turned with a flourish, like a model at the end of the catwalk.

'So, gentlemen, first off, are you familiar with this kind of thing?' All bar one – her CIA guy – shook their heads. She looked at him. 'You know what this is supposed to be?'

He nodded confidently, and Avery knew he was looking directly back at her although his eyes were hidden behind the shades. 'It's like those places where you park your car at the foot of a hill, put it in neutral, and it seems like it rolls upwards?'

'Exactly. The mystery spot. Perennial of the classic Yankee road-trip. Quintessential roadside Americana. Engineering experts from our Dream Technicians' department visited every mystery spot from sea to shining sea, gentlemen, before they set about constructing our very own version. And may I say, we all feel that we've actually succeeded in *improving* upon it. People are not going to be disappointed.'

CIA-man spoke again. 'It's an optical illusion, right?'

'Essentially. Or rather, it's a *combination* of optical illusions that add up to give the distinct impression that you're defying gravity, rolling uphill. These can occur naturally or, as in our case, you can study nature and replicate the effect. But as far as I know, this is the first man-made mystery spot in the US. Possibly the world. And like the real ones, it's going to have a suitably hokey legend to go with it.' She paused to receive her laughter. 'And a good name. Working title is Spook Hill, but there's a real Spook Hill near Lake Wales, so they'll probably change it.'

Avery looked around, enjoying how impressed everybody looked at the depth of her knowledge. They all exchanged glances with one another and one of them, a small, balding, cherubic man, scribbled something in a notebook before looking up at Avery again.

'And this is one of the restaurant locations that's still available?'

'Yep. Right there.' She gestured at a vast, single-storey building a little way away from them, artfully constructed to resemble an oversized version of a tumble-down shack, all wraparound porch and overlapping, hand-weathered planks that appeared to have been affixed with cartoonishly large faux-rusty nails. 'As you can see it's already fully themed to tie in with the area, but yes, it's out for tender. And I think whoever takes it gets a say in naming it, too, if I'm not mistaken.'

The men exchanged looks again and now CIA-guy spoke. 'Yeah, well, we're definitely looking to branch out. We're definitely not, like, locked into doing just the talking gargoyles and mad scientists kinda milieu. Has anyone put in a proposal yet?'

Avery felt frustrated that she didn't know. 'I'm afraid I don't have access to that information myself.'

He furrowed his brow. 'I tell you the only thing that concerns me? Isn't there going to be a risk of people rear-ending each other here? I'm kind of surprised that this is something Dreamworld would get into, something with a risk like that? The real mystery spots, they're in the middle of nowhere. You never get more than a few cars at a time wanting to try it out. Here, well, you could wind up with some kinda mayhem, no?'

Avery bristled slightly. 'I can assure you, sir, that our Dream Technicians – our engineers and attraction planners – are the best in the world. They leave nothing to chance. They think about everything that could possibly go wrong, even the most far-fetched scenarios that nobody else would even *imagine* plausible, and they come up with a solution to it. They ask, *"what if?"* It's the core of how they work. Their trademark. The Dream Techs, they call it the fallback protocol.'

'The fallback protocol. I like that.'

There was a murmur of assent from the others and CIA-guy smiled, baring perfect white teeth and looking more enticingly malevolent than ever.

Avery sashayed up the porch steps towards the main doors of the restaurant and opened the door. 'Shall we?'

The interior was cool and dark, lit primarily, even after she'd flipped the main lightswitch, by the dappled daylight that streamed in through the many irregularly shaped windows and the slivers of space between the deliberately rickety woodwork of the walls.

CIA-guy peered at one of these gaps, the stream of light beamed onto the floor alive with dancing dust particles. With some trepidation, he guided his finger between the planks, then registered surprise to find it met by something solid.

Avery smiled, bewitched by Hayes's skill as a designer

and innovator, the passions that she'd felt for him at that conference a thousand years ago thoroughly rekindled. Her words were breathy, dripping with this rush of emotion. They sounded somehow almost pornographic.

'Custom-treated glass. Same kind we used for most of the aquaria at Atlantis. Tough as hell – keeps the elements out – but you can hardly see it. 'Less you look really close.'

CIA-guy was duly impressed.

'That's nothin',' said Avery, affecting a slightly backwoods accent the better to enhance the restaurant's theming. 'Gentlemen, check *this* out.'

And with great verve, Avery led the group through a tumbledown door at the far end of the empty restaurant space and into the catacomb of rooms that spanned the entire north side of the building.

Each had been built using the same principles as the mystery spot, but here in miniature the effects were astounding. Each chamber had been set-dressed to look like a different room of a homely shack, with a little poetic licence, and Avery was delighted to find that all the appropriate props were still in place, as they had been when Hayes had proudly given her a private demonstration one night. It must have been just four weeks ago, she realized now, but it seemed like another lifetime.

The tour group complained only once or twice of nausea brought on by the skewed perspective in the little rooms, but they soon adjusted, as Hayes had assured her most people would. And they were appropriately captivated as Avery demonstrated each exquisitely designed trick. They watched as she poured the jug of water into the sloping tin gutter in the washroom and gasped when it flowed upwards instead of down. They ooohed and aaaahed when she tossed a handful of balls onto the apparently flat pool table and waited while each rolled, as if drawn by some unseen, unscientific force, into the top lefthand pocket. And in the last of the three chambers, they looked at one another dumbstruck after Avery took a couple of dainty steps backwards from the floor and appeared to be standing on the wall, leaning into the room, virtually parallel to the ground, as if defying gravity.

Finally, she led the group into the final cubicle before the egress back to the restaurant and remembered that here, so turned on after this extended demonstration of Hayes's imagination and engineering expertise, she'd pulled him to her immediately and they'd wound up making love on the floor. The memory made her blush; made her garrulous and rapidly spoken in her desire to cover up her embarrassment.

'So I've just shown you a few of the things – I think there are about eight demonstrations in total? And we're going to have a host or hostess collect parties of diners from their tables and take them back here on tours. Everybody will get a turn.'

She kept talking over the impressed silence as she led her captive audience back into the main restaurant floor.

'And people can take as many photos as they like. And we'll get volunteers up for some of the tricks. Should be quite a memorable evening for visitors, then, to say the least. What we have here, folks, is essentially a restaurant with an attraction attached to it, absolutely free. So we fully expect that within a very short space of time, this is going to be one of our most popular destination dining locations.'

There was a murmur, rich with assent, and Avery was just beginning to think how much she liked this job, and searching her mind for some killer follow-up remark, when she saw a flash of movement outside the window closest to her. It was in the corner of her field of vision, and far, far away, over by the crazy golf course. But it was unmistakable. And unmistakably human.

She noticed that the men were looking at her expectantly, and wondered for how long she'd fallen silent. She started to walk towards the door, stumbling slightly as she did so.

'I . . . er . . . I wish we had a, um, car here so I could get you guys to try the actual, uh, Spook Hill? I did it myself when they first built it and I tell you, uh, it's . . .'

The light in her eyes, and the heat, as she threw open the double barn-style doors and stepped onto the porch, threw her senses briefly out of whack. But not enough to stop her from noticing the streak of movement again. Still on the crazy golf course, only now at the part closest to them, between the pink fibreglass dinosaur and the traditional windmill. And this time the VIP tour group followed Avery's eyes and stared with her in the same direction, perplexed. She looked around sheepishly.

'I'm sorry. I thought I saw –'

Her eyes widened as she saw the movement again, or rather, saw a figure who was unmistakably Trey Clowes, running from behind the windmill and out of the crazy golf fairway altogether, towards the giant orange sphere that would be the juice stand. Towards where she stood. Panic began to rise within her.

'I thought I – would you gentlemen excuse me, please? I think we might have a trespasser on site and I'm going to need to have someone look into it.'

The men exchanged concerned glances.

'If you'd like to walk back round to the west gate in your own time, back to the parking lot, I can meet you there momentarily, yes?'

Avery had begun to back away from the group and to reach down to her walkie-talkie, which she wrenched from her belt. She walked calmly but briskly until the men had begun to move in the other direction and she was sure that they couldn't see her. Then she broke into a run, darted quickly behind the back wall of the restaurant and crouched low. She began to fiddle with the walkie-talkie, which was clammy with the surprisingly chilly perspiration from her own hands.

As she had feared, the security channel was inaccessible. What had she been thinking when she'd decided to tackle finding Trey alone? He might still have the paint-gun. Had anyone found it? Or he might have something else; the entire site was filled with potentially lethal equipment and gadgetry and he'd had all night and half a morning to take his pick. Meanwhile here she was, unarmed, wearing high heels . . . What the *hell* had she been thinking? Her fingers trembled and she threw the walkie-talkie into the dust, raked her now empty hands through her hair, then massaged her scalp as if doing so might make some fantastic plan crystallize in her mind.

The first thing Avery concluded was that she didn't want to die. Hayes had been right, she *did* have a teenage sense of invincibility. Immortality. Or rather she *had* done. Now it was gone, and she felt very mortal indeed, and very, very scared. She was just trying to figure out whether to stay put or whether to run when the decision was effectively made for her.

'Avery.'

Trey Clowes's voice was too quiet, a nasty low hiss, and his eyes seemed to have receded into their sockets, the whites and the lids shaded so deeply by the browbone as to appear indiscernible from the jet-black of the lashes, the irises and the pupils. His walk was inhumanly speedy for a mere walk and the gait, the shoulders and the balled fists – all this shrieked a piercing and terrifying testament to his determination. Avery scrambled instinctively to her feet and began to run for her life.

Thirty-Seven

The Portakabins stood in two dirty, soulless rows on either side of a scarred and muddy pathway, a macabre parody of a residential street in miniature. Avery tried the door of the first grim little abode, but it was locked, and the sweat on her palms greased the handle, making it slip painfully from her grasp at the first impotent rattle. She stumbled through the dust to the next cabin along, hacking her shin on the low metal step as she scrambled to try the door. This was locked too, and now from her slightly elevated position on the stoop, able to see into the windows of each cube-shaped structure that formed the bleak little alleyway, Avery realized with nauseous dismay that not one was conspicuously occupied.

She was a fast runner and the adrenaline had compensated for the unsuitable footwear, so that Avery had been able to put some distance between herself and Clowes before her lungs had started to burn and she'd begun to think in terms of tactic rather than speed. Had he seen her dart down here? She wasn't sure, but she couldn't take the risk, couldn't go back the way she'd come. She dashed down the central pathway between the cabins, kicking up clouds of dust here, gloopy sprays of mud there as she ran, heart thumping, ankles threatening more than once to jar or twist as she landed on the dainty heels of the loathsome court shoes.

Left or right here? Left or right? The growling hum of a generator somewhere nearby fogged her internal radar and in panic she threw a blind left. The impact occurred simultaneously on her left cheekbone, her left shoulder and her right knee – although which had made that sickening crack, she wasn't sure – and Avery reeled back, doubled over and whimpering in pain. A rush of endorphins hit her like a tranquillizer dart, turning the curses on her lips to slow drunken laughter when she saw the great rusting hulk of the generator and realized that she had run into it. She took another stumbling step backwards, her mind running in slo-mo, still dazed. Okay, not left. Go right. But from here she could see now that the alley was blocked to this side, too, by – the hell was that thing? Another generator? One of those inhumanly filthy temporary toilet facilities?

Trapped here by the wire fence at the end of this desolate, ungodly cul-de-sac Avery stood cold and broken and scared, her legs buckling and betraying her like Bambi taking his first steps, while her eyes called to mind those of the cartoon fawn's mother, caught in the hunter's cross-hairs. Trey Clowes was at the mouth of the alley. He had seen her. And, as if knowing that she had no means of escape, he was making his approach with cruel languidness.

Once again, Avery felt herself noting with some interest that the two of them shared the same height, and a not dissimilar build. Only now the reasoning behind this thought could not have been more different from when it had first struck her, back when they had first met.

Head down, shoulders squared, Avery ran towards Trey, making like a quarterback. Her left clavicle, which she now suspected had sustained a minor fracture when she'd run into the hulking metal generator, sang bitter agony as she made full contact with his chest, but the run up and angle had been sufficient to knock him off balance, send him flying to the ground.

Clowes landed heavily on his back, his skull striking the dirt with a hollow crack, the breath forced from his lungs in a powerful rush less than a second later, when Avery fell heavily on top of him.

She scrambled up onto her hands and knees, straddling him, her initial response of fear dangerously marred now by distraction: the way his eyes had rolled back into his head, exposing the whites; the gurgling groan escaping his lips. She held her breath as she watched the eyes slowly close, wondered if he was concussed. She'd switched back to a logical, contemplative state, the primal animal in her locked away once again in the recesses of race memory, instantly losing Avery her advantage. Eyes open suddenly, focused and raging, Clowes's hands flew up from his sides and grasped Avery's wrists; before she'd even had a chance to register this, it seemed, it was now she who lay prone and trapped.

Avery writhed and kicked beneath Clowes, her fear stoked by the taste of blood, although it was merely the result of biting down on her own lower lip on landing impact when Clowes had flipped her over. She had become vaguely aware of a piercing noise, too, a scream, but realized that it was her own only when it became muffled, at the same time that she felt his hand over her mouth.

Finding one of her own arms free now, and fighting for breath, Avery clawed desperately at Clowes's right hand for a while before she succeeded in seizing his little finger in her entire fist and yanking it backwards with the same force; a motion, and indeed gleeful determination, that one might use when engaging the level of a particularly high-paying fruit machine.

Now the screaming was coming from Clowes, definitely, and wriggling out from beneath him and scrambling to her feet provided Avery with little challenge.

It took her a moment to figure out what had happened next, however, when she quickly found herself on the ground again, this time face down, the taste of blood in her mouth now combined with the taste of dirt – perhaps because the pain in her left cheekbone and knee, both horribly bruised from her earlier collision with the generator, hurt so desperately when she landed that she could barely register any other sensation, including that of Clowes's hands around her ankles in the tackle that had felled her.

Her laminated ID, the line-jumping cards and Debbie Kitchen's ballpoint pen had all spilt out of her pocket when she fell, and even now, as she felt Clowes throw himself onto her back, the fury rose within her as the memory returned of the last time she had felt a man's weight on her, pinning her down, when she was a child . . . Even through this she knew exactly what she was going to do.

Despite the fact that she had very little leeway, not much room in which to draw back her arm, the howl that came from Trey Clowes when Avery plunged the ballpoint pen through the web of flesh between his right thumb and forefinger was quite the most unsettling thing she'd ever heard. Except perhaps, she mused, for the meaty crunching of the penetration itself.

Clowes reared backwards, away from her, and sat back down on the ground, staring in gaping shock first at his hand, then at Avery, then at his hand again. Avery stalked carefully towards him, a lioness approaching a fallen zebra, and, closer still and now behind him, sprang into action, pinning his left arm behind his back with her left and hooking her right arm around his throat, yanking his head back, with just a little pressure on the oesophagus, enough to constrict his breathing but only lightly. Her cheek was pressed against his, making anything more than a whisper unnecessary.

'That was for Perdue, you fucker. And believe me, I haven't even got *started* . . .'

She felt Clowes's body tense in her arms, then felt him shudder, wracked with the first of a series of sobs and then her own face growing wet from his tears. With his injured hand, he pawed gingerly at the arm around his neck, his voice strangulated and indistinct.

'Avery, please don't hurt me . . . I didn't do it . . .'

She tightened her grip and he tensed again. 'Shut up.'

'Please, listen . . . Please . . . Perdue was . . . They set him up. Set *me* up . . . You have to believe me, please . . .'

The dawning possibility that Clowes was telling the truth made Avery recoil in horror, but she didn't loosen her grip. She had to be imagining it; mustn't fall for this trick, no matter how sorry she felt for him.

'You attacked me! And you expect me to believe . . . ? Forget it. You're finished, Trey. I'm taking you in.'

'I . . . ? *You* attacked *me*! I thought you were going to kill me! I was defending myself! And I didn't want you to scream because I didn't want them to . . . They're after me, Avery! You have to help me.'

There was something primal about the instinct stirring in her, the instinct that told her of his innocence. Though his words left her neither convinced nor unconvinced, the language of his movement against her body was something separate altogether. It was as if communication was taking place on a different level, in electrical pulses and nerve signals, in muscle and flesh and skin. The weakness and fear and naked honesty in the way he struggled weakly, then stopped, struggled, then stopped . . . her own fear signals had wound down, the giddy klaxon scream in her head whining low towards silence. Her reflexes were no longer on alert. His heartbeat was racing thunder, hers grew ever more steady, the two rhythms slipping into some kind of syncopation despite their warring paces. At some fundamental physical level, a message had been received loud and clear: she was not in danger.

Before her logical mind could protest, Avery found herself letting go of him. He slumped forward heavily onto the ground and she watched the erratic rise and fall of his back beneath the dirt-encrusted sweatshirt, as he coughed and sobbed and struggled to regain control of his breathing. She watched, kept watching, afraid that he would turn and assault her again, but more afraid, somehow, that he wouldn't. He didn't. Avery put her face in her hands.

'What have I done?'

He turned his bloodshot eyes to her. 'No, no . . . I . . . But God, did *I* hurt *you*? I'm so sorry. I was scared.'

She shook her head bitterly before reaching for his right hand. The wound from the pen was surprisingly bloodless, but it was raw and dirty and clearly swarming with bacteria, beginning already to swell and turn a livid purple from infection. Clowes winced and pulled the hand away before Avery could touch it, drawing it into his chest as he rolled onto his back and stared up at her.

She opened her mouth to speak, but he had reached towards her with his left hand already, and now he placed a finger gently to her lips.

'Shhh . . .'

'But I –'

He hushed her again, then noticed something, looked more closely at where his finger lay. He ran the tip lightly over the flesh where it was darkened by dried blood.

'Did I do that?'

Avery shook her head. 'Not really. I bit it. Forget it. I'm okay.'

They sat in silence, staring at one another for a while until Clowes rose to his feet, wincing, leaning only on his left hand as he got up, holding the right one out and away from him as if it were something that he were carrying to the trash can. Avery noticed now that the puncture wound was not the only damage sustained: his pinkie was limp and swollen, and jutting off at an unnatural angle.

'Christ, I think I broke your finger, too,' Avery muttered as she slipped her arm around his waist to provide support as they began to walk. 'Trey, before we do anything else, let's get you to hospital.'

She felt him tense again, stop dead in his tracks.

'Avery – *you* may believe me. Dreamworld security . . . Last night they definitely didn't. I don't want them to find me. Not until we know who's really behind all this, till we can give them an alternative. Take the heat off me.'

'But you ran away, so of course, they –'

'Avery, I ran away *because* they didn't believe me. Perdue had me wait in the car while he checked up on the call. When he didn't come back, I went looking for him and I – I found him.'

Clowes closed his eyes briefly, as if to blot out the hideous image; as if the picture were before him right now and not in his mind's eye. His voice wavered as he continued.

'I was still standing here, just, like, in *shock* when the patrol guys arrived and these guys . . . They thought I did it, Avery. Thought I killed one of their own. There were three of them. Emotions were running high. I'm putting it politely. I think they were going to take me to Osceola County PD, but I'm not sure I'd have been conscious when we got there.'

The involuntary sharp intake of breath sent a stab of pain through Avery's chest, the first real reminder of her damaged clavicle. She shook her head in disgust as she noticed that one of his eyes was swollen and that his left cheekbone, collarbone and both of his arms bore livid bruises.

'They . . . I can't believe it . . . Not here . . . I . . . That's terrible!'

'It's human nature.' Clowes shrugged. 'Even at glorious Dreamworld, public relations capital of America.'

Avery stopped again – *public relations capital of America* – a nasty thought coming clear in her mind.

'Trey, I . . . I'm not even sure if they *were* going to take you to Osceola County. You're right, let's get you somewhere safe. Then we can talk. I think I know who's behind this. I just need to work out how to prove it.'

Trey dabbed at the beads of sweat on his pallid temples, looking grave.

'Perdue's plan. He never told me what it was. *God*, I wish I'd asked.'

'Nah, it's okay. Doesn't matter,' Avery told him. But she didn't mean it. She had to know. Had to work out what it was, this plan so decisive that someone saw fit to kill Perdue to prevent him from carrying it out. She had to know what it was, and see it through herself.

Thirty-Eight

'Is it just me, or is freezing in here?'

Clowes lay palely in the back seat footwell of Avery's car, looking up at her, hugging himself and shivering. He looked about twelve years old.

'It's just you. Hang in there.'

Avery sparked up the engine and turned the heating to maximum before shrugging off the air hostess jacket and passing it back between the front seats. Clowes used his good left hand to draw it gratefully around his shoulders.

'Better. Thanks. So, go on, you were telling me about the tape you found.'

'I told you everything. It's not enough to go on yet, I know. But I'm so sure now that I was right. And I realized something else. This morning, I was telling the VIP tour group about the fallback protocol. It's a Dreamworld thing. You heard of it?'

Clowes shook his head and after Avery had given her succinct explanation he motioned for her to go on.

'I'd been thinking about Lucas again. Lucas bit off his own tongue. But there were no signs of a beating. Or a fall. Nothing. That had been bugging me.'

'How so?'

'Look, I don't know a ton about this stuff, but I know enough to know that it's not something you usually associate with a shooting. And that's when I twigged. I think they were using the fallback protocol. I think Lucas died *at the centre*. I think something went wrong: a seizure induced by Daetwyler's machine, something, anything.'

'"They" being Daetwyler and Homolka?'

'Exactly.'

'You think he was dead already? When they shot him?'

Avery nodded decisively. 'No matter how great a place you think you've found to hide a body, there's always a chance that it could go wrong. And it did. So where's your fallback?'

'You make it look like a murder. Deflect attention from the centre. Nobody is any the wiser.'

'Bingo.'

'But it still didn't work.'

'Nope, still didn't work. They hadn't bargained for you and Lisa and Leon to show up. They tried to deal with that and got even deeper into trouble. Daetwyler and Homolka, they knew we were onto them, big time . . . me and Perdue.'

Avery hesitated, thrown again momentarily by the almost incomprehensible realization that Perdue was no longer alive.

'But Hayes believed them. Believed their story.'

Avery shook her head.

'Sure. But he *wanted* to believe them. More than anything in the world. They knew that. That project, it was his baby too. And he wanted to protect Daetwyler, didn't want to be responsible for him losing custody of Devon if there was a chance that we were wrong. But equally, I think Hayes's last visit tipped them off to the fact that if he ever knew the truth, he wasn't going to protect them. Not for the sake of the project, or Devon, or Dreamworld's reputation or anything. And I think they knew that none of us were going to drop it, we weren't going to stop looking for the truth. And I think Hayes told them everything. He trusted Daetwyler, remember? They're friends. So inadvertently, Hayes told him what he wanted to know: who you were. The last witness to what he and Homolka had done; the one they'd been looking for. And they decided to pin it on you, threaten you, drive you into the security HQ for cover, then lure you and Perdue out. If it looked like you'd killed Perdue, the whole business would be over.'

Trey Clowes was deep in thought. 'Perdue . . . Or you.'

Avery looked at him uncomprehendingly. 'What do you mean?'

'I mean it could just as easily have been you who answered the call. Not Perdue.'

Avery's cellular phone had been resting in her lap as she spoke, and now she seized it and began to punch the keys with grim determination.

'What are you doing?'

'I'm going to get those fuckers. Obviously.'

Trey sat up, excited. 'Have you figured out Perdue's plan? What it was?'

She shook her head, but without chagrin. 'Not yet, Trey. But I will. And in the meantime, I have another idea.'

Despite the dirt stains, and the run in the hose, Avery's air hostess outfit was a very big hit with Officer Brett Toback and many of his colleagues at Osceola County PD

– particularly minus the jacket and several shirt buttons, which had gone missing during her struggle with Trey.

'So this VIP tour, when do you think I might be able to come down?'

Toback looked away from the VCR momentarily to address this question to Avery's breasts. Although she was used to this kind of thing, it was rarely quite this blatant, and she stifled a grin.

'Whenever you like, Brett. I owe you one. Big-time. I haven't forgotten about your Kit-E-Cat watch, either.'

Toback beamed to himself, hit the fast-forward button on the VCR before him, then looked Avery up and down again, a more concerned expression on his face this time.

'You have a fight or something?'

Avery let out a little laugh which was slightly more hysterical than she'd intended. 'Yeah, right! No, uh, I've been showing some folks round a construction site this morning. Took a tumble. But anyway, then I had this hunch, and I thought I might . . .'

She stopped talking as a tall, familiar figure popped into vision and then out again. Avery leant forward, tapped the screen. 'Wait, go back. I think that's her.'

The image spun giddily backwards, then ran forward in real-time. The figure appeared in the lower righthand corner, as if from nowhere. The head low, then higher, standing upright, then ducking down again and to the left. She was getting out of one car, into another. But the cars were just out of shot. Understandable, then, that no one had noticed her: there was nothing to connect her to Lucas, to the case.

'Can we get a printout?'

Officer Brett Toback checked surreptitiously over both shoulders and checked out Avery's chest again before nodding vigorously and getting down to business.

The story Avery had spun for Toback in order to check whether Catherine Homolka appeared on the surveillance tape taken in the parking lot of Emanuelle's was so convoluted that she'd been stunned when Toback accepted it without question. The missing buttons counted for a lot, she supposed.

Needless to say, however, they counted for nothing with Catherine Homolka herself, who now sat behind her desk, scowling across at Avery.

'Hayes told me you guys were going to quit bothering us. This had better be good.'

Avery lapped up the scowl, relishing every moment of awkward silence, drinking it in, before she spoke. 'Oh it's good. It's very good.'

Homolka could barely contain her irritation. 'So shoot. Daetwyler needs me in the lab. I was told this was urgent, so get on with it.'

'Do you like looking at naked babes, Catherine?'

Homolka slapped the palms of her hands down on the desk in exasperation. 'Do I – the hell is this about, Sylvia?'

'It's about I was wondering what you were doing at Emanuelle's. The night before Jerry Lee Lucas was found dead.'

Homolka sneered furiously. 'Emanuelle's? What is that? I don't even –'

Avery held up her hands. 'Please, don't bother. I don't have time to check out your lame acting skills today.'

She reached down into her purse, withdrew the surveillance printout and threw it across the desk. 'Listen, Catherine, you're nowhere near interesting enough to

321

be a lesbian, and something tells me you don't have a part-time job there.' Avery stared pointedly at the decidedly modest swell beneath Homolka's MIT sweatshirt. 'So unless I'm very much mistaken, I'd say you were there because you were dumping a dead volunteer's car in the parking lot to make it look like he'd been there. Whaddya say?'

Homolka stared at the picture then back at Avery with hatred in her eyes. 'Does Hayes know you're here?'

'What difference does it make?'

'He's not going to shut us down, Sylvia. He cares too much about this project. Trey Clowes is gonna go down, and I think you'll find that Hayes is pretty happy with that outcome. It would take a lot of evidence to convince him otherwise. And frankly, I don't call *this* evidence of anything.'

Homolka threw the picture back across the desk towards Avery. It sailed past her, landing on the floor. Avery swooped down grudgingly and picked it up, very tempted to leap to her feet and stuff it down Homolka's throat. She fought to stay calm, however; succeeded.

'You think Hayes cares what happens to this project? Dreamworld has plenty of money. Someone will come up with something else. He'd see the project go tomorrow, pull the plug himself, I can assure you. Whaddya say you get real, Catherine? Then we can talk.'

Homolka gave a nervous, enigmatic smile. 'No. *You* get real. You seriously think Hayes doesn't care what happens to this project?'

'I think Hayes, for some misguided reason, doesn't want Daetwyler to lose custody of Devon. Family is sacred to Hayes, don't ask me why. Probably because he's never had one. And it's blinded him to what's really going on.

Believe me, I don't have the same problem. That real enough for you?'

Though she hated to admit it, Homolka's reaction caught her off guard.

'If you really want to know, Richard already lost Devon. It's over. Yesterday. She's gone already. Okay? You happy now? The court ruled that since she had an IQ of three fucking billion she was capable of choosing for herself.'

Avery sat speechless for a moment, then laughed, although she hadn't intended to.

'And she chose . . . Well, she obviously *has* got quite a brain on her. She certainly made a pretty fucking sagacious choice.'

Catherine Homolka stood up, leant over the desk and slapped Avery relatively hard. It stung, but was more annoying than painful and Avery studiously ignored it, pretended that it hadn't happened.

'Oh, *grow up*, Catherine. You know I'm right. Daetwyler's an asshole. If you can't see it now, I promise you will one day.'

'No, Sylvia, it's not me. It's you. *You* don't know anything about Richard Daetwyler, what he's like. And you don't know Hayes for what *he* really is, either. He might have told you that he wanted to protect the project because of Richard, Devon, all that stuff, but that's pure crap. Did it never occur to you that he told you that because you wanted to hear it?'

Avery wanted to shift in her seat, but fought the urge; couldn't stand to let Homolka know that she'd succeeded in making her uncomfortable. She didn't want to speak yet, either, in case her voice betrayed her. So she let the increasingly hysterical tirade continue. And continue it did.

'Huh? You think he cares about people? Hayes cares about Dreamworld. Period. He cares about it being the first, the best, the most perfect. You think he'd risk letting this project go knowing that someday, somewhere we'd be back, somewhere else? That Disney or Universal or someone else would get the glory?'

Now Avery stood, putting her face very close to Homolka's before she let rip, definite, slow and very, very loud: *'That – is – utter – bullshit*! Do you think Hayes would risk installing something in the park that could go wrong? Could be potentially lethal? Could kill some tourist the way it killed Jerry Lee Lucas? Are you serious?'

Rather than moving back, Homolka stood up too, her face now in even closer proximity to Avery's as she sputtered her response, choking back tears.

'That's not what killed Lucas! Don't you ever, ever, *ever* fucking suggest that there's anything wrong with anything Richard's built! It was the drugs! Jerry Lee Lucas had no business volunteering for a trial that involved chemical work, he must've been so fucking full of God knows what else, he had a reaction, it wasn't our fault!'

Avery sat back down, temporarily stunned by the confession she had not dared hope to hear. She tried to lower her cadence to a simmer, but coming from a raging boil it was nearly impossible.

'But you didn't call an ambulance, Catherine, did you? Because it would mean an investigation. You'd have been shut down. No matter what you say you believe about Hayes, you *know* that he'd *never* have backed you under those circumstances. So tell me, how long did it take Lucas to bleed to death after he bit off his tongue, Catherine? Twenty minutes? Half an hour? More? Did you watch? Or did you just close the door, let him get on with it?'

Homolka's face crumpled and she began to cry. It was quite the most frighteningly elaborate display of lachrimosity that Avery had ever observed – body wracked by spasms, tears coursing down her face, thick mucus running from her nose. Eventually she wiped some of this on the sleeve of her sweatshirt, took a gulp of air and emitted more wailing protests.

'It wasn't like that! I *wanted* to call an ambulance! He wouldn't let me! He told me not to!'

'And you cared more about Richard Daetwyler than about saving a man's life? It's easy to see when somebody's got a crush on her boss, Catherine, but that's some pretty obsessive crush, that you'd go that far to –'

'Noooo! It's not like that!' Homolka howled, flinching physically at the words as though Avery had hurled acid over her. 'You don't understand.'

'So what is it like? Why don't you tell me?'

Catherine Homolka sat back down heavily, buried her face in her hands. 'I can't. What I did, my part in it . . . He said if I ever told anyone he was involved, he'd make sure everything I did . . . Came out. That it'd be me who'd pay. I can't . . . I can't say any more. Except that I know you don't understand. Whatever it is that you think, it's not . . .'

The pity that Avery suddenly felt for the girl was overwhelming. 'Did you shoot Lucas, after he was dead?'

Homolka wailed again. 'No! I found the gun in his car. It was Lucas's gun. But it wasn't me. I wouldn't do it. Couldn't. I dumped the car. That was all.' She wiped her nose on her sleeve again. 'Why have you made me tell you this? What have you made me do? My God, I'm . . . I don't know what he's going to do to me . . .'

'Trust me. You're going to be fine. Just tell me one more thing, Catherine. You have to tell me one more thing. Was it you who took Leon LeGalley to Dreamworld that morning?'

Catherine Homolka just stared. Then, 'I can't say any more. I'm . . . I'm scared. Things have changed now.'

'Now that Daetwyler has nothing to lose?'

'Yes – no! Look, I – you don't realize . . .'

'Was it you, Catherine? Just say yes or no.'

Catherine Homolka shook her head.

'Then I think you can leave it to me. And I think that I can promise you that you're going to come out of this okay.'

If Avery's mind hadn't been so full of so many other things, she might have noticed the figure silhouetted behind the frosted glass panel of the interconnecting door between Daetwyler's office and Homolka's. But it was, and she didn't, and, somewhat ironically, this was to be both the first and the last thing that the two women would ever have in common.

Thirty-Nine

'Hey, sleeping beauty. Wake up.'

The slam of the passenger door had failed to rouse Clowes at all, so leaning back between the front seats of her car, Avery now gently shook his arm. He stirred groggily, shifted position and winced in pain as his now grotesquely swollen right hand made contact with something. He took a few controlled recovery breaths, like a woman panting through labour, before fixing Avery with a sly smile.

'Sorry. I just had a horrible dream that you tackled me to the ground and stabbed my hand with a ballpoint pen.'

Now Avery winced, and gestured over to the passenger seat, whose occupant stared at Clowes, then at Avery then at Clowes again in some bewilderment.

'Trey, this is Mitch Ducek. An old friend of mine. He's going to help us out. Mitch, this is Trey.'

Mitch Ducek nodded in awkward greeting at the somewhat battered young man lying in the footwell. He focused his concerned gaze back on Avery. 'You know ... about that date you promised me? I think maybe I'll pass.'

Avery was surprised to see a shadow of irritation pass over Clowes's countenance, and spoke quickly to him before he could interject.

'It's Perdue's plan, Trey. He knew there was a way to find out for certain who brought Leon LeGalley to ImagiNation that morning. Concrete evidence. All we knew was that Perdue said he couldn't act on it, whatever it was, until the next morning. So I realised that it must have been something connected with someplace that he couldn't get into at night. Someplace in the park. And from that, I finally figured out what it was. And it really was fail-safe, just like Perdue said. Now I know that the killer was Daetwyler, Trey, and I know how to prove it. Right now. Mitch is going to help us.'

'Who the hell is Daetwyler?' asked Ducek.

Avery ignored the question, as did Clowes, who smiled weakly at Ducek before closing his eyes again.

'Hey, Mitch – thanks, man.'

'My pleasure,' said Ducek, in a voice indicative of the fact that this was not entirely true.

On the drive between Atlantis – where Avery had picked up Mitch, forcing him to spin some convoluted yarn to his co-workers – and ImagiNation, their destination, Mitch Ducek tried repeatedly to get Avery to explain to him what was going on.

'It's a long story. Long, long story,' she told him.

Ducek folded his arms. 'You'll tell me later, though, right? You have to.'

Avery kept poker face, her eyes on the road ahead. 'I will. I promise.'

He sulked a little more before his face lit up as if illuminated by a cartoon light-bulb, and he cracked a leering grin. 'How about over dinner?'

'Pathetic,' murmured a voice from behind them in the footwell, and Avery smiled.

'Sure, no, we owe you dinner, Mitch. Hayes is going to be so grateful to you for helping me out. He's going to want to thank you himself, I know it. And I know you'll really like him.'

She looked back uneasily over her shoulder at Clowes, who lay motionless, eyes tight shut in what she was sure was feigned sleep.

Mitch Ducek was still sulking somewhat when they arrived at the ImagiNation photographic centre, fleshy lips set in a petulant pout most unbecoming to one of his age and gender. He watched Avery conversing, low and urgent, with the manager, gesturing over to the back-room door and then to him; watched as the manager disappeared through it and returned momentarily with two rather confused-looking employees.

'Mitch? It's all ours. You're on.'

Avery bounded to the doorway of the now empty room and gestured to him to follow. He walked as slowly as he could in the vague hope that she might find it irritating and was dismayed to note that she didn't appear to. She smiled at him brightly as she kicked the door shut behind her and pulled out one of the chairs set before the row of computer terminals.

'Okay, maestro. Ready to do your thing?'

Mitch Ducek sat down without saying anything.

'It's the same, right? Same system as they have over at Atlantis? You know what you're doing?'

He peered at it, nodded. 'What date are we looking for?'

Avery told him, and he seemed to forget about sulking as he warmed to his task, punching the keyboard and working the mouse, keen to showcase his competence and flair again. Avery might have been affected by the pathos, the poignancy of this misdirected primate-like behaviour – like she could give a shit at this juncture – but she was breathless, utterly focused, a hair's breadth away from finally receiving the proof she'd been waiting for, for so long. In just a moment she would see the evidence that would – along with Homolka's testimony – indict Daetwyler, vindicate Clowes and see justice done for Lucas, LeGalley and Schaeffer. It was nearly over. Nearly over. She could scarcely believe it. Avery tapped the screen impatiently, hopping from foot to foot like a kindergartener on the verge of peeing her Rugrats underpants.

'Outside Hansel and Gretel! On the path to the cookie house! You got it?'

Mitch Ducek ignored her, flipping through the on-screen options until he could truthfully answer that yes, he had found the cache of digital souvenir pictures taken on the correct day and at the correct location.

The numbers – 0901 – in the top righthand corner of the screen indicated that the shot currently displayed was the first of the day. A handsome young family beamed as they posed for a picture with Kitten Caboodle: a pretty young mom, pregnant; her husband; their beautiful little girl, chestnut-maned, four, maybe five years old, eagerly clutching Kitten's soft furry paw.

Avery stared at the picture. There was something sad

about the joy and innocence of it, juxtaposed with her purpose for being here, and she felt a sudden dirty sense of imposition merely in observing it. She took a deep, wistful breath. She was grateful when Ducek's voice interrupted her thoughts.

'Now, what time? Roughly?'

Avery took another breath before answering him. Back to business. So close, now. So close.

She put her hands on the back of the swivel chair and leant over Ducek's shoulder, watching as he zipped the digital clock forward and then began to flip slowly through the pictures.

Kitten Caboodle and five Japanese girls.

Kitten Caboodle and an elderly white couple.

Kitten Caboodle and a numerous African-American family all wearing matching yellow sweats.

'Quit breathing down my neck, Avery,' Ducek said, finding her tension unpleasantly contagious. 'Can you tell me what we're looking for?'

She stood back reluctantly, not taking her eyes off the screen.

Kitten Caboodle and a little boy with chronic sunburn.

Kitten Caboodle and three gorgeous red-haired children.

'It's not the foreground we're looking at. It's the background. See the door there? To the right of the candy cane drainpipe? Set back? That's the stair access down to the utilidor. And any minute . . .'

Kitten Caboodle and two dangerously overweight eight-year-olds.

Kitten Caboodle and a gang of German backpackers.

'. . . someone is going to . . .'

Kitten Caboodle, a handsome man and a blonde girl in a wheelchair.

'. . . come into frame and . . .'

Kitten Caboodle and a tired-looking woman with twins.

'. . . open that door and . . .'

Kitten Caboodle and a stunning Hispanic Lolita holding a raven-mopped baby. 'Mitch! There! Stop!'

Avery dug her nails into Ducek's bicep, causing him to holler in pain, but by now he was too caught up in her fervour to be angry.

They both stared at the screen, neither one breathing. In the lefthand corner a figure who was, without doubt, Leon LeGalley had come into view. He looked dazed, distant. A male hand, its owner still out of shot, rested lightly on his shoulder. Avery tapped the screen.

'That's him.'

'You want it printed out?'

'Not yet. I need to see who's with him. That's what I need. Keep going.'

'I hope they were having a busy morning,' said Ducek. 'If there was a long gap, he might have gone down already by the time the next picture was taken.'

Avery bit down hard on her lip, tasting blood as she inadvertently reopened the split she'd sustained earlier. The next picture flipped onto the screen.

Kitten Caboodle and four little girls. Leon LeGalley close to the door, his companion's identity now obscured by the head of the tallest child.

'Shit. Keep going,' Avery murmured under her breath. 'Come on Daetwyler, you *fucker*. Your ass is *mine*.'

Avery fell silent and began to pray as Ducek hit the advance key one more time.

And then it was there. At last.

In the foreground, Kitten Caboodle posing with a skinny man in a lovingly ironed Phantom Menace sweatshirt. Behind them, Leon LeGalley by the utilidor entrance. And next to LeGalley, the man who had lured him to the Research and Development Complex that morning. The man who had drugged him and brought him to ImagiNation to kill Lisa Schaeffer and kill himself. The same man who had ordered Catherine Homolka to let Jerry Lee Lucas bleed to death and to dump his car at a strip club, and who had used Lucas's own gun to put a bullet in the body before dumping it in a ribbon of roadside swamp. The man who had carefully plotted the murder of Felix Perdue when he learnt of Perdue's plan to check the very pictures that Avery was looking at now. The man who had terrorized Trey Clowes into seeking refuge at Dreamworld in order to frame him for that murder. The man to whom Daetwyler and Homolka had been saying goodbye on the tape that Avery had listened to and who had coldly manipulated and deceived every unfortunate soul trapped within the deadly sweep of his radar.

She staggered backwards, now, away from the screen as if she'd just taken a sledgehammer to the forehead, her hands grasping at nothing, her legs threatening to give, her lungs empty and burning.

The man in the picture was Hayes Ober.

Forty

'What happened? Avery, tell me! What is it?'

Clowes was right behind her now, behind her where she stood at the rear of the jeep, awkwardly straddling the jet ski trailer bar. The tailgate was thrown open and she was leaning in, her hands scrabbling as she threw aside the items of sports equipment and other leisure ephemera that crowded the vehicle's capacious trunk. She flinched as Trey touched her, stopped her frantic efforts momentarily to try and swat his hand from where it rested on her shoulder. She turned to him, eyes bright with horror and brimming with tears.

'Leave me alone, Trey! Get back in the car, they'll see you! Just let me do this. I have to see –'

'Do what? What are you looking for?'

She tried once again to elbow him away with little success before resuming her quest. She flung aside the sports bag that contained Hayes's winter wet suit, using her pitching arm to jettison it over the headrests and into the back seat. The blue plaid picnic blanket – the one Hayes had bought at the Scotch House whilst on a business trip to London – had formed the base strata of the compacted contents of the trunk, and now it was exposed and no longer pinned down. Moving it, she knew, would require little to no physical labour, yet more emotional effort than she could imagine being capable of mustering.

Avery stood listening to her own breathing, and, behind her, Clowes's breathing, and, more distantly, the happy screams of the people riding the Niagara Falls Adventure and the footfalls and the happy chatter of tens of thousands of mothers and fathers, grandparents and children, lovers and friends.

Lightly, she ran her fingertips over the edge of the rug closest to her, feeling the buttery filaments of the cashmere, thinking about the turf in her backyard, and earthworms and weevils and earwigs and beetles, and the thundering AVAC garbage pipes and the decapitated cartoon creatures and Lisa Schaeffer and Leon LeGalley lying dead on the floor of the disabled restroom in the utilidors just below the surface of Dreamworld.

Finally, she gripped a corner in either hand, looked back forlornly at Clowes for a moment, and tugged it with a powerful flourish, an elegant snap, like a magician whisking a tablecloth from beneath a full set of high-tea crockery.

She didn't really need to see it, she knew that. She had known in all certainty – however grotesque and unbearable and unthinkable the thought – that it was there, and she had known that if she sought to unearth this final proof, to see it for herself, she would find it. And now she had. And as her thoughts swam in a slow, churning, unreal sort of way, Avery acknowledged briefly that she didn't really need to look at it now. But she looked at it anyway.

The blanket fell to the ground from between her fingers.

The bullet hole, a tiny, neat ellipse, would almost have been unnoticeable had it not been for the burn in the carpeting at its circumference. Or, peppering a broader radius beyond this bright ring of charcoal, the spots of cordite. Or, for that matter, the broadest ring of all, a dried dark-brown halo that was all that was left here of the fluid that had pumped from the chambers of Jerry Lee Lucas's heart and through his raddled veins and out of the exit wound in his lumbar region before it had trickled through the tiny hole in the bottom of the picnic cooler that she should have noticed had been missing from where it always stood in the back of Hayes's jeep.

Clowes took a step back, his mouth open long before he blurted out his words. 'Holy shit . . . Hayes.'

Yes, Hayes. Not Daetwyler. Hayes. She had wondered at first why the poisonous truth of her erroneous suppositions and his evil deception should have sunk in so quickly, so easily; the demise of her history and her future with him a swift and efficient little death, as sure and sterile and expeditious as a death-row injection.

All her life the enemy, the threat, the fear had never been a faceless stranger, but one familiar to her. Familiar and close. She knew this feeling well; just as intimately as she knew betrayal and denial and lies. This wasn't anything new. This was – in a foul and bitter and putrid way – like coming home.

Avery nodded before embarking on a dignified retreat to the driver's door, pausing before she used the handle. 'Close the trunk, Trey. And get in.'

When she was left alone at home, as a little girl, Avery often used to dial 911 on the phone. Just to see how it felt. The nine. Then the one. And the one again. She knew it was silly, even when she was very young. Figured that it maybe wasn't the right number to call, even supposing that she had been calling with the receiver up, in her hand, not down in the cradle, where it always was. But it was the only number she knew for people who were good and kind and righteous and who would care – and would *believe* – that in a perfect little house in Cassadaga, Florida, which looked like something straight out of Mayberry, a heinous crime was being committed. Again and again and again.

Sometimes Avery would whisper the words she would say to somebody, to the somebody who would answer the phone, if ever the receiver had been up when she dialled. The words she would say to somebody who could save her. The introduction, her name. Her age and address. The initial apology that this wasn't really an emergency, not exactly, not really, but maybe just maybe they could help anyways. Sometimes she'd whisper these terrible, wonderful, forbidden words, but mostly she'd just dial 911. 911. 911. Over and over and over until she felt a little better, a little brighter, a little more capable of drawing another breath, eating another meal, climbing into her pyjamas and her bed again. Switching off the Banana Splits lamp and pretending, just one more time, that tonight perhaps she wouldn't hear the rattle at the door, although she knew that it wasn't true.

She knew so well how it felt to dial those numbers, how it felt to jam her tiny forefinger into the heavy dial of the black rotary phone they'd had when she was very little. How it felt to punch the smooth, square buttons on the mushroom-coloured trim-phone of her more vividly remembered youth. She knew perfectly how it felt in tactile terms and she also knew how it felt metaphorically. It felt like having her hands on the handle of a detonator. Three little movements, a few words, and her family, everything she had ever known, would blow apart, crumble and crash to the ground like a building reduced to rubble. Just rubble and, buried beneath it, the tawdry detritus of destroyed lives; the lives of those who once had sheltered between those four shattered walls.

Our little secret . . .
If you think they won't see that you're guilty too, guilty as
*   hell, then you're crazy, Sylvia Avery.*
Do you really want everybody to know?
Do you want to break this family apart?
Do you know what will happen?
Where will you go?
What will you do?
You'll have nothing.
Our little secret.

Avery raised her forehead from where it rested on her arms, on the steering wheel, and said something too quiet for Clowes to hear.

Gingerly he touched the back of her neck. 'What did you say?'

'*I said,*' she enunciated, smiling gently as she turned slowly to face him, '*not this time.*'

Forty-One

'Where *are* you, Sylvia?'

Avery cradled the walkie-talkie in the crook of her neck, flinching slightly at the decibel level of Debbie Kitchen's voice, its trademark perky cadence notable by its absence.

'I – look, Debbie . . . Like I said, I'm sorry. I'm really, really sorry about the tour group, leaving them there. But there was some trouble – security related – and I really needed to deal with it, without . . . I didn't want them to see it. You'd be glad that they didn't, I assure you. But, Debbie, listen, this is urgent. I need you to call security for me, have somebody tell Calum Asch to meet me out here in the ImagiNation lot. It's really, really important.'

A long, crackling silence reverberated through the earpiece.

'Debbie? You there? You hear me?'

There was a reply, but Avery didn't hear it – at least not succinctly, not beyond being vaguely aware of a burst of human noise issuing from the walkie-talkie where it lay on the ground after she dropped it from her trembling hand. It lay there at her feet as she stood staring in abject alarm across the parking lot, through the shimmering heat haze, watching the male figure climbing out of the fawn Lexus Coupé that she had just noticed standing several rows away. He was, without a shadow of doubt, making his way towards her.

She stood frozen, long enough for Hayes Ober to catch her eye, his gaze a tractor beam, brilliant with menace; trapping her, paralysing her.

Forcing herself to move, she banged frantically on the roof of the Cherokee.

'Trey! Quick! Drive!'

Clowes scrambled into the driver's seat, panicking. 'Drive where? Where shall I go?'

Avery leant urgently into the window. 'Drive to Atlantis. The lot where you left the note on my car. You've got the permit right there, Ray'll let you in. Then run. Straight to the Biodrome and you need to see Dr Gwen Bissette. Got that? Gwen Bissette. In the Biodrome. Tell them, bad news: Scully's dead. They get Gwen right away, you tell her everything. *Everything*.'

Avery glanced urgently over her shoulder as Trey turned the ignition key, a look of confusion on his face.

'Why?'

She avoided his eyes. 'In case anything happens to you, Trey. Fallback protocol.'

'That's a cheerful thought,' said Trey, but Avery had already stepped away from the car, was already watching Hayes Ober, waiting for the burst of speed, the change of direction back towards his own car, the pursuit. Waiting. But it didn't happen. Now, Hayes took his eyes from Clowes, racing away in his own jeep, and fixed them back on Avery, still walking towards her. Closer. Closer. He pointed slowly at her, and then at the plaid blanket that lay on the ground behind the Cherokee, smiling a sly, determined smile that turned every millilitre of blood in her veins to liquid helium.

Run? Stay? Before she could decide, he was there before her, locking his gaze with hers in a dizzy, polluted silence. Although her mouth was dry, her body rigid, electrified by fearful adrenaline, it was Avery who broke it.

'I thought you were in LA . . .'

A malicious grin. 'Nope.'

'Where were you?'

'Following you, Avery. And you're so predictable it hurts.'

She wasn't sure why she'd looked down at this point, but that was when she saw the gun. The gun that she knew somehow – incidentally and somewhat incongruously now – was the one that had once belonged to Jerry Lee Lucas. And fixing her sights on the sloping ramp that led down from the parking lot into the utilidors, Sylvia Avery began, once more, to run for her life.

Forty-Two

Nothing bad ever happened at ImagiNation. That simple fact was as fundamental a truth, as vital a component of Hayes Ober's existence as breathing, eating, shitting. Stay in the park, stay above ground, and Hayes Ober couldn't, wouldn't dare do anything to hurt her, Avery knew that. And she began to feel a cloak of safety enveloping her as soon as she had flung open the door to the first available exit from the utilidors, and began to break for the surface, taking the stone steps two at a time. This burgeoning sense of relief grew stronger still as she plunged into the thronging crowds on Central Avenue. The elements that now flooded her senses, the sounds and sights and smells, felt to Avery like a comic-book force-field, surrounding her, protecting her. She knew that as long as she could hear the clamour of people and the tram conductor ringing his bell, and the clattering hooves of the ImagiNation Clydesdales and the trundling wheels of the colourful drays they pulled, nothing bad could happen to her. The sun on her skin and the artificial piped aroma of doughnuts that wafted continuously from a vent hidden above the entrance to the Central Avenue bakery – all these things meant that she had nothing t fear. She was in ImagiNation, where nothing bad ever happened, and she was safe.

Hayes would also take the first exit up from the utilidors, she knew that, and like her, he would turn right on Central Avenue, travelling away from the turnstiles. She could have second-guessed him, she knew, but heading towards the exit would put her in a wide-open space, a thinner crowd, exposed and easier to pick out. Besides, Avery knew exactly what she intended to do because whenever she'd watched a movie in which someone was being chased, she'd always wondered why the quarry kept on running. She'd always known what she would do instead: stop really early on, take advantage of her lead and hide somewhere so that the hunter would pass her by, still speeding onwards in the initial burst of his pursuit. Up a tree, if the chase were in a forest. Into an alley or a shrubbery, if it were a residential street. If she'd been Robert Donat in the original *Thirty-Nine Steps*, for instance, she always thought that she would have hidden in a clump of Highland bracken. If she'd been Dustin Hoffman in *Marathon Man*, she'd have hidden in one of those really big city trash cans. Or Keanu Reeves in *Point Break* – if she'd been him, she would have stopped in one of the beach houses, run upstairs and locked herself in a bathroom. (And she definitely wouldn't have stopped to pick up a dog and throw it at Patrick Swayze, *that* was just stupid.) Avery had always thought that she knew better than most characters in most movies, in fact, and now was her chance to put her theory to the test. Deftly weaving through the crowd, she ducked into the Central Avenue bakery and took a seat in the last booth, the one at the very back of the store, planning to remain there until she felt sure that Hayes had run past, up Central Avenue.

Something felt wrong, though. Something about the other people in the bakery, a pervasive sense of stress and disappointment and discontent that she'd never noticed before, and that – although she was not by any means superstitious – gave her an unexpected and nasty sense of premonition, a sense that her magical force-field was being gradually eroded as she watched.

At one table, a stressed-looking young couple tried desperately to force a muffin into the mouth of their wailing baby, who appeared to be far too small for the highchair into which she had been wedged by a diaper bag and a balled-up denim jacket. At another, a husband and his sobbing wife appeared to be having a quiet yet brutal argument whilst two of their three children stoically focused on their complimentary ImagiNation colouring books and the third repeatedly hollered at them to quit fighting.

'Are we having fun yet?'

It was the second time that the person sitting closest to Avery had said this, and this time Avery looked up to match a face to the voice. The speaker was a woman, addressing her oddly androgynous table companion. Both were urgently overweight, and Avery found particularly ghastly fascination in the pair's undulating arms, which bulged from the sleeves of their identical *Touched by an Angel* tank tops, the stark white cotton providing a hideous contrast to the skin and its livid shade of sunstroke. She looked at them surreptitiously, with warring measures of reluctance and compulsion, much as one might when cruising past the location of a fresh car wreck, until her attention was distracted by a sudden howl from across the room.

A little boy of about nine had clapped his hand to his mouth, which – Avery could see between the splayed fingers – was a stinging red. He stared at a woman – his mother? – with a poisonous fusion of shock, hatred and heartbreak before turning tail, running out of the café and onto Central Avenue. The woman, whose mouth was frighteningly slack and wrinkled, turned indignantly to return the stares of her fellow diners before turning back to her companion: a tiny, brassy blonde a decade or so her junior.

'He always gives me trouble, whenever we go any-where. Then he'll start saying –' she affected a whining falsetto – '"I miss Daddy."' Her voice dropped back to its natural snarl. 'It's like, he can't use that excuse for ever, you know? He's grounded. And that's it.'

The woman gave an exasperated sigh and got up from the table to find the sobbing child, and after a while most people stopped staring at the blonde she'd left behind, except for a pair of pretty twenty-something girls, who made loud and persistent remarks until the younger female rounded on them.

'What did you say?'

The girls exchanged glances, indignant, yet relishing the promise of confrontation. One of them, olive-skinned and thoroughly poised, replied in a resonant English accent, smiling benignly. 'I said, I wonder why people bring their kids to theme parks to hit them?' The blonde appeared to revel in this opportunity to play her trump card. 'That little boy just lost his father. *She* just lost her husband.'

The British girl gave her shiny black mane a nonchalant toss. 'May I suggest, then, that they go for some family counselling?'

Avery turned away, tried to tune out, but couldn't shake off the pervasive sense that there was some-thing rotten here, something she'd never seen before.

Something she had perhaps been tuning out all along, and was no longer able to. It was as if the earthworms and weevils and earwigs and beetles were swarming to the surface, visible now in the grass, turning the green blades brown. And she found herself wondering whether maybe somebody in her childhood *had* known about her own family. Had been able to see beyond the perfect veneer to the blighted wood beneath. Perhaps it wasn't as easy as she had thought to maintain a perfect surface when there was so much that was bad to cover. Maybe eventually no matter what you did to make things look right, the rot would seep through. And had Avery not buried her face in her hands at this point, she would have seen Hayes peering through the window of the bakery, walking in. As it was, he was already at her table by the time she knew she'd been found.

He slid into the booth beside her, smiling. She tried to smile back, and spoke through gritted teeth.

'What are you gonna do? You can't do anything to me here.'

But now she wasn't so sure as she had been.

'No, quite. Which is why we're going back down into the utilidors.'

'Thanks, but I think I'll stay here.'

'I don't think so. Come on, honey.'

Hayes Ober reached around Avery and lifted her up, like a man carrying his wife across the threshold. She squirmed and struggled as inconspicuously as she could, something within her still regarding ImagiNation's veneer – or what remained of it – as a sacrosanct thing. Because if she didn't, would Hayes? And if *he* didn't, she was dead.

Avery laughed loudly as she battled to get free, aware that the eyes of the bakery patrons were on her. Ever the sobbing wife and her angry husband had stopped fighting to watch.

'*Honey*. . . Put me down!'

She elbowed Hayes hard in the ribs, trying to giggle playfully as she did it. Not a convincing giggle, she knew – it sounded more like a death rattle – but she had to try. Hayes only tightened his grip, successfully pinning her arms by her sides as he carried her towards the door beside the serving counter and backed into it, using his body to push it open.

Avery tried desperately to make eye contact with any of the three girls working at the counter, but all were embroiled in taking orders from customers.

Hayes threw the bemused crowd a jocular smile, a playful salute.

'Bye, folks!'

And the door slammed shut behind them.

The stairwell down to the utilidors seemed darker, damper, colder than usual, and quieter, too. Silent, in fact, bar some echoing footsteps in some far off segment of the catacombs, and the unnerving gaiety of the nostalgic, patriotic piped brass-band music that identified the Central Avenue section of the utilidors.

Hayes Ober's face was set in concentration, obvious concern at the risk of missing a step, since some of his view was blocked by Avery herself, still struggling in his arms. She took advantage of this, kicking her legs as hard as she could, trying to throw him off balance. The hardness of the concrete, the steep incline of the steps . . These things scared her too, made her think of smashed teeth and broken noses and shattered skulls, but such fears were nothing at all compared to the cold, cold horror of her current captive position.

She bucked again, hoping to throw Hayes off balance, and succeeded to some extent, scaring him enough that he instinctively let go of her legs and grabbed the metal banister with his left hand. Seizing the moment, Avery planted her feet firmly on the ground and jumped, launching herself into oblivion, taking Hayes down with her.

Avery's head struck the concrete once, twice, three times as she tumbled down the stairs, and although it all happened so fast, she found herself with time enough to wonder how often – and how hard – one needed to hit one's head before suffering a concussion. Or whether she might break her spine, or her neck. Had she just authored her own demise?

The ground was graveyard cold beneath her bruised back and she hurt in so many places that she could barely distinguish one pain from another. But she was alive. And she could feel her legs, her arms. This was good, very good. And she could see. In fact, she could see Hayes where he lay, not far from her, on his front, sprawled in what was coincidentally – ironically? – almost a perfect example of the recovery position. His eyes were closed, however, and a bright puddle of blood was beginning to pool around his head, oozing from some unseen wound of indeterminate gravity. Even as she began to gather herself, get to her feet, get moving, she felt a pang of remorse, grief. A horror that the fall might actually have killed him. She looked at him one more time, her eye drawn to the stray curl of brown hair on his shirt collar. And then she ran. She'd been to the Cineplex often enough to know that you didn't stand around waiting for your apparently-dead pursuer's eyes to snap open, or for the hand to shoot out and grab your ankles.

Avery had been running – or thought she had – for several seconds when she distinguished a pain in her left hip from the myriad agony elsewhere, and realized that she was limping dreadfully. She slowed to a stop, doubled over, panting, wondering if she'd be able to speed up again. Gingerly taking a step, which sent a blinding lightning crack of white pain from mid-spine right down to the knee, she found herself having to admit that this wasn't going to work. And behind her, as she'd feared – expected? Hoped? No, not hoped, not really – Hayes Ober was stirring.

Covering distance, achieving speed; these things were now out of the question, and Avery realized that this physical disadvantage left her with no choice but to revert to using her mind, using tactics, in lieu.

Like a novice ice-skater, Avery hugged the corridor wall as she rounded the corner, vowing to duck into the first doorway she could find.

It was marked Dreamworld Engineering Personnel Only, and when she swung it open, she was surprised to find herself at the top of another set of stairs. She paused, her bearings, her entire sense of place, thrown out of kilter. Technically, the utilidors were ImagiNation's first floor, the park the second, built on top because – as she had always understood it – Florida's soil precluded building down. And yet here she was readjusting to the idea of the utilidor level as some kind of mezzanine; looking down lower still, into a level she hadn't realized existed; into the pits of the swampy earth that lay beneath her Eden. The glaring Hadean symbolism of this, of the prospect of making a further descent, didn't elude Avery for a moment. And didn't fail to hamper her enthusiasm for doing so. But the sound of Hayes's lumbering steps, and the sinking realization that the door behind her was a fire door with a slow-release safety closure mechanism, still drifting shut even now, left her with no choice.

At the foot of the stairs, which Avery negotiated kid-style, on her backside, in order to avoid using her left leg with its dislocated sacroiliac joint, was a second door, leading to – what was this place? There was no safety hinge here and the heavy soundproofed door slammed shut almost immediately, making her jump, despite there being no doubt as to the source of the noise.

Whatever this space was, it was dark here. Pitch dark. And as the gift of vision became obsolete, Avery's other senses kicked in and she noticed that the music had changed.

'. . . May live far apart

But never forget it – you're my neighbour at heart . . .'

It took Avery a moment to discern, however, that it was not just the sudden and unwelcome recollection –

Heat of leaping flames
Sound of crumbling masonry
Tiny sinews from a torn shoulder like anemones on
    coral
Incisors on viscera
Screaming
And this? This is your home . . .

– of her nightmare that was infusing this particular rendition of 'My Home is Your Home' with such sinister discord. No, there was some kind of delay, some kind of an echo, or was it something else? Was it –

This is my house . . .
Won't you come on inside . . .

Avery limped onwards, blind, feeling the music in her
bones and her skull and her teeth until something that
felt like many smooth, flat tentacles brushed against her
face and yielded to her groping hands. And then all at
once she knew. The echo became two distinct versions
of the song: one tinny and distant in the speakers overhead, the other clear and local.

Not giving herself time to adjust to the light which,
admittedly, was still excessively dim, after passing
through the black curtain of rubber ribbons Avery took
another step forwards and found to her dismay that there
was no ground beneath her feet.

A short fall, a foot or two. Impact on her hands and
knees. More pain momentarily and now blood too? On
her legs, on her hands? No, not blood. Good. Not blood.
But wetness, yes. Shallow water.

. . . home is your home
We may live far apart . . .

And Avery began to wade slowly through the ankle-
deep water, knowing now exactly where she was.

Forty-Three

> My home is your home
> We may live far apart
> But never forget it
> You're my neighbour at heart

The water in the maintenance slip was cold and pearly-black in the darkness, and it was already up to Avery's thighs when she reached the line of brightly coloured boats that were stored here for repair. She studied the one closest to her, and finding no obvious damage, inched her way round to its stern and began to try to push it back into the slip, onto the submerged guide-rails.

Meeting with resistance at first, all straining muscles and brutal war of metal against metal beneath the water, Avery struggled again and again to engage the wheels attached to the plastic hull of the forty-passenger skiff. When at last she hit the correct angle, it slid into place absurdly easily, and she barely had time to realize what was happening when the boat began to glide along the tracks, away from her, slipping from her hand, robbing her of her balance, leaving her to fall face down into whatever the mystery liquid was that flowed through the waterways of the Global Village Cruise.

Avery's face stung with a chemical bite as she leapt to her feet, gasping for air, shaking her wet hair like a dog, and she gave thanks – with a spiritual flavour and yet to no one in particular – that she'd chanced to hold her breath and close her mouth before she fell.

The boats, once on their tracks, travelled faster than one might have imagined they did, and by the time Avery – wading frantically – caught up with her vessel she was thoroughly out of breath and it was just beginning to penetrate the curtain of black rubber ribbons that separated the maintenance slip from the main channel of the ride itself.

Her wet clothes providing little purchase, Avery slipped and slid as she tried to board, but she succeeded in composing herself just in time to join the other vessels of the pastel-hued armada that carried Dreamworld visitors on their fantastical journey through an innocent vision of international comity.

> *Esta es mi casa!*
> This is my home
> Won't you come on inside?
> It may not look just like
> The place *you* reside
> But the world is a village
> When love is your guide
> So come on in, neighbour!
> My door's open wide

The little adobe houses. The burros. The tiny, perfect village marketplace with its minute baskets of tamales and bright mounds of chillis. *Esta es mi casa*. So the maintenance slip was near the start of the cruise, Avery figured. Only one room in from the beginning, in fact.

But that was okay. It was okay. Nothing could happen between here and the exit, and then she could disembark and get back out into the park and safety.

> My home is your home
> We may live far apart
> But never forget it
> You're my neighbour at heart

Nothing could happen. She breathed deeply, stole a glance behind her. Drenched and bedraggled as she was, it came as little surprise that the boatload of passengers into whose path she'd cut were staring at her in mild alarm, but she gave them a smile and the universal hand signal for *no problem here folks, don't mind me*, before turning her back again. She repeated her actions for the people sitting in the boat in front, most of whom had craned back to look at her gesticulations. She hoped desperately that she was right, tried to assure herself that she was. Just sit tight, wait, and everything would be okay.

> *Ni yen'ka so' ye!*
> This is my home
> Won't you come on inside?
> It may not look just like . . .

Avery watched the Thai dolls waving and singing from their pretty houseboats, studied their shiny little faces as she floated past, listened intently to the delicately accented voices singing the English-language part of the song. She'd never listened this closely before, and was suddenly dismayed to notice that when you passed within a certain range of the dolls, the melody was under scored by the sound of their animatronic mouths flipping open, snapping shut again. It was one of those sounds that could elude you for a lifetime, but one that – once heard – made you wonder why you'd never heard it before and made you know with all and instant certainty that you'd never be able to tune it out again.

> The place *you* reside
> But the world is a village
> When love is your guide
> So –

Snap. Snap. Snap.

She'd been trying not to listen to it – a fruitless effort, but one requiring so much concentration that it took Avery a few moments to register the concerned murmur running through the passengers in the boat in front of her, from prow to stern, an auditory Mexican wave. Now, briefly, she wondered what had sparked it, but when it was her turn to sail past the sparkling scale model of the Grand Palace, she understood all too well. For on the sloping surface representing the Na Phra Lan road to the east of the minature compound, was something that shouldn't have been there: a thin, curving tide of fresh water, staining the cerulean blue flooring a damp shade of midnight. And if you followed the streak to its source behind the Wat Phra Kaeo chapel that housed the tiny replica Emerald Buddha, clearly visible were a pair of shoes, and the cuffs of a pair of pants, both dripping wet.

> – in, neighbour!
> My door's open wide

Avery tried not to scream when she saw this, nor when – straining to look back as the boat drifted into the next room – she noticed something worse. That the figure which had been hidden behind the building was *no longer there*.

> My home is your home
> We may live far apart
> But never forget it . . .

The next glimpse she caught of Hayes Ober was behind the Eiffel Tower, where he looked straight at Avery and gave the head of one of the little singing can-can girls an affectionate pat before leaping across the mirrored surface of the miniature Seine and darting back out of view again, concealing himself artfully behind the chateau of Versailles. He knew his way around the Global Village Cruise as if it were his own hometown, or perhaps better than that. After all, he had headed up the team who designed it. And since his mistake behind the Grand Palace, he seemed to be timing his movements and planning his route so that only Avery, and no one else, could see him as he deftly stalked her through this perfect little world, a great, wet, malevolent Gulliver amongst its tiny inhabitants. Checking the faces of the riders in the boats that flanked her, Avery grew ever more sure of this fact. They looked concerned, intrigued, distracted yes, but now the cause seemed not to be Hayes, but merely her. Her own discomfort; the way she fidgeted rigidly, looking this way and that, never sure where she would catch a glimpse of him next. She tried to smile in reassurance at a small boy in the front row of the boat behind her, who was clutching his mother's arm, pointing. But it made little difference, her fear was pungent and contagious, and seemed to be spreading through the cloistered atmosphere of the Global Village Cruise like Ebola through a sealed-off lab facility.

You're my neighbour at heart . . .

Was that Hayes behind the Alps? This time she wasn't sure. He was moving so swiftly now that she had ceased even to be able to gauge whether he was ahead of her or on her tail. What was that behind Prince Leopold's fairy tale castle? Avery stared at the little architectural confection, feeling the arteries in her heart pumping at a rate that seemed to her dangerously fast, dangerously erratic. A streak of motion? No? Yes? No, wait, there, on the other side of the waterway – what was that?

Won't you come on inside?
It may not look . . .

She definitely saw him in Ireland, and again behind Stonehenge as he crept low, all tarantula legs and burning eyes.

. . . world is a village
When love is your guide . . .

The last time she saw him was in Red Square, just a tuft of light brown hair behind one of the minarets of the Kremlin. And then he was gone. And now she wasn't sure how much of what was rapidly drying on her skin beneath the blasts of turbo air-conditioning was sweat and what was mystery liquid, but regardless it stung and made her skin tingle and crawl with cold electricity. Even over the din of 'My Home is Your Home' Avery knew that the occupants of the boats on either side of her had fallen into an uneasy silence – *her own* uneasy silence.

And yet one through which neither the music itself nor the snapping of the little doll mouths could even begin to eclipse the sound of her ragged, fearful breathing.

> So come on in, neighbour!
> My door's open wide . . .

When she heard a collective gasp, she knew. And yet instead of searching for the exact location of the catalyst, Avery found herself scanning the faces of the people in the boats; the men and the women and the children who had all believed as passionately as she that nothing bad ever happened in Dreamworld. It was the sound of illusions shattered. And by the time she tore her eyes from this horror, this sight that had numbered amongst the greatest and darkest of her dreads, the sight she should truly have feared more was right there, at her side.

Hayes Ober, waist deep in the water, hair wet, blood pouring from the superficial gash in his forehead that he'd incurred when she'd thrown them both down the concrete staircase, stood beside Avery's boat, both hands planted firmly on its side, ready to invade.

> My home is your home
> We may live far apart . . .

This time, she didn't have the opportunity, nor the capacity, to stop herself from screaming, so she screamed over the music, looking back at the tourists behind her, their mouths gaping like the mouths of the singing dolls when they flipped down into their open position. And she thought about what they must think, and what they would think – of her, of Hayes, of Dreamworld. And then she thought: *tough shit*! And with all the strength she could summon, she punched him full in the face.

But never forget it . . .

For what seemed like a very long time after Hayes went down, there was no sign of him in the water. Avery and two boatloads of reluctant witnesses watched the surface without motion, without words or sound, bar the sobbing of some lone child and the comforting hushes of the adult accompanying her. The outbreak of excitement from behind Avery when finally he erupted from the water and launched himself with one vaulting leap onto the back seat of her boat was drowned out mostly by Avery's own cry of alarm and the tidal-wave crash of water that Hayes brought with him.

The boat rocked crazily as he rushed across the rows of empty seats towards her, slipping once, getting up again immediately, slipping again, and then he was there at her side. She flinched, closed her eyes.

You're my neighbour at heart . . .

When Avery opened her eyes again, she found that Hayes's own eyes were just inches away. Too close to see his face, but close enough to see that he was glaring, and to note that there were two channels of blood now; one from his forehead and a second from his right nostril. The two of them sat still for a moment, panting, saying nothing, the anticipation of the crowd around them growing. Avery's knuckles stung, and she stared at their raw redness, then up at Hayes. And then she spoke.

'Now what? What are you gonna do?'

She gestured behind them and again, beyond the stern of the boat, to the passengers in the boat in front, who were craning their necks, equally keen and afraid to see what would happen next. Avery smiled, her confidence growing.

'I think we have an audience.'

Hayes glared again, still not moving or speaking. He sat dripping beside her, silent, his sense of defeat nourishing her burgeoning courage.

'*Now* who's so predictable it hurts? You can't do it, can you? Not here. This place, it means so damn much to you, doesn't it? You're finished, Hayes. I know what you did. All of it. And as soon as we get off this ride, it's over. You're going down. I'm through protecting the guilty, I'm through protecting you and I'm through protecting Dreamworld. I don't care what happens any more. This whole fraudulent hell-hole . . . I don't care if it's my home. I don't care if it's my family. And I don't give a damn if comes crashing down around our ears, Hayes. Let it burn . . . And I tell you, I'll dance in the fucking ashes. This time, I'm going to do the right thing.'

> *Akax utaxawa!*
> This is my home
> Won't you come on inside?
> It may not look just . . .

Avery didn't like the amused look on Hayes's face. It wasn't the reaction she'd expected. Not by a long shot.

'What?'

'What "what?"'?'

She wasn't in the mood for this.

'"'What" as in *what's with the fucking smirk*? I wouldn't

be smirking if I were in *your* Bruno Maglis, I can assure you.'

'No?'

'No. I'd be bending over and kissing my ass goodbye.'

Hayes chuckled.

'Oh yes? And that would be because . . . ?'

'Because you're finished. Because when you and this place you call home are done being dragged through the courts, it's all going to be over. It hasn't sunk in yet, has it?'

'And who, may I ask, is going to be testifying for the prosecution at the trial of the century?'

So that's what this was about, Avery thought. He didn't know she had proof. She answered with a certain amount of relish.

'Well, it looks like Catherine Homolka grew a conscience, for a start. You scared her pretty good with your threats, Hayes, but with you out of the picture I have a feeling that she'll be prepared to do the right thing. She was coerced, after all. I don't know much about that end of the legal system, but my guess is she'll get off pretty lightly. And Richard Daetwyler. I don't know if you heard? He lost Devon already. So I think we're looking at a man with nothing left to lose.'

Hayes stared dreamily up at the pink cotton-candy clouds that concealed the turbo air-conditioning vents in the cavernous ceiling.

'Nothing left to lose.' She didn't like the slow, mocking, singsong tone of Hayes's voice one little bit. 'No, on the contrary, he *did* have one thing left to lose, Avery. Just one more thing. So did Catherine.'

Avery's face fell; words failed her as the meaning of his words dawned.

'Yeah, hon, it was pretty tragic. They were both *so*

depressed. The way you and Perdue kept hounding them, accusing them of God knows what, and then the custody case, and of course there was the fact that Richard never loved Catherine, he was still crazy about his ex-wife, and he felt pretty damn bad about that. They must've ingested just about everything they had in the lab cabinets. Talk about overkill. But like I say, we're talking two *very* unhappy campers. You should read the joint suicide note. Breaks your heart.'

Avery's mind whirred and clicked its way towards dreadful clarity.

'You gave them scopolamine. You made them do it.'

Hayes winked at her.

'Not scopolamine. A scopolamine *derivative*, hon. Get it right.'

'Oh, I'll get it right. Believe me. Every last detail. About that. About Lucas. About, about –' She fought to speak over the lump that had formed in her throat. 'About Perdue. You *bastard*. Watch me.'

Perdue's name had cracked her voice like a mallet to glass. Hayes rested his arm on her shoulder. She swatted it off with every available ounce of force in her body.

'Oh, Avery. Avery.' Now Hayes was staring up dreamily again, the nasty singsong voice returned.

'Hayes? What the hell are you doing?!'

He had moved closer now, slipped his arm around her shoulder – firmly, inextricable this time – and was nuzzling his damp, bleeding forehead against hers. He whispered softly in her ear.

'Fallback protocol, honey. I solve problems for a living. I get paid to make believe. Silly girl. You really, really should know better than to fuck with me.'

And then she felt his other arm around her too, enclosing her in a tree-python grip, felt her cheek burning with chemicals from the water that dripped from his hair, and clung to his lips as he kissed her softly, once, on the cheek. And then she felt him pushing her back into a supplicant position and only seconds into this menacing and deadly embrace, she felt his right hand creep gently up her sternum and close around her neck.

Shit, Avery thought as she began to feel the restriction in her windpipe. And yet in the last few minutes it had come to her fully formed, this thought that had actually been there all along, feeding her courage and her confidence. She'd known Hayes long enough for the fallback protocol to infuse the very nature of her thinking. Or perhaps it ran through her veins, part of the blood that somehow tied her to this place. The fallback protocol. It was there, and this – this was hers. She'd had enough evidence, she'd been sure, to indict Hayes and to destroy him, and Dreamworld, and she'd have been prepared to do it, if she could have made it back out into the park. And she really had thought that she'd manage it, too. She'd been so sure that Hayes wouldn't do anything to hurt her in public, for fear of spooking the visitors, cracking the façade, setting free the demons that swarmed beneath. But if she didn't make it . . .

Avery let loose a strangulated cough, recovered enough to force a smile and a few words. 'I've . . . won . . . anyway . . .'

Hayes Ober's expression loudly betrayed the fact that he didn't understand immediately what she meant. Didn't understand that letting him kill her was another way – in fact, the only truly certain way – to author his downfall. And ensure that he took Dreamworld down with him. To commit a crime in public. Right here. In ImagiNation. No room for doubt. He was damned if he did it and damned if he didn't. Wasn't he?

Shit, thought Avery again, when it dawned on her that Hayes had a fallback of his own. Why hadn't she realized before? No one was panicking. No one was shouting. No one was coming to help her. Because Hayes had ensured that his own body obscured any view of what he was doing. And now, as if to confirm this crushing realization, Hayes leant down and Avery felt his mouth on hers, and the eighty or so riders who had wholly lost interest in the Global Village Cruise and were instead observing the denouement of what they must now have pegged as a particularly passionate and outré lovers' tiff – burst into spontaneous applause.

Okay, she told herself as her head grew light and her ears began to ring. So the witnesses were going to be a bit confused. But it shouldn't make any difference. They might think we're making out *now*, but afterwards, there would be no doubt. Everyone would know the truth.

Afterwards. Avery tried to tell herself what she meant by this, but the whole notion of no longer being alive seemed patently ridiculous.

> . . . world is a village
> When love is your guide
> So come on in, neighbour!

The pressure had been minor at first, but as Hayes gained purchase against the damp skin of Avery's throat, it increased. Soon her vision began to blur and her face grew hot and the playback of 'My Home is Your Home' began to sound sticky and sluggish and low and distant, just as it had in her dream.

> My home is your home
> We may live far apart . . .

364

Though her ability to see was now at quite the most elementary level she could ever remember it being, Avery was aware that they had sailed into the final room of the Global Village Cruise: the United States of America. And now she couldn't think about anything but dying, and it was getting harder to remember how it had felt so unreal to her a moment or two ago, because now as it became ever more inevitable she was beginning to feel bitter and sad and very, very reluctant to stop being sentient. Maybe, just maybe, Trey would have raised the alarm by now. Trey and Gwen. He must have reached Gwen, and she'd know what to do, she always knew what to do. And whatever happened, Trey and Gwen would not rest until everyone knew everything, until justice was done. And then she began to think: *fuck the fallback protocol*, and to tell herself instead that if only she could survive until the boat reached the crowded terminus, Hayes would have to stop. Nearly there now. Yes. Look. There was Kit-E-Cat. In his little dinghy. Not like in the dream. No. Wearing his sailor's cap. Waving goodbye. Just as he should be. Nearly there. She wished Hayes wasn't still pretending to kiss her. But nearly over, anyhow. What was nearly over? Avery knew the real – what the hell was the word? Her mind was starting to go blank. The real . . . What? The real . . . *answer*. Sleepy, now. Warm. Sleepy.

> But never forget it
> You're my neighbour at heart.

It hadn't escaped Hayes's notice that he was, in fact, well and truly screwed. Now his continued efforts to kill Avery were borne more of anger and frustration than of any tactical plan, and for the first time in his life, his logic was swallowed whole by his instinct. He released his grip for a brief moment, so as better to resume, to finish what he'd started before it was too late.

> *Au revoir!*
> *Shalom!*
> *Sayonara!*

The quick gasp of breath she'd taken when she'd had a chance switched Avery's senses back on momentarily. Long enough to hear the dolls of all nations expressing their parting wishes. Here in the exit tunnel, where it was dark, however, Hayes was now free to drop the pretence of the embrace, to place both hands around her neck and simply choke her. And by the time her limp body dropped to the floor beneath the bench seat, where in a few moments the ride attendants and the crowds of people waiting to embark would find her and the screaming would start, she was barely aware of anything. Certainly not aware of anything external – not of Hayes letting her go, or of her head hitting the deck beneath the seat, or of him getting out onto the narrow ledge beside the waterway and walking through the dolls twittering their multi-lingual goodbyes and out through the emergency exit, back into the utilidors.

But through the lights and the shadows and the din and the silence of the random firings of the neurons and synapses in her oxygen-starved brain, some small internal dialogue continued. She was going to die here. But she could live with that. *Live* with it? If Avery had been able to draw a breath at all at this point she might have laughed. It wasn't exactly the kind of irony that Lisa Schaeffer went for, but then, for all the changes Avery had undergone, no matter what, she and Lisa would always be worlds apart. And as it dawned on her now that 'My Home is Your Home' was probably going to be the last earthly sound she'd ever hear, all she could think was that, given the choice, she wouldn't have changed a thing.

Forty-Four

Avery's heart leapt when she felt her eyes opening, watched her vision kick in lucid, bright; tasted the air. Either being dead was a lot like being alive – enough like being alive not to herald the intense emotional onslaught of mourning and loss and catastrophe that she'd feared – or she had, by some wondrous chance, made it after all.

'Take it easy there, breathe easy,' said the paramedic leaning over her.

'I'm alive,' said Avery in extreme wonderment, realizing only when she heard how muffled her voice was, and felt the area around her mouth grow hot with her own breath, that she was wearing an oxygen mask.

'Yep. You made it,' said the paramedic, gently smoothing back a sticky tendril of Avery's hair. 'Don't try to talk, though. Take it easy. We're only about twenty minutes away from County General. Okay?'

He looked far too young to be a paramedic and had a great bedroom voice – as soft and rich as chocolate mousse, a hint of Canadian news anchor, pure and alive with erudition. He also had, Avery noticed now, perfect outsized white teeth and the most bewitching blue eyes, delightfully offset by the sky-blue of the Dreamworld emergency services uniform. She nodded her compliance, unable to stop herself from grinning beneath the oxygen mask. If she was feeling well enough to notice these things, she figured, she was going to be just fine.

It was only when she closed her eyes again, still smiling, that she heard another voice, realized that there was somebody else in the ambulance with her.

'Can I talk to her?'

'Trey? Is that you?'

Avery opened her eyes again to see Clowes's worried little face peering over her. His eyes were slightly bloodshot, his hair sticking up erratically.

'Oh God, Avery . . .' He moved his hand awkwardly towards her and she thought that he was about to touch her face, but at the last minute he opted to lightly lay his hand over hers instead. 'It was horrible. They, uh . . . I think we, like, *lost you* for a bit.'

The idea of this seemed bizarre, inconceivable.

'Ohmigod, did I pee myself? I saw them reviving this old guy once. He was wearing white golfing pants and –'

Clowes was aghast at Avery's apparent immunity to the horror of the memory he was currently reliving. '*Avery*! I was like, *oh my God*. I was going nuts!'

Avery turned her eyes to the paramedic again and raised the hand that wasn't under Clowes's to the mask on her face.

'Can I take the thingy off?'

The paramedic pondered for a moment, looked her over thoughtfully.

'You're not having any trouble breathing now?'

She shook her head *no* and pre-empted his consent, slipping the plastic mouthpiece downwards, feeling a momentary shock of pain as it came to rest on her bruised throat.

'That's better.' She turned to Clowes again. 'So, where
. . . Did they do it in front of everyone, the paramedics?
Did people, like, see what was going on?'

'Kind of. They moved everyone out pretty quickly,
though. And stopped the ride until they took you out so
no one else could see.' His face clouded over with barely
controlled frustration and he retracted his hand, quickly
and desperately like someone who had accidentally
touched a burning skillet. 'Jesus, Avery, I can't believe
that after all this you're still bothered about this "nothing
bad ever happens in Dreamworld" crap. You're fucking
lucky to be alive!'

She met his angry glare with a twinkling smile. 'Wrong,
mister. I'm not bothered in the slightest. Not any more.
I'm just thinking about witnesses. They got Hayes, obviously, right?'

Clowes and the young paramedic exchanged uneasy
looks and Avery squeezed her eyes tight shut. This
couldn't be happening.

'Well, I can't imagine he'll get far. Will the police be at
the hospital already? I want to see someone right away.'

Clowes looked quizzically back to Avery. 'What are
you going to tell them?'

'What do you think? Everything.' Her face fell. 'You
. . . You think *I* would protect Hayes?'

'Not Hayes . . . I just thought. You know . . .
Dreamworld . . . The publicity . . .'

'Screw that. I mean, I don't think I've got enough to
prove his involvement in Lisa and Leon's death, but I
think they could get him for his part in the Lucas
business, even without Homolka and Daetwyler alive to
testify. And . . .' She swallowed hard. 'The Perdue . . .
stuff. And threatening you. And, obviously – Well . . .'

She gestured to her neck, and although she didn't her-

370

self know to what degree she was marked by evidence of violence, she knew enough from Clowes's reaction to know that it wasn't a pretty sight.

'What's going on?'

The ambulance had swerved into the hard shoulder and slowed to a stop, and now, it seemed, they stood idling on the hard shoulder. Both Clowes and the paramedic shrugged in response to Avery's question and there was a moment of silence before the driver turned around in his seat.

'Cop flagging us down. We okay for a minute?'

The paramedic looked at Avery, said that they were, and swung the back door of the ambulance open.

Officer Brett Toback's shoes and the legs of his navy pants were splattered with vomit that smelt distinctly of salami, cheese and vinaigrette and appeared to contain a generous peppering of pickled jalapenos. He wiped his mouth before he spoke, and reeled slightly as he did so, clutching the door-frame for support.

'You didn't have your siren on. You're not on an emergency, are you? I radioed already to County, but I think it might be too late.'

The paramedic hopped down onto the tarmac. 'Okay. What have we got?'

The conversation grew fainter, inaudible in fact, as Brett Toback and the paramedic walked away, towards whatever it was that had made Toback vomit.

'Car wreck?'

Clowes shrugged again and swivelled round on the little bench seat to peer through the windscreen. Avery watched his eyes alight on something.

'Car wreck?' she said again.

Clowes didn't speak.

'What is it?'

Clowes chewed at the inside of his cheek and finally spoke in a tone which was almost as hard for Avery to hear as the distant clamour outside.

'It's Hayes.'

Instinctively, Avery tried to sit up for a second, but flopped down again, unable to. 'Car wreck?' she said for the third time, only this time with more trepidation.

Clowes didn't stop looking through the windscreen. 'No.'

Through the small back windows of the ambulance, Avery was able to catch only the most fleeting of glimpses of the Lexus as the ambulance drove away. Hayes himself was not visible, but the splashes and spatterings of his blood on the windscreen and driver's-side window were.

'Fucking coward,' muttered Clowes.

Avery stared up at the white ceiling of the ambulance, spoke softly. 'No.'

Clowes looked at her blankly. 'I think *so*.'

'No. He isn't. *Wasn't*. He just couldn't have conceived of letting his actions destroy Dreamworld. If *any* of this came to trial, it would be the end. But he's dead, Daetwyler and Homolka are dead, I'm dead and it can't. A few things wind up in the press but none of the terrible details ever get out.'

'But you're not dead.'

'Makes no difference, does it?'

Clowes sat brooding, and then he muttered quietly, 'The fallback protocol.'

Avery sighed. 'I guess. Only I have a feeling that Hayes relished doing it. What greater glory could he have wished for than to die protecting Dreamworld? It's the quintessentially Hayes way to go. He'd probably have been pissed if he'd missed out on the opportunity to do it.'

The silence was endless, just the sound of wheels on the empty road, and very little of their journey was left when finally Clowes spoke again. He was holding Avery's hand properly now, had been for the last few miles, ever since she had closed her eyes and appeared to have fallen asleep, and he looked down at her fondly before addressing his question to the paramedic.

'The guy back there – was he dead?'

The paramedic looked over cautiously. 'You knew him?'

'Yeah, but I didn't like him. So don't worry. Was he?'

The paramedic nodded. 'Very.'

Clowes wasn't sure what to say next; heard himself making a nervous quip. 'Police guy looked like he needed a little help, though.'

The paramedic smiled generously. 'Yeah, right. No kidding. There was an ambulance on its way from County, though, so that's okay.'

'He looked like he was going to chuck up again.'

'I know. Fortunately the guy happened to decide to stop and shoot himself *just* outside of our catchment area, so someone from County can have the pleasure of getting covered in partially-digested sub sandwich.'

'We were off property already?'

'*Just*. Lucky for me. Literally *just* over the boundary line. Maybe I'll send a wreath to the funeral, thank him for that.'

And Avery, not really asleep, just enjoying holding Clowes's hand and listening to the sound of the road and the conversation, thought: literally just over the boundary line. Of course we were. And she wondered why Clowes had even bothered to ask.

Forty-Five

The university campus was teeming, and even leaning out of the driver's-side window, scanning the clusters of co-eds who were talking and laughing and lounging on cars or just soaking up the scorching afternoon sun, Avery began to doubt whether she'd ever be able to find Trey.

She looked at her watch again, and was just beginning to wonder if he'd forgotten their arrangement when she spotted him on the steps of the main faculty building, demonstrating his hacky-sack skills to the great delight of a decidedly coltish group of girls. Even as he spotted her, pocketed the footbag and began to sprint towards her, Avery couldn't help scrutinizing the girls – the tossing of shiny manes and silvery glints of belly-rings and flashes of impossibly long, thin, brown legs – even when she realized that they were staring back at her. She who looked as alien to their eyes as they did to hers.

'Hey there. How's it going?'

Trey Clowes leant in through the window and planted a kiss on her cheek. She stared straight ahead.

'Hey, fine. Except I feel like Mrs fucking Robinson here. But apart from that, great.'

Trey laughed, kept laughing as he walked around the

front of the car and finally climbed in beside her. He slammed the door shut, patted her on the knee, and grinned.

'So, are you gonna seduce me, or what?'

Avery stared at him. 'You grew that goatee quickly.'

He touched his chin. 'Oh? Not really. When did I last see you? Gotta have been, what? Two weeks?'

'Really? No, I mean, I think you're right. God, it's just been so manic. Lynda Young – my new boss? – she's amazing, but *boy*, does she work you! She's decided to make me her main protégée, which is great, and she's gunning for our division to take on the bulk of investigative, which essentially seems to mean that I don't get home until fuck knows when every night. But I guess I shouldn't complain. God, is it two weeks really? That went *seriously* fast.'

Clowes looked away. 'Yeah? It went pretty slow for me, actually. Pretty much the longest two weeks I can remember now I come to think about it.'

Avery picked an imaginary piece of fluff from her uniform pants. 'Did you see the piece in *Florida Today* about Leon's funeral?'

'No. Was there a picture? I would *love* to see his family. Genetic mutations ahoy, don't you reckon? Full-on duelling banjos territory.'

Avery laughed. 'Probably. No photo, unfortunately. But they mentioned the coroner's verdict. Murder-suicide. Like we thought.'

'Didn't they say that two weeks ago?'

'No. Yeah. That was the preliminary hearing. This was the final whatyoucallit. So that's it. It's over.'

'No mention of Dreamworld?'

Avery shook her head slightly wistfully. 'Just that Lisa worked there. No mention of Leon being a volunteer or anything. And nothing else. No connection with Lucas's death, zip. God knows where Lisa's van is. Maybe *that*'s under the arcade at the Americana, who knows? And they changed the registration records, remember? So that's that. And, of course, there's no clue to say it happened at ImagiNation. County just took it as read that the whole thing happened in the orange grove off the 192. Right where they found the bodies. Hayes Ober – master of illusion.'

Clowes raised his eyebrows. 'Yeah, really. No kidding. I noticed they even managed to keep Perdue's death out of the press.'

Avery flinched slightly at the mention of Perdue's name.

'So how's your thesis going?'

His face lit up, and he shifted excitedly forwards in his seat and grasped Avery's arm. 'Fucking amazing! My professor? The one I told you about? He says he wants to publish in one of the journals when we're done. He says it's the first opportunity he can ever remember having to observe a legend spreading right from its inception.'

'Wow! And not just one legend, I guess.'

'No, right. He can't believe it. He's been making noises about all sorts of amazing stuff after I graduate. But I don't wanna get my hopes up yet.'

Avery squeezed Trey's hand, making sure first that it was his *left* hand. She didn't mean for her voice to sound as hollow as it did.

'Congratulations. It's really exciting.'

He winced slightly. 'Oh God, Avery, I'm an idiot. I feel like . . . I don't know. What you've been through . . . And here I am getting all happy about it.'

'No, no. Not at all. I *was* just thinking about Perdue again, but it wasn't – it's not you.'

She squeezed his hand again, and he returned the gesture gratefully.

'I *am* sorry, though. I guess at least *something* good came out of all this, yeah? Is that one way of looking at it? For me, anyway. I'll always be grateful to you for that.'

She released his left hand and picked up the right instead, lightly ran her fingertip over the tiny circular scar in the web between his thumb and forefinger and gave him a sly smile.

'And this too, I hope. I hope you'll always be grateful to me for this.'

He gazed into her eyes mock-romantically. 'Very. Very grateful. Always.'

They both laughed. Trey was still laughing when Avery stopped, struck suddenly by a thought.

'So how *is* it spreading? What are people saying? How far has it travelled?'

'Oh, man,' said Trey, coming alive again. 'God, I'll give you everything I've written so far, you can read it later, but you just wouldn't *believe*. Let me think. The furthest away is, let me think . . . Well, since it hit the Internet, God, you name it. There have been postings from, like, Washington State, California, British Colombia, England, even. And it hasn't just been the folklore sites, either – there's been stuff on most of the Dreamworld newsgroups, even a couple of the Disney ones. Someone on alt.disney.the–evil–empire even proposed starting alt.dreamworld.the–evil–empire.'

'Jesus! What about *before* it hit the Internet?'

'Oral vectoring? God, it was *extreme*. We're talking, well, I'd say if you had a map you could pretty much draw a circle with the middle being Orlando and have that stretch down to Miami in the south, right up to Raleigh in the north, and over north-west to, let me think, Baton Rouge,

New Orleans. In the space of less than a week. Early on there weren't a lot of variations but we're beginning to see them now. Started a few days ago.'

'Like what?'

'Okay, um . . . That there was serial killer going round Dreamworld killing people with a paint-gun and he'd killed seven people, but it'd been hushed up. I guess even though the Perdue stuff wasn't in the press, word got out from someplace. Got exaggerated. Whatever.'

Trey looked at Avery nervously, wishing that a different example had sprung to mind, but she seemed to be okay.

'Seven? Why seven?'

'Oh, in urban legends it's always seven. Three, seven or fourteen. No one's sure why. Just is. Something in the societal psyche. People just like those numbers. Anyway, there's that – oh, and actually just yesterday there was a new part on the end of that one, which was that if you look very carefully at the third ticket booth on the left as you come into ImagiNation, you can see a big splat of paint from the paint-gun, and blood, where one of the victims was killed, because no matter how many times they paint over it, they can't cover it up properly.'

Avery laughed. 'Because why? Like some type of paranormal thing?'

'It's interesting you say that, because my professor said he thought it was going to start mutating that way, and it looks like it is. The version I heard yesterday? Verbally? It was just because they didn't do enough coats. But today on alt.folklore.urban there were a few posts from people saying they heard from someone who worked at the park or whatever that no matter how many layers of paint they put over it at night, the stain is always showing again in the morning. The prof says he wouldn't be surprised if by Friday we start to get mutations where people see or hear paranormal phenomena by the ticket booth. Actually, if you're over by there, if it's not too much trouble, maybe you could keep half an eye out, see whether anybody's stopping and looking yet? It'd be really handy for me to know when that starts.'

'Sure. Will do.' Then it hit her. 'Actually . . . You know . . . The paint over the bloodstain that can't be hidden . . . Had it occurred to you that that's a pretty cool analogy? For Dreamworld? For what happened? That's sort of weird.'

Trey stared at her with a look in his eyes that turned her bare arms to gooseflesh.

'You're smart, Avery, you know that?'

'Yeah, you said that before, Trey.'

'No, but I mean . . . I don't think I've ever met a girl as smart as you.'

She fingered the air-conditioning switches on the dash panel, eventually adjusting the main one down a few notches before turning to him brightly with another question.

'So, what about the centre? Has there been any . . .'

Part of Clowes was equally relieved at the change in emotional atmosphere, which, he thought to himself with some amusement, Avery seemed to have managed to alter via the air-conditioning switch. As if it had invisible secondary function notches marked with things like, 'Uncomfortably blatant sexual tension' and, 'Jovial camaraderie'.

'*Loads.* Nothing about drugs, oddly enough, but there's been a fairly strong thread about, like, the serial killer was a volunteer who went nuts because he used this virtual reality machine they'd been developing and it was so real that he, like, went nuts.'

Avery laughed. 'That's the scientific diagnosis, is it? But the fact that there are volunteers, that stuff is out. That *is* interesting.'

'Yeah. Give it a week or so and I think we'll start hearing more stories about accidents at the centre itself. I mean, there's been one on some newsgroup or other, I think it was someone said their friend was a volunteer and they heard that the virtual reality machine made somebody's head explode. But I think everyone studiously ignored that particular post. Stories that are too far-fetched just don't spread, we know that for sure.'

'So what else? Anything about Hayes?'

Trey regarded her carefully before speaking. 'Um . . . Yes. And you, actually. Not by name, obviously. But the part about him being a really high up exec has got in there somehow, which is interesting.'

'So what's the story?'

'It's not far from the truth, actually. That you were on the Global Village Cruise and he tried to kill you. We're not really following that one, precisely because it is so close to the truth. It obviously came from a witness or an employee or the police and has spread a bit, but it hasn't mutated much.'

'Much?'

'Well, uh, there was a bit of a flourish, came up end of last week. I think it was on rec.arts.dreamworld.parks. Or alt.dreamworld.secrets. Or maybe I heard it from someone at the Bamboo Lounge, I can't remember.'

'Which was?'

'Which was, er, that he did it because he was jealous because he found out that you were, uh, having an affair.'

Avery giggled. 'Trey, you're blushing.'

His hand flew to his cheek, as if he might be able to

gauge whether this was true merely by touch. 'No, I'm not. Anyway, that's about it.'

'Yep. I am legend. And who was I supposed to be having an affair with?'

Trey answered slightly more irritably than he'd intended to. 'I don't know. Another employee or something.'

'Can I spread it that he found out that I was screwing the entire Orlando Magic team, please?'

Relieved that Avery had moved the subject along, Clowes grinned and wagged his finger at her. 'Don't you *dare* pollute my nice clean data. If you do, I'll kill you.'

'Maybe I won't and maybe I will.'

His smile melted gently and he turned to her in earnest. 'You know, I was really worried that telling you all this would depress you. The fact that people are saying all these things about Dreamworld? I mean, I know it's probably not going to make much of a dent in their revenue, if any, but it does dirty the pristine image a bit. To say the least.'

Avery ruffled his hair, rather patronizingly she realized with some regret, and smiled. 'No, Trey. Read my lips: *it doesn't bother me.*'

'I just thought . . . You loved Dreamworld, and a lot of what you loved about it was how perfect it seemed to be.'

'Yeah, but how things *seem to be* are . . . I've changed. I *do* love Dreamworld, though. And I love it even more now that I don't have that creeping feeling that I'm walking around on a very thin and exquisitely decorated crust that someone built over the bowels of hell.'

'You still love it?'

'Yes. I do. Still. Something doesn't have to be perfect to elicit love, Trey. And sometimes there's no rhyme or reason, and maybe it's wrong and maybe it's not, but you still feel that love. And you can't change that.'

There was a long, heavy silence before Avery finally gave voice to the thought that popped sharply into her head like a migraine. 'Do you miss Lisa?'

'Sure.'

'No, I mean . . . You know what I mean.'

'Oh, God. No. *No*. It would never have worked out. At the end of the day, it probably saved me.'

Avery looked surprised. 'How so?'

'I don't know. Some people, you just know they're going to destroy you. There's a song, a really old song, by my favourite band. There's this line in the chorus, goes: "I've got a match: your embrace and my collapse." Me and Lisa . . . It always reminded me of that.'

Avery smiled instinctively at the reference to the old schoolyard taunt before thinking again and falling silent, touched by the poignancy of the lyric. Then something else struck her.

'Hold on, that song . . . It sounds familiar. Who did you say it was by?'

'I didn't. I doubt you know them. I hardly ever meet anybody who does.'

'Try me.'

Trey Clowes sighed a what-the-hell sigh. 'They Might be Giants.' He scanned Avery's face, misread her pensive expression. 'See, I said you wouldn't have heard of them.'

'Wait . . . Two guys? One wears glasses, one plays the accordion sometimes?'

Trey's eyes widened. 'Yes!'

'I saw them play live. Years ago. I loved them.'

And she had, it was true. And not just because of the ccordion player's superb forearms.

'You did? I don't believe this! They're, like, my

favourite. . . Really? This is incredible! Okay, come on, who else do you like?'

He began to rifle enthusiastically through the CDs in her glove box; produced one. 'Barenaked Ladies? I love these guys! I mean, I loved them *way* back! Before they got really big.'

Avery felt vaguely defensive. 'So did I. Years ago. Gwen's from Toronto – where they're from? – she got me into them. She gave me *Gordon* right when it first came out.'

Trey peered at the remaining CDs and frowned when he saw that they were also by the Barenaked Ladies. 'Come on, tell me someone else you like. Go on. How about Victoria Williams? Or Frank Black? You know him?'

Avery held up her hands in protest. 'Whoa, whoa, whoa. Hold it right there. I don't like the sound of this. Next you're gonna start asking me if I put mayonnaise on my fries.'

He laughed. 'I *hate* mayonnaise.'

Avery laughed with him, and slowly met his gaze.

'Now you're talking, Trey. Because you know what? *I* hate mayonnaise too.'

Florida Roadkill

Tim Dorsey

As Sean Breen and David Klein head out from Tampa Bay on their long-planned trip to the Florida Keys there's nothing on their minds except fishing, beer and baseball. But when five million dollars is dropped into the boot of the wrong car, a whole convoy of homicidal wackos sets off in pursuit of the two unsuspecting men, leaving behind a bewildering trail of bodies.

From murder by shrink-fit jeans in Tampa, via mayhem at the World Series in Miami, to a convention of Hemingway look-alikes in Key West, *Florida Roadkill* is an unforgettable ride through the wildest corners of the Sunshine State – a kaleido-scopic crime spree taking in sex, drugs and Satanist rock 'n' roll, lap dancing, extortion and a dozen of the most unusual forms of murder ever seen in fiction.

'This one rocks. Like Carl Hiaasen on acid, Elmore Leonard on speedballs, this doesn't let go from the first to the last page. I loved it.'   *Independent on Sunday*

'Over-the-top, absurd and hilarious . . . all the right ingredi-ents are present in this manic kaleidoscope of bizarre may-hem. Supremely entertaining.'   *Time Out*

'Fiercely energetic, outrageously funny . . . imagine Hunter S. Thompson sharing a byline with Groucho Marx.'

Tampa Tribune

'Jittery, bizarre and utterly charming, it reads as if Quentin Tarantino wrote it on a rum runner-and-speedball binge after baking too long in the sun.'   *Miami Herald*

'Vulgar, violent and gaudier than sunsets on the Keys, Dorsey's roadshow is some fun.'   *New York Times*

SBN 0 00 651305 0

Only Forward
Michael Marshall Smith

A truly stunning debut from a young author. Extremely original, satirical and poignant, a marriage of numerous genres brilliantly executed to produce something entirely new.

Stark is a troubleshooter. He lives in The City - a massive conglomeration of self-governing Neighbourhoods, each with their own peculiarity. Stark lives in Colour, where computers co-ordinate the tone of the street lights to match the clothes that people wear. Close by is Sound where noise is strictly forbidden, and Ffnaph where people spend their whole lives leaping on trampolines and trying to touch the sky. Then there is Red, where anything goes, and all too often does.

At the heart of them all is the Centre - a back-stabbing community of 'Actioneers' intent only on achieving - divided into areas like 'The Results are what Counts sub-section' which boasts 43 grades of monorail attendant. Fell Alkland, Actioneer extraordinaire has been kidapped. It is up to Stark to find him. But in doing so he is forced to confront the terrible secrets of his past. A life he has blocked out for too long.

'Michael Marshall Smith's *Only Forward* is a dark labyrinth of a book: shocking, moving and surreal. Violent, outrageous and witty - sometimes simultaneously - it offers us a journey from which we return both shaken and exhilarated. An extraordinary debut.'
Clive Barker

ISBN 0 586 21774 6